Pinatubo II

by Les W Kuzyk

Our Near Future
https://0urnearfuture.wordpress.com/

Climate Fiction Short Stories

Blown Bridge Valley
Tribe 5 Girl
Green Sahara
AlberTa's Gift
Next Door Data
Storm Punchers

Other Short Stories

Brother's Keeper
A Future History of the Environment

Other Novels

The Sandbox Theory

Pinatubo II

Les W Kuzyk

Climate
Reality

For my family

I want to thank my wife Dragana and daughter Lana for their patience during the writing process. I also want to pay tribute to the IFWA and Salty Quills aspiring and accomplished writers for their support and reviews, and to specifically express my appreciation for feedback on this novel by Justin Acton and Michael Gillette. I also want to thank the scientific community for their published research on the global phenomena of climate change.

How about replacing science fiction, the imagining of fantasy by a single mind, with new worlds of far greater diversity based on real science from many minds?

E. O. Wilson
The Meaning of Human Existence

I could perhaps like others have astonished you with strange improbable tales; but I rather chose to relate plain matter of fact in the simplest manner and styles' because my principle design was to inform you, and not to amuse you.

Jonathan Swift,
Gulliver's Travels

Table of Contents

Pinatubo II

Chapter 1

Blazing orange patches melded with the purple laced yellows of an exotic sunset. "So...*a painting, from 1883*." Vince read on the visiscreen.

"Six months after Krakatoa," Tami nodded. "This atmospheric spectacle *will* be noticed as one side effect...the sky will change colour. Not just sunsets for the gawkers, but the daytime sky too—an overall faded blue from the extra haze."

"But this artist painted an English sunset, not Indonesian. Anyway, we're calculating global for reference only, right?"

"Vince," she looked to him, "I wish I could tell you everything, I do. But Her Excellency only releases so much. To each of us. So I can't."

"Right. It's just, well, disturbing." He frowned, but then brightened. "So we speak only to project Phase II, the Niger national scenario."

"Yes."

"Any other side effects?"

"Oh yes. The most frightening is, we don't know all the side effects. We do know the ozone layer will take some beating. But politically, we use this project and any predicted side effects to negotiate."

"Someone's military has us on their radar, we know that." Vince leaned forward. "Say they start zapping tonight's balloons with their drones...that could affect our release."

She glanced up from her jPad visiscreen.

"You're one of the engineers. You tell me," she said.

"Well, Brad's the aeronautical, but we've designed a nocturnal release. He insisted on that for calmer winds—facilitates balloon recovery. Reduced night-time visibility also keeps us hidden. No doubt they have night detection capabilities, but for those he says we count on our distribution—we have release points spread out all over the Ayăr Mountains. So for any military, we speculate a statistical nightmare."

How had he ever come to think like this? Had he become an eco-blackmail strategist? Contractors like him were listed as personnel drone targets; his mind flashed to that day at the storage yard.

This contract had taught him a lot—a totally unique design project, nothing like back in the Alberta oilfield. Even talking of drones felt so other world. His base line contingency plan assumed drones—the word made him queasy—took out ten percent of their release. He would replace those losses. Even fifty percent. With their sulphur supply line they'd have that replaced in a week. Brad said same with any balloon damage. If either of them took a personal Hellblazer missile, well not easy to say, but in the abstract engineers were replaceable. That they had a thought out plan, though, diluted his unease with excitement.

"Good." She smiled. "They wouldn't respond immediately anyway. Politics."

"What about who's financing? Can we talk about that?"

"Short answer, no."

"So Tami, who really is financing? I mean, so many payments are Asian. The Chinese have a high climate change risk index, and other countries bordering China too. India's high, Bangladesh the highest. So it fits."

"Open trust fund. Any country, or individual for that matter, can make anonymous contribution. I can tell you the total truth on this, Vince. Any country can leverage any financing towards its own political agenda. Nobody knows who contributes, but everyone knows our target outcome. One exception to that short answer; we can emphasize the small budget size." She beamed. "This project has no wealthy-nation-only restriction—a country like Bangladesh has equal say."

He nodded. He knew the cost was low, very low, from his sulphur tonnage calculations. He had priced out liquid sulphur dioxide with only one border crossing, trucked in from the oilfields of next door Nigeria to local storage tanks here in Niger. Brad invoiced slightly more for shipping in balloons and helium from Asia.

"And why did we pick my country again? Why Canada to deliver this message?" He knew, but he needed to confirm, to hear it again. Out loud. Many arguments ran laps in his head lately.

"Take it from a global business outlook. Say Her Excellency chose from the five northern countries claiming Arctic rights, as the polar ice recedes. Take military into account, consider nuclear armament, and say environmental record as well. Who dropped out of Kyoto?"

"Yeah, Okay." He scratched his cheek. "You know Canadians are pretty attached to their lifestyle, carbon based or not. Our economy grows northward. Our Prime Minister even has this quip—he says less ice gives us more Canada."

"Well, you know what you tell a child in a sweets shop. You can't have it all. Pick vacation lifestyle or healthy planet, one or the other."

"I feel like a rat." He had grown up in an Alberta oil town, played hockey as a kid and listened to his grandfather's stories of pioneering. Everyone found the better life in Canada, the story always ran that way. Trees to hew, water to draw and land to break and farm. Then came drilling rigs and pump jacks, and now the latest Arctic drilling and fracking technology. Everyone flew south for a winter vacation.

"Think of future generations."

"Eco-blackmail, that's what they'll call this."

"Your daughter."

"Yeah..." His little daughter had caused none of this! Yet she would be paying the piper.

"Ready?"

He didn't answer, shuffling over to the window.

Vince stared along the bridge at the dim twinkles spread along the south shore. How much had changed since he first saw the dirty Niger River. Only weeks ago he'd stepped off the plane into the African heat, pissed at everything. He had since come to look at people under the light of a reality check. Like Tami's gawkers. Most global attention now focused on the Martian pioneering drama. Most could put name to face of the eight resident Martians and the minute details of the Jackie and Haydon romance. The fantasy of escaping from the crib, Brad had said, leaving the poopy diaper planet mess behind. People preferred denial and distraction.

This contract had started out simple, yes, just an atmospheric test. Now these politicians would arrive any minute. He had never before engaged a federal cabinet minister, especially in high end global politics. Who else would talk on topics like drones?

His eyes scanned the edge of the horizon, but in the dark he could only imagine their designed balloon eruption. He knew their release ascended that evening, fleets of balloons rising loaded with their sulphur release systems. Enough payload to theoretically cool the regional Sahel climate. But nothing real world could be that straightforward.

He turned back to the room.

Tamanna sat in one posh chair, focused on her jPad. Her beauty made his heart flutter, but that was only ever his to know. He wandered over to sit next to her. She looked up to smile, giving a reassuring nod. During their patient wait, they practiced pitch rehearsal mixed with ongoing strategic discussion. One thing was sure, they were about to bring on a bad day for the diplomats from his home and native land. The door clicked opened, and they both looked up. Vince watched the three men file in, evaluating each face as they took their seats.

THE HEAT

Chapter 2

The dull grey tinge of the city slipped into view, displacing the patchy reddish terrain as the airliner descended to his final destination. *The City of Niamey* Vince scoffed—not the official name, but as he stared down, this one appeared as his City of Calgary sliced through by a river flowing from the northwest. Not a narrow brilliant mountain-blue, this river ran wide and dirty mudsand-brown, flowing not down from westerly foothills, but in from somewhere beyond that god-forsaken emptiness. All ran flat and even here to a hazy horizon, missing his home city's reach-for-the-sky rocky peaks framing a distant western sky.

He pulled his gaze from the window and collapsed back into his seat, letting his eyelids fall closed for a moment. Peace—if only—he struggled for any fragment of tranquility. Travelling for what, almost forty hours now? And, he scowled, he had lived for almost forty years as well. What seemed an endless struggle to keep it together, to endure a trip like this, in a life like this; now this place. One clear difference between back home and down there was the searing African heat.

God.

His mind restarted its subtle persistent churn, thoughts sneaking insidious in the back door. He pulled the reins in hard. Focus! Concentrate. On something, on anything, on what's right here in front of you. Local geography, that had worked earlier. This Niamey had no trees to speak of, unlike that last city. Abuja. He pictured the words for that airport: Nnamdi Azikiwe

International. More humidity around Abuja. Two lakes lay in the rough terrain just to the north and clouds floated in those tropical skies over patches of green trees. One lake was a reservoir, not natural at all. The telltale straight edge cutting through the hills gave it a manmade signature. A smaller reservoir graced the city's core, perhaps an urban park where some local resident might feed birds from a bench.

He relaxed, almost.

In Abuja he had de-boarded Lufthansa and transferred to this aged Ethiopian Airlines jet. Abuja had a polished clean look, while this City of Niamey had the scratches of desolation etched across its arid barren landscape.

He felt the plane bank and leaned to snap a photo with his Jeenyus. As the airliner straightened for final approach he looked to his mini visiscreen. He sent the photo, texting his daughter. *Hey baby, daddy's coming in for landing—you spell this city N I A M E Y in Google maps.* He had sent her the same from Abuja. Hesitating, but only for a second, he decided not to cc his wife. She could wait for her official email once he got settled.

As the plane touched down he watched the sun burnt grass rushing past. Two traffic control towers loomed against a bright cloud free sky, one tall and one short, but both built of baked brown brick. The Jeenyus buzzed and he read: *I am eating brekfust daddy. Whit mush.* He felt his face relax, naturally almost, a moment of internal relief. Seven hours difference, he'd have to keep that in mind.

He clicked his seat belt and grasped his travel bag from beneath the seat. The crowd shuffled down boarding stairs to the parched afternoon tarmac. He forced his way through the sweaty sun's heat to escape into a waiting bus. A weak fan blew, and he turned his shoulders towards the cooler air for the ride to the airport entrance. Beehive roofing cells gaped at him with open mouths from beside the airport signature—Aeroport International Diori Hamani. He reread the sign...that would be French. His lip twitched, the language sparking recall of a youthful summer in Montreal. Something new to keep his mind absorbed, to help defocus his plague of invasive mind mutter.

Past customs, a taxi carried him along through light traffic. He read a street sign—Boulevard du 15 Avril. A pattern of stark social contrast stood out in the streets. The few newer SUV's passed amidst throngs of ragged pedestrians in sandals or many even barefoot in the dust. Some rode creaky bicycles. He habitually translated peoples' lifestyles into a data set he could never help noticing.

His driver pointed out the hippodrome as they motored past. *Horses race*, the driver voiced in his English. *Course de chevaux* Vincent parodied back in French. *Oui* the driver smiled. A series of N roads, N25, then N6 and around Rond Point Kennedy. As they navigated the roundabout, he caught more words on signs *Aide et Action: Programme Niger* and they veered onto the Boulevard de la Republique. A long curving wall of windows loomed down from the *Office National des Ressources Minieres*, across the way when they pulled in at the Hotel Gaweye.

Paying the driver, he stepped out into the sizzling sunshine and hurried up cobbled brown steps. Passing through the tinted glass door entrance, he again escaped *la chaleur*. Yes, this thinking in a different language helped keep his troubles subdued.

At the desk he asked for his room key in French, and that having worked, he spoke the more complicated request for the meeting room pass card. He took the elevator up, walked along the hallway to his numbered door, opened and stepped in to toss his bags on the bed. His new abode for the next, god, who knew how many weeks? He scrambled to locate and test the air controls. The fan blew out extra cool and he flopped into a chair breathing shallow.

His Jeenyus began a soft scheduling reminder and he rose robotically. Out the door and at the corridor end he took the elevator to the bottom floor. The lower hallway heat hit hard and he sprinted to the meeting room, entering and slamming the door behind. He banged his finger hard into this air controller, holding back from punching a hole in the wall.

Fuck! Everything!

He took a deep breath, then another and his eyes focused in on the coffee machine. Nothing was okay. Trapped in a lifestyle he hated every day, one he wanted so bad to drop out of but could not.

Not if he was to live up to his father's wish, and his wife's demands. And keep his daughter in his life. To get through, he needed toe the line. He just had to do what was right, for that fractal math angel if no one else.

He absorbed himself in the routine of pouring a cup. He checked the time—the meeting was scheduled in twenty minutes. Leaning back against the wall, staring at the floor he sipped the hot liquid over the rim and counted. *Un, deux, trois...*but the numbers transformed into that extensive list of remissions he had with life. One was the *warehouse* mentality he supported back home, two, the endless crunching of meaningless numbers to support that warehouse. Now, three, God knows how many weeks in this hellhole contract. Then especially *quatre* the fucking heat. He sank into his accustomed level of rageful despair, his familiar modus operandi bordering on depression. He fumbled the pill bottle from his pocket, fingered out two relaxants and threw them to the back of his throat followed by hot coffee.

Godforsaken, surely a word defined by this place.

Okay, repeat that in French, how does one say godforsaken?

He swung a chair to the table and pulled his jPad, glancing over the almost interesting numbers one more time. Boring in a way, but they came as a long familiar mental exercise. Another welcoming distraction. Where had he left off in that airport Starbucks hour in Frankfurt? Before he caught the ICE train. A spreadsheet, no matter what the numbers had their soothing effect. Had the words or the numbers caught his attention there in Frankfurt? He had just started a review. His Jeenyus buzzed lightly: *me and mummy ar going shoping now daddy*. Of course, what else would his wife do? Back to the review—he would read the scope and purpose. But, he frowned, how could these figures be so low? And the impact so high? Like a catalyst ...

The door banged opened behind him, interrupting his number crunching reverie. Unable to ignore whoever was the invader, he swung over to face them, struggling to downsize his grimace.

A fellow maybe his age bounced over, beaming out a white toothed grin. "How the hell are you, man? I'm Brad." He stepped up to Vince with hand extended, his grin piercing through Vince's being like a sprinkle of sharp children's glitter. *Jesus* Vince thought, you do not want to know. "Hi." His voice cracked. "Vince."

He fumbled the coffee cup to his other hand, and took the handshake, struggling to clear his throat.

"Cool. Where you from?"

"Calgary." Vince coughed. He raised his hand to his mouth, but choked out more. "The City of...you know—the Stampede."

"Hey, my wife's from Canada." Brad bubbled on. Would this guy not shut up? "That's not too far from Spokane. I flew the Bow River valley just out of your city, off Lady MacDonald. You know that peak? Magic air's excellent; spectacular sunset."

Vince glanced hard at the wall, then back. Focus. "Magic air?" Please don't make my head hurt.

"That magic air gives you extra loft in the evenings. I do high mountain flights with a paraglider. Aeronautics, that's my engineering background." His face shone and he shrugged. "Quite an interesting flight getting here. Thirteen hours in Monaco after New York. Across the Mediterranean on Royal Air Monaco and then over the Sahara. Man, those dunes look awesome from forty thousand feet. Started off from Spokane, via Seattle. What route did you take?"

Vince stared at the grinning teeth. He picked out the slight wrinkles around the guy's eyes and his mouth, the type that spoke of one of those permanent smiley faces. Happiness forever in his daughter's talk.

"Lufthansa from Calgary, twenty three hours in Frankfurt, then Lufthansa to Abuja in Nigeria, just two hours there, then Ethiopian Airlines here."

"Holy shit." The face beamed a look of delight. "Long time in Germany."

"Yeah, I got in five hours sleep there, anyway."

"You the chemical guy?"

"Yeah." Vince scowled.

"Well, you know, when I take a look around this place, there's one thing that makes me happy."

No really, Vince thought.

"Sure glad my family's still back home. This seems one rough looking piece of the world." The smile dimmed slightly, but flashed back in full. "But hey, instead of my wife I brought my wing. You always gotta have a backup option."

"Yeah." Vince stared at the grin. He couldn't help feel a tinge of infection and he sighed, "I'm glad to work away from home too. Wouldn't want my little girl here, that's for sure. Nor my wife, well, that's another story."

"You have a daughter? Cool! We have two boys, Josh and Jimmy." Brad poured a coffee. "They would be eight and ten. How old's your girl."

"Seven." He couldn't keep the mist from his eyes, and he felt a strange hurt at the corners of his mouth. "Yeah, she just turned seven. One of the bright spots in my life, for sure…we text all the time." Vince looked closer at the listening eyes of this new acquaintance. He didn't know why, but he went on, "My marriage hasn't been all that great for a while."

"Yeah, I hear you, married life can be a tough gig." The smile didn't dim one bit. "Always some compromise or other."

"Compromise?" Vince curled his lip. "Yeah, right."

They sat at the table. Brad, not stopping had them swapping stories on their engineering backgrounds. Stories told, they turned to figuring out how their positions integrated into this project. Their roles as defined in the contract said Brad would calculate lift for the load while Vince took on supplying the tonnage at the load end. Sulphur dioxide, just another chemical to Vince.

"You like your job a lot?" Brad asked.

Vince grimaced, staring. His lips parted but he clenched his teeth.

"My dad always said you make your choices." Brad casually folded up a piece of paper into what looked like an airplane or some version of a flying device. "You know, there're some doings I find appealing, but a lot don't work for me at all." Brad looked at him, shrugging. Vince watched as Brad stood, stepped up on his chair, then right up onto the table. He scanned the room as he lifted the paper craft above his head, thumb and finger stretched high. Giving the little craft a flick, he set it free to navigate the room's air currents.

"You gotta maximize your elevation for an unpowered craft."

The paper aircraft glided downward gaining speed, and then rose along a slowing arc. But before stalling, it tipped to the side and spiraled around near two complete circles before touching down on the floor. Vince glanced back and forth between the plane and this other engineer. Easing back down from his perch, Brad looked as if he were reviewing the general trajectory in-flight equations in his head. He stared at the airplane where it had landed on the floor, his face content.

"If there's a to-do list item I like, that's anything to do with flight." He grinned. "In fact, I love to fly." He bent and picked up the paper plane, handing it to Vince. "But you know, I didn't always know that. And...I never thought I'd be flying the kind of payload this project calls for."

Chapter 3

Brad talked Vince into a beer. They tracked down the hotel bar and found a corner table to talk over project details. What the specs called Preliminary held top priority, yet they agreed that the Preliminary made up such a tiny component of anything you'd call a project. A hundred kilos of sulphur would be nothing more than an equipment functionality test. Any Phase mentioned after that remained undefined. Should have it done in the next few days. They'd be flying home in a week, as far as they knew. But looking at each other, they wondered why the client would bring them all the way to Africa just for that.

They both shrugged.

"Whatever."

"Yup."

"Brad, you got me curious." Vince took a swig from his second beer. "How *did* you get into flying?"

Brad beamed. "You play crib?" He dug into his device bag, and tossed a game board shape of a number 29 on the table. "Work time's done and now I will tell you my tree climbing story. But only if you fill me in on your life."

"I got no life, but yeah sure. You got pegs?"

"Yes sir, check the bottom of the board. Here, cut for deal." He pulled out a deck of cards and tossed them over in front of Vince. "High card deals. Sounds like you've played."

"Maybe." Vince felt a glimmer of the mischievous.

"Six cards to start, look at them all and keep four. Two down in the middle."

"Right."

Brad told of how as a child he would climb any playground equipment up to the highest point. When they camped up at Priest Lake in Idaho his father said right on to climbing trees, up high where branches thinned to twigs. He'd stay up in that treetop 'til his butt felt sore—he didn't know why. When the wind blew, swaying him around at times he felt like a bit of the breeze. Birds hung out up there, tweeting and scolding, and he looked down on them as they flew by instead of up.

"You flew the treetops." Vince pushed his finger at the card deck.

"No." Just a feeling, there, Brad told him. "That's not flying." More like something he could never put words to, but kinda like when you fit in with everything. Some kind of an up-in-the-air freedom, like those birds. You know, when you feel totally connected with who you really are. "You never feel like that?"

Vince glanced up, staring. "Not really. Maybe. No." Authority had said not allowed, and you always listen to authority, he knew that. Except he spent that summer in Montreal.

"Cut?" Brad split the deck. He brightened when Vince declined.

"Well whatever they supplied us here for a balloon, you gotta come up. That Preliminary requires basic atmospheric tests and they have to take place at elevation. It's cool, man, up there in the sky. You look down, I mean straight down! Like those guys that jump from the edge of space. I'd never go up where they go but still it's a top down view of our planet. And if you like the balloon, I got my wing with me and another shipped and on the way. Come up for a flight, Vince."

Vince looked at him, unconvinced. "What happened after the tree."

As Brad dealt out cards, he told of his teenage discovery of gyrocopters. Only on a movie screen, but when he first saw that pilot in Mad Maks flying that little gyrocopter Brad was blown away. "Now that guy had it all. So much better to be a pilot up in the air than stuck down on the roads in the Maks truck. I never forget that image of a machine flying deep into the blue sky beyond the truck tractor. Why would anyone not want to fly? No way a kid's gonna get a vertical prop unit, but wow!" A couple years later when he and his buddies hung out at the motorbike shop, he heard the owner talking about the weekend coming. A trial-and-learn guy was coming from Seattle with hang gliders.

Now that turned out to be flying! He got his hands on a wing he could pay for then, and found a local hill for launching. His friends stuck with motor-biking, so he learned to fly trial-and-error on his own. Genius that he was, he trialed an install of wheels on the control bar to smooth out awkward landings. One time, he ran at top launch speed and tripped over frontwards dragging all the way down slope with those safety wheels just a spinning. No brakes, so he was dodging rocks all the way. Exhilarating maybe, but definitely poor design.

"We learn." Brad grinned. "Some things by just trying them out, hey?"

"I suppose." Vince picked up his cards, recalling the how-to of this crib game. He looked at Brad. "You got a lot of guts."

Brad's bright grin widened.

"I play first, right," Vince said.

"Yup. Try it out 'til it fits," Brad said. "That's what my dad would always say."

"Four." Vince placed said card.

Brad looked at him, following with his own four and pegging two points.

Vince laid a seven down. "Fifteen two." He pegged. "So your father knew you did all this. And he told you great."

"Never told him about that down slope drag, but yeah, dad's great. We're buds." Brad nodded as he placed a King. "How about you?"

Vince sighed. "My father's the Senior Engineer and CEO of GeoChem, that's the company I represent here. He lives on an acreage out in Rocky View just north of Calgary."

"Oh." Brad raised an eyebrow. "A successful man."

Vince stared at the cards dealt to him. This game had predefined rules, like every other game. Like life. "When you're the type who needs to boss the company, you are the type who needs control. Of everything. My father wants to keep his son, that'd be me, in the company. He has decided he wants a family run business."

They played out the rest of the cards, with no more pegging but for last card. Brad picked up his crib hand.

"My father had a lot of influence on my career." Vince sighed. "He knows exactly what everyone else should do with their lives."

"Fifteen two, fifteen four." Brad pegged his points along the twenty nine route. "And the rest don't score." He threw in his hand, face up.

"You know," Vince said, gathering in the cards for his deal. "I can tell you one thing I find interesting about oilfield engineering. There's no linear equation, and I don't have any stats either, but just looking around Calgary I could rattle off a long list of people working at their oilfield jobs who are not very happy. But you know what? They're trapped in that world of unhappiness. They have a high income lifestyle coming with oil and gas work and they have no idea how to get out."

"Sounds like a kinda suck-ass way to live," Brad said. "And, sounds like you have an interest in people."

"Yes and yes." Vince said, touching his finger to the pain at his mouth corners. "The redesign challenge remains people. How would you reengineer people?"

"Oh yeah," Brad said. "You got yourself one major design challenge there."

As they pegged their way around the board, shuffling, dealing and strategizing, Vince felt a memory stirring. Yes, at times he'd felt free, almost like a bird up in the air. They ordered another beer and started a new game.

"You gotta come up to cloud base," Brad said.

"Define cloud base. I'd venture there's clouds at a lot of elevations."

"Ten thousand feet. Above that, aircraft regulations require oxygen. You can go that high without oxygen, no matter where the clouds are."

Brad continued his come-for-a-flight pitch to Vince. First things first, they would have to head over to the warehouse and check out what they had in storage for a research balloon. For balloon flight you had control over elevation but not much else. Now for paragliding, you had to find lift. You needed to know the atmosphere to ride up on thermals or magic air. Another way to launch easy and find lift off was from a cliff edge. "You're hangin' up there, and you look down, Vince," Brad said. "Like a space station view, just a smaller piece of the planet." Birds know the atmosphere. Raptors use thermals; they need them. That's why they don't migrate across the Gulf of Mexico. No thermals over the ocean. Other birds live and nest on a cliff so they're always set for any next launch.

Brad's eyes sparkled as he spoke. The guy looked set to explode with this insane inner joy, Vince thought.

"You know what astronauts spend most of their free time doing?"

"No." Vince shook his head. "I don't."

"Looking out the window," Brad said. "At their blue green home rock."

Vince nodded, counting his cards and pegging.

"You mention planet a lot."

"Yeah, I've been thinking lately. On how we live."

Vince mused. He leaned back. "You ever live in a warehouse?"

Brad looked at him, blank.

"You know what women like my wife spend most of their free time doing?"

Brad appeared attentive.

"My wife believes in a committed consumer participation plan, that holds supreme reality in her life. Which means we live in a warehouse, and she keeps the consumer items shipping in and shipping out. My position is finance, I finance the whole operation by maximizing our household income. Thus—oilfield engineering."

The home warehouse had a high turnover rate when it came to inventory, with regular stock rotation, Vince explained. Carloads of new merchandise rolled in at their Calgary home, from a set schedule of forays out into the shopping world. Shipping out remained an unresolved issue, which brought up the need for storage space expansion. "Then we need a new house. Often. And each time we move, we make sure we find more storage." Which meant a larger house, Vince emphasized.

"That's quite the analogy," Brad said. "You tell a mean story, dude."

"Yeah, whatever. I mean how did I end up in this warehouse? Well, there I sit in university Engineering class with high school voices in my head telling me over and over that's where I otta be. I aced those math exams, so engineering they kept saying. My father's voice concurred of course. Him and his dinner table business equations. Then along came my wife. She lived then as the pretty receptionist shopping at the time for the lifestyle that comes with an engineering income."

"We all make choices."

Vince stared at Brad.

"Well," Vince said. "Not really."

"No? Look Vince, for me, engineering teaches you how to think," Brad said. "When you're done with that, then you decide what to think." He waggled a finger Vince's way. "I do think about flight design, but I think about a lot more too."

Vince scowled. He pushed the cards about on the table. "So, up in a tree you can be a free bird." His finger stopped suddenly. "You know what I remember most, Brad? From engineering? First year and first year only they give you an optional class. You know what I elected? Archeology 101, The Origin of Humans. Now that was one fascinating topic! Did you know we all came from right here; that our species developed here in Africa? We humans came out more than once, you know, but always out of this place. Africa."

Brad watched him, listening.

"I played this math game all through engineering with a running analysis of my grades. I don't know why but back of my mind said keep minimum grades for grad school. I always put just enough effort into engineering to hit that admittance target. Most amusing part of engineering was tracking my own grade point average. Stress and strain equations were, oh god boring."

"I bet that arky class helped with your GPA."

"You got that right—I got an A." Vince massaged the corners of his mouth. "And there's no A+ on that grade scale."

"Let me tell you something, Vince." Brad leaned towards him. "That, my friend, was passion. When you put your whole being into something, that's what it is. Not because of what some school teacher tells you. Or even your dad. You're never gonna feel happy following directives. Unless you're a soldier, which counts neither of us."

"Yeah, well anyway I did fly free." Vince sighed, staring. "Once or twice."

"That archaeology class?"

"Nope, more." Vince looked at him. "I worked one summer job in Montreal. Nights at a punk bar, *Foufounes*. Nothing to do with math, just wild dancing and a lotta French."

"Cool."

"Never forgot. So a decade of engineering, and I walk into my father's office one day and quit. Kind of. I went back and did that graduate degree. Man, so many optional classes. I learned how to structure grammar in French. Of course who speaks French in an oil patch job? I heard that over and over. And an ancient civilizations class, so cool. My wife screamed of course." He winced. "But I crunched the people numbers and wrote a thesis on human behavior. Anyways, I had that bit of free bird time."

"Fits with your reengineering people idea," Brad said.

"My graduate supervisor told me one thing I'll never forget. In anthropology, there're beliefs and there's behavior. These two human factors correlate at times, but often they don't. They are independent variables, and both measurable. Did you know that? People say one thing and do another."

"Some might just say 'no shit' to that," Brad said.

Vince stretched his mouth sideways, realizing he would have to work out the pain of this persistent unfamiliar smile. "But all the time at home it was, 'What are you gonna do with a degree in arts? *For christ's sakes*. Should have got an MBA.' My father would say that. My wife went on a silent spending spree. She set us back a couple years on the next house mortgage. Oh well, that's what I did."

"Yeah."

"I tell you, forget chemistry." Vince went on. "We need a faculty of people engineering. You know you can analyze social issues, and evaluate trends in human behavior? You know human behavior is so complex you best run statistics? You can analyze a lot of the story of that species that came out of Africa."

"You never switched careers?"

"When I said 'kind of quit', well, my father had a compromise. I do the degree, then I come back to the company. Anyway, getting a Calgary job in social science would not pan out. With maximizing income as primary to meet my wife's lifestyle, engineering was the best option and holding shares in a private family business. Voila, GeoChem. Anyway, I want my daughter to see a good family model."

"Is she seeing that?"

Vince shut his eyes for a moment. When he opened them, he was staring down at the table.

"Maybe you were meant for something else."

"Yeah, no shit. No shit. Look, bottom line, I got a daughter, and I just want to keep her in my life. Just gotta toe that line and pay the bills."

"You know, Vince, I got a feeling about this project." Brad tapped his finger lightly on the table. "You just might get yourself a whole new line to toe."

Chapter 4

Next morning found them looking over outdoor patio breakfast options in the swirling aroma rising from cups of Ténéré Dark. The aqua blue of the Gaweye pool glinted in the morning light from its oblique corners. Vince at first reacted to the hot morning sun, but sitting at a parasol shaded table he relaxed as a gentle breeze rustled cool through the palm fronds.

"Just guessing from last night, Vince, don't get me wrong," Brad said. "But I would say you've got a reengineering design for your wife."

Vince threw his menu down on the table, squinting at Brad.

"Man, we used to talk." He shook his head. "But she can be so harsh."

"Maybe you're too sensitive."

"You my mother?"

"Nope."

Vince took a sip of coffee, and a deep breath.

"Listen up on this Brad. Take a typical day when I'm at home. I get up in the morning real quiet like and start working on a project or two. That's my most productive time of day, first thing in the morning. But as soon as my wife gets up, she's on my case with her issues. Like she needs me to go get groceries or whatever. And when she wants something done, that means not some time that morning or what would work best for me that evening, not even in two minutes but right fucking now."

"I see." Brad nodded. "But why doesn't she get the groceries?"

"She doesn't feel like it! But I'll get to more on that."

"So off I go with her grocery store list or whatever," Vince said. "And that's how it goes through the rest of the day. She gets what she wants and I get pissed off. Passive aggressive, that's my psycho adjective. Being subconsciously passive, I fit what I need to do in when I can, and always last. There I flounder in the evening, my least productive time. By then I'm so pissed—my aggressive part has set in."

Brad pulled his chair in a little closer.

"I think Haydon and Jackie have issues like that."

"The Mars pair bond," Vince said. "You part of the voting audience?"

"No. But you hear about them everywhere. They're the latest romance story around, am I right?"

"Classic case of people living in fantasy. Jackie's the first woman of child bearing age in our grand extraterrestrial experiment. I wouldn't call it romance. But everyone sure knows who they are and the details of their lives and their launch date. People love stories, and a *love* story in some faraway place or now a faraway planet catches everyone's attention."

"Well, they get the Planet B option untainted by any climate crisis."

"Climate crisis?" Vince's voice dropped to a hush. "No one back home talks about that. In the news its change isn't it...not crisis."

"Really?" Brad's look lost some gleam and he spoke softer. "Maybe not your guys' end of the planet." But he shrugged and nodded at Vince. "So give me more on your love story then."

"Love...yeah, maybe when we first got together." Vince looked at Brad. "Look my wife just doesn't like grocery shopping. She just doesn't like a lot of things. When I hear that, my deep psyche kicks in...always try to please and appease those around me." He paused. "You and my mother got it right. Extra sensitive, that's another psycho analysis of my personality type. It exhausts my type to set required boundaries, to make it clear to others what I find fair. Or not fair!"

Vince bounced his fist on the table, staring at a palm frond dangling from the roof of their sunshade.

"The thing is, I can't fucking change my personality type. Why doesn't science devise psycho surgery, the more invasive the better? Instead of this Mars Mission technology. Anyway I go along with what she wants, and that stupid naïve part of me hopes she'll realize she needs to do something in return for me later. Yeah, forget that."

"You ever talk about it? With her I mean." Brad said. "I hear Jackie and Haydon have a relationship counsellor. Gonna be remote from Earth when they get to Mars though."

They handed their menus to the waiter as they selected breakfast orders.

"To have effective results from a counsellor, you have to hear the counsel. My wife's type, whatever that may be, has one distinct trait. She does not listen well. I mean that's another issue. I detest repeating what I've just said. Or getting cut off in a conversation— which she does all the time."

Vince paused, jiggling at the arrangement of his knife and fork on their napkin.

"The thing that comes out of her, once we get on talking terms for a while is 'can you do this whatever-it-is for me?'. I feel like a servant boy with a task, or a dog on fetch duty. She always finds a chore for me to do, every time I'm in her presence. Okay if she were doing something in return, something meaningful to me ..."

"How do you feel in your relationship?" Brad cut in. "First thing in your mind."

Vince's hand paused with the cutlery. "Manipulated, man, not just that but controlled and used. Yeah, that. You analyzing me? Thanks. I mean she couldn't give the slightest shit about what's important to me. She's good at manipulating and controlling. I'm pathetic. I have no energy for the power struggle and in the end ninety percent of my life energy goes into playing out her script."

Brad took a sip of coffee, nodding.

"I'd be long gone from this marriage." Vince pushed his fork and knife apart off the napkin edges. "The thing is," he choked, "sorry...I just want my little daughter to have a good life, and a stable safe home."

"Yeah, I hear you. Kids are everything."

"But look at the way things are now! My daughter's back in Calgary, I'm here in Africa and I see her camera image in a Holo-Skype cube or I hear her voice or we text." Vince half smiled through wet eyes. "She loves texting words, you know. I'm not sure what I'm supposed to do for her. I mean I do appreciate what my wife does for our daughter, don't get me too wrong, and maybe she's growing at her own pace. My mom and dad are at least friends in their own way; it hasn't come out that way for me yet, for us."

"Each relationship has issues. Could be there's something else you can do for your daughter."

"Like?"

"Well, as my wife would say, check in with the universe," Brad said. "She's like that. I'm kinda more down to earth. I mean I fly, but rarely above cloud base."

"The worst of it is when I'm the target, not other people. When my wife talks and even her parents say she has a sharp tongue, it feels like hanging in a sack kicked with a sharp pointy shoe. When she has a project going—she's the project manager and no one rests unless and until she says so. You're exhausted it's your regular day to do something else, well tough shit. You do it and you do it now."

"That's one of Jackie and Haydon's issues," Brad said. "She is the commanding officer." He looked at Vince. "My wife can be the boss, but only sometimes."

"Really?" Vince went on. "Yeah well, the thing going through my wife's mind any given day is her house sized up against others nearby. Life is all about the neighbourhood and the neighbours. There're some neighbourhoods you wanna move to, and others you keep far away. Her grand plan is we make a move out to Rocky View into an estate house like my father's. We've moved what five times now, always to a larger house and not just for storage space. The money coming into her household has to show like a billboard to those around—it's all about look at me. The house you occupy scores you points or takes points away. No use any of my social science talk in our household. I get firsthand experience on beliefs translated into behavior."

"You sound kinda like my wife," Brad said. "She calls the consumer outlook pure hypnosis with a big boost by advertising. She talks about starting a business, like 'The Party's Over: The Gift of a Low Impact Lifestyle' counselling service. With a program de-contaminating the mind from advertising."

"How do you get clients?" Vince brushed his eyes with his napkin. "Can I send my wife your way?"

"She says advertising doesn't sell on usefulness. Instead the business model seeks to keep people dissatisfied. What we see in Holo cube adverts, show you in your dream-come-true role, right along with the advertiser's product. She says self-restraint has potential."

"Self-restraint?" Vince scoffed. "Yeah, okay forget that."

"My wife also says you wanna change. The client's motivated by some kinda trauma." Brad said. "You know people. They gotta lose a job or go bankrupt or get a divorce."

Vince looked him straight in the eye for a second.

"Life's tough my friend," Brad said. Then he grinned. "But you know, depends how you look at things. Like my cousin in Idaho always says 'won't matter in a hundred years.'"

They sat back as the waiter set their meals before them.

"I wish I could have half your way of looking at things," Vince said.

"Hey hey hey." Brad dug into his eggs, "There's nothing you can do about what other people do anyway. You might as well take it easy, do what you can and have fun with it."

"Yeah."

"You know, sounds like the best thing you've got is your daughter." Brad shrugged. "Hey, you become her storybook hero."

"Hero? That's bullshit—life's not a fairy tale."

"Might be for her," Brad said. His smile dimmed. "And there's plenty of room for meaningful action in my version of the near future world."

Vince glanced at Brad.

"You know what our project's really about?" Brad's voice changed.

"Atmospheric tests. Reaction rates. Someone needs data for that Terraform Mars operation."

"Terraforming creates an atmosphere," Brad said carefully. "Geoengineering adjusts an atmosphere. Like fine tuning the climate."

"Geoengineering." Vince raised his eyebrows. "You think that's what we're doing?"

"Someone wants data on adjusting our atmosphere."

"Bullshit."

"North American air regulations would totally prohibit any of this back home. So that's why they want us here in Africa, unrestricted."

Vince stared, and his Jeenyus buzzed. He read the text from his daughter, now completely ignoring the pain of his fully emerging smile. "Hey check this out. My girl says they're using the SMART board at school today but they encountered some problems, look here, read." He showed the visiscreen to Brad. *Teknologee issues daddy. You draw and the line goes in the rong plas.*

Brad scanned over the message more than once, glancing at Vince. They beamed at each other as parents who dream of their children's tomorrow.

"Hey, we gotta get over to that warehouse," Brad said. "Check out the balloons."

Vince felt a rising excitement on the flying idea. And a sinking chill as he realized he'd have to listen more to Brad's take on their project.

Chapter 5

Aahil awoke to the din of the pre-dawn city. Rising in the broken shadows from his rooftop mat, he touched Hilal's shoulder. His son, feeling his father's hand, rose to wipe at his sleepy eyes. This eldest son would come learn the ways of the world today; the other children must attend classes and assist in the restaurant. Hamina would organize the household. He stepped down through the rooftop portico, one hand on the wall and each foot seeking out the next familiar brick step below.

On the main floor he felt the shelf where Hamina had left Taguella spread with goat cheese wrapped in a cloth. His Hamina, his eyes softened, his Tin Hinan. They ate as they walked through the door to the plaza. "Open the gate." He spoke English to his sons by rule. French only when necessary out there in the city. Tamajaq was a language to be spoken among family from the Tinarimen, the deserts of the north. English, the world language of business must be one stitch in the fabric of his camp.

His father had made business the way of Aahil's childhood. With insight he had journeyed from the desert tents into this city of Niamey. Food, he knew all people must eat. The restaurant along Avenue de l'Afrique became the centre of life for his mother and father. They negotiated and jostled out a life, dealing in meals to support an urban lifestyle. That restaurant had for him been a classroom, as there he learned not only lessons on how money changes hand, but the languages of the world. At every chance he spoke with government workers in French, those on their lunch breaks and he mimicked their etiquette. He paid attention to the television English, picking up on the mannerisms of Europe and America. The official classroom may help others speak foreign but for him the words of another mother tongue translated as he simply listened.

He slid into the front seat to start the Nissan, pulling out into the street.

His son pulled the steel gate closed behind, and scurried about to jump in the far seat. They turned left from their compound onto the side street, circling the block to check on the restaurant. His mother wanted Ténéré, the true desert, for a restaurant name. But his father told her Drakkar was French, the title of a European warrior ship from the north. Now the wooden carved sign with the sailing ship beside Drakkar had gathered many clients. His father had insight into people and business. In another land, he would say, we must fit with how those who live take in each day, there in that place we go. Leave the ghosts of our desert past to swirl among the dunes; his eyes would twinkle as he spoke.

They stopped for fuel. Aahil explained to his son how the new contract credit card worked. For this one, he had only to walk into the Minister's office and speak to the Asian at the project office. The card would last for all the time of the contract. As had that contract before—escorting the young white haired Canadian some days after the rains of August. That one had been two weeks; this one will be two weeks absolutely and perhaps extend longer. The rule: always keep the fuel tank full, as when they decide the contract finishes, the card will no longer purchase. The Asians made good business partners though, truly good. They at times paid in advance, they paid always, they accepted no tips and they paid well.

The Minister's office had been abuzz that time. Not just the election coming, but something other was causing a stir. Connected to these recent contracts he suspected. He would need to keep talking with those he knew. As a Berber, he would never sit at a government desk, but there were those others he knew, the ones who spoke openly. More than one language helped in many ways.

He turned the Nissan into Hotel Gaweye to park. Leaving Hilal to guard the vehicle, Aahil walked up the steps and in through the main entrance. Speaking softly with an attendant, he followed the gesture through a wall of crystal windows. He walked up steps to push opened a glass door leading to the dog leg angles of the tourist swimming pool. Shifting his glance carefully, he picked out two white men sitting in cushioned chairs, each with a jPad before him. He walked directly into the shade of their thatch table parasol.

"I am Aahil," he announced. "I am your driver and I will answer your questions."

Vince and Brad looked up and came to their feet. Aahil shook each hand as was the custom of Europeans. When the one called Brad motioned to a chair, he took a seat on the edge.

"You want a coffee?" Brad said. American, he would say by the voice.

Aahil raised a hand to decline, yet also shook his head as he had learned. He respectfully took in these two, not looking directly their way, but remaining attentive. He watched, as the silent Vince took a sip from his cup. Not quite American, this other one, close but something else. He gave them time to adjust to his presence, patiently setting for them his own image.

"We were checking out your bridge." Brad showed many teeth as he spoke again. "We're engineers—well known for building bridges."

The smiling engineer pointed through the poolside grove to the green steel-railed bridge crossing the wide waters of the Niger River. They had been discussing, he told Aahil, how and when the bridge was built. How its stick-in-the-mud construction crossed the wet earth-bank island in the middle where the water spliced the island into smaller ones.

"That one has the name Pont Kennedy," Aahil said. "The first built, yes."

"The U.S. built that bridge," Brad said. American, yes, Aahil was sure now.

"When we cross you will see better. Look past, two kilometers more distant. Pont Chinois the second built."

"Chinese Bridge," Vince said. This one spoke French Aahil detected.

"The second bridge has two lanes each way," Aahil said. "The bridges are Niamey's way to ocean ports. China now builds a third."

"So why," Vince asked, "would a country like China or the United States build a bridge in an African country?"

"People here call the second bridge Pont Chinois," Aahil told him. "But the bridge has an official name that may explain. The China Niger Friendship Bridge."

"There you go, they want to be buds." Brad winked. "Strategic friendship."

This American spoke so lightly of things that Aahil relaxed. What another takes as serious. "You have not come to build a bridge." He allowed his eye the slightest twinkle.

"Nope. We don't do bridges." Brad grinned. "We do atmosphere."

"You will change our air?"

The American looked at Vince, smile fading. "That's what I think."

"The Chinese own mines at Agadez," Aahil said. "They require transport trucks to carry cargo to the ports."

Vince nodded.

By the voice of this other engineer he was European Aahil thought. Or with French, as that white haired Canadian. But the American spoke again, pointing. Aahil followed his gesture to the horned animals grazing in the tall green river grass closer to the water's edge and as far along as they could see up and downriver. "Those cattle look thin. They live here in the city?"

"Yes, the rain was small this season," Aahil explained. "The Hausa graze their herds where the grass grows."

"Droughts come with climate crisis," Brad said.

"Seasonal variation," the other white man spoke back.

Aahil waited for the whisper of tense air he sensed to settle.

"You speak French?" Brad broke the silence.

"*Oui monsieur. Et vous aussi?*" Aahil's eyes twinkled brighter at Brad's blank look. English preferred for this smiling one. "Yes, I am available to translate for you. I speak English, French, the local Hausa dialect, local Zarma and the Tuareg language if we need. The Tuareg language has the name Tamajaq."

Brad turned to Vince. "You're on top of French, right?"

"Maybe not on top of, but I can get by." Vince nodded. Then he looked to Aahil. "I'm Canadian, where the French colonized along with the English, so we are officially bilingual."

"Wild, man, we are set to communicate."

Aahil's ears perked. Two North Americans from two countries. He took in these two more closely. This American connected well with people, one he could enjoy being around. But he had guided many foreigners, and knew trust was earned. What to trust would come with time. "I am available to take you where you wish, any day, any time of day," he told them. "My Jeenyus number is here." He pulled the phone from inside his loose colorful jacket and showed the visiscreen. The American Brad looked, and spoke the digits into his jPad.

"Come. I am to take you to the storage compound today." Aahil rose from his chair. "We will cross the bridge you are talking of and go more past the city's edge on the Boulevard du Gourma." He stood waiting beside the table.

The other two finished the last of their coffee and gathered up their devices. They came to their feet beside Aahil, and he led them back out through the glass door.

#

Vince followed beside Brad and their new guide as they left the hotel entrance. The heat seared more intense in the front, than the shaded pool. Down the steps and walking across the asphalt they approached an attentive teenager standing with crossed arms beside a waiting SUV. The guide and youth looked both to be of medium height, dark, and with brown eyes. Strands of curly black hair poking out contrasted with their blue turbans and bright colored clothing. Aahil, that was his name, and his introduced son was Hilal. The father held his head straight and true, his chin up and his gaze appeared terminally calm.

Vince found himself in the back seat beside Brad, and he watched out the window as their guide drove them from hotel parking out onto the street. They turned, then circled the Rond and pulled onto Pont Kennedy, the long green bridge.

"This bridge gotta be a half mile long," Brad said.

"Yes," Aahil said, "A small amount less. Seven hundred and ten meters."

Brad laughed. "You guys are metric here too." He looked at Vince.

"Only Americans still count feet and miles," Vince said.

"Hey, no problem." Brad grinned. "You guys may be the word language experts, but I can speak metric. Zero point seven one kilometers."

As they passed over the bridge Vince gazed out at the many people walking back and forth along sidewalks on either side. Brad pointed, and Vince also noticed a well-dressed man in a suit beaming at them from a poster hung on each sequential light post.

"Who's that guy?" Brad asked Aahil.

"The president of Niger."

"Lotta posters."

"He promises a miracle to his people—the Green Sahara will be returned to us."

"Sounds bogus," Vince said. "How could anyone do that?"

"Our president has ideas and an election to win."

Vince felt Brad's eyes on him, but he turned to stare far along the river not wanting to hear that atmosphere word again. Not yet...yet he had talked of Mars followers living in fantasy.

Crossing the bridge Aahil told them of the picture alongside the bright smiling face—the Dabous Giraffes. There had been a time, long before recorded history, when the Sahara was truly green. But not all records were written in words. The Dabous Giraffes had been etched in stone at that time and the famous pictograph remained to this day. Carved some seven thousand years past, the giraffe pair told of the time when the desert had not been desert, but grew grass enough for hoofed animals. The people listened when the president spoke of this age. Other records neither in words spoke of a green Sahara, but the image of those two giraffes caught the peoples' attention best. Beautifully carved into the stone of Dabous, the male beside the female, they stood a full five meters high, life-size.

"The Dabous Rock is half way to Arlit from Agadez close to the Aïr Mountains." Aahil told them. "But a few kilometers off the tar road. We will go, if you wish to see."

"Mountains." Brad grinned, nodding.

They sped up as urban development thinned. The road became the N6 which, Aahil told them, would take them to the border of Burkina Faso. The N1, the other way before the bridge, back past the airport would take them to Dosso and from there the N7 south to the border with Benin. There would be the closest ports on the Gulf of Guinea. Uranium flowed to port that way. Oil wealthy Nigeria sat to the east of Benin, with all its peoples and all of its oil companies. Prosperous times there now, for some.

"Nigeria," Vince repeated. He turned to Brad. "That's one potential material source on the list they provided. Storage tanks, steel pipe and liquid sulphur dioxide. If this thing goes anywhere past Preliminary that is."

They pulled up to the compound entrance. Aahil introduced them to the guard, speaking lightly in one of the local dialects. The guard smiled broadly, opening the gate to let them in. "Green Sahara," he said in English. Vince and Brad looked to Aahil.

"This man dreams—he believes you have come to bring the miracle," Aahil said. "But as you now know him, you have access to this compound. At any time."

They drove into the compound and over to the warehouse building. The guard had followed and he unlocked and pulled open one of the warehouse doors. They all stepped out of the vehicle, and the two engineers walked inside, looking around.

"Hey, this looks like a passenger balloon with a basket," Brad said. "Probably helium. Should work."

"So cloud base right? "Vince looked sideways at Brad. "Ten thousand feet you said." He paused, scanning the plastic and metal containers stacked against the walls. "So what's that in metric?"

"Fifty meters more than 3 kilometers." Brad beamed. "Like I said Vince, you really gotta come along. You'll love it up there; if you don't mind heights. The views, the freedom. Fantastic." He turned to their driver standing in the doorway. "We're gonna need you guys, Aahil, to follow this balloon with us in it and pick us up for a ride back here. We'll use GPS to coordinate locations. A lot depends on the wind direction that day."

Aahil lifted his chin to acknowledge, nodding his ascent.

Vince walked over to a large steel vessel. The red paint characters SO2 were stencil-painted on the tank. The pressure gauge told him liquid sulphur dioxide and the float gauge showed the tank full.

"What prevailing winds you got around here this time of year?" Brad asked.

"The winds blow this season from northeast," Aahil said.

"So we'll be drifting southwest. We land best as close to a road as possible for pick up. Somewhere along that N6 highway you say goes down to Burkina Faso. We definitely don't want to cross any international borders." Brad asked what kind of road pattern there was along the highway. Almost none, Aahil told him, but Brad listened close when their guide talked of the wadis. They would drive off road best along a drainage. There the exposed rocks kept any vehicle out of the sand, acting almost as a road.

"Hey Vince, almost like we're a second shift." Brad mused. "I mean my specs told me all of this equipment would be here. We've got the helium launch balloons, the helium tanks, those 100 litre PVC vessels must be to carry test sulphur. I'll check with the inventory details on what's here. But, just like someone was here before us getting things prepped."

"Yeah same," said Vince. "The sulphur dioxide volume we need for more than one test looks like it's right here. This vessel holds three tons. I don't know where the sulphur was sourced, but we easily run Preliminary multiple times. We're set for that, anyway."

They looked at each other, and back and forth at Aahil.

"Okay, so we take this passenger balloon up to cloud base, test a batch of those pop valves and carry out the Preliminary release. Try out the dispersal hardware." Brad shrugged. "So basically, we debug the release procedure."

"Yup." Vince nodded.

"Hey Aahil," Brad said. "I've been having a look at those ridges just to the south. What say you drive us over there and see if we can make it to the top. Anywhere up high. I left my wing back at the hotel, but looks like those could be some excellent launch sites. Easily a couple hundred feet of vertical. Can we get over there to check them out?"

"We can drive there, maybe two kilometers," Aahil said, looking. "We will search for the wadi there."

"Excellent," Brad said.

"You have interest in mountains." Aahil looked at Brad. "You may wish to go east and north to Agadez. There in the desert we have the Aïr Mountains. Those are the true mountains of Niger."

They drove from the compound down the N6 highway, turning off onto a local street. Not much further the street opened up to the sand of a dry drainage. Aahil shifted the Nissan into four wheel drive and they followed the rocky stream bed up towards the point on the ridge Brad had picked. On a weaving path between boulders, Aahil wove a careful way partially up the ridge. But not to the top.

"No more," Aahil told them stopping on a level spot.

Vince turned to Brad.

"Excellent," Brad said. "We hike up."

As Vince stepped out he watched Brad orient their position relative to the edge of the rocky outcrop. Aahil lifted a hand from the window as they walked away. Brad picked a route for their upward trek, crunching on the rocky sun baked ground between scattered drifts of sand. Vince fell in behind. He could feel the day heating, but a cooling breeze blew up the ridge.

"So how do you see us packaging the sulphur?" Brad asked over his shoulder. "For Preliminary."

"Ah, it's liquid and low pressure," Vince said. "One of those hundred litre plastic cans. A liquid litre being a kilogram, one of the wonders of the metric system."

"Yeah, okay so your hundred kilograms that's two twenty pounds no problem with the lift there," Brad said. "You can rig up the dispersal hardware?"

"Yeah yeah," Vince said.

They came to a set of protruding rocks almost like stairs, and they stepped along keeping single file.

"So we're up in the helium balloon." Brad turned back, stopping for a breath. "From there, we dump the plastic can with dispersal hardware and a helium lift balloon that takes it up up and away. We give a wireless call signal for release and we watch. Should work."

"Two or three days and we report back on Preliminary."

"Mostly a procedural test."

"Yup."

Brad grabbed a stone, and winged it up over the edge above them. They could hear the rock chip rattle and clatter out of sight. They went on.

"What we said back in the warehouse," Vince said thoughtfully. "The contact lists, the project design specs. Someone did run through this before us. I mean everything's there!"

"Yeah. And this is Africa," Brad said. "My co-design guy Keith does developing country work and he says deadlines are typically a joke. Nothing on time and the schedule can be a mess. Hey, you'd like the guy. He's got a daughter just like you."

Brad brought up an infogram from Keith with his photo ID on the side. "You gotta meet the guy some day."

"And he still does overseas work?"

"That's his trade off, yeah."

"Well, this plan's been thought through." Vince kicked a rock to the side, listening as it bounced and rolled behind him.

"So then I wonder if they got the right people. You and me I mean." Brad said. "An American and a Canadian. Maybe they screwed up there. Could be they wanted a couple Chinese engineers."

"Yeah, whatever. Just another contract," Vince said. "Overseas bonus lets me pay the bills."

An extra high step took them up and over a pinnacle. The natural rock surface lay flat before them, near level as the concrete floor back in the warehouse. Brad walked to the edge and looked down. As Vince edged closer to catch a glance, he could just make out the diminished figures of Aahil and his son standing by the Nissan far below.

"So dude." Vince could sense that beaming face beside him. "You stand near the edge and inflate your wing. Right here. You got this nice little breeze coming up the ridge, that gives you lift, and so you step off into that wind like a cliff top hawk."

Vince turned to stare at this fellow, shaking his head. But for the crazy climate crisis talk, this was beginning to feel like an adventure in the making.

Chapter 6

Harry followed his son down their concrete front drive, each lugging a duffel bag with protruding hockey sticks through the crunching fallen leaves. Glancing back to view their Ottawa home, he waved at his wife behind the French doors. He touched Release and the Lexus LS back doors slid to the sides. He threw his bag into the plush carpeted compartment breathing in that new car interior smell. "So this'll be your side this season, Jase, and the other your brother's." Jason mimicked his father, heaving his bag up into the SUV. "Okay dad." They climbed into swanky front bucket seats and Harry backed out onto their street. "We'll keep your hockey bags in the Lexus the rest of the winter. You boys each have a game or practice every week and this'll work for tournaments too. Should be good." He ruffled his son's hair.

He drove towards the local Durrell arena. The cold blustery day brought a sure sign of a Canadian winter on the way. He engaged his son in banter. Who was playing on Jase's team this year and Harry's memories of his team back when he was fourteen. Jase's younger brother Sten just had his thirteenth birthday. "How are the new skates?" They had shelled out seven hundred dollars for the boys' new skates this year. Each! A bit of a kick but hey, they always found a way to pay. The new sticks were a ninety dollar set back too, but the best quality Harry had heard. Not too many broken this year he hoped; he'd appealed to Angie's soft spot. Who, as a mother, could deny her boys what they deserved? Not a problem, the game came first and a slap shot could always score a goal. You gotta take a chance out on that ice—he could feel the surge of the game rush through him. They'll need new pads this year. Growing boys he'll tell Angie; that line helped hedge her resistance.

Harry got Jase talking on his new school. After grade eight at Vincent Massey in their Riverview community, he and Angie applied for their son's admittance to Ashley College up in chic Rockcliffe Park. Many Prime Ministers' children had attended that prestigious school. "Hockey school was great this summer, eh?" Best to keep up skating and stick handling skills. "Yeah dad." Balance that out with the other month of summer they spent at the lake, water skiing and ripping around on the sea-doos. The motor home stayed parked this year and they opted for the rental lake house. There was always next summer. That lake turned out great with their friends and friends' boys renting the other half of the beach front home. The bush crashing motocross trails for the not-so-hot days were great for the boys. Tentative support of their friends' mother for boys out on bikes helped console Angie on the danger. They both took a riding safe riding course, but, well, boys will be boys.

Harry turned in at the sign—Jim Durrell Recreation Centre—and found a parking spot. Touching a wheel button with his thumb, he had the back doors slide apart into slots. He loved this new vehicle! They grabbed the bags and walked in through the front doors. When Jase headed off for the change rooms clutching both bags like the little man he was Harry found his way to the ice rink benches. He needed to make a few calls and the unheated yet quiet rink area worked excellent as a communication base. Close to centre line he parked himself in one of the blue plastic seats. Scrolling down his contacts list, he selected Allan, the workmate who didn't mind going to every NHL game he could.

"Hey Al." The guy answered right away.

"Hey Harry. What's up?"

"Just at the rink—Jase has a practice. Hey, you remember last time we talked. I was telling you how Spezza checked Glass in game five. You know, Eastern Conference, semi-finals last season. You remember how they went on to win that game. Now that was a turning point I'm never going to forget; that's what got the Sens into the playoffs. They have to be hitting back and hitting hard, man. That's the way they gotta keep playing this year."

"Yeah, okay Harry, I'll give you that Spezza's a good player but his line could definitely use some help. Coach needs to play more Chinsky time on his line. Even Don Junior analyzes that line option."

"Yeah, well, Mr. Don Junior has a lot of opinions," Harry said. "Many of which are not too accurate."

"So Harry," Allan said. "You got those tickets for the home opener Saturday?"

"Yes, in fact, I picked up season tickets yesterday. You got yours?"

"That other friend I was telling you about did, so yeah," Allan said. "He got something going that evening so I'm in on his ticket for the game. Should work out again this year, four of us splitting two season tickets. You gonna pick me up?"

"Sounds good Bud," Harry said. "You get the parking and I will get the beers."

The Ottawa Senators would be starting the season at home, playing their rival Toronto Maple Leafs. Home team always played a great game, and he'd especially be following the new team captain. Jason Spezza had been traded to the Senators a few years ago and kept getting better and better each year. He'll have to pick up Allan where he lives just off the Queensway on the way out to the Scotiabank Place.

"We gotta talk shop a bit Allan," Harry said. "So first, did you set up that meeting for tomorrow with Climate Minister Kendall's office? We have to confirm the position they want to take at the OECD negotiations. We have to make sure we are clear on that." Allan affirmed this had been done. "I glanced over that infogram you forwarded from Lewis over at Braunstein and Eichel," Harry went on. He could picture the man with his shock of premature white hair. "I don't know what to think, brings a chuckle to me in a way. I mean, they weren't even negotiating! Seems more like influence peddling, but based on what? Why would they want to take Lewis on a ground tour of some obscure part of Africa? I'll have to give him a call and see what he says." Allan agreed it was worth a follow up call. "Right, on my list if I get a chance. We can talk more about that after the game, okay? We have some other high priority issues over the next couple weeks, do we not? Are you up on that Harden presentation next Wednesday. I am going to have André in on that one."

"Good idea, Harry," Allan said. "André catches the real gist of what's going on. Who is ICFSC again? Do you want me to be totally up on this Tim Harden?"

"Make sure you know the basics. Mr. Harden is the director. ICFSC, you know, International Friends of Climate Science Coalition. Been based right here in Ottawa for a few years. Professor Harden taught climate change classes at Carleton from quite a meaningful perspective. He reminds me a lot of my graduate advisor in Montreal. He takes an open ended outlook on climate change. Basically free enterprise will solve the climate change issue if and when it proves true in the eyes of the market and voting citizens. Based on every-day-evidence. So that would be what a real life person like you or me can see, not from the obscure theory of some lab scientist. Most importantly, Minister Kendall's office has expressed an interest." Harry had finished his degree in political science at Carlton and then a Master's of Sustainability Negotiations at McGill.

Allan was new to the climate change negotiations side of the consultancy business but his political negotiating skills are pretty well honed. He had been with the firms' national team before, so Harry was filling him in on their international tactical team. The guy picked up fast, retained detail well and definitely had a unique demeanour so far. A likable way of speaking went a long ways when things get hot under the collar at the table. Even went so far as reading up on extra research sources. Good fit, Harry had let Harold Heine their CEO know more than once. In his first weeks with H&S Harry had come straight into international negotiations but with some helping guidance to start.

Harry felt the grin on his face as he clicked off this workmate connection and selected call home. As the phone buzzed, he looked out through the plexiglass across the rink. Jase came out on the ice and lifted his stick as he skated past his father. Harry gave a little shoulder-up-in-the-air signal as his son looked back to watch.

"Hey babe, how's things?"

"Oh, hi honey," his wife answered. "I am just getting dinner on the table for Sten and I. Oohh Harry, guess what? I went for lunch with Sylvie today and they're just moving into their new Lindenlea place. She really loves their new house, and she was telling me *all* about it. It just sounds so gorgeous."

"Right, wow, cool. As good our kitchen reno? Was that just last year, babe?"

"I know honey, I know. I like our kitchen, I really do, it's just when I heard Sylvie talk ..."

"Yeah, Angie. Listen you'll like what I've been thinking."

"Tell me honey."

"What we've been talking about, you know, our place is getting kind of old. So how about we really start looking for a place closer to school for Jase. From the way he talks, he's fitting right in at Ashbury College. So if Jase still likes it there later in the year, say, well you know how Sten likes everything his brother does, so he should be able to follow his brother over to Ashbury for grade nine next year. I mean Riverview has been a nice community, but we should be looking at a place closer. Up in Lindenlea too or Vanier North. Even right in Rockcliffe Park, hey babe?"

The phone was silent, but he knew he had used his convincing tones, so he waited.

"Oohh Harry, we would barely qualify for that kind of a mortgage. You know that. And we still have payments on our Toyota. I still don't know if leasing the Lexus LX was such a good idea."

He knew when to wait, and when to listen. He shushed lightly to not leave a silent blank.

"I really do want to drop in on Sylvie though," his wife continued. "I'd just love to see her kitchen. The whole place sounds so cute, marble counter tops, beautiful hardwood floors and a built in Jacuzzi out on the deck. You just step out the Montage doors and into the hot water with a glass of wine in your hand." Harry could taste that sigh in her voice.

"Angie, c'mon babe, we needed the Lexus, remember, we need the space for the boys' hockey equipment. The Highlander's just too small. And you like to drive the Lexus, right, especially when the roads get icy."

"It's just so big Harry, and awkward." She sighed again. "But, yes, I do feel safer. I guess it's one of life's little trade-offs."

Harry smiled.

"Contracts are looking pretty good at the office," Harry said. "I know I'll be gone for that week in November, the COP negotiations again. But hey, in Florence this time. That's in Tuscany, babe, you know, the kicked back wine drinking lifestyle. *La vita.* You'd love it I know but don't worry, we'll all go one day. And then bonuses come out in December, I mean looks like they'll be pretty good this year. We should start looking around at places the next few months, babe. Something newer, definitely bigger."

"Do you really think so? Oh I love you Harry."

"Sten has his first practice tomorrow. You gonna come watch?"

"Oohh Harry…maybe. Honey, I have to get Sten's dinner on the table while it's hot. I'll leave you guys something on the stove."

"Okay babe, love you."

Harry put the phone back in his pocket. He stood to balance like a kid on his blue formed seat looking over the glass down the ice. Jase and his team were lined up across the other end of the rink and their coach had them in a quick start, skate fast and stop hard drill. As he watched the line of boys each take a turn, he thought of work again, and of his time with Heine and Samson. Things had been quite good the last few years, no question there. The government's stance on climate change had brought ongoing negotiating contracts to his firm. Good old H&S.

He never forgot that moment when Harold asked about his political persuasion, off the record of course. What insight to have had in his portfolio a photograph of the campaign sign from the last general election right there on his front lawn with his family standing next to him. Harold had leaned in for a glance. That political party that had brought so much business the way of Harold Heine's company. That had been a Stanley Cup moment. In the political consultancy business, you had to keep your cv current and pertinent to who had been elected; he picked up on that from his professors at McGill. His father had always supported a national security, low tax economy and family focused voting history. So it was easy for him to talk with Harold about market based solutions with a small government keeping a distance.

He lifted a fist, waving his son on as the boy stick handled the puck around the rink.

He wondered about white haired Lewis and that peculiar trip to Africa. What had any country in Africa got to do with real climate change negotiations? They didn't even fit into the picture as they had no voice at the negotiating table. So why would anyone want to travel there let alone even talk about such an obscure part of the world. He'd have to call and chat.

Bizarre.

Chapter 7

They carried the launch components one by one from the warehouse out into the yard. Vince found the balloon surprisingly light to carry wrapped up tight in its bag. "They got us high quality," Brad said. "That's the latest feather-web fabric, super strong and near zero weight. Needs to be impermeable to helium molecules—that's it dude!"

The carrier basket they would stand in was just as light, but more awkward, so they each grabbed an end. The steel helium tanks had to be rolled out on a dolly. "This heavier part of our load actually supplies our lift," Brad laughed. "The sulphur will be the heaviest, each of us next." Wanting to simulate a prototype procedure, they had Aahil parked on contact standby at a randomly selected location. He would track them down by GPS that morning after they signalled ready.

"So we can launch from the middle of the yard." Brad pointed. "Should go near straight up in this little breeze. Trickiest part will be getting everything back here again."

Brad had been telling Vince of his time at Boeing. He'd been in the flight design department for a few years, then some months on military contract as a civilian design engineer—never do that again—and now he ran a one man consulting business. He knew other engineers who did the same like that Keith guy, so they worked at times as a team on joint contracts. But each kept their independent business status. One contract had involved designing these lift and release systems—some kind of urban air pollution absorbent. For some Asian company—he co-designed with Keith on that one. He believed the Asians picked his design for its summary conclusion: adaptable to multiple scenarios. All testing on that project had been in Washington State. Lab testing only. No way air space restrictions there would allow what they were about to do here.

"That same client sent me a request for proposal for this African contract." Brad shrugged. "I dunno about Keith but I submitted."

Vince noticed Brad lifting an eyebrow at the organization of materials orders. Someone had precisely and efficiently moved his design proposal through to ready phase, the helium, the balloons, the valves, and the dispersal hardware all in place. All flight materials had shipped in from Asia, and he received a full contacts list with prompt delivery times guaranteed on any further orders. What would come post Preliminary—they could only judge by the extra warehouse stock.

Vince too had been supplied a list of links and direct contacts with major suppliers and refineries in the Nigerian oil industry.

"Why the three tons of liquid sulphur?" Vince wondered.

"Interesting."

"Yeah."

Vince held the carrier basket steady while Brad clipped on the balloon.

"Sounds like you like design," Vince rambled.

"Here's a story, you story guy." Brad glanced at him with a glint of mischief. "I was in high school and we got this bio assignment. I mean, biology man, not my science of choice. But I came upon this idea somewhere in whatever I was reading at the time. So I got an empty plastic Javex jug from my mom, wandered around in a field just down the road filling that jug up with cow shit. Way more shit than I needed. Shit everywhere." Brad waved around. "Tap water rehydrated that shit and I totally forgot that jug in the bio lab. The teacher never forgot though, and he wanted results. So I took a chance on the design theory and stood up right in front with the whole class watching. Hey, I opened the valve, struck the lighter and got a constant flame! Methane, yes, from cow shit. So an alternate energy source got me through bio. Yeah, I like trying things out—potential design options."

They positioned the basket vertical at yard centre. Brad blasted some helium into the balloon and the feather-web rose to hold, swaying gently above. "Helium. Specific gravity zero point one three eight. So helium weighs one seventh as much as air. Excellent lift." The early morning heat swirled around carrying the smell of dust. Vince dragged the sulphur tank on edge through the basket door and let it fall back upright. He pulled over the low pressure hose from the three ton tank and clicked the connection, then opened the valve to fill the small tank.

"So you're into shit research," Vince said.

"Any shit, man."

"Natural gas comes out of gas wells. That's mostly methane."

"Must be some shit down those wells."

"Yeah, well that wouldn't be the primary source. Most gas formations in the western Canadian geological basin are Cretaceous. Deposition occurred at the bottom of an inland sea. So if there was any shit, it was not from cattle."

Brad showed Vince where to position himself in the basket for their ascent. They were going above cloud base. "If there are any clouds today," Brad said. They would remain above ten thousand feet for about half an hour, peeking near fourteen thousand. Brad explained to Vince how to pop on and adjust a nasal cannula connected to their oxygen supply tank. A case of pop valves had been set to open at twelve thousand feet, and Brad threw that box onboard. An onsite manufacture warranty test. They needed a near total success rate on those—humidity had an effect and the air did not carry much vapour around here.

"You know they called gas 'natural' when town gas got replaced?" Brad said.

"So what's town gas?" Vince asked. "And why would you know something like that?"

"Town gas was a syngas, made mostly from coal. Technology was all there to convert coal into liquid fuel or gas. The process takes a lot of extra energy, but like the Germans who didn't have much for oil resource during WWII, they did it. Now our U.S. military keeps the idea on hand for backup energy." Vince looked at Brad to catch the rare glimpse of a diminished smile.

"I come upon that kind of thing when I do background research on my near future plan," Brad spoke softly. "You wanna learn how to survive the climate crisis world that's a comin', you call my office."

Vince stared at his jPad, silent.

As they stood in the basket, Brad released more helium into the balloon above. They each ran through their check lists on jPad confirming all required items on board.

"A plan?" Vince frowned. "On survival?"

Brad looked up from his list. "My survival plan has more than one scenario." His smile snuck back. "One bright side scenario says the world adjusts, keeps humming along and we all get along just fine. You know, no resource wars. But pick any indicator; take gas and coal. You replace coal with natural gas to power the electric grid, and that about chops the carbon dioxide emissions in half, assuming no methane leakage. That would be a smart carbon reduction move, right?"

Vince closed the list in his jPad and looked at Brad.

"Well, has coal burning stopped?" Brad asked. "Tar sands tag along close on the heels of coal, so how's that project goin' in Alberta? Right here and now, Vince, you and I appear to be running some kind of CO_2 emissions test, wouldn't you say? When it comes to global priorities, we got politics and corporate interests. So…anyway, most of the time I think about a higher risk scenario. For my kids too, a survival plan."

Brad opened the helium valve further and turned to a dashboard of gauges. The basket began to shift under their feet. Vince grabbed at the edge while Brad kept his practised feet slightly spread. They lifted off with Vince staring down speechless.

The landscape spread out in a receding picture below, rooftops diminishing and the horizon expanding as the balloon raised them aloft.

"God created all this," Brad said, waving his hand at the ground below.

Vince peered straight down over the edge. "God?" He stopped humming.

"Yeah, my wife talks." Brad looked straight down too. "Not religious, mostly spiritual."

"The universe thing?" Vince asked.

"Could be designed you know," Brad said. "She reads up on the creationist theory. I mean, she's got some science behind her.

The moon keeps our planet tilted and thus our seasons. How far our planet is from our star, our sun, in the habitable zone. Statistical probability says random chance would be suggestively small. But what I need evidence of is universal compassion—to have any influence on my survival scenario."

"So," Vince said. "Any evidence Brad?"

They pulled on light jackets as they ascended and the air cooled.

"Religion isn't too helpful," Brad said. "Except for the basic God idea. Too many wars. And the laws of physics alone in no way show a compassionate creator. So I'm lookin' for something else."

Vince shuffled to the side getting a feel for balance in the swaying balloon basket. Brad tapped the surface of one of the digital gauges.

"Okay, tell me how God fits in on this one," Vince said. "I did some research on those Dabous Giraffes. A Green Sahara did occur historically, but the causal reason was a wobble in the Earth's axis. That allowed more direct sun to come down and heat up the Sahara."

"C'mon." Brad looked at him. "That's more heat, not less."

"Surprising, right? But that extra heat actually reduces the desert," Vince explained. "'Cause what happens is, extra heat rising sucks air in off an ocean—that's the basic monsoon effect. For the Sahara, more heat stimulates the West African monsoon drawing more humid air in off the Atlantic. And all that humid ocean air dumps a lot of extra rain. That's what made for a Green Sahara back then. So anyway, here's the question. Was that God? I mean Africans around then would have found compassion in all that extra green desert."

"Yeah, I dunno. God's a tricky idea," Brad said. He zipped his jacket a little higher and Vince copied. They were drifting south, further from the city of Niamey.

"I mean, I hear you on the God thing," Vince said. "I've noticed a thing or two."

"Yeah," Brad said. "Like what?"

"Assume the universe can be defined. Mathematically."

"Okay."

"And you said it, right, religion makes war. But religion stories are still acceptable, and they have ideas that people really get attached to. Everyone knows the Adam and Eve story or something like it. So...I need an acceptable story as background to certain things I notice—otherwise inexplicable."

"Yeah."

"So I've decided on an angel. Angels are popular, right?"

"A mathematical angel?"

"Look, math has always been a breeze for me. Engineering was a cinch." Vince looked at Brad. "Okay, I admit it doesn't say too much for compassion, but say this God doesn't care about me specifically or any of my little issues. Say this God has a grand plan but say that plan does include me. Religion goes with that, right, God's will not mine? Anyway, I've decided to call what I notice an angel helper. Helped me ace all those math exams, maybe more. I get that impression sometimes."

"Your angel tell you that? Your angel talk to you?"

"Not really, kind of..."

"Like?"

"Like I keep getting told there's a reason for everything. 'So what's that reason?' I always ask." Vince's face darkened. He stared fiercely at the ground below, and then took a breath. He didn't look at Brad, but kept talking. "My personal analogy fits the Christian soldier idea. You know, onward. Like suck it up buttercup." He paused. "So I say 'what's that purpose for me specifically? Give me a hint on what to do with all this math'. All I get for an answer is 'Wait'. Or 'Good job. Keep going. Stick with it.' But the main message is wait. So you're American, you'd get that I'm in the reserves or waiting in the barracks or something military like that."

Brad zipped his jacket all the way and glanced at the dashboard. He handed Vince the nasal oxygen supply and slipped his own over his head. "Your daughter has a lot ahead of her, so she fits in there somewhere."

Vince took a breath, squinting at Brad.

"So forget about proof, but just say we were created," Vince said. "And then say we were created in the image of—pretty anthropocentric—but just say. So add to that, just suppose that we

are spiritual beings, and that we all are children of this creator, this
God, then we are all having a human experience just like the Son,
you know, Jeshua bar Joseph. Jesus. Well, that guy did not have a
wonderful life, right? Anyway, that I can take."

Brad knelt to open the case of pop valves.

Vince went on. "Assume the creation process was
evolutionary, so I watch myself, Brad, and I notice a lot of
instinctual behaviour, the monkey or the hominid drives, the
ingrained survival tendencies going through my mind. A lot of it
not really useful towards say being more like what this God of pure
love wanted. So I am pure spirit stuck into a monkey's instincts
and told to deal with it day to day. That, yeah, that is my life.
That's a design I can believe, based on simple observation."

Brad nodded. They were drifting further south, and Vince
could recognize the wadi they had driven up with Aahil, with its
rocky outcrop ridge. The highway wound its way through the dry
landscape.

"There's two kinds of deer, did you know that?" Vince said.

"Whitetail and mule deer."

"Naw, think psychoanalysis. Most deer come to the edge of the
forest and rush out into the meadow to eat right away. The other
type holds back at the edge, has a look first. People are like that, a
four to one ratio. Some rush right in, and some hold back. Those
first deer eat first, and eat best, but once in a while they get eaten."

Brad nodded.

"I'm the second type, the more hesitant."

Brad glanced his way. "Yup, I would say you pegged that
one."

"So species can be genetically similar," Vince said. "Yet still
psychologically distant."

"Wasps!"

"What?"

"Take wasps. The wasps around Spokane do really well in the
heat, but nobody wants them around. You kill wasps best with a
hot water and soap spray. So I hang around their nest entrance with
my spray bottle and knock them off. Most of those wasps fly
straight in without a thought. And they die. Not that I'm saying
wasps think a lot, but these others act the opposite. They buzz me

or fly off. I always wondered which wasp started rebuilding next day—wouldn't be those dead ones. Would be the ones that made some atypical choices."

"Interesting. Insects would be even more genetically similar."

Brad put his hand on Vince's shoulder.

"There's gonna be two types of people," Brad said. "The ones that adjust to climate change, in a get friendly way. Those ones I want to come live in my mountain valley. Then other ones, I dunno, I hope they get in the lineup for the next Mars mission. The only Planet B we've got so far."

"You have quite the outlook, Brad." Vince looked at this guy, this incessant grin while he talked of the end of the world.

"My research says get prepped for a transition. A few scenarios are possible. You know the gyrocopter pilot in Mad Maks? How the heck he kept an aviation unit going in that screwed up future world fascinates me. Anyway, the world he lived in is one scenario. Pretty barbaric, but possible. No matter what scenario plays out, it's all gonna be exciting. That's what I tell my boys."

"That's scary."

"Yeah, kinda," Brad said. "Hey, we're at height."

Brad checked the dashboard, then switched open the top flap to release the lifting gas from their balloon. He motioned Vince back to the edge of the basket and touched a visiscreen button. The trap door in the floor of the basket fell opened, releasing the sulphur package bundled with small helium tank and bagged balloon. At another touch the package lowered on a thin winch wire to hang below them. One more signal, and the small helium tank opened, filling the other balloon trailing below. Brad smiled, winking at Vince to grab the basket edge. He dumped more helium from their balloon as the rapidly inflating small balloon lightened their load. Balancing off their reducing load, Brad had them slowly begin their descent.

As Brad touched the visiscreen for a side blast of gas to get them clear, they watched the sulphur canister come up hanging beside them. As they sank past, the small balloon ascended further above and Brad touched a final detach signal to let the winch wire drop.

"So, we go no farther," Brad said. "The pop valve on the sulphur tank opens at 15000 feet. As the apparatus loses weight, it'll accelerate due to lightening load. We could optionally remote control the valves, but this time everything's pre-set."

"Cool," Vince said.

"We could add special effects color and make like a shooting star. If this president wants a daytime show for his people. On a clear day, they'd follow near vertical lines up into the stratosphere," Brad said. "But I've been thinking. The wind's calmer in the night time, so I'd design a release in the dark."

Their next task would be guiding Aahil to where their balloon came down. After that they needed to find the landed smaller balloon—the GPS trackers would help. Terrain will be the biggest problem Brad said. They stood, watching the balloon above shrink as it ascended. Once full sulphur release was detected, another pop valve on top dumped helium to atmosphere and started that balloon's decent, Brad explained.

As they passed through cloud base—there were no clouds—Vince felt Brad's tap on his shoulder to remove his oxygen supply. He stared at the distant dry horizon, unzipping his jacket unconsciously as they sank back into the heat.

"We redesign our planet." Brad looked at him with his broad adventurous grin. "*We* are God, my friend."

THE PLAYERS

Chapter 8

Tamanna gazed out towards the east. The fourteenth floor window framed London's late afternoon traffic clipping miniature along the Chiswick High Road. And there amidst the flow the Gunnersbury reserve sprouted, a tiny pre-industrial relic of tranquil English woodland. Woodland William's site tracked nesting birds in the reserve, and now Mediterranean larks came north as ecosystems shifted. Had a climate tipping point passed? She strove for clear thought, and her deep resolve. Her lifetime commitment since Copenhagen to climate action hung again on today's critical choice.

They needed a decision by day's end.

Her business partner Jake entered the room and she turned from the window to sit across at the meeting table. He gave her that squint as he looked up across the top of his jPad visiscreen. This afternoon strategy review would be the last.

"Decision outcome format, then," Jake said. "Topic discussion, opinions and options, then resolution on each issue. First...legal."

Tamanna had spent the morning listened to legal counsel speaking through a Holo-Skype cube.

"Mind it, Jake, I can at best partially understand their legal jargon. Much of our decision will be guesswork," Tamanna began. "Let's see, they do have our contract classified nicely into issues pertaining to risk. So whilst we do entertain certain peril, our project locations on overseas foreign territory, god, how do they phrase it? Here, let me read...*presuppose the legalities of each such nation state to have legislated determination.*"

"So our involvement in contract outcome is governed by local laws," Jakes said. "To our advantage, that sounds."

"Yes, well, in ways," she said. "Listen...*certain articles of said contract wording remain open to interpretation by local authority*...I mean, that reads totally vague," she said. "And," she read on, "...*issues of international environmental legislation vis-à-vis the United Nations constitute no recognized jurisdiction over the stratosphere. Air space remains classified as sovereign vertically, that being directly upwards from the borders of any recognized nation state.*" She looked up, pausing.

"Non-issue," Jake said. She knew of her partner's special interest in atmospheric geography. "That's the same type of jurisdictional airspace agreement entered into by any airline or any business jet flown internationally." He squinted. "That portion we take a face value."

She looked at him, and then read on. "*Reasonable assumption suggests extension to the scientifically defined top of the atmosphere precludes infringement. All stated clauses of said contract determine the airspace of interest to the client.*"

"Yes, correct," Jake grinned. "Spot on for us, Tami."

"Right then." She glanced at her screen. "There's more, listen to this on conflict. National *conflict of interest may be or may arise as an issue.* Case in point—*any forthcoming litigation may consider the UK, rightfully* so they say, *as a full member of the OECD.* Yet on and on, okay...*in contradiction to the aforementioned, any party may content that the United Kingdom remains legally an active signatory to the Kyoto Accord.* That, we know."

"Potential conflict of interest," Jake said. "Look, we have a standard clause for that in any of our contracts."

"Conflict then Jake." She looked at him. "We may be escalating conflict and not that of the interest type. We may heighten the state of combat between one country and another."

"Not for us to say." Jake dismissed the idea.

"Lots of media chatter on the climate change factor in the Middle East now." She looked up from her screen. "And those latest Asian conflicts."

"Off topic." Jake returned her look, spreading his hands wide. "Look Tami, I know you have a personal interest especially in Bangladesh. But we need stick our noses only into our business. So we function at a legal distance. We act as a third party."

"Drones then." She eyed him. "We will be operating in active drone land. They're zapping political targets anywhere outside a country with a known agreement. Meaning any country below a certain wealth and power level. That, we know."

Her American friend kept her up to date on high altitude drones—the UK and many other countries now launched missiles from on high. Selective targeting was the running term used.

"What's legal say?"

"They state that issues may be raised on risk regarding my own personal safety and they rank the potential risk to our business integrity." She glanced up. The business interests of their joint consulting firm were on the line. They could be classified as eco-terrorists and entered into any country's drone target list.

"We've talked at length on overseas hazards, Tami." Jake sighed. "As we agreed, the final go or no call will be yours." As she would be in the field on this contract, he had left the final decision up to her. Entirely, but by tomorrow. They went on with the legal jargon and all its ramifications.

"Conclusion, partner." Jake looked at her directly. "Worth our legal risk, yes or no?"

"On legal…yes." She nodded. "Worth the risk."

"One down. Now let's skim our climate status."

They glanced over their firm's standard infogram with ever glaring climate numbers. Carbon dioxide that caused seventy percent of anthropogenic warming continued rising along the Keeling curve. Methane and nitrous oxide had their knock on contributions. The only greenhouse gas exception was the chlorofluorocarbons, the CFCs, due to the historic Montreal Protocol. Tamanna knew Jake would need to update that. Though contributing but two percent to planetary warming, those gases had immense potential for impact on the greenhouse effect and fed

Jake's pet political wild card. A rogue industrial nation forgoes all benefits of the ozone layer, builds a CFC production plant, and unilaterally accelerates planet warming. Russia, for one, wants a warmer north. Current technology gave people control over any future ice age.

"Two CFC sites remain on the Climate Watch list in Kazakhstan," Jake intoned. "Others in Siberia hold suspect status with very little knowledge we can access."

"Intentional climate heating would be near insane as pushing the nuclear missile button." She spoke softly. She had her own pet topic specific to people. "People must learn to focus on managing themselves," she said. "Not so much planetary resources. We do need a crisis but that one would not be my fave Jake."

After her dissertation defense, Tamanna read up on humankind, and came to understand people needed motivation to learn. History showed a crisis brought on an action response. Human nature was prone to crisis management, not to wise planning of the future. With this contract she told Jake, they had a real opportunity to craft a manageable crisis. *If humanity wanted to preserve the planet on which civilization developed and to which life on Earth was adapted, paleoclimatic evidence and climate change suggested action...*she'd memorized that. But motivation remained.

"Your CFC plants would be sitting duck drone targets, Jake." She eyed him. "Think on that."

With their air-to-surface missile striking ability, drones circling high above could destroy any plant. The newer surface patrol drones now assisted in target identification to fill in missing knowledge. Not the first time she told Jake his imagined CFC plants would make an easy target for those disagreeing with a rising temperature.

"Right," Jake said. "Cancel any thought of mine on our business decision." They had taken many another business risks in the past Tamanna knew. "Have we reviewed the numbers then?"

Tamanna nodded, keeping silent.

"That's two then," Jake said. "Other politics? Anything from our client?"

Tamanna spoke yesterday for the first time to Nishat Jabbar. As the Minister of Negotiations for the High Impact Climate Change Countries, the HICCC, she lived in the political thicket.

"The HICCC set up a Science and Research fund with a board of director scientists having no political affiliation," Tamanna said. "So scientists make all decisions, at least officially." She smiled. "So cool, Jake."

"Minister Jabbar will be our speak-to person?" Jake said.

"Yes," Tamanna said. "For that fund, anyone invests anonymously."

"So we don't know who's paying us?"

"Precisely," she said. "At the same time, they don't officially accept donations, or contributions. They call the fund an investment."

"Brilliant."

"Any concerned citizens group can invest or any billionaire." Tami went on. "Or any country, so now the politics. She so much as said major Asian political interests have likely made financial contribution. Remember our Chinese contract a couple years back?"

"Right."

"Recall the conditions? All our fees paid for up front and in full," she said. "And those extension options, so clearly defined."

"Yes."

"The way Nishat talks, this Science and Research fund has something similar. So we function at arm's length from real interests but we'll have no billing issues."

"So we're working for the responsible." Jake nodded. "Or possibly Asian politicians."

"Think on that political strategy Jake…they keep their hands off the fund—no official association. That's the way Nishat wants to run this project. Any country, even a non-HICCC member, could have climate crisis influence in their policy."

The HICCC strategy would trigger loud voices at any Conference of the Parties get-together, but Tamanna no longer attended COP. This African contract excited her, bringing out a new negotiating voice and so much potential.

Jake nodded.

"Nishat gives this spiel. Any country that takes on climate cooling alone will be seen as good guy or bad. By the citizens at home or in the eyes of the world. Play it safe, she says, and invest in a mutual hands-off fund."

"Any of those wealthy OECD countries you love?" Jake asked. "The UK?"

"Netherlands or Denmark," Tamanna said. "Both small, wealthy and high risk. Japan has a huge budget and significant interest. But in the end, who knows?"

"Our British M5," Jake said. "Or the American CIA."

Her American friend did not believe the CIA would fund anything without specific ability to decide on each spend. The United States was stuck in a climate change impasse for years helped in no way by its political system endlessly mired in two opposing traditional ideologies. The American climate change impact was not quite as high as China's or India's, but up there. Recent media covered extreme weather events, sea level rise and food prices affected by agricultural loss. All that reached out to even the least discerning general public.

"Is China an HICCC member?" Jake asked. "Or India?"

"Nishat says they have a partnership list where those two fit. Neither makes any real push to join officially."

"Those two keep building cheap energy coal burning power plants," Jake said. "Dumping lots of carbon. That, we know."

"At the same time," Tamanna said, "China leads the charge developing solar, biochar and wind technologies. Nishat talks about how they're penetrating the global market."

Jake glanced at the time.

"Any political player would be wise to keep eggs in more than one basket, Nishat says. That way they keep their business options open while they negotiate climate change terms politically." Tamanna paused. "She talks about power. She says any poor country with a high climate crisis risk sends a powerful message to the rich OECD countries to cut emissions. They enable negotiating those reductions on their own terms."

"The rich have become so by dumping more than their share," Jake said. "That, we know."

They were both so aware that the Organization for Economic Co-operation and Development had contributed the bulk of carbon emissions. Carbon emissions over time and emissions per capita gave Asians a negotiating advantage. The UK was at the top of that cumulative over time list, having begun the industrial revolution in their backyard. An offsetting argument added in a knowledge factor. For how long had a nation been emitting carbon dioxide knowing of the climate change impact? This outlook softened the historical UK damage cost and increased the carbon responsibility of currently planned Chinese coal burning.

"So we know a bit and we don't know a lot," Jake said. "That's possibly good."

"We know one thing Jake," Tamanna said. "Our contract includes balloon manufacture and shipping by an Asian company. Another takes care of sulphur storage facilities. All we know are shipping points and times."

"We are near out of time Tami," Jake folded his visiscreen. "Any final inspiration?"

"Nishat knows science."

Tamanna had explained to hearing ears how the paleoclimatic record showed quick flips of the global climate in the past, knowing that critical information never came up when politicians talked. The climate record did not show nice smooth transitions from ice age to warm period, there was no nice-to-show on an economic graph transition to allow for comfortable politically adjustment time. That had been one of Tamanna's reasons for dropping out of COP negotiations—the tortoise speed. Minister Jabbar had listened.

"She understands passing a climatic tipping point would easily wipe out the effects of any political action. She's aware of the situation in each high impact country, and she's quite savvy on the global situation."

Climate change was accelerating faster than the worst case IPCCC scenario and there is nothing good about climate change no matter what eccentrics claimed. Even if growing seasons were extended, the droughts and floods that killed off fields of grain far more than offset any crop increase. Once the climate switch was thrown there was a solid possibility of no option to go back, economic standard analytical methods didn't work with the physics and chemistry of climate.

"She gets the no going back scenario?" Jake slipped his jPad into his device bag.

"Yes she does," Tamanna nodded. "We talked on that. Humanity does not have the option to globally overshoot and then go back and patch it up later."

"She have any hopes?"

"One, yes."

"Not COP Florence," Jake made a face.

"No, not COP," Tamanna said. "The HICCC scheduled direct negotiations with the OECD. The poor will petition the rich."

"Hasn't worked before," Jake said. "That we know."

The remote possibility of a negotiated OECD agreement with the HICCC still lingered, what with the latest talks. The world remained sitting on the fence awaiting specific tough decisions, but they had been for decades. Anyway, how much better had COPs worked? She remembered her naive excitement during her attendance at COP 15 in Copenhagen. All, in her juvenile mind, would be worked out through good will agreements. The first ethnically diverse American president jetted in to show leadership. The first week held a string of rock concerts and she recalls the bitter sweet excitement of those bells ringing 350 times. Then when negotiations started, she and many others faced locked doors, in fact all NGOs were locked out of the meetings. She shook her head.

"We hope for that too…but no impact on our decision today," Jake said. "Three down, and end of discussion. We go ahead on our decision independent of any politics."

"Yes," Tamanna said. "Agreed."

"That's it then." Jake ended the discussion with one of his forced laughs that signalled an end to business.

"How's Anna and the children?" All children's future motivated Tami but she kept sensitive to the pain in Jakes' eyes, whenever they talked too far into the future. About what they knew. Jake and Anna had their two but Tamanna's cousins in Chittagong had others, and she needed speak strong to their dire situation. She put off the thought of having her own, or she often thought not. She would first need a husband, anyway.

"Superb," But Jake touched his cheek. "Jolie has an owie tooth. So I need be off to attend on that."

"Anna talking at all?" When Jake's wife had her first child, even though active at the COP conferences—where they all met, she stopped talking. A shift to the classic stance of climate silence.

"She sees no point," Jake said. "You had your moment. Anna's taking a break in the safety of denial."

"She's counting on us, Jake."

Jake picked up his jPad, looking straight at Tamanna. "Send me a note if you decide before you sleep." She twittered her fingers in a wave as he walked out.

Folding her screen down, she remained at the table.

Her moment. All those years back at COP Copenhagen. Sitting around outside those doors, deflated, she met Jake and his then girlfriend Anna. They got on right from the start. Anna told the ice bubble story, and Jake sent her literature she read there on the sidewalk. The Volstok core became her research, leading her career path as a paleoclimatologist. Her research showed what climate modelling could not—the ancient climate record revealed. That was one of her moments, actually.

She rose, moving back to the window.

As her deep gaze immersed her being among the Gunnersbury leafy branches she could not ignore the imposing urban sprawl— her peripheral vision glimpsing flats and towers along the high road. Yet the forest green allowed her the clearest glimpse into what needed to be, merging her enchantment with the harsh contrast of the cityscape all around. Her thoughts touched bottom, and then scattered. Armed with a dose of green intuitive, she allowed her deducing, rationalizing thoughts to set in and have their say.

Her gaze ran off along the M4, that high road would take her to Heathrow, her departure point. This contract offer. An opportunity not only on career—perhaps that of a lifetime lay before her. Yet was she prepared for the land of high drone risk?

She walked back down the hallway to her office and plopped down at her desk. Her fingers drummed on that stack of reports supplied by the HICCC. What they knew. They copied back to that IPCCC Fifth Assessment Report, the AR5, and the RCP scenarios she followed since release in 2014. Projections of carbon reduction targets out to 2050 and how close they were to being met. Way off, to be succinct.

She stared into her Holo-Skype cube saver. Her eyes followed the NASA climatologist's dancing graph, by far the simplest infogram on a changing climate. She watched the infogram dice roll, recalling his scientific voice warning of the new climate forcing load. However much people wanted to kiss the luck of their desires into those dice, modified forcings played a part in each roll. And those modified forcings were people.

She'd never been to Africa. The client through a peculiar clause wanted that she evaluate the people, the personnel—mostly engineers—hired for the field camps. Nishat sought specific traits among those employed, anomalies in the stereotypical engineering personality, pending further political negotiations. Whatever that was about.

She had to leave and wrap her mind in the mundane.

She walked out of Chiswick Tower to her bicycle racked in front. She unlocked, and slowly coasted past the adverts. Down the road she tucked in to grab a Take Away dinner, a veggie pie with jacket potatoes. The three kilometer ride to her flat would stir her appetite. Her net zero flat, with its feed in tariffs supported a reduction in the carbon impact. Yet all for what?

As she straddled her bicycle, she became motionless and took a deep breath. Her moment, that moment, then and now. This project needed happen, no question, the African initiative must begin. This contract would swing their consultancy business solidly into the international. HICCC would become a major consulting client into the future, a new entity for her and Jake.

But all that was business background. She had to go, she knew in her heart. She'd ring her mum that evening, to talk of trips abroad over the next weeks.

Chapter 9

Brad seated himself on the cushion. He watched as Aahil waved his hand in a demonstration of how to rest one's back lightly against the mud brick wall. As they settled in, Brad felt an exuberance at having been invited up on the roof of his new friend's home to enjoy the cool evening with his two sons. The sun slipped under the painted green of the distant urban bridge and touched the darker leaf color of the riverside trees beyond.

He asked Aahil more about the other white men at the hotel. Near four weeks ago, Aahil said, since he drove them out in the countryside to look on the rice and peanut fields. They then toured along a preselected route of the streets of Niamey. Their official Asian guide seemed intent on impressing something upon them. How the price of rice had been rising higher each year; how there was not so much rice; how the Hausa were bringing their cattle closer to the river as the grasslands shrank. Aahil drove them last to the Minister's office where the Asian took them inside.

"That curved government building?" Brad said. "Across from the Gaweye?"

"Yes, it is so."

"*Ressources Minières*, father."

Aahil nodded, approving his son's knowledge.

The Caucasian tour group had not stayed long in the office building. Whether they did meet with the Minister or an assistant was difficult to know. When they returned to the Nissan, the Asian was speaking directly of the changing climate. In a manner similar to how those more educated Nigeriens spoke, Aahil said. Those living in Niamey who had been to university would say the situation was unfair, much as it had been with the Europeans of Niger's past. The Asian insisted the white men pay attention to this in particular. Even at times the Asian alluded to how the Europeans and their North American descendants, who first came to Africa to colonize and to take resources, now were the ones who caused the desert to expand. The white men had been much more interested in the horse races. But the day of the week had been wrong.

"I will take you there." Aahil's eyes widened ever so slightly.

"A horse track. Sure."

"Friday, in two days."

Brad nodded. "Do the people of Niger talk of their future? How things will be with changing weather patterns and a dryer Sahel."

"Some do, many do not." Brad noticed Aahil's shoulder shrug. His chin shifting forwards seemed to come more natural. "Many say Insha'Allah. It is the will of Allah."

Aahil's wife Hamina came up through the portico and Aahil rose to assist her. She brought them tea on a tray with a bowl of sugar and as Aahil took it from her and put it before them, he softly said "But we drink tea in our home now. We speak no more on business."

Brad slowly picked up his steaming tea to sip. "Yeah, sure, no problem." He found this man in the bright multi-colored jacket easily likable. He spooned more sugar into this tea cup and grinned watching it dissolve as he stirred. The man sat tall with his two sons respectfully beside as if there to learn. Brad spoke again. "So can I ask how many of you live here? In this house?" Aahil's face softened at the America. "We are I and my wife Hamina, my sons here and our other children, my brother and his family, my sister and her husband; they have children, our mother and father, and then also our mother's uncle. We are one family."

Brad had realized before how important community would be in his speculated mountain valley. This model before him had miniature community written all over it, right here in one household. "Cool. And you get driving contracts for the government? And you run a restaurant?" Aahil nodded, telling how since his father's thinking had slowed, his brother and sister and Hamina mostly ran the restaurant. All the children went to the school that was close along the same street. Everyone contributed of course to the camp—camp was a desert word, urban household now—everyone did something that was helpful.

They talked more of cousins, of relatives, of family. Brad told Aahil of how his Canadian wife had cousins living in the river valleys in the mountains of British Columbia, a province of Canada. His family lived in Washington, one of the states in United States of America. Where they lived, the border with Canada was very close and friendly to cross and the land varied from lush to near desert. Spokane was his city in Washington State.

"As Tillabéri father." Aahil's other son spoke. "A state, like a region."

"Yes son," Aahil said. "Tillabéri is the region that encloses Niamey. Our capital district."

"In America our capital city is separate from all states."

"As our capital Niamey," Aahil said.

"Washington DC is our capital. Washington State, where I live, is a long ways from the capital, opposite end of the country."

They both nodded.

Brad told of his wife's village named Osoyoos, a native Syilx'tsn name but with the first O added by later settlers. "When Europe colonized." The Osoyoos Lake valley crossed the border and was the north end of the Senora Desert stretching all across America from Mexico.

Aahil had more family to the east and a little north, up close to and in the Ayăr Mountains. Closer to the Ténéré, the true desert. "In French or English, you will hear them as the Aïr Mountains. We are Tuareg." His eyes lit up. "We are desert people." Some relatives lived in Agadez, but many lived still in the villages deep in the mountains. Where dates from the palms could be eaten with the meat and cheese of the goat.

"All Tuareg?"

"Yes, it is so."

Brad listened closely as Aahil spoke of the times past when an Amajagh, a Tuareg man, was a freeman and a Tamajaq, a Tuareg woman was a free woman. "Tamajaq, the word for woman, is the same word for the language we speak." Unlike many Muslims, women are important among our people. As you see, I wear the veil while my Hamina does not." Aahil's eyes glistened.

Brad nodded. He felt a warm peace sink in from more than just the tea. Many natives, the First People of the Pacific North West whose culture developed over millennia also had a great respect for women. That would certainly fit in as a trait to have in the model he envisioned of the future. A future his sons' would inherit would be well served by the inherent affection of women.

Aahil motioned to a goat skin, hanging on the wall of the rooftop storage house, where a dark stained imprint read a poetically balanced script. "My father left the desert with his Tuareg story song." *Imidiwan ma Tennam.* He pointed to each word in that title, reading and speaking the same in English. "What have you got to say my friends?" Aahil sighed. "The song written here speaks of how our people have left the dried up desert, how the power of ignorance now holds strong." Aahil looked at Brad to explain. "That ignorance does not hold always true." There had been a time when Tuareg and horses and grass and water all ran together with great pride. But, the song also says, Aahil told Brad, how green lands exist elsewhere.

They fell silent.

Brad followed Aahil's practiced gaze to where it fell on the distant cloud free sky. As the blue darkened, the sparse scatter of street lights began their twinkle, illuminating the buildings and streets along the river bridge and out across the city. The sun dipped below the urban edge and as darkness settled in deeper, the touch of a cool breeze wafted in about them.

Aahil broke the moment of peace. "We have story of another way to make the desert green—not the president's way." Brad's look swung over to the dark eyes of his companion. Aahil spoke softly. "Come. We will go below. This one will be our mealtime tale."

They rose and Aahil waved him ahead as they made their way through the portico to the drifting aromas of food from the home cooking space. As he walked past Brad glanced at the song story written on the hanging goat skin. He would have to ask Aahil for a full translation.

As they descended, Brad wondered how it could be this extended family, this community of the Tuareg modeled here in Aahil's house fit so well with the world. If there was a way he could transfer some of this, of what he saw before him to his mountain valley community. The help-each-other-out and cooperative attitude would fit so well in any model he would want for his sons. And household incomes from whoever was employed at the time—no questions asked! What a blow away idea, but man, why not?

#

Aahil led the American down the stairs to the lower seating area. He felt comfortable with this new acquaintance, but any real friendship took time.

Many past stories among his people told of the comings and goings of the rains, of the wet years and the dryer times. The older ones spoke endlessly of the ancestors living in the greener times, before the recent droughts and even longer before the French came. But the recent story of his cousin he thought would fit best for this white man.

His cousin Aksil, he told Brad, had listened intently to those stories of greener times, tirelessly searching for crumbs of wisdom. As he heard the yarns, he would also watch closely the water pools along the Anou Mekkerene. A place among the Ayărs where even the palms and acacias grew. He saw where the last of the green would hold out before it too would return to sand. Always after the rains had poured down and rushed away.

They sat in a circle on cushions around the lower room. Hamina set a plate of meat in the centre before them and a steaming platter of rice beside on the mat. Their evening meal. And a basket of crusty Taguella.

"Fire roast goat." Aahil waved to his guest.

"Taguella, our bread." He took a piece and dipped it in a sauce bowl to show his guest.

Aksil was Aahil's mother's cousin's son, and had only three fewer years than Aahil. Brad nodded. "Aksil, my cousin, has stolen a piece back from the Ténéré, in a mountain pasture, in the Ayărs." Aahil's eye twinkled. "We, the Tuareg, have a reputation for plunder." His cousin had turned a sand meadow into grazing grass with large herds. "Listen, and I will tell you the story of Aksil."

As the American dug into his meal, Aahil told more.

As a boy, Aksil would follow his goats up the valleys to the higher places. Everyone knew he was a clever young man. He noticed those things around him that were important, and he was always trying out other ways as a boy. He would rush out into the rains when they came, and yet even the heavy rains would wash away by the next day. The light rains would simply disappear from the hot rock and sand. How could he capture that water he wondered? He discovered how the wet stayed longer under fallen palm leaves, and how in the odd spot even in the high valleys, a plant would grow. A tiny patch of soil developed around the plant and the water stayed a little longer. As long as his goats did not get close, at least at first, for they would chew it down to the sand.

One time he decided to build a wall of blue marble stones across a small ravine, and to catch the rain water in a pool. A place he could stay through the night, keeping the goats close and safe from cheetah and fennec fox. The water stayed but only a few days in the beginning. He found if he kept the goats and their droppings close to the sometimes pool the grass grew and the soil grew also. And with soil, the water stayed longer. But he had to move the goats, and let the grass grow before they ate too much.

Now Aksil sounds like only a goat herd boy, but he grew to be a man in the times of a wireless connection to his cell phone. He followed other ideas, other projects combating desertification across Africa online. He learned about managing his goat grazing land by dividing his pasture into pieces, and keeping the animals close as a herd. And from watching his first at times wet pond and goats, he knew to move each tight herd from one pasture to another. Never allowing the desert to return.

As he grew older, Aksil raised more animals, lots more. One might think fewer, in a dry desert, but bigger herds were good he learned online. Websites said mimic the wild where large groups of hoofed animals stayed in a tight herd, yet moved about the grasslands. One replaces the predatory big cats with people, consumers of milk, cheese and meat. Now, he has spread his pasture from the little ravine where he began, down and out across a valley bottom. What at one time was a patch of barren sand now was a green pasture. Even the water trickled along the bottom of the ravine for months at a time.

"Wow," Brad said. "Sounds like an answer."

Aksil had tried to show other Tuareg people, but most even in family did not listen. Most saw him either lucky or blessed. "As my father would say," Aahil said. "Better ways often lay hidden in the sands, waiting long to be discovered. Even then, only a few at first can know them."

"You got that right," Brad said.

After the meal, Aahil invited his guest to lean back to rest, while he rose to help his Hamina clear away the plates and bring out the sweet dates and coffee.

This white man showed his teeth often as Europeans did but he did carry himself with honour. Aahil felt respect shown to his family, and the American held respect for his own family far away. In his way, in the European manner.

Still, how far could he trust this man?

The Green Sahara president talked to his citizens of one idea. The balloons would rise into the air as a spectacle for the people. But Aahil had heard more rumour buzzing about the Minister's office. Anyone, it sounded, who could influence the engineers' numbers would find esteem in the eyes of the president. More rain would bring more votes. If the president could cool his country of Niger even further, the people would cheer even louder. There were future contracts to be had, Berber or not, yet he needed be careful. Aahil knew enough about North American culture to avoid talking directly about a tip, a bribe they would say. But tips had never held honour with the Taureg. And he liked this man.

Chapter 10

Vince awoke in a cold rank sweat to a scatter of disjointed thoughts. The chilling stickiness drove deep into his empty zone, his absence of anything. The night time, that time when the unconscious ruled all and when anything went. When there was no one home, but you. Alone. With all focus disabled, dream space was exposed as an easy target. A dream had rushed him directly at cliff face, but without smashing there he had been stopped abruptly. By what? He swore under his breath. A theory of relativity moment maybe—he frowned—he didn't do physics. The nuclear world since Einstein had an alternate power source but people also dropped bombs and entertained Cold Wars.

He blinked at the dim ceiling, gradually tuning in to the air fan whirl.

This project was pure engineering, no theoretical science or was it? If not research the design tests were certainly attempting something. For Preliminary, they had effectively manufactured an artificial mini volcano. In effect, they had released a sunshine shield, a parasol to cool one tiny part of the planet. A sulphur dioxide release to atmosphere for Initialize could be classified as first trial of a major release process. They were certainly running their tests out of lab in a country with minimal atmospheric restriction.

He needed focus, on engineering. An infogram brief had reminded him sulphur dioxide could be bulk sourced from oilfield operations, anything like a refinery or gas processing plant. You sprayed emissions gas with sodium hydroxide or soap to wash the sulphur out of gas form, and the sulphur gas was then stored as a low pressure liquid. Sulphate gas had industrial uses, like a PH controller or a heat transfer refrigerant. Most produced in Alberta was simply released to atmosphere, and what was captured was shipped out of province.

His mind drifted to picture that cliff face, one of those fractal dreams. His fractal angel. A warning of danger, or message hope? From God?

God. How could there be a God, there had to be gods. One god put together the laws of physics, the rules that held the universe together, but those laws did nothing to fill his emptiness. All that scientific evidence for a creator, and even one with vested interest in those created. He needed a personal god, not just a belief or so-called faith, but a real angel helper. A friend on his side. He needed a peace of mind god, or even the god of that much lauded love. Dream on, he thought, affection maybe, but he would settle for peace of any kind. But, rational thinking suggested a god might use assistants, angels, perhaps his angel had kept him from collision.

A designed universe needed be bigger than physics. There could be help for humans. Maybe. Take the whole story of energy. Just when people deforested Europe, they discovered coal, and then oil and gas, and other hidden energy sources like nuclear. People believed in their own ingenuity of course, but take the ozone crisis timing and now the carbon dilemma. Had the time been allowed? Allotted? From what he was learning about climate change, maybe there *was* help-along design. If most proven hydrocarbon reserves had to stay in the ground—he had missed that International Energy Agency report a couple decades back. To stay below two degrees. But a lot of high profile decision makers knew. So, were people being gifted with a soft crisis, an attainable adjustment? A meteor or an all out nuclear conflict would end it all in a flash. But to be given a time frame along with technology allowing awareness, well, that could be guidance. The timing was Goldilocks, just right, allowing people a chance to cooperate and even bring on one of Brad's positive scenarios.

Was there a global fractal angel guide? Focus, engineering.

People needed to play around with what they knew like they always did and see if they could find an easy way out. An easy chemistry fix in this case. Their project release was to upper atmosphere, the stratosphere, that he now knew was very low pressure and very cold. But there, once dumped, the SO2 mixed with naturally occurring water to form sulphuric acid. Which then gradually formed into an aerosol. Which diffused some sunshine, and like these historical volcanic emissions, cooled the planet. Temporarily.

He sat up to grasp the water glass from the bedside table.

So what was he doing here? He had a feeling a big decision was coming on, and he would be the one deciding not just on the sulphur supply.

The optimal scenario for his engineering task of setting up the sulphur dioxide supply was pretty clear. They'll be releasing three tons that morning, the Initialize phase, but they've been completely stocked for that by whoever had been there before. If they continued, next was Phase I. Now for that he would need to have a lot of tonnage in place. But basic engineering, he would reverse calculate to supply side and ramp up the Initialize. He took a drink and sighed.

His mother had always chided him on his sensitivity, his indecision, and on being so slow to grow up. The tears came so easy to him, for any sad song, any touching moment, so easily influenced by the needs of those around—he needed a thicker skin, a rhinoceros hide. That never happened yet, if anything with his daughter now around, the reverse. But there had been a couple times, in traumatic moments when everyone else was freaking out but everything for him became fractal and calm and the best path to take was crystal clear.

All that said, was his math angel attempting a calculated reality check? Was his math angel an engineer?

He never forgot how as a boy he heard his father talking to his uncle. They were drinking late and dad talked about his experience. That one time he had seen all in calculus. "You look at something moving and you see freeze frame pictures. Fractals. You have no choice, you see everything defined by pi," his father told Uncle Lou. "Then you start to love everyone. Too much for me." He got another beer. But Vince never forgot—'cause it explained what he had seen as a young man. More than once. When he saw a rainbow from time to time he literally looked into the geometry of the number pi. His pi angel. And his empathy level intensified until he couldn't stand it anymore. Pi was the root of everything mathematical, his fractal angel. Pi turns up everywhere, in the formula for the period of a pendulum, or the force between two electric charges, or the power of a shockwave. And that's only the beginning. Not that he could talk to anyone about it.

Images flooded in of the meeting in Calgary with that foreign service company. Whatever name they used, their front had been first contact on this project. The specs they supplied were limited and the project rationale vaguely specified. The extensive non-disclosure agreements were business overhead, but the pay and the sequence of potential contract extensions brought bonus sparkles to his father's eyes. He signed a confidentiality agreement with a Nigerien government department—he hadn't heard of the High Impact Consortium before arriving in Niamey. He had covered GeoChem sideline government contracts in the past classified as atmospheric. His father knew of his interest, and had perhaps made the business decision calculating in the extra thrill to hedge keeping him in the family company.

He needed an angel, but more than just math vision. His default feelings had ever been programmed negative, his dreams endlessly crashing into solid wall endings. Optimism was a choice; just focus on happy thoughts the psych people said. Brad had that wired in solid. Theoretically, he had heard, it took as much energy to hate as to love. But how do you quantify either of those? One could, through fierce determination, control how they thought and then influence how they felt. In spite of it all he had never had any option but to struggle to escape, always an uphill struggle, slipping and sliding. His target unfairly was Brad's natural setting. With pitted endeavour, he achieved brief forays into the foreign wilderness, glimpses of happiness beyond that cliff wall.

He remembered now, this dream had been a train, rushing at the painted image of a non-existent tunnel entrance. Yet the train had transitioned in a flash of light, and the light became more German than math angel. He had made that decision in Frankfurt, or had the decision been made for him? The Calgary client left that promo Hologram, timed to peep him at Starbucks. Come to Vauban Holo-characters danced and sang of a bullet train ride at triple highway speed. No cost. And he had gone. With nothing in mind but more distractive focus, he boarded the Intercity Express, that ICE train to Freiburg, mesmerized by the outside zipping past. Whatever got him on that train, the focus transitioned to what he could now picture. Citizens well dressed, living in fine housing, certainly with at least a Calgary lifestyle. But so many differences. The sidewalks were crowded, there were streams of cyclists and the cars buzzing about the streets looked so miniature. Not one SUV, certainly no four-wheel-drive, not one dual axle ton-and-a-half like he saw in Calgary streets. What every southern Alberta cowboy minus a horse needed. He had wondered, as he found needed distraction in the pamphlet tour of houses. Producing more energy than they consumed, net zero the Hologram repeated. A message of hope, but fear too—not good for Alberta energy companies. He felt deeply peaceful in Freiburg, and after eating checked in for a shower and five hours sleep. But on the train back to Frankfurt, his gripe list of his wife's spending habits set back in, extra intensified.

He could picture his daughter living a good life in that German city. Maybe that god of angels sent his fractal messenger to get him on that train.

At times he had invited whatever was out there to help fill his emptiness. Fractal angel visits were sporadic. At other times he screamed at it, loudly. Whatever god doles out in unconditional love to his inner being.

What path you choose, you can always justify. That much he knew from listening to his father and watching other people. If a big choice came up he could make it and then come up with a reason. A reason that felt right and one he had discussed with his imagined angel. Could this Brad guy be another angel messenger phase? The guy knew math. He would understand that nothing does not break down into pi. He would get it that pi was an irrational number and could not be expressed as a function.

He just needed bide his time focused on this project. Back to engineering. So then, the chemistry. At ten degrees below Celsius and at normal air pressure, sulphur dioxide condensed. But when compressed to just over car tire pressure the gas would condense at thirty degrees above. So you move sulphur product in bulk by the tonne which required railcars or tanker trucks. Once transported you stored it under low pressure in liquid form. He felt the relief of his focus. To keep his mind on one topic, that was meditation. Like a standard twelve foot diameter vessel seventy feet long held two hundred and sixty tonnes. So a storage yard contained horizontal cylindrical vessels easily holding hundreds or thousands of tonnes.

He needed to get enough sulphur available in storage for whatever phase came up. Setting that engineering calculation task solid in mind he dozed off.

Chapter 11

Vince trailed along the basement hallway after Brad to the door, and as they entered realized this was that meeting room where he first talked with his new friend.

"Hey, Vince." Brad called back over his shoulder. "Our number three has arrived."

They walked in to find a very North American woman sitting at the table nursing a coffee. Brad walked over with a broad smile and an extended hand.

"Jeri Able," she said, rising stiffly. "I'm the modelling analyst."

Vince glanced her way again, forming the impression she was an attractive enough older woman. He wandered over to the coffee machine to refill his cup, glaring briefly at the air conditioning controls. His harsh look softened. What had it been, ten days now? Could be he had adjusted to the heat, to the situation, to other realities…somewhat.

"Did you just arrive?" Brad was asking.

"Yesterday."

"Right on." Brad's eyes wrinkled into his smile. "How were your flight connections?'

"Acceptable."

Vince and Brad walked over to the table and found places in the hard chairs. They looked at each other, then at their newest team member.

"So, Jeri, you'll be running our climate model?"

"That's why I'm here," Jeri said. "They want onsite impact estimates of our little smog project. You guys have some data for me, or so I'm told."

"Well, we've run a simple lift so far, mostly testing the mechanics and the release process." Brad spread his hands palms up, shrugging. "And now, we're expanding our design based on that. So what'd we release this morning Vince, three tons? That's it, that's our Initialize. We're working on a way to retrieve the balloons for reuse. So we haven't really moved much load upstairs yet at all."

"Yeah," Vince agreed. "Three tons of sulphur dioxide. On top of that Preliminary hundred kilos."

"Well, excellent," Jeri said with a flare. "So you guys just give me the data you've got. With that, I start calibrating the climate model." She tapped her finger at the visiscreen in front of her. "Three tons fits in loosely with what I've got for a project description, says here 'a preparatory test involving several tons.' Any numbers on any release make for a starting point." Her face eased. "We'll be setting most of our initial parameter estimates based on the Initialize phase—that was one of the reasons for it. Also helps us get a finer adjustment on some other standard model definitions. For a final run, output quality would not be up to par." She shrugged. "But we can do a functional run now and we extrapolate from there."

Her face stiffened towards Brad. "So get me that data."

"Right, sure, okay. How would you like to connect?"

"An infogram works." Jeri gave them an address, then pointed to a large data traveller beside her jPad. "This software takes up significant memory and then each run output is humongous. Depending on how things develop, I can give you guys directory access."

"Cool," Brad said. "What kinda software you run?"

Jeri told them about her Coupled Model Intercomparison Project, her CMIP5 climate model. "I speak to my code with a gender touch...and I classify her as female. So she's my pet chimp." Jeri shrugged. "Good to have a relationship with your work." She told the engineers that her chimp allowed a variety of hypothetical scenarios and could also process the impact of regional variations. Like small or large local artificial volcanic simulations. "Obviously very important for our little smog-on-purpose project. You guys probably know sulphur dioxide at ground level is the primary source of urban smog." Brad and Vince looked at each other. "So if carbon dioxide were visible like smog

I wonder if we'd notice the greenhouse gas effect better? We being people in general. You know we dump forty times the weight of carbon into our atmosphere as we dump in our landfills. If carbon were visible we'd have cleaned it up long ago."

They looked at her, neither speaking.

"People." She half sighed, shaking her head grimly. "Anyway this is our climate model. So after the output we get based on your Initialize data, the model runs become iterative. Our little chimp will apply the output from that run to help define our first phase. An improved definition in the model. Then, after we get numbers from the Phase 1 release, the input helps us calibrate for Phase II. And so on. If and when they ever give us a definition of those phases."

They nodded, relaxing a little.

"Now back to people. What do you guys think of all this?" Vince noticed Jeri getting all revved up. "All these partially defined phases; you guys got a feel yet for how this experimental project is gonna really play itself out? Out there in the wide world, I mean."

Vince and Brad gave her a questioning look. She went on. "The way I see it, this little sulphur experiment of ours isn't all that different from our global carbon experiment." She shook her head. "And when it comes to how people operate…you can easily say, wow, look how that one's turning out."

Vince's eyes widening as his heart pumped an extra beat. "Absolutely," he heard himself say.

"People," Jeri repeated.

She looked back and forth between the two, while they waited, almost as cautious schoolboys.

"You know, Jeri," Brad said grinning. "You sure got a way with words."

She went on. "Listen, did you notice cigarette smoking's not allowed in this hotel meeting room." Her look turned severe, and she jabbed her finger into the table. "Here. In this obscure desert country somewhere out in Africa. Even here someone's learned that human caused smoke in the air turns out to be a health problem." She let that sit for a moment. "At the same time, people dump spent hydrocarbon emissions into public air anywhere out there in the world." She waved her hand around. "Now tell me, does that make the least bit of sense?"

"Not really," Brad nodded.

"You guys into psychology?" She asked. "An expanded study coming out of the Argosy school of psychology says when it comes to climate change people need to be convinced of four things. The first would be that a problem exists. So for you guys, do we have a climate change problem? Or what?"

"Yeah well kind of," Vince said. "I mean I'm from Alberta. Canada. The primary industry in Alberta is still oil and gas. You know, the tar sands. So what you are talking about isn't exactly a popular topic."

"Well, I'm from Chicago where there are some pretty prominent psychologists. People who wanna understand people. People who've gotten a little past that 'let's pretend it isn't happening' stage, and want to have a good look at reality. So the second thing people need to know is that it is bad for people to do nothing about it."

"Right."

"You had extreme weather in Alberta not long ago, am I right? Like flooding? Droughts? Wildfires?"

"Well yes." Vince nodded. "Alberta's adapting."

"Then the third thing people have to accept is that people caused the problem. Now that's the one that gets a lot of push back. So where do you guys stand?"

"Yeah, no doubt." Brad nodded. "In the Pacific North West we talk that way."

"Just a minute, though, I am not sure I get the relevance. I mean does it matter who or what caused a problem," Vince said, "when you know the problem exists? Would you not want to solve the problem, independent of the cause?"

She stared hard at Vince for a moment. "Good point, we should talk more on that one." She glanced back to bring Brad in again. "And then number four, now listen to me on this one, 'cause this is the one that should grab you. People have to know that the problem can be solved. Hey, you guys are engineers, right? Solving problems, that's what you do. And that is what this little project we are working on is all about."

They sat quietly for a moment.

"People." Jeri touched her visiscreen.

"You guys know we developed around here? People, our species I mean, on the plains of Africa?"

"Absolutely." Vince chimed in. "We sure as a fact did. Our species' registries would have Africa marked in as place of birth."

Jeri stared at Vince, her eyes shifting back and forth. "And somewhere along that path of progress we developed in a way so crisis management comes a lot more natural to us than wise future planning." She enunciated each word. "A change in behavior still has to feel right according to what happened out on the savannah." People only transition when they have to, not when it's a wise idea. They only do something different if 'necessary'. Jeri was explicit. So the question glared: how do you make it necessary? Her voice trailed off as she talked towards her jPad visiscreen, half under her breath. "Gotta make you fit for that clever biological chimp, that monkey species with the enlarged brain ..."

"Okay, so I got your data and I'll start this initial run." She made a final touch on screen. "Could take some time."

She looked up at the engineers.

"You guys ever heard of Dunbar's number? That would be about one hundred and fifty individuals that make up your tribe. They'd be the who-you-know group. Or the us part of us-versus-them. Now that is a number that comes straight from the savannah. Inside our one fifty group, we need empathy and ethics and communication so all of us become one and stay on the 'us' side."

She looked directly at Vince. He nodded cautiously.

"There's another Argosy study," she went on. "That one concludes we need to make the major leap out of being a small group animal directly into the status of a global animal. And with our climate crisis, like now. The whole us-versus-others world approach just does not work anymore. We've got some serious fast track evolving to do in a fast paced timeframe. *Them* has to become part of *us* and then on top of that our behavior has to be the new common enemy. What we *do* has to become the new *them*."

"Yeah, I see it that way." Brad brightened. "Nuclear family first, extended family as much as possible. Then local community fits the Dunbar tribe if you want to call it that." He looked at the others, smiling. "And I like how you put that, we need a global animal. 'Cause the way I see it, we have a real opportunity to do just that. Lots of motivation for a much better world…so cool."

"You're one of those goddam optimists."

Brad beamed at her.

Jeri didn't stop. She went on to highlight her critical view of the human experience. She shook her head, not tiring. Brad and Vince eyed each other across the table, carefully sipping their coffee.

"You play crib, Jeri?" Brad asked finally.

"What's that?"

Brad pulled the deck of cards from his carry bag.

Chapter 12

Tamanna checked the late afternoon time in her London office. Britain was six time zones back around the globe from Bangladesh. Evening would have settled in for Nishat in Dhaka. Tamanna's plane for Africa leaves tomorrow morning and she had hoped for a final update on HICCC contract instructions. She felt comfortable speaking with Nishat. "Your mother is well?" Nishat enquired. "Yes, she lives healthy," Tamanna answered. "I will have tea this evening with her and my father at their terraced house." She hesitated, but went on. "The UK feed in tariff works so well. Their house creates more energy than it uses so they live comfortably in a country like England yet emit little carbon."

"Yes, a valiant effort. Many will soon follow." Tamanna heard such a confident tone in Nishat's voice. "Your mother was born in Chittagong?"

"Yes. And of course I was my mother's Dita. As a child she would tell me stories of life on the Bay of Bengal. Many of my cousins live there even to this day."

"The carbon for a citizen of Bangladesh carries little weight. Also to this day."

"Yes, I have come to twig that quite well," Tami said. "My cousins live in such a way they contribute almost not at all to our planet's climate demise. Yet they will bear the brunt of the storms."

"Yes," Nishat said. "We must speak again on science and politics. I hope you will not mind."

"Yes, of course."

Nishat briefed Tamanna on the latest geopolitical outlook on climate change from an HICCC perspective. Lately backroom talk revolved around the Russia factor, a nation showing a disturbing take on accelerated global warming. The Russian perceived advantage translated into relative disadvantage for their rivals, the Americans and Chinese. Analysts classified climate change risk into extreme weather events, sea level rise and agricultural impact. While China showed high vulnerability for all, Russia was less susceptible to extreme weather events than the United States though Russia and the US were near equal in risk of sea level rise. Although Russia did carry risk on existing agricultural land, the food exporting country may have been calculating potential farmland further north. More likely, offshore Arctic energy sources opening up added to that calculation.

When Tamanna mentioned Jake's stupefying idea of Russia constructing CFC production machines, Nishat only nodded, that manufacture was simple. "Chlorofluorocarbons have an extreme greenhouse gas effect as a carbon dioxide equivalent," Tamanna said. Russia's public voice ignored all rumour, maintaining highly critical language on any such idea as HICCC climate engineering. The Russian voice built on public revulsion, and tapped the fear among people of disrupting the natural climate. As well as whatever sway scientifically analyzed dangers held in the public eye. A rumour in the mill ran that Moscow had secretly approached Canada suggesting negotiations around their common global warming interests.

Tami wondered if Russia had considered migration issues in a potentially chaotic world. Asians could swarm that sparsely peopled nation with dropping birthrate and expanding energy and food resources. She mentioned the scientific estimates of a perhaps twenty percent increase in cultivatable land in northern latitudes. Desirable perhaps for Siberia or Canada. "But, Minister," Tamanna said. "Many soils lack fertility. Thawed tundra would not readily turn into grain fields." Also, Tamanna wondered, had the northern leaders considered the fast approaching methane release threshold for Canadian and Siberian permafrost? This climate tipping point put climate change on an out of control path. Run away climate change means no one wins.

Politics, again politics Nishat pointed out. The general populace at any cold Siberian or Canadian moment thought no further than a warmer day. "Indeed, this issue is one of our greatest barriers to international agreement," Nishat said. "The everyday desires of the common people for local reasons have significant influence on our decisions. When decisions must be global." Canada, like Russia, had the polar advantage. Yet the North American country outpaced Russia when it came to economic base. And rather than follow the way of the economically strong Nordic countries of Western Europe, Canada defined its own path. American's northern neighbour took full advantage of its polar geography, developing global exports of one of the dirtiest energy sources. The world knew of the bitumen or tar sands.

"Yes, I was at COP Durban," Tamanna said. "Canadians took the Fossil of the Day award."

Tamanna could so tell of Nishat's real interest in science. She reviewed the ongoing summer sea ice loss that was so much a part of northern countries. Such an obvious visual indicator of climate change. With a view to economic interests over the planetary environment, the Arctic nations saw only hydrocarbon reserves and shorter shipping lanes. The loss was not all obvious Tamanna emphasized; there was a hidden environmental change when sea ice lost thickness from year to year. The ice typically remained frozen for one or two years and even up to five year old ice stayed solid, yet each layer was thinning. This loss did not show in any satellite view. Also, Tamanna went on excited with her attentive audience, transformation of the polar ice cap was highly visible in any polar image, and this climate transformation showcased a classic feedback loop. Science could easily explain this loop to even school children—bright white ocean ice melted away into dark salt water, converting a highly reflective surface to a darker ocean blue. Dark water absorbed much more light and heat than the mirror effect of white ice, and this compounded the warming effect. Over three quarters of Arctic ice now warmed into seawater by the time of September minimum and reliable satellite mapping imagery showed this event easily. Any online hologram played out the story of recent arctic ice cap history.

"Why do people not notice this?" Tamanna lamented. "I have never understood, auntie."

"This type of event may be too distant from their everyday lives. The image on a screen is distant and they do not pay attention to what happens so far away," Nishat said. "People notice more that which is under their own front step."

Five more years. Tamanna had seen the latest statistical extrapolation projected for an ice free North Pole in September. Depending on climate noise, maybe in two or three years. Nishat appeared to appreciate statistics. Would that be noticed by the people, though? Tamanna wondered how many would hear the scientific say-so. She realized her voice had to shift from the scientific.

"The North Americans notice their Santa Claus has a home swimming pool installed," Tamanna said. Would that make climate change noticed? Nishat seemed unsure. "North pole sea ice retreat should be one of the climate change canaries in the coal mine." Tamanna tried again. "Could a bird story catch public attention?"

Nishat brightened. "Perhaps the polar canary will remain a distant ghost, my child," she said, picked up on the story. "However another canary, Bangladesh, sings a chirping song, or a chipping song as she pecks at her seed. This song bird will be our concern. Much more than half, over seventy percent of Bangladeshi land will be inundated by a one meter sea level rise. Our canary must sing louder, much louder, and begin chipping and pecking at more than just seed."

"Yet we begin in Africa?" Tamanna said.

"Yes, my child."

The discussion turned to the information they each had before them. Tamanna and Jake had submitted a technical proposal.

Had Bangladesh been with the HICCC for long Tamanna wondered. Well, yes, Bangladesh was classified as one of the Lease Developed Countries, the LDCs, and together with the OASIS, the Alliance of Small Island States, they had put forward a one point five degree limit at COP in Copenhagen.

"At Copenhagen we students were not allowed into the meetings."

Nishat told her, the AOSIS and the LDCs and other states had come together to form the HICCC. Now they represented the interests of the country where Tamanna's mother was born. You speak for the people of Chittagong who wish to keep their seaside property just as it is now, or more truthfully, as it was decades in the past.

"Minister, our consultancy proposal addressing the terms of the HICCC request is based on recent publications and climate model runs," Tamanna said. "For the Sahara regional initiative, we suggest injection of sulphates at the top of the troposphere, our weather zone. The sulphates will drift northward from their release points towards the poles. To meet the HICCC defined regional effect, our models show that we best inject at an elevation between fifteen and seventeen kilometers at the latitude of the Sahara. Although a lower elevation than the ideal modelled for any hypothetical global project, this height assists in keeping the project regional. Our model shows that sufficient mixing of the reflective aerosols with the weather of the troposphere will draw fifty percent of the sulphates back down within months, before they drift north of the Sahara, and that eighty percent will never make it across the Mediterranean leaving Europe mostly unaffected."

"Yes." Nishat nodded. "Your proposal has great promise."

Tamanna looked at Nishat. "Regional climate modification gets tricky. I don't know about the politics, but yes for climate engineering. Background science has been determined and well defined, so we term this exercise as an effort in engineering. For any global scenario, sulphur injection would be up in the stratosphere proper—above twenty kilometers. At that elevation, retention time in the atmosphere would be maximized. Most aerosols would circulate all the way to the poles and remain aloft for one or two years. The acid rain effect of sulphur in the weather zone would be kept to a minimum." Tamanna looked at Nishat. "That would be for the hypothetical global scenario, the one HICCC wants for reference only."

"Excellent," Nishat said. "We will still have some effect on Europe?"

"For the regional?"

"Yes my child, we speak only of the Sahara region."

Tamanna nodded. "All factors considered, this proposal makes up our best compromise for regional. We argue that any acid rain will be minimal over an extremely arid and relatively uninhabited desert. We have emphasized an alternate scenario that shows significant improvement over our regional model run but those benefits can only be added with a mid-Atlantic sulphur release. If we create an aerosol cloud to cool the mid-Atlantic, this would greatly enhance the west African monsoon."

"Unfortunately," Nishat looked to Tamanna. "Any operation carried out in international airspace holds too much political risk. We appreciate that scenario, but will have to retain that as part of the global for reference only."

Tami stared down at the desk before her, frowning, but nodding.

"Does any other thought come to your mind, my child, on assisting us in catching the attention of the world." Nishat smiled. "To the plight of our canary?"

Tamanna looked up. "Well, as morbid as it seems, people do pay attention to death tolls."

In any news cast, a story with the word fatal caught attention. And, Tamanna had noticed, more increased attention was paid to the drama of tragic death in a safely faraway land. The British public would know of the search for a plane crashed and missing, or ship sinking, while at the same time local deaths remained hidden in backstage traffic fatality statistics. Climate change fatalities had been catching attention to a certain degree. Europeans had been informed that eleven of the hottest summers since 1500 came about in the last three decades. Maybe a boring fact, but the heat rang in a death toll of over seventy thousand French just after turn of the century. Then another fifty thousand Eastern Europeans less than a decade later. Including eleven thousand Muscovites alone—would that not catch the ear of heat seeking Russia? Of course the deaths never were of the affluent, but rather the sickly, the old and the poor who lacked air cooling systems. That latest year of death caught the most attention, the extreme heat that saw over two hundred thousand dying across Italy and Spain. America had had its woes too; the Texas heat wave and the U.S. heat waves after.

"We can shift terminology to replace extreme weather events with say a hurricane, or a super hurricane. One that strikes not only the Philippines and then Bangladesh, but New York City and up the Chesapeake Bay to Washington DC, then that gets noticed. Beijing has hurricane potential."

"Our canary's song must sing of storms then," Nishat said. "But of rising seas even more. Our Bangladeshi song bird, along with her bird friends living by the sea, must find a spot to peck. That spot may need be economic."

Nishat pointed out people noticed lifestyle while politicians talked to them of jobs. All in a global growth economy. Yet, Tamanna pointed out, carbon emissions graphs showed economic "recessions" to be the most effective human events that actually slowed carbon emissions. At the same time, people struggled and strained to return to the celebrated economic boom of high carbon output. Events could be compared. There were historical events— the UK 'dash for gas' converting coal-burning electricity to gas by end of last century translated into a one percent annual reduction over a decade. Yet the unplanned economic collapse of the USSR showed much better—a five percent decline for the same decade. The best news for a climatically stable planet came from an economic recession, while people struggled for the opposite.

"Perhaps global growth is no longer a viable option," Nishat said. "That growth and associated wealth remains so uneven. Globally. Our canary must sing of how some have grown too much."

"Yes." Tamanna nodded. "Economy and people aside, most scientists agree we will surpass the two degree danger zone. And I don't think I need too much economics to understand the economic cost. Damage is the underlying word, not a nicer day in warmer weather."

Nishat wanted to know how people viewed the idea of climate engineering. Tamanna could speak for the scientific view—one global survey revealed half of scientists agreed geoengineering will be necessary as cutting emissions continued at a tortoise pace.

"Good." Nishat said.

"One large political risk in the wealthy nations has been policy towards adaptation, superseding mitigation," Nishat said. "Politicians score points by saying 'let's adapt'. That touches people more deeply, as they have often adapted in the past. This does not assist with efforts to address the root of the problem...the emissions of wealthy nations."

"Even the two degree rise creates a mess," Tamanna said. "Adaptation does nothing to stop the acidification of the ocean. The Great Barrier Reef of Australia and all other ocean reefs are now seriously bleached, half dead one report states. So that's one side effect they would get along with the adapt-to-two-degrees attitude."

They talked of the billionaires. The wealthy and likely self-interested would react in ways of little benefit to most. When they knew fully of climate change threat, they would attempt to impose their version of an answer on all others. They will use their power to attempt to control dwindling resources, actions not to the benefit of most people. These people were the ones of significant concern. Though equity was known to be a true solution to global sustainability, where everyone was better off, and everyone had an equal vested interest in the wellbeing of the common planet, the ruthless among those powerful would have no interest in this solution.

"Our canary will sing to them also, my child. And more. She will peck, not drawing blood, not to start. But to be consistently insistent on gaining attention."

"My mother always shared gifts with me. As a paleoclimatologist, I can tell you Nishat of what I now see as a gift," Tamanna said. "The Holocene has allowed us to have everything we have today." One NASA climatologist pointed out how fourteen thousand years ago the temperature rose 5 degrees C and the sea level rose one hundred meters and people were gifted with the Holocene. "The Holocene allowed us time to develop agriculture, and based on that stable food source and the specializations allowed we built cities. We gradually became civilized."

"Now, we must become even more civilized," Nishat said.

"We need keep our life support system, our gift." During the Holocene, the carbon in the atmosphere varied by no more than five percent from the preindustrial. The 350 ppm limit would be necessary to keep the planet similar to the one where civilization developed. Yet they crossed over that line way back in the 1980s and were now living on the slow inertia of carbon impact. Many facts and figures define our problem, but enough science, I am sure."

"We are glad to have found you, Tamanna, your scientific knowledge most impressive," Nishat said. "I sense people are important to you as well as the physics of the climate."

"Oh yes, there has to be more," Tamanna said. "What would you have if there were only the laws of physics, a pretty cold empty world I would say."

"You have no children?"

Tamanna felt her face warm as she shook her head.

"The future may not welcome children. But a woman, a mother must be responsible and think of the lives ahead."

"Just a word, Minister," Tamanna said. "You describe our mid-Atlantic scenario as politically risky. Could I suggest you approach aircraft design companies at this time for quotes only. Our research shows the hardware exists, so quotes would be a matter of business jet design modification. Our company has research interests, and the benefits of that scenario would then be much more feasible...for reference only of course." Tamanna knew the most effective manner to carry out this mid-ocean release would be with special aircraft, and the design process would take time.

"I see." Nishat hesitated. "Yes, I will have an assistant initiate that suggestion."

"Thank you Minister."

"I have a special request also, my child," Nishat said. "First, our canary will sing through our fellow birds in Africa. Yet, I must ask that you not reveal any aspect of what one HICCC bird sings into the ears of any other bird."

"Each national contract runs independent?" Tamanna looked to Nishat.

Nishat returned her look, steady and firm. "I trust that you will do this, Dita. You must await my instruction on what precisely to say and when to speak. Each African country will operate as a separate entity for the first contract phases. We must plan out the optimal point to direct the first peck of our canary's sharpening beak."

Tamanna smiled at her childhood name. "Yes Nishat, that will not be a problem."

HORSE TRACKS

Chapter 13

Vince stepped with Brad from the cool Nissan air into the swirling dusty heat. He squinted around at the crowd of jumbled traffic-of-all-sorts leading along the approach road to the Hippodrome. Many stood tall and thin wearing white turbans and shirts of many colors. Tattered clothing covered most, many barefoot but some with sandals. These mixed with a sprinkle of shiny business shoes below tailored suits. A few stood beside bicycles and threesomes sat squashed astride motorcycles. The odd man sat high on horseback or lower on donkey back.

"That was good of Aahil to drop us off." Vince fell into stride beside Brad. "So Friday would be a day off for him, kind of like Sunday for us?"

Brad nodded his head emphasizing their driver would spend the day with his family. "They keep a few months' supply of food in their house, you know that Vince?"

"Who?"

"Aahil."

"And?"

"Food would be a first concern, absolutely."

"Your survival cell?"

"The Pacific Northwest looks good for any climate change scenario." Weather patterns and soil conditions in his mountain valley made for local food production, Brad explained, and the precipitation trend though erratic was on the rise there while the prairies baked. Without a greener thumb Brad felt more motivated to help develop a strong community. A tight family first, like Aahil's. For basic adaptation, you wanted your family around you and extended family made things more tribal—cousins on your side was a good thing. And then the local valley community. He rephrased Jerry's Dunbar number into a future-aware tribe you found, formed or joined.

"Which country will your valley town be a part of?" Vince humoured his friend.

Strategically best not to rely so much or really at all on any distant federal or state government. As a last resort Brad speculated. National government would be good to keep, but not the insanity of a worldwide military. Who beat their chest the loudest, like really, who or what really was the enemy? Back on the plains of Africa, but not in a modern context. Aside from the hypothetical, how current were the national governments now? So who knew what they would do, a traditional track record didn't bode all too well for the future. A local community could keep that national thing on the sidelines in case they did actually grow up. If they could sort out their differences without a war, that was a good sign. But not for the basics of everyday life. Think local, like venison would do as a protein source; the mountain valley white tailed and mule deer lived quite well among people with their intermittent fields and forests.

"You've got yourself a plan," Vince said.

"Getting a lot from Aahil," Brad said. "You know, he says they're trucking biochar from the south to Agadez."

"Who is?"

"The Chinese. You have to have a bio source where lots of vegetation grows—that would not be in the desert. One way of replacing the desert with grasslands is biochar. Takes carbon out of the air, and stores it in the ground almost permanently. Helps create soil, which is what you want on top of the desert sands."

"So, our project has competition."

"You know what else?" Brad shifted his eyes around. "That Taureg man says if we pay a little extra, we get a seat in the shade." Aahil had described the economy of the race tracks somewhat, a little world of business mixed with struggles amongst young and old over alms turf. They walked through the crowd towards the roof covered stands.

On their first weekend free, they'd come to watch the horses race at the *Champs de Course*. Brad had convinced Vince of the need to celebrate their successful field test release—after working day in and day out for over a week since their arrival. How to celebrate? The glimmer in the eyes of their driver spoke to them of the free spirit of the Sahara horse racing through his Tuareg blood. Friday at the Niamey tracks, he told them. Now they found their place in the shuffle progressing across the stony parched ground towards what they judged to be the entrance gate.

A young boy hobbling up to them, calling out his services in French at first, then English as he caught the emptiness in Brad's eyes. Falling in beside them, his one crutch acted at least as well as the missing leg from the knee down. Vince felt his heart swell and tears rising in his eyes. This boy couldn't be more than a few years older than his daughter.

"*Je m'appelle Antoine ...*" Then his English spoke of how he would be their guide. He would find them the best seats, and for a small amount extra he would find them soft pillows to place on the hard bench. He would show them, he confided, where to place bets on their favorite horses—not at the official booth. Or, his voice dropped another notch, to the only good-luck seats in the stadium.

"All desert horses today, sir," Antoine spoke in a normal voice again. "Good race, very good race, sir."

"Good-luck seats?" Vince raised an eyebrow in fun. "How do we get luck out of a seat?"

"*Bonne chance.*" Antoine noticed the interest and led them through the crowd. "Come."

His services proved true and the two engineers found themselves sitting on cushioned seats in the shade. Antoine pointed out the repaired seats just next to theirs. The boy then raised his finger up at the shading roof above. A circle in the roof looked refitted with different colored metal sheeting.

"Patron Abul Malik," Antoine said. "*Feu de l'enfer.*" He lifted his arms, shaking his hands as they rose and shushing deep in his throat. "Missed."

"What's he talking about?" Brad said.

"Where these seats get their good-luck," Vince said. "Say a meteor struck. That'd be extra luck if it missed you."

"I get you *bière,* now, yes?" The boy asked.

Vince nodded, handing Antoine paper money to pay.

"*Feu* means fire. Or flame or blaze," Vince translated out loud. "But *enfer,* that's literally inferno or could mean hell." He looked at Brad. "So the fire from hell came down through that roof. Meteors come from hell?"

"What? Oh shit." Brad stared at Vince. "Not a Hellblazer. That's a military missile from a Marauder drone."

They looked at each other, stunned.

"You sure?"

"Yeah, that's military flight talk."

"Okay, so you wouldn't want to join al-Qaeda. Not around here," Vince said, glancing up at the roof. "You would not want to become a drone target."

Brad hung his head to check down under their wooden bench seats and Vince followed his down under gaze. Below the replaced seats the charred cut edges of an old metal frame twisted around into a bowl, laced with half melted bolts and a scatter of charred wooden remains.

"Had to be using surface drone assist technology," Brad said. "To get a target lock underneath a metal roof."

"True then." Vince laughed nervously. "You would be lucky sitting over here next door to not get blown to pieces over there."

"Yeah man." Brad shook his head. "Lucky."

Vince felt his chipper outlook surge, a strange feeling he couldn't keep down today. How absolutely abnormal. And now he felt a extra tingle over this latest.

"That drone surface assist is fairly new," Brad said quietly.

With his daughter flashing to mind Vince clicked a saddled horse photo with his Jeenyus, sending it directly with a text...*hey baby, look at Google maps and find the horse tracks in Niamey. Look for daddy down there beside this horse... ha ha!* Almost a moment of silliness—where had that come from? He still hoped to be home for Christmas, but at the moment, he felt fine anywhere. He could even stay in this place for a while.

Antoine brought them glass bottles of Bière Niger from one of the booths.

Vince accepted his, condensation covered and half cool to the touch. "Fire-from-the-sky?" he said, pointing up at the roof repair. "*Feu de l'enfer.* Hellblazer? Missile?"

Antoine bobbed his head avidly in agreement, gapped teeth showing.

"Foreigners try. They miss." He winked. "Abul have cousin double that day."

"Abul did not die?"

"No no no," Antoine shook his head. "Cousin look same. Abdul lives!"

"So that's the good-luck," Vince said. And a local hero found in the boy's tone. "Abul had a lucky day, even if his double didn't."

"Yeah," Brad said. "The luck of the draw."

Brad clinked his bottle against the one Vince held. "Well, success, man!" The incessant grin today went well with his toast held high. "We lifted three tons of sulphur dioxide into the stratosphere within vertical distribution specs." Brad took a swig. "And, we successful landed and retrieved all three balloons." He had let Vince in on his personal retrieval policy on all aerial equipment. No balloon left behind. Vince took a long draw from his bottle. He could feel the African bubbles snap the sides of his throat and foam this dry city's aroma up into his nose. He nodded...what would come next?

Across the tracks, order appeared amidst the confusion as horses assembled into a line. Mounts of pure black or desert ghost white, some painted mixed, others dappled, each saddled with an equal diversity of turbaned riders.

"That Jeri sure has character," Vince started to chat.

"Yup, she has a lot on her mind." Brad heard him, nodding. "She sure knows how to speak that mind, though, doesn't she?"

"Yeah...you know, if you listen, a lot of what she says sounds like she's been doing her homework."

A couple of the things their analyst said had caught Vince's ear. "She says people see nature as chaos, especially engineers." He shrugged, looking over. "So, Brad. You feel a need to conquer nature? Do you hold within you an inherent desire to redesign ecology?"

"I dunno," Brad said. "I mean I don't have any grand plan past my survival ideas, but I sorta get what she's saying." He took a long pull off his bottle. "Like engineers design and build a bridge, say. Well, better than crossing the river on a log or even those big river boats they got here."

Vince nodded.

"But when you design a wing, you've got inspiration and initial design coming from nature, from a bird say. After that, you can come up with a lot more…no bird can fly like a jet."

"What hits me hardest would be her take on human nature," Vince said. "People *did* develop here on the plains of Africa, and our brains *are* built around the stages of evolution we went through. I never heard of that Dunbar number, and I never saw it from a psychological perspective, but what she says, that's true. We have an outdated decision making process based on survival of our tribe at the expense of that other tribe. But now we have a new situation. We've used up our one planet and we don't have any Planet B."

Brad looked at his friend, an eyebrow raised as if in surprise at this new Vince energy.

"So us lifting those three tons, is that gonna help us share the planet?" Vince said. "Or is this gonna bring about tribal conflict, just at a global national level?"

Brad shrugged.

"'Cause climate change is gonna hit a kid like Antoine just like the kids in Bangladesh…a lot harder than our kids back home— already has. And now I see numbers on how much planet our kids use up. A lot more than Antoine ever did. While we sit back and say a place like Niger has a population problem. Like I kwikread an infogram last night on that equation, and you gotta add in affluence. The real equation becomes Population times Affluence equals the real People Planet pressure. You actually classify people *larger* depending a lot on that Affluence factor. Take us for example. When we get driven by our chauffeur in an SUV—we measure a lot bigger than these young guys working the horse tracks. Then there's technology."

"Yeah." Brad looked at him. "C'mon Vince, let's watch these horses."

"The total equation includes the Technology factor." Vince's voice dropped. "Infograms says don't count on that, like a wildcard."

"Well, horses are the technology today." Brad transitioned focus to the race. "Good old horses—with a lot longer history in the Sahel than automobiles and balloons."

"So true Impact actually equals," Vince spoke quiet to himself, then thought. "Population times Affluence times Technology." He snapped another photo.

"Look at that tall black horse. If I was gonna bet, I'd be watching that one. Got freedom written all over him." Brad clinked bottles again. "D'you know freedom *is* the name of the Taureg?"

"Really." Vince switched gears. "Yeah, freedom. So cool!" By the third bière he was laughing deeply as they watched the black horse rider sparing for position as his mount galloped the track.

Chapter 14

Vince listened to Brad talk in the back seat of the Nissan as Aahil drove them past the warehouse. Their project supervisor would arrive next day, but for now Brad expanded on his survival cell plan. A guy had to have a worst case scenario, Brad told Vince, based on how people were reacting to climate change. You could say people were overwhelmed and mostly inactive. So there was a chance, an ever increasing chance they may not do what they really needed to. In the end Brad figured the trade-off really came down to giving up the lifestyle or struggling to hang on. Most people back home remained averse to giving up much, more typically into self-centredness. As they muddled along with their consumer lives, a long list of potential upsets seemed possible—political, economic, social—ending in some last ditch chaotic effort to survive. A lot of climate refugees could be looking for a new place. For not just his sons' future, but his too, that scenario was not too appealing. So for his own peace of mind, keeping a background hope people would eventually all become friends or at least politically cooperative, he was strategically casting his dice.

"Brotherly love would be nice," Brad said. "But kind of idealistic."

"Yeah," Vince agreed. "Not likely."

"I see people as a bunch of goofballs," Brad said. "And any goofy person learns as they go, right? That learning means making a lotta lousy choices to later say, oh yeah ha ha, I get it now."

So while the goofiness goes on Brad believed best to have a place to get to where a guy could survive the fall out. The snow disappearing from the Sierras and the San Joaquin valley in California drying up had already pushed people into moving north. Still in an organized and peaceful way, though the Idaho locals were not overly welcoming. Say the next goofiness turned into a quick move. "Say they meet resistance, or say the military even gets involved." Brad figured best to lay low for a while, until the big shift blew over. What he called the transition was going to happen one way or another.

They turned off at the street that led to the wadi and Aahil switched into four-wheel-drive as they drove out into the sand.

Best to get off the most likely northerly travel path—many would be thinking Alaska. "So I got this small but livable building. The land is actually a two acre piece of forest on a hill." Think maximum efficiency, Brad said. Think what do you really need to live? Think as if this were some chaotic moment in the transition, or alternately, how you really could live on the planet if you wanted a one planet footprint. What do you really need? Solar panels, a water system catching rain off the roof, enough space cleared for a healthy garden. "You can't see the cell from any road. You have to know the turnoff where you go up and over a little rise to even see the place." Brad had imagined a wartime-like scenario with soldiers on the search. They'd have to be awful meticulous to find this hideaway. He could even cut trees down to block the road, further discouraging access or making the place look abandoned. He waffled over the thought of digging in an underground bunker—kind of extreme. Who wants neighbours in bunkers? Minus the bunker idea, you fade away into the forest while the soldiers snoop around. History says they don't stay long.

Vince watched Brad's eyes light up when he told of the first time he drove into that mountain valley, and looked up from the valley floor. The east side rose near vertical with rocky cliff patches exposed in a forest that climbed to almost cover the peaks. The valley spread out wide across intermittent farmland to a gentler sloping west side. When he stepped into the wind from one eastern peak to lift off, his first flight had been spectacular. Flying straight out towards the valley centre what caught his eye poking out from the grid of farmers' fields had been the hills, old worn out mountains or the remains of the last glaciations he was later told. The little knolls were covered in remains of original forest, yet still had easy road access. Circling to take a closer look and even catching some lift above the dark soil fields, he was amazed at the huge trees at one hill bottom fading to grassland on the hilltop.

What a place to lay low for a while if need be his thinking told him at the time.

Brad's buddy met him at the prearranged pickup point, and they drove back up the forestry service road for his friend's turn to fly. Later he drove those farmer roads, checking out the real estate signs. That had been back then—now he was a registered owner.

Vince nodded, absorbing his friend's outlook. Aahil had discovered an alternate route along a side ridge, and drove them directly to the flat rocky outcrop this time. Dropping them off, he headed back down to their prearranged meeting point.

They left their backpacks on the stone platform, and walked up to the edge. Leaning into the breeze from the outcrop, Brad pointed out the warehouse roof. Brad's look told Vince conditions were favourable and Brad showed him how to open the pack and roll out the wing.

"Hey Brad, you see that SUV," Vince pointed. A dark vehicle had driven part way up the wadi along their path.

"Yeah, huh," Brad shook his head. "They're just parked there."

"Would they be able to see us?"

"We see them, so...they'll notice when we get our wings up."

"Tourists?"

"Chinese engineers working on that third bridge—they got time off just like us," Brad grinned. "Or Aahil talks about the president's men."

"I'd say Aahil can't see them from where he is down there."

"Yeah, I'd say not," Brad said. "But from up here, we get to see it all."

Clipped into his harness, Vince's eye followed the tangle of strings leading to his wing. The rag as Brad called the spider web cloth lay lengthwise before him where at its centre a half bubble of fabric stood erect in the blowing wind. "So just like I showed you, Vince," Brad told him. "A nice little tug will pull the whole wing up in the air straight above you. So you'll be reverse flying. You can flight practise standing right there on the ground but the wing flies just as if you were up in the air. Then it's so easy to do a one eighty, but not yet, that's next."

Vince gave the upper edge strings a tug, and the bubble began lifting the wing off the rock. He released his pull and the wing fell back. He had control.

"Pretty good time at the horse tracks." Vince needed to talk. "We go on Aahil's day off Friday, now we take our day off Sunday."

"Those good-luck seats worked great." Brad walked his bundle of wing cloth spreading it wide across the cliff top. "But I was up pretty late Friday, and then got final reports together yesterday. See what big boss says tomorrow."

"A hand shake and a ticket for home." Vince tugged his strings.

"I doubt it. I think they got a lot invested in this project." Brad dragged his strings back to his harness and clipped them on. "Aahil says the president's gonna want the balloon launch right by Niamey. For all to see."

"We're pretty much running test stages so far," Vince said.

"That's what I told Aahil. This president's got some kind of political agenda on the go. The guy sounds good when he floats a rumour the rains will be coming back to the Sahel and even to the desert. He looks good if he shows he's doing something for his people and their lousy rice crops. Bring back the rain, bring back the Green Sahara."

"How about we color the sulphur gas? We add copper sulphate and he's got green shooting stars—just in reverse—they shoot upwards. That'd give them a spectacle."

"Right Vince, I dunno if that's the show they're looking for. Like Aahil says the Tuareg celebrate what they call the Wodaabe. That's the Festival of the Nomads, and it happens when the rains' finish." Brad clipped himself into his harness. "That's at Cure Salée up on the edge of the Sahara. Green pastures everywhere, president says, even better than they had a few decades ago so he keeps connecting to those Dabous Giraffes."

"Giraffe politics," Vince said.

"Those Dabous Giraffes rock carvings are up by the Sahara. So Aahil thinks the president wants a release up there. Around this place called Ingall. But if they catch it on Hologram video, that puts the president right there in the Sahara beside those stone giraffes reaching out to all of Niger."

Brad caught Vince's eye and pointed out past the outcrop edge.

"Zero effort. You just ride the air," Brad said. "Should be some lift coming up this embankment. Remember, you pick a place to land but you have an alternative spot in your mind. Always. The breeze is strong enough so I'm gonna catch ridge lift for a bit. I fly back and forth a couple times and then land right back here."

Vince listened like a fledgling.

"When we fly out there where there's no ridge the idea is to find a thermal. You ride the rising air up, but never past ten thousand feet. Watch your altimeter. You dump the thermal by flying a straight line. If you want to go cross country you catch the next thermal further along." Brad pulled his upper strings and his wing snapped into position above him. He pulled his goggles over his eyes. "The heat in this place says there'll be thermals for sure. We'll look for a darker colored patch on the ground, where the heat gets absorbed, and a thermal comes up."

Brad spun around. Taking two steps right off the edge, he lifted into the wind. The paraglider rose aloft taking him up-up-up a few hundred meters above the cliff and he turned to follow along the edge. Vince dropped his strings and sat down in on the warm rock, arms wrapped around knees. This guy was telling him he can not only do as he was seeing done, but that he will be able to fly out across the plains, picking and choosing like a bird where to land.

His mind was so busy the need to find distraction lately was near gone. He'd been reading up on some of the infograms Jeri sent, like why, unlike birds, people poop in their own nest. Birds are smart, yet another infogram site challenged the intelligence against lemmings. Over the cliff without a wing or a second thought. Or even people compared to their own ancestors. How can we allow ourselves to repeat Easter Island? Or the Mayan civilization. To trash our whole natural support systems…take the Sumerians. Where once Sumerian irrigated agriculture flourished there now was nothing but desert.

He watched Brad soar.

The guy has such enthusiasm for flying. Triggered by a childhood movie experience—he would mimic that Mad Maks pilot instruction 'now you gotta understand the basics of aerodynamics'. That aerodynamics caught kid Brad's mind. Knowing it had to do with flying, he researched the word right off. Inspired by the gyrocopter hero arriving by air to the rescue—kids notice that. Or rising to safety—Brad's hidden valley was a safe place—above the Max truck down on the road. Vince felt inspired by his dance floor time in Montreal, that another cultural model was possible, but the rest of his life got in the way.

Vince squeezed his brake handle as he watched Brad pull a brake line on one side. He leaned the direction of Brad's wing, and saw Brad hold the turn until he had spun ninety degrees. He waved down and Vince raised a hand back.

Getting to his feet Vince took a deep breath. He pulled that launch bubble up for the breeze to catch, and pulling both lines of strings, he stepped backwards a couple paces. His wing rose above him and he braced against the harness pull. As the paraglider lifted into place directly above, he could feel it balance and fly on its own, just as Brad had said. The upward pull lifted his feet as the wind strengthened and he skidded over the rock. He yanked the bottom strings and the wing deflated—he still had control. But ready to step off?

Brad glided back out of the sky, touching lightly onto the flat outcrop and deflating his wing. His face held a spectre of wonder.

"Edge of space?" Vince looked at him.

"Oh no," Brad said. "Cloud base is a lot higher than you get soaring a ridge."

"I wonder what the carbon footprint would come to for space travel," Vince said.

"Yeah, interesting question." Brad popped out of his harness. "Wasn't in that spreadsheet so I had to extrapolate. That Jackie and Haydon carry a whopper if you include travel over a life time. They might get services remote, but groceries and hardware come delivered to Mars. You do not want to know the carbon cost."

Vince stared. "They finance through crowdsourcing now."

"Yes. And they are well financed. You know the rumours, but I'd call it true. I mean is Jackie a good looking woman or what? How much influence did popularity have on audience vote for their team? Then everyone followed the mating contest, how she picked

Haydon. Mission Mars knew how long people followed Apollo and the moon missions. Strategically stage a crew competition to keep world eyes on Mars. Who's gonna be following any research on ancient hydrological cycles. All eyes will be on Jackie and Haydon."

"My wife could never tell you Mars is fourth planet from the sun," Vince said. "But she knows what Jackie wears."

"So that's what people do. They follow the Martian soap opera. As our planet goes to shit," Brad said. "I gotta keep that survival cell in my hip pocket, Vince. Take my boys out there. Get them used to the place, so they know how to live a different way."

"Carbon footprint—like driving an SUV equates to driving down grandchildren."

"That's a harsh thought."

Vince stood on the outcrop edge beside Brad, their wings inflated.

"Okay, you ready?" Brad asked.

Vince nodded nervously.

"Follow me."

Brad lifted off again. He caught the rising cliff face air to go up and then struck out straight away from the outcrop. As Vince took his first step off the cliff he felt his foot's last touch before totally lifting off. Watching the ground recede below, he instinctively searched for a known and did notice the dark SUV gone. No balloon basket around him, but Brad told him, many more flight options. Hanging his hands from the brake handles like Brad he flew after his friend who was already circling in a thermal and on his way up further. Vince followed.

When Vince looked down the exposure brought on terror but the view ecstasy. The mix turned to an amazing calm. So this was cloud base, though not a wisp of white in any direction. He couldn't keep the widening grin off his face, no matter how it hurt. This was angel country. Closer to the edge of space where astronauts have their epiphany, Brad said, with their view of the planet below. If not rising to some higher plane of consciousness, he was sure catching a moment of elation.

Chapter 15

Tamanna sank deep into her Sunday evening Air Deccan seat totally knackered, yet sparked by an underlying glow. This contract suited her quite well; just the schedule intensity got her. Near every contractor on site seemed not at all to catch the urgency of climate change—they needed only fill out terms of contract. That feeling prevailed here in Mali. The plane taxied down the Bamako-Senou runway, circled about and lined up between the rows of reflectors for takeoff.

When speaking with Nishat today she felt her heart sing along with large scale ideas that played tunes of potential. Solar power arrays spanning the Sahara, supplying carbon free energy from North Africa for Europe would create jobs everywhere. It just made so much cooperative sense. That message should totally satisfy political figures and their talk of employment. But pragmatic reality interfered when Nishat spoke on such issues as national security. What were people afraid of? For HICCC members, strategic interests revolved around waves of disruptive environmental refugees. Simply adapting to climate change would be such a brutal transition for most citizens of High Impact countries come to that. Their politicians had no time for grand global dreams.

Whoever suggested adaptation, ignoring mitigation, as anything of a solution should be strung up. High. The Bangladeshi government projected severe ocean flooding, and major food shortages. Extreme weather events including talked-of super monsoon rains brought plagues in a tumultuous aftermath. Millions in Bangladesh, having already lost their delta farmland to the sea, had moved to the slums of Dhaka. The challenge was to the world, yet reality kept that world divided into national interests. Horrid.

At Nishat's direction Tamanna concentrated on how to message onsite project personnel. Different people heard in a different manner and needed be spoken to as such. One major wild card in predicting climate change outcome had always been climate sensitivity, a piece of cake to her. How much climate change comes from how much interference by what climatologists term as forcings. Tamanna knew a forcing to be an imposed perturbation of the planet's energy balance, but how did one translate that into engineering language? Further to that, what version would communicate well to a non-scientific politician? The Asian engineers in Mali, and Mauritania before, had been a challenge, politely nodding at anything she said. She felt certain they got the numbers, but then showed no further interest in the broader climate change context. Meticulously following design instructions, their interest ended there. She'll need keep numbers simpler for the politicians, as they'll understand figures less than the engineers. And have political pomp as a part of their agenda. Nishat emphasized that.

She leaned back to rest, but could not. Out the window, she peered through the cloud free atmosphere at the semi-arid land below; such contrast with the rich green of Britain. The surface cover down there could have been that of another planet, or out of some long ago time on this planet. Planet Earth had passed through so many phases, many tumultuous for living creatures, people among them. The Paleographic history of climate had been written into her dissertation Volstok ice core among other records.

She loved the data held in the Pleistocene section of the Volstok core. Nestled within that paleoclimatic record lay confirming evidence for measuring climate sensitivity. And a simple measure too, for anyone to understand. A side by side comparison between the last glacial maximum, the Ice Age everyone knew of, and the most recent interglacial showed it all. Twenty thousand years back, planetary energy or temperature had been a constant deep freeze. But conditions were in balance, quite stable, unchanging as one would want in their kitchen freezer. Just as the also balanced and stable pre-industrial Holocene. The Holocene allowed civilization to develop under much balmier conditions, a gift to humanity being removed from the freezer.

Animal domestication and predictable weather allowing agriculture brought about cities and ever advancing technology. Technology allowed such a convenience as a kitchen refrigerator. This Holocene—she liked NASA's word gift—became climatically stable by eight thousand years ago. Though written history recorded freak weather and traumatic storm events—there had been the Little Ice Age in the middle ages—the Holocene actually was a period of measured climatic balance. Long before the industrial revolution...and noticeably warmer than the Pleistocene Ice Age.

The figure to know was five degrees Celsius—everyone could understand five degrees. The climatic forcing for each of the Holocene and the glacial deep freeze before were known, the difference in global average temperature was known, and from this, one could infer change in temperature dependant on change in forcing. The difference between Ice Age and the pre global warming times of the Holocene had been that five degrees. A surprise to most especially those from more temperate climates, this was much less than a day to night or seasonal variation in temperature. But this was climate measurement, not weather! With a glacial to interglacial difference in forcing of 6.5 W/m2, simple calculation showed that every watt of forcing gave you three quarters of a degree change in temperature. The maths were not difficult, but would a politician be able to follow? Her PHD dissertation argued in detail how the same numbers were confirmed by the Vostok ice core. These effects came only through fast-feedback processes, though, and the warmer or colder the planet got, the greater the sensitivity. But that was another topic. She had only so much presentation time for these science lessons. And they needed be sunk hard into other minds.

Turning her gaze from the window, Tamanna leaned her head back, closing her eyes. The Niger field test should be complete. Like the two cities before, she'll gather Sahel climate model data in Niamey, and forward the reports via infogram to Jake in London and Nishat in Dhaka. After connecting with the Niger project professionals, she'll send that special appraisal the way of Nishat. A time's waste so far, but the Minister insisted on face-to-face evaluation on the type of person within each engineer. Nishat avoided full disclosure on the purpose of this contract task, but promised to reveal more over time.

Her head nodded as her thoughts blurred.

#

Wheels touching the runway startled Tamanna awake. Invigorated by her light sleep, she focused on Niamey, the third Sahel city. In Niger. Sitting up straight she checked her hair. When the airliner fully stopped she grabbed her device carrier and stood to file out after other passengers from the plane. In runway heat no different than Mali, she followed African travellers through the terminal door. The queue was short but slow at the airport baggage claim. "Yes sir, I have two bags and my devices," she told the attendant. With luck she would sleep well that night.

Riding a taxi to the Gaweye Hotel, she glanced at the people walking the streets of a world as threatened as that of her Bangladeshi cousins by a problem they had in no way caused.

She found her room, dropped her bags there and made her way to the hotel restaurant. Throughout her meal her mind wandered over further options on how to speak the science of the climate. Take watts. Everyone knows of watts from their monthly energy bill. The planet needed energy, just as any home. With an energy balanced planet, you had near 240 watts from the sun to power each square meter. That was your comfortable thermostat setting, but how does one tell that story? She needed a story teller.

She finished her meal, and ordered a coffee. Checking her device, she found an infogram from Jake. The link took her to an advert for, god, drone missile insurance. Rates varied, depending on your travel plans. The man had warped humour at times...his text read: Serious? Or bullocks? He posted a happy face in the image corner. She half smiled, and hit return—Yes, let's buy!!

Storytelling. Say you imagine a 240 watt light bulb switched on at the centre of each square meter of the planet—most Westerners can picture a Christmas tree. Simple, she thought. Politicians would find value in a Christmas tree. Using this imagined light bulb world, one could describe to any person what the AR5 8.5 forcing did. Eight and half extra watts for each kitchen table sized area of your Christmas tree planet. You clipped on an extra 8.5 watt light bulb beside each 240 shining energy all across the globe. Still, that eight and a half read small. Right then, talk about degrees Celsius. Take three quarters of the eight and a half watts number and you had near 6.5 degrees. That much warmer. You should be hearing a deep rising scream at that figure. Recall, the temperature rose only 5 degrees after Britain melted out from under a kilometer of ice. And two degrees was the conservative IPCC danger line, way too hot with many arguing for lower.

She'd have to run the eight and a half watt Christmas tree lights idea by Nishat.

As she settled in her room, she checked her schedule on the meeting with the engineers and analysts of Niger. Their first encounter was early next morning. Another possibility.

#

As she walked into the meeting room, the lively chatter of mates fell off. She shook hands with Vince, the Canadian engineer, Brad the American and Jeri the climate model analyst also American. A North American crew, peculiar, those in Mauritania and Mali had been all Asian and more difficult to read. Jeri had hard lines on her face, late in her forties, but she appeared to be taking care of herself.

They showed her a chair and settled in at the table.

Tami asked first for the model run results, listening as Jeri briefed her on the Preliminary. The engineers then told of their balloon release—the designated three tons of sulphur dioxide up into the stratosphere. She paid careful attention, noticing something creative in their approach to this field test. "You designed that balloon process." She looked at Brad. "Sorta," he said, shrugging. She nodded and asked. "And what would either of you give for a Phase 1 launch time estimate?" Vince stared at her for a second, eyes shifting. But he fell into a meticulous answer, citing container tank readiness from sources in Nigeria based on expected delivery times. She watched his face as he spoke, sensing a certain distain for details. "And what percentage of Phase II could we have in the stratosphere in three weeks time?" She spoke quickly. Vince fell silent and Brad took on the question, citing inventory of balloon launch capacity and time frames necessary to scale the project up. All synchronized with the sulphur supply, he nodded at Vince. These two seemed a team.

"Okay." Tamanna folded her screen down. "Those Phase I and II scenarios will become our new focus."

Vince and Brad glanced at each other, neither saying a word. They fell with Jeri to listening.

"You will be required to calculate phase estimates," Tamanna said. "The client wants a Niger regional test—that's our first focus, Phase I—and from that an estimate of how close we could come to a Phase II. That's our Niger national target. As you may be aware, there are local political reasons for this national target." She pursed her lips, sighing. "Although, as one might deduce, the laws of climate physics do not tend to recognize political boundaries." Tamanna spoke carefully. "What our client refers to as Phase III will be the Sahel regional. And then Phase IV, the abstract idea of a global scenario. We determine these simply for theoretical comparison of course." She looked to Jeri. "And to help calibrate our climate model."

She noticed Vince's face brighten as she spoke.

Tami went on to overview the standard global numbers as she had for each national team. The carbon outlook went by the budget approach. "We have room for 1 trillion tons of carbon in our global atmosphere to keep under two degrees. We are near three quarters of the way there and not deescalating anywhere close to fast enough. To be more precise, we will have emitted 745 gigatonnes by the end of this year. At least forty percent of carbon remains in the atmosphere a thousand years later, that is a given. For the purposes of this project, we consider other greenhouse gases to be offset by reflective particulates, a variable expected to decrease as people clean up visible pollution, but nevertheless an offset at this time. Current projections predict we hit our CO_2 budget maximum in less than nine years. Our client is significantly concerned."

Tami took a breath, pausing a moment. She looked into each face in her audience. She felt comfortable with this numbers based dialogue, these were engineers and analysts. She studied each face as she went on, keeping her ear and intuition open to any inner signals.

History was boring, she said. She told of the NASA climatologist testifying before Congress way back in 1988 citing scientific evidence that climate change was happening. Her audience attention faded only slightly, so she tried out her light bulb analogy. The Canadian's eyes lit up as the numbers became a decorated Christmas tree. "Other color for the 8.5's," he said. Empirical fast-feedback climate sensitivity had been mathematically defined by several sources—including that NASA fellow's research. "Fast-feedback processes can be water vapour, clouds and sea ice. The math is fairly simple. Our Phase I project tests how much fast-feedback climate forcing we can offset with a sulphur dioxide release. We know dispersal will have a major impact, so we need precise timing to measure a short term impact." She paused, watching. "We also have the cryosphere, all parts of the planet covered by ice and snow and frozen permafrost ground. We calculate the cryosphere as a forcing and translate into degrees."

"So what about slow-feedback processes?" Vince asked. He looked directly at Tami.

She returned his penetrating glance, probing deep into those brown Canadian eyes for an instance. "Right, I am so glad you ask." This type of question was atypical, that was a given. She grew with the moment as it turned into a little lecture on climate science, with an attentive audience.

Of course when fast-feedback was isolated, slow-feedback sensitivity remained, she explained. Slow-feedback would be a process like modification of major land based ice sheets. Like Greenland or Antarctica. And then changes in forest cover, where forests transitioned to grasslands. For these, climate sensitivity actually increased. Slow-feedback processes guaranteed extra warming in the pipeline, so to speak—she smiled when Vince did. The climate record showed ice sheets collapsing in the past and planetary sensitivity to climate change to be defined allowing accurate judgement of what to expect now. "These processes played out over the long term, centuries, and though we will be aware of these, we focus on the immediate future, the next decade. Our primary presumption holds that the carbon cycle is now distinctly out of balance due to human activity."

"I can forward you more if you are interested." She caught Vince's eye as he looked up from keying in to his jPad. The hint of a smile crept across his face.

Tami tried out another analogy on sea level rise. The northeastern portion of the United States had been identified as a hotspot where sea level was rising higher than global mean. She described the reasons. First, how the sea level was neither flat nor uniformly distributed over the surface of the planet. Ocean bottom mountains, deep-ocean ridges and even ice sheets threw off the planet's gravity field, giving the ocean surface its own valleys and high places. Wind and ocean currents further influenced the outline of the sea. "Kind of like global politics," she said dryly. Only politics varied even more around the planet than the ocean, not adhering to an overriding law of gravity.

She noticed Vince nodding, his lips twitching as his fingers flew at his keyboard.

Sea level has the most impact on members of the HICCC. This explained at least partially their extra interest in membership. By end of century optimistic predictions caste the whole world as a version of the Netherlands, expensive but manageable. "But not just sea level, severe ocean weather events will become the new normal. Conservative media alludes to more intense hurricanes, but reliable sources speculate on super storms as yet undefined."

"So who exactly is the HICCC?" Vince asked. "Say politically?"

"Right. I'm only just finding that out myself," Tamanna said. "Basically, the HICCC wants to negotiate a climate change mitigation agreement with the OECD. Negotiations are ongoing, but let me see, I will be returning in three weeks to see how our regional test turns out. The High Impact/Economically Cooperating, the HI/EC conference will take place another three weeks after. I can forward you an Infogram with a list of countries involved." She looked at him and he nodded.

Tamanna rose as she spoke, signalling a close to the meeting. She had a good read on this team face-to-face. She could write up her Niger personnel report for the Minister on her flight that afternoon to N'Djamena in Chad, one hop further along the Sahel. She nodded a goodbye and quickly found her way back to her room to organize herself and schedule a taxi to the airport.

Chapter 16

Sitting on the Gaweye cobbled front step Brad tapped at his jPad while awaiting Aahil. A client supplied guide was taking him on a project background infogram tour. He couldn't help nudging his tour follower interests towards the changing climate back home. Both history and projections.

An overview had shown the speed of altering influences worldwide. What had recently been voiced as a grandchildren's problem, well, no question that was way off now. Today's grandchildren were going to experience situational overload with their new normal weather patterns. A tour stop emphasized the crushing contribution of the way of living back home to the problem, while the way Aahil and his family lived in Niger added so little. Heating a northern home read lame excuse. Next stop showed growth as the consumer habit that needed to be broken. But yeah he winced, tell that to most anyone back home. How would you get people kicking the habit of their own lifestyle? The ingrained recreational shopping thing? One side infogram detailed how consumption could be classed as more than just a habit. As a true addiction the gram highlighted the negative impacts on the participant. The guides took him on another side tour of economics. Economic recessions had been one of the few influences that relieved the insanity of carbon emissions acceleration. Then further historical data showed lower recessional hydrocarbon prices at the pumps kick starting the economic cycle again. The guides pointed repeatedly to the problem as people-based, that Vince and Jeri topic. Most folks don't want to be bothered with a future other than the one they have planned. Ever since they were a kid. Like those oil company workers in Vince's Calgary. To avoid any change, those guys simply avoided the conversation.

How smart was pretending he wondered, glancing up at traffic and checking the time. An SUV pulled up to the steps but not the Nissan. He looked back towards the Kennedy traffic circle.

No question, he had to stick with what he had concluded—that a fellow had to keep a survival tactic in play. As time passed, his outlook turned more into Plan A than B. A big ruckus would hit and folks needed a strategy on how to get through. That was key. How to live like Aahil's family made so much sense. Before his eyes, an excellent low risk model. Their background survival skills developed under harsh desert conditions and they were now living in a world of significant climate change impact. How could he transfer their strategy back to the Pacific NW?

Folks needed think of the basics for a year or a few years or longer. You needed water for one. Unlike a desert, plenty came from the sky in the back home mountain valley. He had a water well drilled so the place had an dependable water supply. And he had that rainwater capture system designed for the survival cell roof. Water was of primary importance.

You needed food—secured for that year or two to make sure. You store high density durable nutrition, a grain like rice. For the longer term any basic design needed a garden, keeping independent of today's global food market. Grow your own he winced or at least make a deal with local farmers. With no green thumb he needed low maintenance crops and to negotiate on the food part. He'd learned a couple things about mountain valley agriculture. Soft fruit could be high maintenance; cherry groves needed regular spraying. So you picked the right fruit. Fruit trees attracted bears—his wife pointed that out. So far he'd planted plum and apricot trees and a patch of raspberries all at the far end of the land in case a bear wandered in. But nuts he reasoned would function better for both attention needed and long term storage. Carpathian walnuts, and hazelnuts and Chinese chestnuts grew in the valley. Blending in as forest, nuts fed folks a highly nutritious diet. The rifle and a supply of shells would make it easy to pick off a deer for winter protein. The gun would be only for hunting hopefully.

You needed a clothing supply. Quality manufactured clothes lasted a long time. Making leather from deer hides came to mind, but that was too old school. That type of clothing took too much effort—ideally the transition would never come to that. Instead, you stock up on and store boxes of extra factory-made clothes. Seasonal clothes, to keep warm in winter.

You needed shelter. A place to sleep, eat and stay warm and dry. After designing, he had near finished constructing the cell, one that turned out to be no more than an inconspicuous cabin. Tiny, but with all the amenities of a house. An off-grid solar panel and low voltage battery system powered LED lights and electronics. He spent time there last winter, checking warmth from the small wood burning stove. With wood everywhere, staying warm should work. While the people of the world made friends with each other. Or gradually learned to, if they needed a while.

As he rose to stretch, the Nissan Patrol drove in off the Boulevard. Aahil pulled up right in front of him and he jumped in.

He shook his African friend's hand. "Hey let's get over to the warehouse and see what showed up." They pulled away, back into the morning traffic. Aahil seemed unnaturally quiet, staring ahead at the road without a word. Brad wondered about interpreting Taureg thinking, but then decided to slide in his questions on Taureg life.

"So Aahil, you think you could live back in the desert?" He looked over. "Just in case of hard times?"

As they circled the roundabout Brad listened as Aahil told how a wise Taureg family had another way. His father had moved into the city, but always kept contact with family in the desert. For him, his connections with his cousins up around Agadez kept a network alive. The way his cousin Aksil lived, that could be done. But all in the city would be missing; he would most wish to stay in Niamey. Aahil fell silent again as they pulled onto the green bridge and Brad glanced around out the window as they crossed.

He sensed an excitement, certainly a tremble in Aahil's voice when he spoke. Brad was surprised when he glanced, catching a look of concern on a face terminally calm.

Brad remained quiet when Aahil finished, asking no more.

#

Aahil had held his peace. Patience was the attribute of a Tuareg, a man of the desert. But the engineer no longer spoke. "I must show you one thing from my cousin," Aahil said after the silence.

Brad nodded.

"A sandstorm blew into the Ayăr Mountains from the east," Aahil said. "One day past when you flew as a bird. My cousin captured the rain that comes before the storm, but Aksil has also found a balloon that does not fit. At first one of his shepherds told him of the balloon that was tangled on the rocks, above his pasture. He believed, ah, only another balloon and he would get the rewards for a return. But a foreign look comes with this one."

"Not all our balloons are stitched together identical," Brad said. "Flight specs yes, but appearance not always. Foreign how?"

"Please." Aahil handed his cell phone to Brad. "See these shots."

"Looks like our design," Brad said. "What?"

"You check out the words written." Aahil pointed. "One language is Arabic; that can be known from the alphabet. English and French too."

Brad zoomed in on the photo and the message marked on the balloon cleared, showing enough English letters to get the gist.

Support...Clima...Stabilization

He stared. "Arabic?" He pointed and Aahil nodded.

"Chinese?" Aahil took his turn tapping at other script.

"C'mon. I only know English." Brad smiled. "So, what country is east of Niger?"

"Chad. As Niger, Chad stretches to the north, across the Sahel into the Ténéré and to the middle of the Sahara."

"Chad, yes, what's the city in Chad?"

"N'Djamena."

Where Tamanna flies to next, Brad was sure. They were not the only team with a project. And a very similar project.

"And further east from Chad?"

"Sudan"

"And Mali is to the west of us, right?"

Aahil nodded. "Burkina Faso also."

"Gotta tell Vince." Brad thumbed text into his cell phone. "This balloon has implications to our project."

"Our ministers make agreements with Chad." Aahil said.

"I dunno." Brad half smiled. "But our HICCC project administrator may not have been telling us everything."

Aahil knew there would be too many concerns. Yet, he thought, all was not bad. Other balloons would make things easier for the president of Niger. And for him, though he would gain no pocket credit. His thoughts of betrayal could be washed clean. The president's extra cooling would come from the neighbouring Sahel countries. To make friends with neighbouring countries, as they together brought back the Green Sahara, yes, that could bring more rain and more election votes.

As he pulled them up beside the storage entrance, Aahil found the way blocked by a transport truck backing in with a container to offload. He parked the Nissan at the side and got out with the American to walk into the yard.

AÏR MOUNTAINS

Chapter 17

Vince fumbled bleary eyed into the meeting room, the only place he could think to find coffee this early. The hotel rustled with four-in-the-morning shifting, but the restaurant didn't open 'til six. He leaned against the counter as the coffee perked, then poured a steaming cup in his new mug. His favourite as his daughter would say. Why finish it here, he decided and he walked out with Smiling Earth cup in hand—he'd take his fave along for the trip. Brad was sitting on the cobbled hotel steps with a happy face mug, his own mirror. "Where'd you find java?" Vince mumbled. Brad shrugged. "Talked with the attendant." Aahil with his son in the front seat pulled up for them in the Patrol, and they tugged the back doors closed. Mornings greetings in various languages mumbled around the vehicle.

Aahil drove out into light traffic passing on Boulevard de la Republique, turning right towards the Rond. Intermittent red and white street edges flashed by on either side, and the four remained subdued navigating the sequence of N roads, first 6, then 25. Vince watched the numbers drift by, his mind habitually searching for pattern. They passed the Hippodrome. Antoine would be staking his young life's gamble on the urban race track business. How life could have been for that boy in some developed part of the world, or here but in long ago times. Riding high and free on a horse of his own across the grasslands of the Sahel.

Vince looked at the dark vehicle driving along beside.

"The president's men," Aahil said.

"Who?" asked Brad.

"They saw you fly your bird wings from the high stone." Aahil said. "They watch you but they will never talk to you."

"Why?"

Vince looked out again, and the window beside came slightly down and a finger flicked out a cigarette butt. He caught a glance in a reflection and could swear the two men were Asian.

"The president has his interests," Aahil said. "They will protect you when you are in Niamey."

"From who?"

"We do not always know."

Vince and Brad looked at each other as the vehicle fell behind and turned a corner.

Past the Diori Hamani airport, they ventured on to never-before territory for the two in the back. As they left city lights behind, Aahil sped into the stretched out high beams penetrating the deep predawn darkness. Vince took his last swallow and set his fave cup gently on the floor. He turned to the sound of Brad's whistle, glancing at the spreadsheet being reviewed on visiscreen. "How're we looking?" Vince asked. Brad gave a thumbs-up. A couple plane loads of balloons and helium tanks from China gave them enough theoretical launch capacity for Phase II. "You definitely got the easy payload end," Vince said. His end involved more freight; storage tanks from an ocean port like in Benin, and liquid sulphur from Nigeria. They estimated 40 kilotons of liquid sulphur for Phase II, make that 45 for contingencies. That list of contacts in Nigeria left by the first shift turned out useful. Surplus and decommissioned oilfield tanks could be an alternate source of storage tanks. Once a minimum storage capacity was in place, it would be a matter of timing to ship the SO2 liquid in truck load by truck load to fill the tanks. A pipeline was certainly out due to time; rail was another would-be-nice for both tanks and sulphur. Air would be too tricky. Trucks looked like the most likely.

"So we still calling our estimates preparatory?" Vince asked. "You say we can offer them enough of Phase I regional to call it Phase II national? How about schedule?"

"Yeah, yeah." Brad nodded happily. "All items hold an expected-to-go status, either option. Just a matter of what kind of efficiency we can squeeze out of the launch process. One potential bottleneck depends on the kind of recovery rate we can get on the balloons. Say they give us 'til the third or fourth week November, we should be able to do that Phase II national."

"So the Phase I launches mostly around Niamey, a lot for show. What the president wants. But if they go for the national, we have a lot of transport up to Agadez. Excellent launch site, they say, just a lot of extra materials movement."

They fell into silence again. Even with the coffee Vince dozed as the highway slipped by. He felt the vehicle slow as they pulled in to a village, past what looked like a military base. "Dosso." He heard Aahil speak. As if on cue, they slowed more to pass through a high barbwire topped gate standing opened beside a guardhouse. "The soldiers sleep now," Aahil said. Further into the village, he pointed to another highway. "This road N7 arrives at Benin. To the ports." Ocean transport remained low on their discussion list. As they left the far end of the settlement, the flaming orange glow anticipating sunrise marked its spot on the horizon. Noting their route veering south Vince checked his GPS map.

As light spread over the Sahel plains they were presented opening curtains on the African semi-arid. Brad pointed at goats passing through the shrubbery. "Needs more animals, right Aahil?" he said. He glanced at Vince, telling him about Aksil's green-the-desert effort. Aahil helped fill in the details, how his cousin had captured a piece of the desert back from the dead sands to create living grasslands, now pasturing goats and cattle high in the Ayăr Mountains. With laptop in hand how a desert nomad by heritage had learned of bio-mimicry, keeping herds large and tight and rotating pastures as nature did.

"Wow," Vince said. "Great carbon storage capacity."

"Yeah," Brad said. "Be interesting to calculate."

Vince fell into thought for a moment. He felt that new and overwhelming sense of frustration with how truly useful their sulphur dioxide project would be. When clearly there were other options, like this, it was nothing more than a political maneuver. Why cover up one problem with another? Except that it gives political gain to the decision makers. The most logical step to take with an excess of carbon in the atmosphere was reduction in emissions. Not dumping an extra blanket of pollution to offset the side effects of the first.

"We gotta have a look at your cousin's pasture," Brad said.

"As you like." Aahil nodded. "A long journey into the Ayărs."

Vince watched out the window at the vast expanses of grassland speckled with trees rushing past. A group of darker dots seemed to move along the horizon in the distance. He strained to see closer. Like Banff National Park herbivores back in Alberta, but this was the Sahel. Gazelles, perhaps here. "Any lions around here?" He spoke to the two sitting in the front. "No lions here. Only in W National Park. To the south of Niamey."

"W?"

"The Niger River there has the shape of W."

They stopped at Birni-N'Konni for a rest, pulling into a yard of parked semi-trucks. Followed Aahil, they walked up to a food bar to order plates of chicken on mounds of rice and greens. He passed the basket of Taguella bread. They were almost half way to Agadez Aahil said, and at this village they will veer directly north. He gestured in the direction of the Sahara. Close to the border with Nigeria here, the other way. "The A1 highway will take you to that country," Aahil told them.

As they ventured down the road after the trucker stop, Vince and Brad chatted about their schedule. "Back to Niamey by air," Vince said. Brad nodded total agreement. They settled in for the afternoon, grateful for the air conditioning, comparing numbers and strategies. They approached an extra secure military check just past Tahoua. Aahil kept his face solid as stone when he passed the letter from the Minister's office to the soldier. The tip he left with the hand shake helped them through to the N25 desert road. As they left the drainage, the stunted trees dwindled to scattered shrubbery and they played tag with wadis, up and down, until even the grass was rare.

Staring out into the sun's brilliance over endless fields of sand, Vince was overcome by an indescribable sense of pure beauty. Numbers popped up where no N highway signs existed, and the scene collapse into a chatter of fractal images, pi dancing everywhere. He wiped at his eyes. His father and that long ago numerical epiphany, now his fractal angel. He resigned to any message. What came warned of the out of balance, an equation calculating iterations of impending error. Vince had to talk and he told Brad. His father had another drink, why couldn't he? Brad listened, nodding in understanding.

Across the sands, still distant from Agadez, the earth color shifted orange to maroon red and the Aïr Mountains smouldered dark on the horizon. The setting sun glared through their back window. Vince peered intensely and fell into talking of his research on recent natural volcanic activity. Before Pinatubo, there had been El Chichón in Mexico—1982—and Agung on Bali in 1963. Tambora in 1815 was huge, creating noticeable climate impact by knowledgeable historians looking back. Certain volcanoes blew lots of sulphur while others did not—he needed find out more. Typically, each that did blow sulphur showed its impact on a global temperature graph but El Chichón had a large El Nino the same year and warming offset cooling. Climate can be complicated—not totally predictable. Agung, however, was a classic and the best documented with its influence of sunlight reflection sulphates dumped high in the atmosphere, so used widely in climate response models. A natural background to their project. He glanced at the sun disappearing.

As they entered the scattered lights of Agadez from the pitch black darkness of the desert, a movement caught Vince's eye out the side window. He stared out into the dimness. As if something had passed them, but on the wrong side. What one of those ground drones Brad talked of could do with camouflage. He glanced at Brad but the guy was snoozing. He rubbed at his eyes, having seen too much today. He was probably just exhausted.

Aahil found a route to a hotel with a restaurant to end the long day with a final meal. A refreshing rest must follow. Tomorrow they needed have a look at the storage yard and find potential launch sites. "Then we gotta find us some magic air," Brad said. "Those mountains got some height to them. We gotta scout around and find us the right kind of valley."

Chapter 18

"So when we dump our SO2 in the thin cold stratosphere, it just hangs there for a while?" Brad raised an eyebrow. With street vendor coffees in hand they leaned back in chairs against the wall of their sidewalk hotel front in Agadez. The air hung heavy with early morning dust mingled with the smell of passing animal traffic. Aahil was to arrive any minute in the scout truck.

"Yeah, the sulphur gas combines with water to form sulphuric acid," Vince said. "The acid forms into droplets and you get an aerosol. The whole process takes a few weeks, so we've got that kind of delay before our sunshade's really in place."

"Huh." Brad sipped his coffee. "And this scout truck?"

The truck, Vince told Brad, was a three ton tanker, one of a potential fleet. Aahil would be bringing one from its parking spot in the storage yard. New from Asia, they were designed for deep penetration of harsh terrain. The idea was to trial a refill and re-launch right from where the balloons landed. The truck crew would refill the sulphur tank, trade the helium tank for one full, relocate the launch point, push a reset switch and have it prepped to send up another load. "Your night time requirement makes it complicated, but the trucks have GPS tracking and nightlight capacity. Works more efficiently for a launch like the Niger national." A few hundred tons would go up around Niamey for the presidential showcase, but thousands more needed launch here by the desert's edge.

"Could turn out pretty good for Aahil, and this family," Brad said. "A lot of his cousins live up here, so they get truck driving work."

"Yeah, we'll be needing crews."

Brad stared down the street. "You know, I got a message from Keith, you remember? We did that joint project on balloon design."

"Yeah. He works out of Seattle, right?"

"He's talking African contract."

"Really."

A donkey brayed long and loud down the way, and the barking of distant dogs came in from all directions. The heat of the day rapidly pushed aside the cold night air.

"Okay listen," Brad said. "Say nothing else changes but we do get a Green Sahara. Could be good for Aahil right? But everywhere else in the world the climate keeps changing. So, I'd say Vince there's gonna be places you wanna be and places you don't wanna be."

"That's the way the world is now. You thinking of moving here?"

"Nope, I mean back home actually. You think this project's gonna fly? Who knows?" Brad said. "Take extreme weather events—floods, droughts, wild fires...you want to avoid hurricane alley for sure. Hard to tell exactly where things will be nicer, or even less disturbed. But I'd hedge my bets on the Rocky Mountain valleys for one. Most of the Pacific Northwest looks relatively stable on a four degree map. Interior, anyway...there's gonna be rising sea levels on the coast."

"So you've seen a four degree map," Vince said, looking over. "How's that look for here?"

"Minus our project." Brad pressed his lips hard into an unnaturally disturbed look. "Well, uninhabitable. I mean I can see why Aahil and his family would be listening close to their president."

"Yeah."

"Look, the way I see it Vince, it's a good idea to pick out a spot. A good spot. Hard to say if it'll be better in the city or out in the country, so I figure best to have two places. A back door option."

"You think things could really get that bad?"

Brad shrugged. "Like I say, a growing risk. Anyway, you gotta come check out our valley when we get back home. Stretches right up across the border into Canada. I'll meet you there and we'll find paraglider lift off the east side mountains."

"I dunno. I mean thanks for the invite." Vince's eyes softened. "You know Calgary has that advantage, no ocean front. We're up at three thousand feet plus; the salt water would never be rising enough there. But now the infograms I've been touring describe typical southern Alberta flooding. Snowpack partly, but it's mostly extra rainfall on still frozen ground that makes for a quick spring runoff into the rivers. Other weird weather, like early heavy wet snow dumps break the tree branches before the leaves fall." He looked at Brad. "Who would have thought? Calgary's semi-arid, so you'd expect a drought."

"There you go," Brad said. "It's gonna be a crap shoot. And we got some global dice rolling here."

"All random chance then." Vince balanced his Smiling Earth cup on the arm of his chair. "Or we got a few angels onside."

"Alright, here's a situation check for your angels," Brad said. "The same ppm of carbon spread all over the world, supplied gratis by countries like ours gives different effects depending where you are. That's some pretty fine tuning when we're measuring in parts per million. And we got a world laced with the business as usual attitude. Carbon from the US or Canada floats around in the African air we're breathing at this moment. So tell those angels that's what we got, carbon everywhere. And invisible too, like them."

"The grand designer's giving us an opportunity." Vince mused, watching a herd of goats walking past guided by a turbaned youth with a long stick. "A common issue bonds young people together. Could that be what we've got?"

"So you alluding to our chance to grow up?"

"Yeah." Vince stared into his empty cup. "Maybe."

Aahil pulled up in the scout truck. They climbed the two side steps and slid in beside on the high front seat.

"To storage yard, yes?" Aahil said. He shifted the truck into gear and gently let out the clutch to roll them forward.

"How about a tour, Aahil?" Brad said. "Your family comes from around here, right? Show us the sights."

They drove a weaving route through the dusty streets on their way to the north end of the city. Mingling in with the camel traffic, they passed stunted shade trees that cast shrinking morning shadows. Diesel fumes mixed with a hanging aroma of animal dung in the thick air. Aahil pointed out the top of a brown clay tower poking above the walls along the street.

When they turned the corner, Aahil let his foot off the accelerator as they passed a gaping burned out chasm in the wall around the tower. "Eight years past my cousin came in to Agadez. Blessed by the prophet, he did not attend Grand Mosque. Khalid was known to meet his wives and children in entrance hall. Two fire-from-the-sky missiles hit the mosque entrance—many leaving mosque that day are now in paradise."

"Christ." Vince said under his breath.

"They never had surface drones back then." Brad spoke softly. "A Marauder carries two missiles, maybe Hellblazer II, the 116R Romeo." He looked at Vince. "So back then, they can't see their target exactly, so they take out a suspected part of the building and everyone in it. Or a vehicle. The military must have really wanted that Khalid guy bad. Now surface drones help achieve target lock, if they're available."

Vince searched for a picture on his Jeenyus, showing how the skyward poking Grand Mosque and blasted entrance building once stood before the Hellblazer. He showed Brad. "So tell me about this drone missile thing again," Vince said.

Brad nodded. "They launch a Hellblazer from an UAV, that's an Unmanned Aerial Vehicle. Often a Marauder. They argue it's more selective and accurate than bombs." Brad shrugged. "Less collateral damage. Say they target us in our vehicle, well, they get Aahil too. Only Aahil would be collateral damage." Brad put his hand on Aahil's shoulder.

"The Grand Mosque has a reborn entrance." Aahil stared at Brad through furrowed eyes. "The main door now opens to the other street".

They passed between the red mud plastered walls to a taller palisade—the Sultan's palace, Aahil said. The rampart loomed above as they jostled in a traffic snarl of other desert trucks, beasts of burden and rattling old cars. "Morning rush hour," Brad tooted.

"Like anywhere." Free of the tangle, they left the city business zone and ascended a gradual slope along a wadi to the storage yard end of town.

"Those surface drones use camouflage Brad?" Vince looked out his window.

"Chameleon technology keeps advancing...real bonus for reconnaissance."

"What could one do to us? Say here and now."

"First step, they snap a shot of our vehicle and plate, you know, like the police camera for a ticket. Then you've been tagged."

"Then what?"

"Depends what vehicle data they got." He looked at Vince. "And their mission objective. Why?"

"I think I saw one. When we came into town last night."

"What color?"

Vince looked back. "Night shadow."

"Next step, they take us out."

"Hmmm."

Pulling in to the walled yard, they discovered an extensive packed earth patch of vacant space. A twenty-five-ton tanker trailer sat tucked in at one end, one thing Vince needed to see. Room remained for many trailers beside, and he could envision larger sulphur storage tanks at the other end. Buildings with warehouse front doors lined the central drive, an inside storage place for launch balloons and helium tanks. The Aïr Mountains loomed above them in the distance.

#

That afternoon, Aahil and his son had laid out a line of ten balloons for launch along a desert road. A recruited crew of two locals helped.

"One ton each," Brad said. Vince nodded.

Brad showed Vince the latest design features of their remote sulphur release system. Each balloon would rise to an elevation of 15 kilometers. Starting there, pressure sensors would trigger an SO_2 release valve as the balloon rose to 17 kilometers. "We'll keep ozone damage to a minimum at those heights," Vince said. Brad nodded. After that, each balloon would vent its helium and return to ground to be located by GPS. "Good. Then the crew shows up in the scout retrieval truck," Vince explained. "They refill the sulphur, disconnect and replace the helium tank and push your reset button, right?" Brad nodded and said. "Yup, then we got remote control again for re-launch. They need to locate those balloons careful to avoid any snag on a shrub." Much depended on the lateral air movements in the high evening atmosphere. Vertical ascent and vertical descent would be ideal for retrieval. But not likely. Aahil would learn the routine and be able to train other crews.

That evening they waited with Aahil as the sun set, watching with night vision binoculars from the Nissan Patrol. "So we'll use the same basic logistics as this for the Niger national," Brad said. Along roads gave best access, but also away from civilization to avoid plastic tanks coming down on the road or someone's house. A little obsessive they agreed with so few houses around here. "Anyone could be doing this," Brad said casually. "Anyone, anywhere in the world." Night time release would avoid high altitude drone detection and any spotter satellites. "We'll see what the world says," Vince said. Drones wouldn't be, at least shouldn't be watching, not this early in the game.

"So we keep two storage sites," Brad said. "One here and the yard at Niamey."

"I'm gonna rename Agadez the major sulphur yard," Vince said. "Niamey will transition to a transfer station. How about the balloons?"

"Yeah, warehousing's good," he said. "For balloons and helium."

More tanker trucks would bring sulphur dioxide from Vince's Nigerian oilfield connections. They'd truck in the stationary storage tanks empty—a hundred and seventy tons each—to this Agadez yard. If the scout truck idea worked, they had parking space for a good sized fleet of those. A good night would have each scout truck coming home empty with all of its three tons released by recycled balloons.

They talked about the timing logistics of hitting target tonnage. Brad calculated a thousand tons a week. "The drone people are gonna be noticing then." Lots depended on the number of balloons, the rate of trucking sulphur in from Nigeria, and the local weather. A few windy nights could make for a setback. Vince thought a random pattern of time release as well as a random spatial pattern would help avoid detection. The primary constraint was keeping close to roads and access wadis for retrieval.

"I sound like a paramilitary strategist," Vince said.

"You do need a new career," Brad said. "That's sure."

Vince stared at him for a second. Then he couldn't help smiling.

"You know, I made this special request once," Vince said. "More like a wish whisper to the universe. Like a prayer, but not really. Just I was out in the mountains that time."

"What'd you request?"

"I dunno, brotherhood of man," Vince said. "Or anything that gives people, not only young ones, a practical chance." He paused. "This maybe."

"What this?"

"This global situation is gonna bring people together. Brothers, sisters." Vince gave a wry look. "Could be a motivation."

"Yeah, don't count on it."

"I suppose not," Vince said.

Brad confirmed the time on his jPad. Double checking final balloon settings, he looked to Vince, and then touched the green square on the remote screen to authorize. They watched along the sand road as the balloons bubbled up from the ground in a line, lifting their sand colored globes like quick growing weeds sprouting up towards the sky. As they lifted off, the sun dipped below the distant desert horizon and they ascended in a weaving trail into their darkening target.

#

Next evening found them on a desert road east of Agadez, traversing the rocky crags of ancient worn mountains. On another Friday and another missed day off for Aahil, they were combining a tour of the southern Ayărs with a search for a magic air valley. Brad explained how daytime heat captured in a valley rises in the evening, like a thermal but spread out. The air of the whole valley ascends, lifting raptors and paragliders alike, magically. "Kind of like ridge lift too, any air going upward slows your descent. Magic air has a more mysterious source."

The road trended upwards from sand bottom valleys, giving way to chattering stone on the passes. Vince hummed as he listened.

"We need the right kind of valley." Brad pointed at the topography on visiscreen. Scouting for ideal terrain, he pointed out a couple promising spots they could ground checked as they passed. A wadi allowing a drive at least part way up would help and then a nice flat launch spot.

Conversation turned to the project—they lost only one balloon the night before, but Aahil tracked the location down today.

"Your guy got to it riding a motorbike."

"True." Aahil said.

"Can the scout truck get in there?" Brad asked. "Or we could rig up a small pull-trailer for a motorbike," Brad said.

"Yes, good," Aahil said. "We recover balloon to scout."

"Yeah, yeah," Vince said.

With little light left in the day, and Brad having marked two promising ridges on the map they decided to tour beyond the Ayărs. Next evening they could return and fly.

On a final descent the road passed through thinning rocks into the sand. As they left the mountains, the track lead them into a desolate nothingness, what Aahil called the true desert.

"I don't see one blade of grass," Vince said, glancing out the window.

Anywhere Aahil pointed Vince saw nothing. But he noticed a stir in their driver's Tuareg blood, more even than at the Sultan's palace. Places he knew, they could not. Where once the barren sand had been plains of green grass covered in grazing gazelles. That age was better remembered back in the Ayărs.

"What makes a true desert?" Brad asked.

For the Tuareg, the Sahara was not one desert, but the Tinarimen—'the deserts'. The name rang with sweeping meaning when Vince looked across the expanse. The road they drove withered into the distance of the Ténéré, the truest desert of 'the deserts'. The uninhabited emptiness, the place where there is nothing, nothing at all. Where the jinn, the spirits of the desert played tricks on your mind when alone, Aahil explained in all earnest. Yet truly, the Tuareg legend told where now they looked upon the purest of sand, there once lay not a mirage, but a water filled lake.

Vince called up an infogram tour—to supplement Aahil's rich desert tribal history. The Taureg had migrated thousands of years ago from the north to the Sahel, after the green Sahara had waned, across true desert sands. They were pushed south by Arabs in the times of horses and chariots. The tour guide added how after the Taureg move the trail they followed became a later medieval trade route, to Bilma in today's Niger.

Touring before the Taureg people lived on the land, the guide told of Green Sahara times. Ahead in the now Ténéré Desert, in those times first the Kiffian people lived with roaming elephants and giraffes, like the president's Dabous Rock carving. Alligators and hippos swam in local waters, and the people had been of the fisher/hunter kind.

Aahil listened intently, as Vince revealed the history.

Later as the lake dried the Tenerians lived in the Aïr Mountains among olive, juniper, Aleppo pine forests, and rivers in valleys teemed with fish. The people ran pastoral cattle on plains of seed-bearing grasses. Still before Taureg, 8500 years ago to 6500 years ago, large mammals roamed the land as in African national parks of today. Aahil told them how the president did not mention the thousands of years that had passed, only that he wanted his people invigorated about this, the times of a Green Sahara. And, many people were listening.

On their return in the dark, as twinkling stars appeared, Vince let his mind drift as Brad traced out possible ascent routes on the terrain map.

"Feels square," Vince said.

"Explain," Brad said.

"You know, when you run the math of a statistical model. You run iterations until you have the error minimized. Same with the world. You can tell when you've done everything you can by how you feel. One feeling equation confirms another. You know, like fair and square."

"That an angel message?"

"Yeah." Vince grinned.

"Okay bud, tomorrow we return. We're gonna find us some valley air out here," Brad said. "Maybe we'll call it angel air, instead of magic."

Chapter 19

Vince sat alone in the newly arranged office space at the Agadez storage site, fist bumping lightly on the desk. Aahil had taken Brad off to the distant mountains to pay a visit to Aahil's relative, Aksil. "Why?" Vince muttered. Why a world with such scarce food here when back home provisions flowed from the grocery stores. His fist beat harder. People! To reclaim a piece of the desert for pasture was a brilliant idea, especially for local food production. And Aksil might soon work less at that reclaiming process, if the rains came back to the Sahara. He smashed his fist into the desk, too hard; he rose quickly. He couldn't think; he needed focus—on something, on anything.

Hands grasped tight behind his back, he stared at the morning light spread across the yard. This inexplicable anger, this rage, this part of him. Such dissatisfaction with the world. What, fractal angel, what? You want me to refashion society's operating manual?

After a moment he took a deep breath and sat again, grabbing his jPad. Focusing on sketching a tanks layout for the yard, yet his mind still drifted. That childhood tree house design; he'd sketched that out on paper—he felt his father's approving pat on the back. Over the idea of sketching, not the content. Turn your mind to something practical, son, I'll get you design work from the office.

Vincent had been born angry, yet what did this anger need? He knew of clues, like mulling anger turning to rage whenever he made a mistake. His grandfather had raged, then his father—he'd watched his father's anger, the lump in the throat, the fist pounding on the table.

His father may have had that fractal moment, but any added concern for others never came about. More like a reversal actually. At his moment of epiphany, his father made a decision—to ignore it completely, to harden his nose in tradition. Had fear been his deciding factor? Fear of change. Fear of being wrong. The non-traditional could always be cast as wrong. Mistakes were not allowed. Tradition allowed you to gloss them over, to ignore them, to pretend they never existed. Psychology said anger hid behind many fears.

What was *he* to do with these inner knowings? The overall sense that, not what they traditionally scoffed at as intuition, but mathematically, things being out of alignment. The out-of-sync sensation now was increasingly tied to what people were doing to their planet. All this shit from the past had piled up on itself and brought him to where he was today. Out beside some mountain range in the middle of the Sahara desert, working on a project that would change the color of the sky.

He touched send on the jPad for the sketches with basic dimensions. The Calgary office would create detailed design drawings, an efficient way to have it done. He grabbed a coffee, touching his global icon cup. Like his Calgary office cup, with a kindergarten photo embossed of his daughter. He turned back to his jPad which peeped out a list of options. A background review caught his attention and he picked his project supplied infogram guide.

The guide connected him back in time to the dated Fifth Assessment Report, the AR5, and numbers associated with the four RPCs, Representative Concentration Pathways. The real on the ground situation they were dealing with could easily be tracked back to the predictions of the original 'A1F1—the Intergovernmental Panel on Climate Change worst case scenario. God, why were people so dense—why did they not listen and learn then. Okay, he knew his wife well enough—one for sure who would be the last to hear. The 'A1F1' was superseded by the AR5 RCP 8.5 radiative forcing scenario. Yet both older reports had agreed; based on strong economic growth and high fossil fuel use their predictions as the most likely scenarios translating into a 3 degree temperature rise. Which, the guide led to further evidence, had become the de facto truth. Three degrees! What had Brad said about that 4 degree map? Jesus Christ, why hadn't anyone done anything back then? Why didn't he know this already? His mind reviewed his life those AR5 years—Fort McMurray tar sands had been booming on high oil prices and his father's business was expanding.

Sweat trickled down his forehead, dripping on his screen and a hunger stirring. He clicked on the fan, and grabbed some packaged food to munch on as he switched infogram to soft absorb mode for the early afternoon. Then he reconnected.

The subsequent AR6 and AR7, and early releases on the impending AR8 fell in line with those earlier predictions. The world was closely tracking the RPC 8.5 representative concentration pathway by all indicators, expecting an 8.5 watts per square meter climate forcing by 2100. These later Assessment Reports had distinctly improved their definitions of Shared Socio-Economic Pathway, in the AR6 and then especially in the AR7. He could not hold his excitement down—he couldn't disconnect from what the reports termed as common but differentiated responsibility. Shared Pathways carried story, real people story, and the projections of key socio-economic factors wrapped his attention into a tight bundle.

The math had been simplified into easy to scrawl on the back of a napkin measurements. The units spoke volumes, radiative forcing in watts per square metre. Watts were simply a standard measure of energy. And they knew the area in square metres of the planet. A bright high school student could calculate this and a first year engineering student should grasp the radiative forcing expression. The concept was simple. A change in balance between incoming and outgoing radiation to the atmosphere was caused primarily by changes in atmospheric composition. So picture a greenhouse, his daughter could do that. Greenhouse gases insulated the earth so more watts came in than went out.

Radiative forcing as a simple engineering concept had always been the type of thing so easy for him to understand, yet boring, dreary on its own. But, yes super big but, these numbers could also be translated from climate forcings into people forcings, into cultural outlooks and political views. The Nigerien national sulphur they were planning to dump would keep more watts blocked, but that would only give breather space for the politicians to get their shit together. And climate forcing created by people, whether by carbon or by sulphur, had to translate into a crisis they could rally around. A people forcing. A reason to shift culturally. A reason to get politically active. They just needed to know about the crisis. Somehow.

More connections informed him the driving forces causing carbon equivalent gases to increase in the atmosphere could be simplified too. And they needed expression as human forcings. Simplified to three, they were economic development, population growth and technology. Different combinations of these forcings created different emissions scenarios or RPCs. You could have rapid economic development or slow, that was a choice. Did people what to work harder or have more quality family time? You could have quick population growth or slow and associated affluence—highly influential on carbon footprint—depending which country and what social status of the children's birth. You could have a rapid switch from hydrocarbon based technology to alternate and more efficient technologies or you could lag along like Alberta and keep digging into the tar sands. Or like Brad said in America, keep mining out that coal.

He felt an excited tingle rush through him. That fractal presence on a rare positive visit. The anger held at bay for now. He could influence these human forcings in a real way. And now he understood better the target so easy to keep in mind. The numbers he could keep background except for other engineers, analysts, scientists. To completely avoid the RCP8.5. They had to, for his daughter, for her life and definitely for her future family, they had to shoot for the RCP 3PD. The radiative forcing would peak at about 2 W/m2 before the end of century and decline due to ambitious mitigating efforts. To get the CO2 equivalent ppm back down to 350—many people got that number. Many more would get temperature, so to keep the temperature increase below 1.5 degrees. The High Impact countries would be relieved and yes, his daughter could live in a potentially happy world, a least not a stressed out carbon trashed garbage dump.

Come evening, he had decided to build a global information database. He stayed up late, building a map model of carbon in a geographic cloudware, tagging each country with what database information he and the guide could find, and grouping each country by its various associations. The most intriguing thing was the global aspect of the project. Pretty much a no brainer when you thought for a moment, that the atmosphere was a global issue. The tingle returned—brotherhood of man. Even though the land base and parts of the ocean were divided up politically into countries. There were the OECD, the G7 and G20 and now the HICCC. He found total annual carbon emissions for each country, and then with population, the guide stressed tons per person emitted. Some countries had large populations with low emissions, while some have small populations with high emissions. So that came down to a for-each-person measure to be accurate. And real. And informative.

Back home, each Canadian had quite a stack of carbon tons, like 20 on average, but that varied by province and by lifestyle. Each Canadian set beside each Nigerien showed a whopping three hundred times difference in carbon dumped into the atmosphere for each resident. A pattern quickly developed—high carbon emitters clearly were not members of the HICCC. One would think a place like the Netherlands would be quite impacted by a rising sea level, but as it turned out, wealth allowed a country to adapt. So a lack of wealth and bad geographic luck highly motivated HICCC membership. He was almost satisfied, when the guide took him to risk index analyses. The climate change vulnerability index was calculated by more than one source, and adding that column to his geographic cloudware model, he stayed awake well into the morning. HICCC membership would also be highly motivated by vulnerability risk.

Exhausted, yet satisfied, he leaned back. Brad and Aahil would be staying overnight in the mountains so his infogram map creation needed await discussion. The infogram map of the world as it was danced back and forth, highlighting the divisions between the HICCC countries and the OECD. The two world segments held no overlap, no true intersection, except perhaps in climate crisis risk. His anger began its familiar surge but the fractal tingle diverted it, and held it back. This model before his eyes connected him to at an excellent global summary of the problem and he knew he had to do something. Now what to do was still the question.

Chapter 20

Harry sat in his downtown office looking out at the snow falling from the Ottawa skies. Large wet flakes settled in a gentle frosty cover over his Kent Street view. He enjoyed a rare quiet moment on a Wednesday afternoon. Initial negotiations with this HICCC entity were going quite well, even Minister Kendall's office agreed. The OECD, with Canada as one of the more outspoken on budgetary responsibility, was certainly losing no ground. Unlike the COP gatherings, these negotiations were being carried out via digital media interface, just as any weekly business meeting. This week's meeting postponement had contributed to this unnatural lull in activity and he glanced down his to-do list on screen. Selecting a wooden pencil from his standing-at-attention sharpened container, he noticed an almost forgotten item. Whirled the pencil into a practiced spin, he perused the forgotten note.

The Sens beat the Leafs that home opener game. He tapped the pencil end on his Senators red with black trim Post-It stickies. When he and Alan left the Scotia Place they hadn't stopped talking about the game all the way home. That's right, they never had talked shop again that evening. What a game it had been though, Spezza scored twice in two unbelievable plays. He smiled at his recall…no wonder this item never came up again that night. Should have been in his mind just by association with that game. Oh well, call Lewis at B&E, he would do that now. He grabbed his office landline and punched in the number with the back end of the pencil.

"Hey Lewis, how's things at Braunstein and Eichel? You in management yet?"

"You are speaking to the new CEO, my friend. You considering a move?"

"Gonna stick with the Harold Heine team for a bit. Quite a few contracts drifting our way. Climate Minister, you know."

"You guys are quite involved with the High Impact meetings, are you not?"

"That's our second biggest contract now. You guys too?"

"Some, yeah."

"On that note Lewis, can I pick your brain? Any chance B&E has a confirmed list of the countries claiming High Impact status?"

"We likely have the same as you," Lewis said. "Pretty vague."

"Really? 'Cause they're all self-designated as high impact, right? I mean after what, an entire year of negotiations we still don't know what kind of hodgepodge we're actually dealing with." Harry tapped his pencil.

"We do know HICCC stands for High Impact Climate Change Countries," Lewis said. "Common sense tells us which countries would most likely make up the consortium."

"Yeah, okay. We know Bangladesh holds the chair right now, but there's this long list of countries like Mozambique, Myanmar, Cambodia. Most of them are so obscure until you get to Thailand. Nice place I hear, I mean our friends have been there on vacation. But what about Pakistan?"

"Nuclear armed," Lewis said. "That states plenty."

"Right," Harry stopped tapping.

"And then would Pakistan be signed up as affiliate or are they an associate member? You guys seen that speculated list of supporting non-members? Not one associate and certainly no supporting non-members participate in negotiations, nor are they holding the chair at any time. The big question is where do China or India stand in the picture?"

"Or Brazil?" Harry wondered.

"We're still trying to find out."

"The Minister has an interest in any booming new economy."

"Off the record, we have those same membership questions bouncing around our office," Lewis said. "Then there's their research fund. That's the issue our CEO wants to know more about than anything."

"Sounds like we sail similar waters."

"Nothing new," Lewis said. "So what's on your mind?"

"Hey, I just called about this infogram I got copied on. You know Allan Turkon with our firm? So this infogram...let me see...from a couple weeks back reads about some kind of African tour you were on..."

"African?" Lewis said. "Yeah that was part of what the HICCC calls a continental educational tour or what they officially call their HICCC global enlightenment program. Ecuador, Niger—that's the one in Africa and Bangladesh, one country for each continent. I probably cc'd Al the Niger summary part of the trip. What do you wanna know?"

"So the tour was focused on informing, right? I mean from what you say I get the impression it wasn't exactly at the table negotiating," Harry said. "So on what are you now enlightened?"

"Okay let's see, that was a one week tour back in the middle of September—a full seven days. The African component was in a city in Africa called Niamey, a French colony in the past so the name is French. Like I said, in Niger. For reference that's geographically sub-Saharan in a region they call the Sahel. The HICCC runs their presentation kind of like a show and tell. They do run a show, but don't tell all that much. You know how their publicity campaigns have been running where they negotiate around ethics and global cooperation. On this tour they attempt to show a connection between their upfront view of local climate change events like floods and droughts with global emissions. And they put the onus on recorded emissions sources."

"But we all know how difficult it is to connect any weather event directly with climate change. Even the scientists admit that," Harry cut in. "Anyone can see our negotiating edge right there."

"Yeah, well, they quote scientific publications...they passed around a few recent studies." Harry let others do the reading, picking up on research through conversation instead.

"Okay, anyway I think we've seen one or two of their high impact climate change brochures." Harry switched pencil for silver Sens pen and leaned back in his chair. "But you say they take you right there. Like they want to bring you right into the action, to share in the experience firsthand."

"That's it in a nutshell. They took us around to a few rice paddies and peanut plantations. Not much of a crop this year, I mean don't get me wrong 'cause I'm not from the farm. But they did show us the crop reports at the Minister of Agriculture's office. That part I get. Then they took us around, you know, to see the faces of the malnourished African children. Around the city, then out in the countryside to the villages."

"Sounds like a sympathy call."

"Nothing new, you could say. A basic ethical argument. Their birth rate is certainly part of their dilemma. "

"Why countries like that have so many kids is always beyond me. A real no brainer when you're short on food, right? Wouldn't you want to allude to that birth rate with their representative? I mean no matter what actually gets heard? Whatever's gonna come out of any African talks anyway? They've been trying to negotiate with this kind of stuff for years."

"They do point out to industrialized countries that if we help educate their people, especially the girls, that that would be in our own best interests. You know the statistics, eh? Education of girls has the highest impact on population control. Anyway they present their issue as a self-benefiting investment. To us."

"So we're given an opportunity to finance their Education Department." Harry gave his pen the maximum spin. "I can just see how that would fly with the Climate Minister's office."

"They had an HICCC representative there. She told us they want to hold the OECD HICCC negotiation meetings right there in Niamey. Like they're petitioning a sign of good will from OECD."

Harry poked his finger down to stop the spinning pen.

"You've got to be kidding. In some obscure African city? Can you imagine the logistics Lewis? Good thing the initial conference was in Paris." Harry smiled, feeling an inner smirk. "I mean international meetings need real airport connections and a drone free zone where you can expect people to show up."

"Yes, if I were the HICCC I'd think about setting up some kind of continental office first. In Niamey if they want. Or they could at least set up some kind of a regional operation there."

"That's a place I'll never go." Harry flicked his pen one spin at a time, wincing. "That'd be the day I come talk to B&E."

Lewis told him the tour report came across his desk just yesterday for final sign off—should be with Minister Kendall's office early next week. But, Harry wondered, what was in that the Minister didn't already know? If they wanted to allude to their idea that countries like Canada caused climate change more than countries like Bangladesh or Niger, where would that get them in the real world? They could say industrialized countries dumped the most carbon into the atmosphere, and that OECD members benefited the most. But how could they take that to the table?

"Truth be told, Harry, I get a feeling they want us to deduce our own fault in the matter. To admit openly to them, to the world saying 'my bad' and even apologize. A developed countries grand mea culpa. A valiant effort on their part. But highly unlikely I would say…"

"…especially when it comes to shifting any budget." Harry picked up on the thought. "That's when the brakes screech the loudest. What grounds do they have to stand on anyway?"

"Let Minister Kendall's office make that call. I mean, how do we interpret China?"

"Ouch! Always working on that one over here."

"You guys too?" Lewis asked affably. He continued. "So after Niger, we were off to Bangladesh."

"Right."

"So tell me Harry," Lewis said. "Are you guys following the HICCC fund?"

"Dunno, we know they can finance a few things."

"Oh yeah, you can tell by their ad campaign. Sounds like that fund's growing too. Anyone, any person, corporation or country can contribute anonymously. That's what they say. We're fairly sure that fund financed this tour."

"China," Harry quipped.

"Dunno. They say a large part of that fund is designated towards climate change research. Officially, anything any OECD country isn't researching, they want to take on. They plan refugee migration routes and likely patterns pending various sea level scenarios. If I recall, one scenario went with an abrupt sea level change if the West Antarctic sea ice shelf slips off all at once."

"Crazy stuff."

"Yeah. Some of its more realistic. Storm surges from major weather events, so British Columbia and New Brunswick and their modified building codes—I think they project a sea level rise of a meter eighty years from now."

"We consult with the Dutch." Harry knew the prescribed response. "Adaptation does create employment."

"You'd like the alternate food sources like insect farming—I could see that in Africa. What's your take on that obscure idea of geoengineering. You guys following that one?"

"Yeah, maybe, no not really. What the heck for? Too many insane ideas out there. None of that's really going to happen so why waste the time?"

"How about the legal end? They really pushed that one when we were in Bangladesh. You must know of the Bangladeshi and who else now, Philippines law suits in world court? Base on that Dutch precedent. They're looking for fines levied on industrialized countries, binding or not, they expect a world reaction. That kinda thing make for real substance for you?"

"Well, depends who can hires the best lawyer, doesn't it?" Harry leaned forward. "That's the way the world works."

"Yeah, I know. The U.S. doesn't even recognize the world court, even if most European countries do. Anyways Harry, good chatting with you."

"Later Lewis."

Harry put his pen down in the open spot, giving it another maximum spin. Kind of a crap conversation—like what kind of crap was all that? In some shithole part of the world where you get snuffed out by a drone missile. And why would Allan be interested? Oh well. He had to give Angie a call; let her know about Sten's hockey practice.

Chapter 21

A rising desert breeze touched Brad's face as he peered down the rocky ridge at Agadez below. Magic air in the valley had been fantastic, but he had time today only for a local flight. This morning he would land right in the storage compound, saving Aahil a pickup trip. Whistling softly, he unrolled his paraglider as his mind switched gears from flying fun to project detail. Tomorrow they'll double check the size of the expected shipment, the big one coming in from China. Three cargo containers were confirmed arrivals at Benin ship docks days ago. One held two thousand crates of balloons, and two were stocked full of helium tanks. The project was ramping up. Transport trucks were scheduled to arrive at the Niamey yard in two days. He and Vince would fly to Niamey tomorrow, while Aahil would make the return drive with his son.

He laid his harness out and clipped in the wing strings. He'd flown with Keith back home when they designed those balloons. He'd have to find out what project the guy had going now.

Vince and this British woman sure seemed to be getting along. Vince would finally get to be around an amiable female. Although, his face clouded, nice she may be, but why did this woman keep dropping in on those other Sahel countries…his whistle turned silent. Those other countries would have interests common with Niger, that made sense. But Brad sort of puzzled over what she was really doing there 'cause she sure wasn't talking about it. And, he scrunched up his left cheek as he did once in a while, what was she not revealing?

Oh well, he picked up on the whistle again. He popped his wing up in the air and stepped up to the edge of the steep rock spine. Gauging the light wind blowing over the top, he embraced the moment as he pushed with toes lightly off into the air. Rising in the breeze, he slipped into prone position to fly in true bird freedom. Letting the wing fly, he adjusted his weight in the harness and relaxed into the tranquility.

That Vince sure had curiosity for Tamanna's paleoclimatic outlook. All very interesting the climate history of the world, but for Brad there was so much more at stake in the right here and now. There were neighbours to chat with in the mountain valley back home. The odd time he caught himself thinking of the past, he imagined a life in the not so paleo, say the times of the Wild West. When a hand shake went a long ways and there wasn't so much dependency on the outside world. He needed to talk to valley neighbours like the cowboys had. How cool to ride the open ranges, and take on adventures in the wilderness. The only flying option back then had been the unpowered hot air balloon. Anyway, reality dictated this was his life to live, his time.

He flew a straight line out from the jagged rocky peak, slightly off track of Agadez to gain needed height from thermal lift to make the distance to the yard. Following the ridge of warm dark stone below, he watched his altimeter preparing to judge the upward boost.

Paragliders had been a fantastic leap in flight technology, and the next couple decades would bring on a lot more innovation. But the near future will be challenging people times too. He always came back to that primary question: just how close will these times a comin' in this rapidly developing global neighbourhood get to those of say Mad Maks? A wince warped his smile for a second. Nowhere close to Maks' world, he hoped but…a smart fellow had to at least be prepared. If people chose to be good global neighbours there should be a nice smooth transition to a friendly situation, the so-cool all-friends community he envisioned. If all people realized their dependence on the same basics of life, they'd know the atmosphere that regulated their climate was top of that list. Really, there should be nothing but opportunity as climate change unfolded. He grinned, knowing there would be some kind of adventure, no matter what.

Letting his eyes slip closed for a few seconds, Brad felt the air brush past his face. This was his purest thinking time on his primary topic of the what-if back up scenarios. He let his mind drift through a reality check warning of that adventure being of the rougher type. Just in case the trend shifted more in the direction of a Mad Maks world. Keith always said a shift to a nastier world would start in the developing world—cause they were already part way there.

To really cover all bases, a fellow needed a survival strategy as independent as possible, like that hidden away survival cell. Now that he thought of it, kind of like Aahil moving back out to his family hideout in the Ayărs. A place to sit tight for a while, just in case things got a little ugly. Many people in the south, in that drying up California, had moved up to Idaho and Washington State to get away from congestion. The reasons to move north were becoming more varied and increasingly insistent as each year passed.

Aksil's sand land grab had used bio-mimicry.   Why not use nature as a model where survival was of primary interest? What would a bear, a white tail or a ground squirrel do to avoid danger or otherwise adapt? Sleep through the cold berry-free winter living on fat reserves. What an idea! Or when deer hunters came, blend in to the forest along quiet hidden trails. Fade into the background. Ground squirrels could scoot down into their borrows to wait out a raging forest fire. He could mimic that wisdom and move his family to the survival cell for a while. Basically wait it out by getting out of the way until things improved. He felt secure about the risk adaptation that cell provided. That inconspicuous place had all the necessities, yet away from it all. He told most non-listening acquaintances of his getaway place, and that fit. And he and his wife had good neighbour connections in that valley, and agreed it to be one cool place to join a better cultural village. Lots of promise for his dream of a place to live no matter what happened elsewhere. Even with the international border bisecting, in fact at times they thought of that as a bonus.

He felt the wing balancing in the breeze, adjusting to wind like a bird. Could people become like an admired feathered friend in flight, find a way to adjust and balance things out?

When the third flood hit, that was a turning point. Watching oil producing Alberta as a barometer, Brad judged his actions. That year he convinced his wife, and they bought a piece of undeveloped valley land. The next year he got a machine in to make a small clearing and he started building the cell. They went there on vacations, such a beautiful setting and lots for the boys to do. Get acquainted and familiar he thought. Their land was in Idaho, but in a valley that ran a long ways into Canada along a huge natural mountain lake. Not a bad circumstance, he had reasoned. People said the waters of that mountain lake kept the valley warm, forming a microclimate allowing fruit trees to grow, and all kinds of other food. The lake never froze. What also caught his strategic eye was the long corridor that valley formed, stretching far to the north past the huge lake to another. His wife's cousins drove north for days finding work in the camps. One fellow he talked to went hunting at the north end of the lake, for grizzly bear. Wild! Say people came flooding north from California, and that caused even more chaos. Depending on the situation, it seemed worthwhile to have another route going even further north. Warmth was shifting that direction, opposite of an ice age. The polar vortex was breaking up too, bringing on heavy snow dumps that broke September tree branches, but you could only account for so much.

His wing reached the darker stony ground, and as he felt the lift of thermal activity from below, he banked. He'd circle here and rise like a hawk as high as he chose. The take off point was only three hundred feet higher than landing, so he needed lift enough to make the overland distance. That dry sand Teloua drainage had to be crossed. He followed his spiral upward, keeping an eye on the altimeter.

As an engineer he analyzed, and at times like Vince and Jeri he crunched people numbers. Say people got played a forced hand—required to cooperate. What might motivate them? What would be their common goal—teams that work together form around a goal. Like winning at sports. Like high school football. How would Coach Arnie have put together a team of not just football players, but say mixed with his basketball guys? Then throw in Coach Sanders and the baseball players. Mix all the sports into one brew. When Brad played football, he joked around with the coach on how he never could find that indoor court hoop. How would he as a player react thrown into some other sport? Then throw in a girls' volleyball team—even more complicated. For the coaches, for the players, for everyone. Then total reality dictated the coach would need to combine not just the jocks but *all* the school kids. The nerds never played sports, nor the smoke pit guys...the smart Asian kids had other issues in mind, and the metal heads had nothing in mind. His wife had been one of the choir and drama kids. What's a coach, they would ask. What a challenge. Kids, like people, split off into groups for good reason.

The thermal lift carried him higher, revealing the extent of Agadez. He could make out the minaret of the Grand Mosque along that distant street. High altitude drones he knew could be used for reconnaissance-gathering, but each carried that deadly pair of Hellblazer missiles. He bit his lip. That would have been quite the pilot decision to blast a place of worship all to get one man. The drone missile trick had always been ascertaining a target from high above cameras, like his view now. Surface drones give a ground level view to lock onto identified targets right in the street.

His altimeter beeped. After one more spiral upward, just to be sure, he judged the elevation good and picked a line of flight directly towards the north end of Agadez and the storage yard.

Global neighbours, like school kids, would have to figure out a way to include everyone. Aahil's family modelled positive aspects—girls fit in there. What had Aahil said, women must be respected. They are the rock of family and community. No matter what the gender outlook, or the mind or skill set. Outlooks of any kind all had to fit. Well, of most kinds. What about school bullies? Good chance the nerds would be strongly drawn back to computer games; the stoners wanting back out for another toke and a lot of girls needing their drama mirrors. Had he put the choir in there, their voices singing unto the most high? How would choir voices ever fit on the sidelines of a football game?

Girls were the best of people. He had learned that from a decade of marriage. Suppose in that high school, just say for a minute you get girls on a creative cheer squad, not traditional pom poms, but leave it to them how to cheer. Say the nerds came onside as not water boys but game strategists. Those stoners, into the audience somehow. But reverse that and picture the jocks creatively sitting in on the drama audience. Yeah right he shook his head. Okay, try a scenario with the jocks playing the computer games, how would they fit there? Virtual football; that could connect them. For a bit. Just...how do you keep the nerds from walking away and back to their visiscreens and the jocks escaping from the drama audience back to the playing field? One conclusion was sure—big challenge. No doubt.

As he circled down closer to the storage yard, a movement caught the corner of his eye. He swiveled his head to look closer, adjusting his wing back for another turnaround. Almost as if a piece of the sand had moved. Must be the jinn, he told himself, Aahil's spirits of the desert. But weren't they only up in the Ténéré?

He circled again, thinking on another hope he had at times. The same lightning storm that kills the lights for the game on the sports field also knocks out the power for the visiscreen game. The trick would be then to get the jocks and the nerds together in an effort to restore their zapped common need. Like a school fire drill when everyone files out in an orderly fashion with one objective in mind. So something had to get the whole world together on this one situation. Still, and he always came to the same conclusion, a certain possibility continued, even a good chance, for at least some, or even a lot of chaos.

He waved down at Aahil, and let out a wild hoot as he passed over. Aahil looked up, lifting one hand at the sky. But as he circled back outside the compound wall, he saw that movement again, more distinct this time. He made out some kind of shape—could that be a military surface drone in camouflage colors?

He could do no more to keep aloft and he came in to land beside the Nissan. He'd have to reply to Keith, get an update on surface drones, and see what he thought of that kind of ground detection snooping around a country like Niger.

Chapter 22

They flew back from Agadez that day for an afternoon update meeting with Jeri. Vince sat with the other two around the downstairs meeting room. When Brad suggested kick around time, they talked Jeri into a game of crib—three way. The ten desert tons at Agadez made up the latest sulphur dioxide ascending, yet when Vince filed the report with Jeri that hadn't stilled her clamour for more climate model data.

"I just don't get it. When's Ms. Meacham going to define all project phases?" Jeri looked at them as she dealt the cards.

"And fill us in on who's got drones snooping," Brad said. "More I think about it, more I'd say that was a surface recon drone. Right outside our Agadez storage yard."

"Whoever has an interest," Vince said. "That's who."

"That's just it," Brad said. "On climate everyone has an interest. So who knows?"

"Russia," Jeri said forcefully. "Communists."

"How about China?" Vince said. "If you wanna talk about democratic or not."

"Who's got the most at stake?" Brad said.

"Any northern country that wants to keep the planet warm." Jeri stared at Vince. "Like Canada. They got drones?"

"Everyone's got drone capacity," Brad said.

"Yeah." Jeri looked at him. "Any drone hits Niger and I tell you guys, I'm gone. Contract or no contract."

Vince and Brad eyed each other, neither speaking.

"Five cards each, right?" Jeri asked.

"Yeah." Brad nodded. "Your crib."

"Anyway," Jeri said. "If they want any accuracy on the Sahara phase III and global phase IV runs, we need integrated model definitions. The model solidifies when we enter real data. But what have we got? Three tons here and ten tons a thousand miles away. That's just not enough to stitch the model internals together."

"Seven hundred fifty three kilometers away." Brad corrected her. "Our direct flight."

"Whatever," she muttered.

"Phase III and IV remain talking points, for hypothetical comparison only." Vince shook his head. "We do the Niger national release, and that's it. The president wants to run his political show around Niamey for the city people. You'll get numbers from that. Then there's the real release around Agadez, to give our client their national tonnage. You'll get big numbers then. They'll be negotiating around that for years. You guys are gonna be home for American Thanksgiving."

"Yeah." Jeri shook her head. She threw the last card down to start the crib pile. "I wonder if the Air Force will see this as a national security threat."

"Whose air force?" Vince asked.

"We Americans," Brad said. "Our Air Force."

"Ah, yes," Vince said.

"I dunno," Brad said. "Don't wanna scare Jeri off yet but I'd say we're on a drone target list. Someone's watching us."

"Yeah right," Vince said. "Like we're terrorists."

Brad looked at him, eyebrow raised. "So what's a terrorist?" He shrugged. "A political label."

"Aside from all your drone talk, say the Air Force does say yes, security threat," Jeri said. "Say they shoot down a certain number of balloons when we're in mid-launch. Now that would screw up our model—we'd have to do contingency runs on a whole matrix of scenarios." She gave them a sordid challenging gaze. "That would be a complex model run, borderline chaotic."

"Hey Jeri." Brad winked, reading her look. "People." He lifted his chin towards her.

She shrugged. "It's possible."

She looked at Brad's face, her eyes drilling into him. Then one corner of her mouth began an upward curl.

"Alright you engineers, here's an equation for you. Say P equals C. That's People equals Children. Both constants. Then throw in a maturity variable, say applied to the children side, so P equals M multiplied by C. And that M is your Maturity factor."

Vince watched as Brad's smile dimmed, and he became attentive. Could he be equating his chipper outlook as goofy, like immaturity?

"What do we know about children? They play with toys, right? For sure that's what my husband does. Boy's toys. Big trucks, ATVs, bush machines—whatever he can load up and pull around; gives him a sense of macho power. He can puff out his chest like at the playground. And the more money he makes—he does quite well there—the more toys he gets. He's always going upstate Michigan with his buddies, where they over and over play out the conquer nature scene. Zero progress—so maturity factor equals one. He is a total child."

"That Argosy school have anything to say on that?" Brad counted fifteen two and marked the points.

"I was really hoping one of you would ask." Jeri sported a half smile now. "Studies show my husband's behavior ranks as typical. The classic America view of the purpose of nature. An archetypal Christian based belief—nature was created to be subdued by man. Man, not woman mind you. His church reinforces this identity...a little scripture goes a long ways on belief support. The right select scripture, mind you, so that same church helps his deep belief that he's a self-made individual. His God sort of kicks around in the back of that church somewhere, not interfering much."

"Yeah, well women too." Vince nodded ardently. "Reverse that gender role. My wife fits right in there, not the church or conquer part, but replace the boy's toys with girl's toys. All she wants is a bigger house. No stopping, bigger and then bigger and bigger. Her M factor would never exceed one either. Drives me up the wall."

"Okay, point taken." She looked at Vince over her two cards. "Anyway, my husband counts how much nature he can squash. Cuts notches into his stick with his bucky-boy knife. He feels like a real big boy when he drives his Hummer around. He shows off to the people on the streets of Chicago, and he gets all kinds of pats on the back from his buddies up in Michigan."

Vince looked at what cards were played. Strategy only went so far in this game, mostly luck. So whatever. "Twenty." He placed his card, looking back up. "All I know is the bigger your house gets the more it's like living in a warehouse." He heard his voice getting louder, louder than he had spoken in years. "And then you get to play warehouse manager." His voice rang with sarcasm. "You have organizational and scheduling tasks by the carload."

"That's a go for me," Brad said. "You got an Ace?" He asked Jeri. "So unless you got an Ace, Vince, peg one for last card. And I start with a seven." She shook her head no and he put his last card down.

Jeri laid down her last, an eight. "So that's fifteen two for you, Jeri," Brad gestured at her peg on the board.

She moved her game token, and sat back, lifting both hands open to the above. "Where is the maturity, dammit? Why are we so adolescent? Me, the big childish me, as long as this climate change thing doesn't affect me and absolutely not my standard of living. How is that attitude going to adapt to the end of the economic growth model? What kind of a maturity factor does that suggest? When I am only interested in myself, my own wellbeing? Ahh, makes me want to scream sometimes."

She pushed her chair out and took her coffee cup over to the machine.

"You know I got a friend in one of those 12 step groups," she said. "And I've been to a couple meetings just to listen—well they got at least one thing figured out. They say the biggest problem is self. And they talk about maturity a lot; the drinkers say when they started drinking was when they stopped growing up. So when they quit, that's where they get to start over on the growing up process."

"People are making a lot of technological progress," Vince said. "Any points there on our M factor?"

"No way. My husband's looking at a hover bike, but that's no game changer on his attitude."

"How about Mission Mars, Jeri." Brad winked at Vince. "How about Jackie and Haydon?"

She walked back around the table and took her seat again.

"Martian astronauts or not, they're still a couple. They've got issues, that's for sure."

"Authority disallows formal legal marriage en route to or on Mars," Vince said. "So they call it pair bonding. Like back on the savannah or even before."

"Let's see how long they stay bonded," Jeri said.

"The thing is, everyone knows all about them," Vince said. "That's one issue with world focus. North American entertainment links—that one's solid."

"Yeah, just wait 'til she gets pregnant." Jeri nodded knowingly. "Then we'll have us an entertaining world story."

"Mission Mars relies on the entertainment factor," Vince said. "Their budget's crowd sourced."

The engineers counted their points and pegged. Jeri let Brad help her count her points.

"Argosy study," she said, watching. "On the inside, we're still trying to please our parents. My husband's father was a rock solid GOP businessman. Driven by fear of not measuring up, discomfort at not appeasing his deep knowing of his parents' desires. Who ever said we need to be like our parents? These aren't the Middle Ages anymore; we don't need to learn our father's trade to survive."

"No shit," Vince said softly.

"The thing is, our parents are our primary model," Jeri stated. "We spend our growing up life watching them and emulating certain traits. You could say the soft genetics of personality, and character."

Vince nodded, musing. How much he does that, he thought, and has done that all his life.

"So you got one chance there Vince, with your daughter," Brad said. "You gotta show her a happy face. The best you got becomes a part of her."

"Well you are helping, you bugger." Vince half grinned, making effort to hold his smile at the thought of his Calgary home.

"What else about people, Jeri?" Brad gave her a creased his brow look.

"People are like a frog in a hot pot."

"Whoa, shit, frogs now," Brad said. "My deal." He pulled in all the cards and began to shuffle.

Jeri stared directly at Brad. "You throw a frog into boiling water and he jumps our right away. Try it. Put him in warm and slowly bring the pot to a boil and he does not notice. He dies. Global warming's just like that on a macroscopic level." Jeri shook her head. "Look around you. You see people, young people, set on mimicking the baby boomer lifestyle, or even more—completely unaware of, and totally uninterested in what's coming. Just look at them; look at what they're doing. Each of them plays along as a cell in the body of that frog."

"Dopy frog." Brad nodded absently, finishing the deal and placing the last card down next to him for crib.

"But people think they're quite clever." Jeri nodded as she spoke. "My husband thinks he's the smartest one around. The ego of the clever ape, that's what I say. That ape, just came down out of the trees and now fresh off the kindergarten plains of Africa."

"A growth spurt," Brad said. "If we gotta grow up, don't even goofy kids grow in spurts?"

"So all of a sudden our child will start having an adult conversation," Jeri said. "My teenage boy husband, clearly with all the power of a man, will grow up? All of a sudden? Forget it— never gonna happen."

"C'mon," Brad said. "Lots of kids goof around for a while."

"Yeah, like say you're a teenager," Vince said. "You get a fast chance, or you get a slow chance depending on your situation. You don't fit in, you get depressed, you think of suicide, you get charged with a crime—then you grow up fast. Alright. Or say you drop out of school, but you go back later—you get a slower chance."

They looked at their cards, each selecting one to place on Brad's crib pile.

"How about counselling Jeri?" Brad said. "My wife's something of a counselor and she says people can change."

"My husband would never talk to someone like that—he's in total denial. That's a typical psychological state and he's stuck in party mode," Jeri stated, placing her hand flat on the table. "The future looking so bright you gotta wear shades makes for a total disconnect from reality. But the little boy wants that bright future, and to have that oh-so-cool look of the shades. How do you counsel someone who's having too much fun?"

"Lotta people gonna need those sunshades for their drive up to Alaska," Brad said. "Lots of people figure they'll head north for a holiday soon, and survive no problem in Alaska. Others are scheduling in one last spin down to the tropics before the last reef dies off."

Jeri stared at him, and Brad stared back.

"So imagine your husband in a self-care group, and they fit that Alaska trip in as a response to climate change," Brad said. "They could get his cooperative pro-social side activated for a climate crisis response. Build up his hope level."

"Yeah, shut up on my husband." Jeri smiled, playing a card. "In a million years. Anyway, hope is bullshit too. Lots of people 'hope for the best', and all that does is drown out the truth. People really have to accept their loss, that being their lifestyle, and process the grief. Get past the denial. Gotta crash first."

"I personally believe less work could be the answer," Brad said. "I've run the analyses and a more laid back lifestyle produces less carbon. So come out gliding, eh Vince?"

"We have to detach from our old future and reattach to a new future," Jeri stated. "Our self-esteem, our status, our image has to come from making things other than money. So I think you got something there."

Vince nodded along listening to the other two bantering. Except for the ideals, and prospects of radical change all of what they said translated into a harsher and more unpredictable future for his daughter, for all children.

"Maybe there's a God," Vince said slowly. "At least a friendly creative force that's going to help us out here."

"Oh, there is a God," Jeri announced. "No question there."

"You go to that church with your husband?" Vince asked. "You talking Bible?"

"That's his thing, not mine. Why piss around with religion?" Jeri looked directly at Vince. "Read the latest proof-of-heaven series. When a brain surgeon goes through a week long near death experience, and then documents the whole thing scientifically, why waste time trying to figure out stories thousands of years old? The most recent evidence should carry the loudest voice."

"I dunno, people like ancient stories," Vince said. "Everyone knows about angels. So I tell this engineer here some kinda force is giving us a chance to grow up." He looked at Brad. "Sure, stipulated as a growth spurt. This climate change is all about an opportunity to do just that. High risk, for sure, depending how adolescent we want to be."

"So God planned this opportunity," Jeri nodded her head, smirking. "Just for us."

"First steam engine started it," Brad laughed.

"Now, if we could just get everyone to experience a near death or something similar, that would wake people up. Near death typically has a real impact on people." Jeri almost softened. "A really positive, beneficial impact."

Vince thought she sighed—he must be imagining. "All that being said," he said. "And I know you don't have any kids Jeri."

"My trucker boy didn't want any. Would interfere with his life."

"All that being said." Vince tried again. "What with Argosy and all, where does that leave kids already born? I mean they never caused this problem any more than the Nigeriens, but they're set to get hit hard just the same."

Brad gave him a rare serious look.

"I'm glad I got my trucker boy. Better not to have any kids," Jeri said. "I mean, yeah, sorry guys, not looking too good. With all that we've been saying."

Vince wondering if humanity as a whole had an M factor of one or anything at all higher. And if his thought were true, that this climate change thing could be a chance to grow up at a global scale. Or, what if like Jeri's husband, there was no interest in growing up? Then a plan like Brad's survival cell carried more weight than ever.

Chapter 23

Vince stepped out of the taxi after their two hour ride down N6 to the Burkina Faso border. Brad exited the other door. Vans topped with high bundles and side access ladders filled the dusty parking area. Vince looked around at multicolored buses loading and unloading people in their harlequin clothing. Many waited on foot in the lineup at the border gate. With Aahil up at Agadez still, Brad had convinced Vince to come meet Keith. His balloon co-designer turned out to be here in Africa, in the country next door to Niger. One of his overseas contracts again, Brad said, but Keith was short on details. Other than he had design work in both Mali and Burkina Faso.

"They're coming from the city of Wagah?" Vince asked.

"Yeah, Ouaga," Brad said. "In Burkina Faso."

They would chat, and Brad figured he'd tease out of his friend what Tamanna refused to talk about—the larger Sahel project. With device bags slung over their shoulders, they found a place in the line.

For most of the taxi ride, no matter how Brad wanted to talk flying, Vince kept him on project details. The thing he did want to hear more on were those surface drones they'd both seen. Keith was aeronautical too, so he would know more.

Brad whistled as the line shuffled forward.

"So he'll be in a white SUV?"

"Yeah, him and another guy." Brad glanced down the line of people ahead, searching through the chain link grid for Keith on the other side.

"So your theory is he's working on a sulphur balloon project, just like us."

"Yup."

"Makes sense I guess," Vince said. "A Green Sahara in Mali would go a long ways politically just like in Niger."

"Green pasture instead of sand. Grass for your goats."

"We signed confidentiality agreements, remember," Vince said. "Your ever think he probably did too?"

"We just got to get the guy talking," Brad said. "We blow the lid on Ms. Meacham and her secrets."

They walked through the border gate, showing their papers to the guards and out the other side. Brad broke into a grin when he saw the doors of a white SUV open and Keith getting out with another fellow.

"Keith, you dog," he whacked the fellow's shoulder. "Got your message and here you are." He gripped Keith's hand, introducing Vince.

"And this is Sanoo," Keith waved to the brown skinned man beside him. "He's on my engineering team."

They walked slowly back to the SUV.

"We needed to see this end of the desert," Keith laughed. "You used to the aridity?"

"We flew south from Agadez, up near the Sahara yesterday," Brad said. "So this, my friend, we call humidity."

The engineers hopped into the vehicle, Sanoo in the front where he spoke to their driver in another language. Minutes later they stopped in front of the Kantchari restaurant and Sanoo guided them in to a table.

"How's the wife and kids?" Brad asked Keith.

"I dunno, wife's working now." He shrugged. "Kids are in school. You?"

"Yeah, about the same," Brad said. "Vince has a daughter, like you."

"Ahh," Keith smiled. "How old is yours?"

"Seven."

"Mine is nine. Cool."

They glanced at the menus and Sanoo gave them a running commentary on the options.

"So what've you got for a contract Keith?" Brad asked. "In Bamako?"

"You know Brad, I'd love to tell you," Keith said. "But we can't. They had us sign the no talk papers on this one. Sorry."

"Nothing to do with our balloon design?" Brad squinted at Keith. "I'm calling your bluff, dude."

Keith shook his head, running a finger across his lips. Brad told him the details of the balloon Aahil's cousin had found. All those languages and a familiar build. Maybe their design, but modified enough to talk about.

Keith kept his poker face, feigning interest but shrugging through the whole story. Keith and Sanoo knew nothing about balloons with Arabic writing blowing around the northern deserts of Chad.

"The country of Chad lies far to the east," Sanoo said. "On the opposite side of Niger across the Sahel." Vince saw Sanoo's eyes light up as he spoke of African geography.

"The probability of finding a balloon drifting all the way across Niger would be close to nil," Vince said.

"Precisely my friend," Sanoo said.

"We just wanted to get outta town," Keith told Brad. "And grab a little social time in this desert."

Brad looked at him. "Humid here," he raised his beer glass. "Good to see you."

Keith clinked his beer glass on Brad's. Sanoo appeared to watch the custom, clearly not his. He busily consumed his meal instead.

"You wanna see desert?" Brad said. "You gotta go up north. Come to Agadez."

"Burkina Faso approaches desert conditions," Sanoo said. "But Mali stretches far up into the true Sahara. Our northern desert city in Mali has the name Timbuktu. That much we will tell you."

"Timbuktu," Brad said. "No such place. Now I know you're full of it."

"Full of what my friend? Truly, a place mark on the map," Sanoo said. "Along our Mali to Algeria road. As in Niger, your road follows from Agadez. Through the land of the Taureg."

"Hey, our driver Aahil," Brad said. "He's Taureg."

"Yes," Sanoo said. "Then he will know."

Brad and Keith got into some chit chat on the good old days back in America and Vince engaged with Sanoo.

"Do you have any kids Sanoo?" Vince asked.

"Yes, my wife and I have three small sons."

"Cool." He had to smile. "Like Keith, I...we have a daughter."

"This is very good," Sanoo smiled. "The wonder of children makes our future."

The coffee arrived dark and thick.

"How about drones?" Brad asked. "You guys seeing any surface recon units around?"

"You in the rich world have been watching us here in the poor world for decades." Sanoo said. "You have satellite imagery through which you can confirm Timbuktu." He turned his visiscreen to show Brad. "And you have drones to take photos of us as we live."

"The U.S. has high altitude drone bases in Africa," Keith said. "The Chinese have more than one—they've got a major base in the South Sudan."

"So drones are common."

"Drones everywhere, Brad," Keith nodded. "Rumour has it the CIA, the KGB and British M5 run recon surface units. The story goes surface drone operation is standard training for any sleeper agent they assign to a developing country. But locals operate them too. That's just a part of life here."

"That would mean drones in any HICCC country," Brad looked at their faces quickly. "You guys heard of them, right?"

Keith and Sanoo looked at each other, but remained quiet.

"The trick then is to know the purpose of surface drones," Brad said. "'Cause I don't think they're taking tourist photos."

"A camera will be taking our picture at this moment," Sanoo said. "Look at the corners above us, or the light fixtures. A camera mounted on a drone becomes mobile, that is all."

"Mobil and communicating with the missile platform above." He told the story of the repaired roof at the horse tracks in Niamey.

With lunch finished, and the afternoon wearing on, they walked back out to the vehicle. Keith and Sanoo would return to Bamako before nightfall, but first they gave the other two a lift back to the border.

"Alright, good talking to you," Brad nodded

With all around waves, Vince walked with Brad towards the line up to border cross the other direction.

"So whatta we got?" Brad said. "Great lunch and Timbuktu is a real place."

"And those drones we're seeing are not imaginary," Vince said.

"The drones we gotta know about are the purposed missile targeting," Brad said. "That would be our concern."

"You think Keith and Sanoo designing sulphur release?" Vince asked.

"Yup, good chance they're doing same as us," Brad said. "And our projects are gonna morph together into Phase III."

As he walked, Brad looked as if he were thinking along another angle, like he could have asked more. Vince was almost surprised this happy go lucky guy could become so intent on proving a conviction. Brad keyed in a message on his jPad.

They passed through the border gate.

"I dunno, wait," Brad said. "We need a way to detect those missile support drones. I should have pushed Keith on that—that's not part of nondisclosure and he knows that."

Brad turned back towards the border fence, and Vince followed him back to the chain link fence. They hung their fingers high in the wire and could see the white SUV still parked in the dust, not moving.

"He likes back seat work," Brad said.

"Connect with him on Holo-Skype," Vince said. "You can read his body language there."

Keith must have been watching them as he rolled down his window to look out. He raised his hand with a thumb up. Brad gave him a thumb to the side signal, and then waved for him to come over to the fence. The white vehicle door began to open.

Vince frowned as all the drone talk seared into a thought of camouflage everywhere—a flash of reconnaissance drone eyes watching from all corners. His mind sliced through quick time as he heard the delayed scream he somehow knew came from above. His picture of Keith and Sanoo both waving, with their children— their children were not here—skipped to the next millisecond frame of a scorching blasted fire hole in the dust. White fender pieces scattering to the sides in a chatter of clicked instance fractals and as real time set back in, so did the real screams.

Brad stood stunned, face ashen. Vince looked, matching his shallow breathing, and knew their world would never be the same. A delayed flush of air blew past their faces following the explosion shockwaves, wiping any vestige of pleasant afternoon smile from Brad's face.

BALLOONS

Chapter 24

Tamanna gazed out this African sixth floor window from the end of a Gaweye Hotel hallway. Searching for something of a High Road down there, somewhere, any semblance of home. The sparse morning Niamey traffic sped along the N6 with its slip roads, almost fitting the picture. The scatter of dry trees inside the roundabout, circular not triangular, brought on minute reminders of the Gunnersbury wood.

The choice remained well taken...she needed believe that. Inspired by Nishat overall, by her strength, Tamanna had listened to Minister Jabbar's view on the Mali engineers. She felt her angry eyes swell, and let out a shuttering sigh. Keith and Sanoo had been HICCC contractors, fully informed of risk—not her fault. She needed remain detached from political implications beyond her control, as Jake put the matter.

Keeping point of mind on her Sahel circuit second tour helped. Starting with a first drop in on Mauritania's capital Nouakchott, she arrived in that Atlantic city direct from Heathrow. Then came the heart crushing stop at the Bamako hotel in Mali—she straight-face briefed the fresh engineers—Keith and Sanoo's replacements. Having met the American and African engineers on first tour, with Nishat's help, she now saw them as heroes in the greater struggle. She classified their families' pain as sacrifices for her cousins' children. She was nearly convinced, yet no question, the stakes of the game were up.

Here in this midcontinent city, she'd settled in for some days in this Gaweye Hotel by the river. With a primary task of finding how close the regional release came to the Niger national target, she needed also further face-to-face personality evaluations Nishat desired. With Mali engineers now deceased, importance had increased on Niger personnel. After Niamey she would continue her city to city leap-frogging across the bottom edge of the Sahara, though never getting as far as the Red Sea.

On this tour, project conversations bounced about in her mind, especially those with the Minister from Bangladesh. Nishat lately decried the wealthy carbon emitting OECD countries with extra focus on the G7. All of these seven nation states could be classified as *overdeveloped* the Minister said depending who was classifying. Some more than others developed above and beyond what was reasonable or to be blunt, carbon fair. Contrasted directly with the High Impact nations, they showed what a discerning eye would term as significant consumption excess, especially when taking into account the limited resources of a finite planet.

Tami had piped up in one talk. A well defined carbon emissions comparison she'd come upon posted measurement of each country. "All countries combined...humanity as a whole crossed the one planet line long ago...in the 1970s," she told Nishat. That crossover stuck with her, so intuitively important. That measure according to the Planetary Footprint Network.

Nishat paid careful attention.

The growth fetish Nishat called it. When all citizens owned what they needed, she challenged, why carry on? Yet material goods took on the status of religion as symbols of success carrying magical powers, and bringing to the believer what could only be had in dream. People have their value system, Nishat said, and that system has created our carbon problem. Tami nodded, with ever deepening passion as she listened. She pointed out how rocket science need not be consulted to find that growth might not, could not, continue. No matter which economic model selected, having crossed the one planet line, the safest option was to backpedal. People had to date debt financed all planetary resource for decades into the future. The Planetary Footprint Network emphasized that. The people of the planet had mortgaged their atmosphere as a free carbon dump. All signals pointed to this search for phantom planetary resources as a drive directly off the cliff. And what chance did the life-giving Earth have, Nishat asked, when religious obsession caste the planet as but a wayside sacrifice?

Tamanna tuned in when she heard the religious analogy. Her Bangladeshi cousins might attend mosque, but none owned an automobile to drive off a cliff.

Determination to acquire possessions became an unreasoning fixation, Minister Jabbar said, not only a sign of achievement, but a symbol of life itself. The very essence of vitality. This mindset brought a huge contribution to the climate change crisis. Luxury emissions rolled over beltlines as an obese portion of emissions, but again that depended on who decided what was luxurious. The lifestyle of a well-to-do Bangladeshi shop owner, having acquired a personal automobile to drive on weekends, could be put up against the carbon spewing trappings of an everyday developed country middle class citizen. An honest portrait of global society, Nishat said. Tamanna nodded.

Tamanna walked up on the windowpane until she could feel her own warm breath. The roundabout circle below valiantly struggled to take on triangular shape, filled by lush green growth. She shook her head.

She felt so on the same page as the Minister in so many ways. Yet still, Nishat refused to confide in everything. She was explicit on what Tami could reveal too. Only so much to the engineering teams. They could only know of certain vague references to the Sahara regional option...that was theoretical to them. And they must know nothing...nothing at all about each other. As far as each team knew they were the solitary experimental team.

"Tell me more on these Niamey engineers," Nishat added. "Take them to me as a vicarious visit to their heart."

When they discussed decades back COP Copenhagen, they agreed the G8 finally settled on that 2 degree target then. "But how near have we come to that target today?" Nishat asked bluntly. However important a political agreement was, she told Tamanna, the primary concern remained that of achieving that target. In measured terms.

At times Tami felt she knew the Minister as her auntie. Even often. She once shared with Nishat a childhood scientific observation on people, and how they think. Many spoke as if the only viable lifestyle options were binary: the mansion or the cave. She'd asked her laughing mother how many people lived in each cave. How ridiculous this thinking was, yet how common. Paleo-peasants, she later gave a name at least to Europeans. Those with ingrained memories of times lived in the medieval hovel, where folklore and fairy tales imagined life in the kings' court. A life relieved of poverty inside that distant fairy-dream castle.

Her voice broke when she spoke of a realization. Her personal effort was meaninglessness or of any other individual, come to that. Living by choice in a net nil housing unit, with the latest British legislated feed in tariff applied amounted to nil. Of what consequence was this personal action when others spit out carbon everywhere else about the planet? Offsetting any carbon measure contained by the more responsible. Such a high need existed for global regulation, where global included each and every global citizen. Tamanna spoke of her own philosophical passion: we can have rich lives, not lives of riches. Nishat murmured concurrence. Strong truth was evident of rich countries' need to live differently, but really, how useless was this to say? They touched on children and maturity. A mature conversation spoke of mortality, and how knowledge of the limits to a human lifespan brought about mature conversation. The older holding more wisdom. Yet climate change would just so take a toll on the longevity of even the richest citizen.

When they spoke of Bangladesh, they truly connected. Their canary-in-common, seeking out a louder voice. Dhaka, the capital at now over 30 million, Nishat said, though no one really knew by how much. A true mega city. The city was nothing like that when Tamanna's mother left making Tami question the population dynamics. Nishat told her of the drop from seven children per woman down to under three over recent decades. The urban citizen count expanded due to severe weather events, much more so recently, with near a million arriving in Dhaka each year. The city birthrate was replaced by a refugee rate. Half of the people in Bangladeshi cities were now climate refugees, officially recognized as such or not. Cyclone Sidr hit, and then cyclone after cyclone, with millions moving away from flooding, and then many or most staying where they moved. The twin super cyclones of mid-decade had been a miraculous near miss; the first making but partial landfall along the Bay of Bengal. Bangladesh had been lucky as the second cyclone raged past, but catastrophic for Manila—the storm struck the Philippines with a fury.

Tami's tone reminder disturbed her review—her meeting would be in ten minutes.

She mentioned Jevon's paradox to Nishat. People with more efficient cars tend to drive more...in fact people consume all they have in one way or another. Depends then on what, and how much they have. While global auto traffic dumped tons of carbon, in Dhaka the bicycle rickshaw was the standard transportation method. Nishat often rode rickshaw to get around her city.

"Perhaps, my child, we can present to the Jevon people the rickshaw as the most fuel efficient." Nishat laughed lightly.

"Yes!" Tami said. "To assist people with their exercises."

Tamanna confided in Nishat the story of the day her grandmother died and how her family grieved. Conversation turned to the Bangladeshi traditional outlook on family-first values. "If OECD family values could only be expanded..." Nishat said.

"...to include all of humanity, the whole global family." Tami finished the sentence.

The final two minute tone sounded, and Tamanna backed away from the hallway window. "I have to go." The sound of her own voice brought her back totally to the present. She pulled her gaze back in, redirecting thoughts to the meeting with this North American project team. Just the engineers would be there this time. She picked up her device case, and walked down the hall to find the lift.

#

"How ready are we to achieve our targets?" Tamanna looked back and forth from Vince to Brad. They sat across at the downstairs meeting table. "And I need to know what contingency storage capacity we have, after we finish the national release." She listened as they summarized what happened with balloon launches so far, and then updates on sulphur supplies. She searched each engineer's face for telltale signs, listening to voice tones, for the Minister's face-to-face update. The joyous American and his cheers-forever-countenance surprisingly scowled today, more in line with the strait-laced Canadian and his routine half sad look. That sad face did brighten, she noticed, when facts switched to concepts, and the topic swung away from tedious detail. Especially when touching on people or storytelling. They both held certain levels of project enthusiasm. Report to me any interest outside and beyond the specifics of contract; pay extra attention to that, Nishat said.

With engineering design reports filed, she gave them an update on their client, the HICCC. The wait was now on, the outcome of specific items being negotiated with the countries of the OECD. Those items would not likely come to resolution before the direct HI/EC conference scheduled to finish in three weeks come Friday. Whatever financial assistance for developing countries, or lack thereof, climate adaptation remained the primary issue.

"So," Vince said. "It's all about money."

"Yes." She watched his smile attempt fade.

"Military interests," Brad said. "Why not talk about that?"

She returned the American's stare. Did he know of the Mali engineers incident? She led the topic off on her chosen wander, one that was hauntingly short in the other Sahel nations. See how they view the world, Nishat told her. Like a general interest interview. Another plan had come up to reverse desertification, she told them. A plan that could be global, one that would bring about a significant reduction in the size of the world's semi-arid areas. The plan included those countries in and around the Sahara. One scientific group analyzed the counterintuitive use of grazing animals in rotating pastures, mimicking the natural order of ungulates on grasslands. She described promising results. Then there was biochar, any biological plant refuse converted to a carbon storing char state, which when added to soil had the impact of retaining moister. The two together made the most sense when it came to least disturbing the natural order. But, agreement was required on financing and that depended on OECD budgetary decisions.

She let that sit.

"Money again," Vince said under his breath.

She looked at him.

Brad started to speak. "Saw a place like that here." Brad said. "Our driver's cousin."

"Is that so?" Tamanna looked to Brad's defiant face. She sensed the guy had a tiff, with her maybe, but he stuck to his topic.

"Driver's cousin reverted a piece of desert to pasture. He runs a lot of goats and cattle on it. Like a little patch of green in the middle of the rock and sand." Tamanna looked at him. His grin remained distant, like the whole idea of global cooperation.

"Unfortunately, there are many successful local efforts, personal efforts, yet the realities of global politics remain," Tamanna said.

Tamanna took Brad directly in now, but he kept silent. His chipper outlook had so diminished. She went on about biochar fitting in better for a place with high volume vegetation biomass, higher than the Sahel. The lower plant growth of this region better depended on storing carbon in revitalized green pastures.

Both engineers listened in silence, so she continued. Many argued wealthier people would ideally eat less meat, however, in the real world, getting their meat supplies from reclaimed desert rather than destroyed rainforest, could be a more realistic possibility.

"Insects," Vince said. "High protein, low fat."

"Possibly," Tamanna said. "Many cultural barriers."

"So as you can see, other methods exist for Sahel countries to reclaim their Green Sahara," Tamanna said. "Besides global cooling with sulphur in the stratosphere."

The desert had been naturally green early in the Holocene, and based solely on this, science theorized a realistic return to that state, she told them. A strong regional plan would have to be carefully thought out and coordinated among countries. It would depend not only on regional, but global cooperation. You could give the people of Niger what was so politically popular. Cultural familiarity with the Dabous giraffes helped, alongside stories of the ancient green Sahara. The final outcome would be good for everyone.

"The president's got posters plastered on every light pole," Vince said. "His image beside the Dabous giraffes. He's catching a lot of local attention on that Green Sahara idea."

"Yes."

"So..." Vince said. "What about those other Sahel countries?"

"Yeah, how about Mali?" Brad said. "Burkina Faso."

Tami nodded, holding a practiced silence.

"They should be seeing the same benefits as Niger."

"Yes."

"So, are they interested?"

"Not everyone wants things to be good for everyone else," Tamanna said. "We must keep this fact in mind."

Not only the Sahel required consideration, Tamanna knew. If one looked at any global map, more than half of the planetary land surface was or was becoming desert. This type of project on a major macro scale could address global climate issues through extensive adjusting of micro climates. Cooperation would be of the essence, Nishat said, including finance. Yet that was the missing piece. The striking lack of interest in cooperation, especially coming to the monetary part.

"The truth be told, the OECD track record of contributing financially to the interests of the LDC the Least Developed Countries has been dismal." Tamanna repeated Nishat's fact. "Now for more than one reason, near all members of the LDC have joined the HICCC."

"So the truth be told, Ms. Meacham, we are telling you what we know," Brad's voice was loud. "Why don't you tell us the truth?"

Tami held her patient silence, as coached by Nishat.

Brad pushed his chair back to stand.

"We say what we can, Brad," she said. "And we do what we must."

The American strode to the door. "I gotta meet Aahil," he said. "We can talk this afternoon?" He glanced back at Vince only and his fellow engineer nodded. Brad walked out.

"He's pissed," Tami said.

"You're not telling us everything."

"I can't."

"Why not?" Vince said. "I'm the one telling Brad *if only everyone told the truth.* I'm the idealist, but just say he heard me."

Tami nodded.

"He's committed to your project."

"I'll take note of that. And you?"

"Should I tell you everything?"

"Maybe not," she looked at him, then said. "I can tell you more, still, if you like."

"Sure."

According to that group of scientists, reversing the trend of only half the global land becoming desert would return atmospheric carbon levels to pre-industrial levels. Bringing vegetation to a place like the Sahel would actually retain surface water, a strategic objective that also resulted in cooler regional micro climates. This would certainly be one of the more preferred options at the table for the High Impact countries when they met the Economically Cooperating representatives.

Wisdom abounded in expanding the planetary living area towards food production and creating local employment, she told him, but the HICCC could not hold its breath on a plan to reclaim the deserts through natural processes. So the consortium of climate change first-threatened countries needed have a range of options on its global choice list. The desert was immense. All that solar energy space invited photovoltaic fields, hypothetically powering European, in conjunction with if not as well as a green Sahara, from a technical outlook...

"Parts per million," Vince cut in. "Carbon dioxide in the atmosphere measures in ppm. The Keeling curve measures in a 423 ppm this year, so what does that mean politically?"

She glanced at Vince, noticing a shifting tone.

"Back in the paleoclimatic record—the Eocene was a thermal maximum," Tami said. "Even if you talk about 34 million years ago, science is pretty secure the atmosphere contained 1000 ppm level. And no Antarctic ice at all. So, yes, your number is correct and chances of our staying under 500 are remote. What would you say that means politically?"

Vince stared. "No Antarctic ice."

"Yes," Tamanna nodded. "In contrast, the Holocene measured 270 ppm and hasn't varied more than 5% during that time. Our current level measures over 55% higher."

"What's safe?"

"Many scientists, but especially the bunch who followed that NASA climatologist, repeatedly published 350 ppm as a need-to-be-below target. Or not above for any extended period of time."

"Why so low?" Vince asked.

"Take ocean reefs," Tamanna said. "Coral ceases to be viable around 360 ppm. Significant, as ocean reefs hold the biodiversity of the rainforests on land."

"The Holocene," Vince said. "That was kind of recent, like the last Ice Age up to now, correct? The last fifteen thousand years or so?"

"More or less." Tami felt a smile creep in. "Better to take the last eight thousand years, as the ice age didn't exactly end gently. Climate change can be chaotic. The Younger Drydas was a warming trend setback, so better to go by the time frame when the climate was measurably stable." Tami noted the spark of energy in the eyes of this Canadian. "According to the NASA climatologist, our stable climate was humanity's gift."

"The Younger Drydas, what was that then?"

Tami sensed intensity spurring his voice. "The primary theory has the fresh water of Lake Agassiz flooding over into the North Atlantic, which drastically slowed thermohaline circulation." She watched his eyes now. "This hydro circulation can also be termed the Meridional Overturning circulation, or...what most know as the Gulf Stream." A science backed storyline brought this engineer to life. "Whatever the cause, cooler dry ice age conditions returned for another eleven hundred years. The point being, interglacial climate did not truly stabilize until about eight thousand years ago."

Vince nodded, lips twitching.

"So if we cause climate change, we bring on something chaotic like that Younger Drydas. Likely a different real effect unknown to us at this time. A destabilized climate could bring up any number of unpredictable events."

"You know I used your infogram list of the HICCC countries. And with that, I put together a set of numbers on carbon emissions at a national level. In a geography software with full interactive map display."

Vince told Tami of the numbers he discovered, and her turn to listen came. How the OECD countries, on average, emitted almost nine times as much carbon dioxide per person into the common atmosphere as the HICCC countries. "Can you believe it, nine times!" And yet, how the HICCC countries are at a much higher risk of climate change impact, even though they had so much less responsibility for the climate change gases. As Vince rattled off his numbers, Tamanna thought how to case this man's outlook for Nishat. The G7 almost fifty percent higher than the rest of the OECD. Canada, his home country, globally among the top five countries per capita and seventh from the top for total annual emissions in spite of being thirty-third by population. She noted indignation rising in his eyes as he spoke.

He went on until his numbers petered out.

"Did you come upon cumulative emissions?" she asked.

"What's that?" Vince asked, eyes shifting alive.

"A cumulative count would include national emissions historically, you know, back to the start of industrialization. The end of the Holocene you could say."

"So there could be a variation over time." Vince stared at her. "Depending on how long a country has been burning fossil fuels. Yeah I see. I'll see what I can find on that."

Tami tapped notes into her keyboard.

"You know, Vince, I'd like a copy of those maps and emission rates. Our client would likely have an interest." She glanced at the time on her tablet, then at her schedule. She had an online meeting with Nishat. "You fancy lunch? I could meet you down in the restaurant around noon."

She noticed his eyebrow rise.

"Umm, yeah sure," he said.

She smiled as she rose to leave.

Chapter 25

Vince took a sip of coffee, taking in the aqua blue swimming pool amidst lazy swaying palms. A tranquil safe place, paradisiacal, the type of place you'd want to set your laughing children free. He'll need to explain the world, and ideal circumstances to his little girl one day. Maybe soon. *What are you doing daddy? Changing the color of the sky, baby. The sky at Africa? The sky everywhere, our Calgary sky, all of the sky. My favourite color is purple daddy. Yes, Annalise, you can see some purple sky at bedtime. When the sun goes down. And a lighter blue sky when you're at school. Okay daddy.* He sighed.

How will he ever fit in a 'sorry about that'? That he had tried his best to somehow keep the blue sky gift unaltered from his childhood. That gift word wrapped around his thoughts, reminding of all those wrapped gifts he'd watched his daughter open with twinkling eyes. A gift. A shining delight when first unwrapped.

Tamanna slid into the seat across from him. "Sorry, I was speaking a little long with Her Excellency the Minister. She understands people so well, really a wise woman." Vince shook his head slightly, "No problem." He glanced her way, then back at the pool. "You speak British or Australian, I'm not sure which."

Smiling, she sank in more comfortable. "Well, I did grow up in Britain, you guessed that one. My mum moved over from Bangladesh when she was a young girl, however, and my father is an interesting mix of Scottish, Welsh and English. I prefer to speak as a global citizen, no matter what ring my voice sounds."

"I see...you've the ethnic mix for that then." Vince relaxed somewhat himself. "You know the Isle of Mull? One of the Inner Hebrides off the coast of Scotland. Anyway, Calgary got its name from a castle over there. That's me, I come from Calgary...the Stampede City over in Western Canada."

"Yes, I am familiar with some of your background. You are the Canadian." Tami watched Vince's half smile. "Sounds like you have interests beyond engineering."

"Yeah." His smile faded, and he paused. "You know, there's knowledge that allows you to work in a place like Calgary and support a family and then there's a whole raft of other things you know because they're so darned interesting." He sighed.

"A raft?"

"Lots or many." His smile returned. "So that Minister is pretty wise to people?"

Tami told Vince how Nishat absorbed not only facts, but the science-supported numbers behind. She also knew how people deal with a crisis or any society threatening situation. Lots of them simply let irrational thought transition into denial. They basically pretend whatever was happening simply wasn't happening, or they have a tantrum and look for someone else to kick in the trousers. Many look elsewhere. Some turn to beliefs, looking for salvation from the man in the clouds. Others simply give up on all things, becoming listless. "So whilst all these stages previous to acceptance have been processing, we the global citizens have run fresh out of time."

"Whilst?"

"At the same time as." The view of concern for 'our grandchildren' lost any reality for its frame of time reference, she said, even parental concern for children no longer made sense. The reality of now, not some future generation had become blaring. Adults alive today have the ball fully in their court. A North American expression, was that not? As the grandparents and then parents had simply kicked the can further down the road, today's people were left with a looming schedule. "Minus the far flung idea that we want to destroy our own life support system, the time to act is now past, and we have been designated as the catch up actors." Even the idea of green growth had become a decades-back missed opportunity. They now had but a tiny time window to work within.

"You know I've been thinking along those lines." Vince sat up straight. "Taking our foot off the gas pedal at one time was a real option. Now we need a safety net spread below the cliff we're driving off, and a trampoline net strong enough to bounce our car back up." She looked at him, nodding. The game really being played matched people, or really human nature, against the laws of physics and chemistry. Those laws of nature that drove the planetary climate. And with no inside intervention, who would you place the odds on? With no change to the rules of the game, who would one think most likely to win?

"Can we actually bring on a Green Sahara?" Vince asked.

Tami looked at him, swallowing. Trusting her instincts, she started to explain. A little more on the reality of the idea of global cooling and bringing about a wetter desert. The naturally caused historical Green Sahara, also known as the Neolithic Subpluvial, had actually been caused by a variation in the planet's tilt and the effect that had on African monsoons. "We can't bring back a tilt variation in our planet. No reasonable person would fathom geoengineering the planetary orbit to replicate that climatic scenario." The Sahara was actually larger during the Younger Drydas, when things became a lot colder globally. "There could be other ways to do it, but those methods depend on a lot, like reasonable people making decisions, which we may or may not have." The idea of recreating the Green Sahara based merely on the Nigerien national volcano was highly unlikely, and the best the local president could hope for on that route was a return to more rain like a few decades ago. Not the Green Sahara of previous millennia.

Vince listened closely.

Unless they could get some activity going above the Atlantic, but that was more complicated, Tamanna explained.

"The Atlantic?"

"To really stimulate the West African monsoon, you would want a regional cooling out over the mid-Atlantic. That would make for an ideal Green Sahara plan."

"So, it is feasible."

"Possibly. But politically, not likely."

"Nishat's a politician?"

And a scientist, she told Vince, with special interest in the science of humanity. Nishat acquainted herself with the most recent scientific papers. She actually read them, and she pointed out the peer review status of her favourites. How *Nature* and *Science* had by far the most references, that they were the top journals. From papers of specific interest she would directly quote science. She would state conclusions like when it came to people and climate, any measure exceeding the safe estimate of 350 ppm of carbon dioxide equivalent challenged the viability of contemporary human society. She would leave quotes like that for her audience to absorb.

Vince turned his visiscreen towards Tamanna. "So hey, have a look, I tracked down those cumulative emission numbers." The half smile returned to Vince. Tamanna watched the visiscreen as he displaying a chart beside a global map. The United States leaped out as by far the largest when total historical emissions were included, with China and Russia next, almost tied for second place. Those of course included large populations and took into account industrial history. Canada, with its much smaller population, still sat up in the top nine countries. His voice took on an excited tone. Canada, with less than three percent of China's population, had dumped over a quarter of China's emissions over time. So even if China was the number one annual emitter now, this carbon debt was still on the books, and China would certainly take this into account. China, the now economically powerful nation, and with a touch higher vulnerability to climate change than the U.S. depending who was calculating, would certainly have an early interest in supporting action towards mitigation of climate effects.

"Exactly. China and now other countries have been making that argument politically for some time now," Tami said. "And as their power grows, their voice gets louder."

"And as they argue on," Vince said, looking at Tami. "Nothing gets done, right?"

"True." She sighed.

"Bangladesh has an extreme risk according to one climate change index, very high according to another." Vince pointed to the visiscreen. "Yet the Bangladeshi emissions for each person are only a quarter even of the HICCC average. Way low. That first index rates them as the highest risk country, and not just because of lousy geographic luck. They don't have the finances to adapt, so that has a lot to do with their extreme risk." He pointed to a graph beside the map, then back. "And look at the map, those other countries all around Bangladesh rate extreme risk too. Bangladesh may be the epicentre of climate change risk—but look at the string of countries on either side." He waved a finger back and forth. "East and west along the bottom edge of China and then they leapfrog over, what's that, the South China Sea to the Philippines. The only other extreme risk countries are in East Africa. And Haiti in the west."

Tami nodded. "Yes, those would all be HICCC members." She looked at Vince. "However, the lack of finances has become something of a mute point. Sulphur emissions can be quite affordable. The cost of the project we are designing right now, right here, is quite low, actually, very low. Which puts Bangladesh in a completely new position when it comes to having a voice."

They glanced at each other, almost directly.

"Right." Vince reclined, looking back at the swaying palms, the aqua blue pool.

"So...I have a question," Vince said. "A few actually. On the climate, our climate. To start with, what is slow feedback sensitivity?"

Tamanna joined his gaze.

"Right. Well, slow-feedback climate sensitivity depends on slow-feedback processes, which as implied, can best be analyzed over the longer time period. So one must look further back into the earth's climatic history, back say to the Cenozoic."

"How long ago was that?"

"Millions of years."

He settled in, fingers before visiscreen to take notes.

"Okay, well, at that time major geological events happened. Like the collision of the Indian and Asian tectonic plates, which raised the Himalayas and formed the Tibetan Plateau. That reduced a subduction source supplying volcanic outgassing which at the time kept the planet much warmer than today."

"Outgassing? Like volcanoes? Emitting sulphur, like us?"

"Yes."

He keyed into a personal infogram.

This being the theory, she went on, planetary cooling then set in. This froze Antarctica for the first time, she told him, a continent that has been glaciated more or less ever since. That would be 34 million years ago, at the end of the Cenozoic. "The record shows a path towards snowball earth beginning then."

"Snowball earth?"

"Oceanic ice sheets reaching to the equator."

"Wow, catchy," Vince said. "Paints a read image—our planet was a snowball."

"Yes, I never thought of it that way."

"Did that ever actually happen?"

"There is evidence of ice at the equator. But during a previous geological age, even further back than the Cenozoic. Hundreds of millions of years ago, in the Neoproterozoic."

"Excellent. Added impact for any story I mean."

"Yes." She looked at him. "Or better yet in the case of a warming planet take the Venus effect."

"The what?"

"Consider this, if you want an image. Picture the earth not as a frozen snowball, but with an industrial furnace atmosphere like Venus." She watched his eyes brighten. "The truth be told, if we were foolish enough to burn all available hydrocarbon reserves, NASA has postulated that theory. That might catch as a real talking point."

"Absolutely." Vince's half smile had long been replaced by a gaping grin.

"You want more?"

"Yeah."

"Okay, there are the much more recent millennial scale events."

Tamanna went over the history of recent Ice Ages and how past sea levels had varied by up to 120m between glacial periods and interglacial warmer times.

"Holy crap. People would notice that, I mean, that would make for a Moses type flood."

The last interglacial, the Eemian, had spanned several millennia but peaked at 122,000 years ago. Then, sea level was up to ten meters higher and the temperature was 1.5 to 2 degrees warmer. This was a time when slow-feedbacks had carried through at a natural pace. The slow processes like continental ice melting down, sea levels rising and forest cover extending polewards. Ice receded enough and growing conditions changed to the point where trees grew on the edge of the Arctic ocean at that time. "Excellent evidence for comparison, if two degrees is now our supposed danger line."

Vince nodded. "Where were people at the time?"

"Modern humans? Mostly still in Africa. A little movement out on the Arabian peninsula. Nobody in the new world, or Europe."

"I see," he said. "So we only compare our climate to the Eemian time, not our human behavior. We mighta been cave dwelling hunter gatherers at best, so not much climate change from campfire emissions."

"Right. And now, we are not in any way on a slow process. As we now live in the Anthropocene, the human influenced epoch, we are dumping carbon into our atmosphere faster than any natural process ever has. Much faster."

"Fill me in on say sea level only," Vince said.

Looking at things right now, she told him, if all the mountain ice caps and glaciers melted, that would raise the sea level by just over half a meter. But then there were Greenland and Antarctica. With only the Greenland ice gone, they would have a seven metre sea level rise. One critical threshold for Greenland melting had been estimated at 1.6 degrees. Although slow feedback meant this Greenland melt off would be over centuries and could be reversed, it brought up another scary thought. The West Antarctic ice sheet alone made for another five meters of sea water. The unthinkable accompanied knowing the world like before the Himalayas were formed. With all Antarctic ice melted, the sea level would rise an incredible fifty seven meters.

"How come I didn't know this? How come everyone doesn't know this?"

"Bangladesh knows. The Maldives know. Tuvalu knows."

"No sea level issue in Niger." He stared. "But they know about a growing desert." He looked at her. "Back home, people don't know. Or they wouldn't want to know."

"And, that would be politicians, who don't want people to panic." Tami looked grim. "Or they don't want them to wake up." She shrugged. "The Minister says human nature has developed people into crisis managers, only motivated to real action by real or perceived threats. So perhaps the best thing we can do is supply them with a nice gentle crisis to manage. The more manageable, the better of course."

"So, this project we're doing. We're gathering research data? For geoengineering?"

Tamanna swallowed, looking away. How much of the project was theoretical research remained a question. Too many. She had to keep her silence with all project personnel for a while longer for sure. Nishat had been quite clear on that.

"Look Vince." She touched his hand. "I wish I could tell you everything, I really do. But Minister Jabbar only releases so much. To each of us. So I can't. What I can tell you up front, honestly, is that I can't tell you everything up front. Just so that you know."

"Yeah, okay, no problem." His smile didn't fade.

Chapter 26

Vince stared from his Gaweye room at the green bridge strung across the Niger River. Divided by support pillars the bridge briefly broke into frames, his father's fractals scrunched ever thinner—Brad's grinning face now pained, Tami's instructing voice and his daughter's fractals expanding into a field of flowers. His own reflected image turned into a running action figure—spewing sulphur atoms into the discolored mix of a once familiar sky. What did they all mean?

Life...so hard-core real these last few weeks. That was it, he felt so damned alive. This project, this place, these people. Fantastic, if he could keep his life going this way—to hang on to this new paradigm, this new energy. The oomph running through his veins had his insides roaring like a Rocky Mountain waterfall. Action, yes, but along what path?

Was Tamanna being evasive? Or truly unaware of the drone deaths two days ago? Brad had talked before on that Arabic balloon. But ever since Keith and Sanoo vanished into a fire-from-the-sky hole, he'd become incessant on back home and their wives and children. His beliefs took a turn, downgrading any benevolence idea out in the universe.

A chasm lay between global action and answers existing. That desert thievery of Aahil's cousin. Greening a piece of the Sahara by managing farm animal pens—when livestock eat and where they crap. Like, yeah! Exactly what Tami had described as the pie-in-the-sky idea of some scientist. Yet there it was, a living grassroots think-global-act-local solution to climate change. Benevolence offered the answer, but free will reigned supreme. Not that Aksil thought global, but he stuck to his guns running counter the wishes and frets of family and community. Later, having proved himself he ended up with a healthy herd to feed his people. Feed them on a high protein diet, no less and in Sub-Saharan Africa. What innovation. African beef, like the Alberta Beef slogan back home yet burgers for all as the planet greened not degraded.

How would he be other than what he was when a world of his father's powerful voice and his wife's demands stood in the way?

Brad's pep talks had turned into calls to war, nearly, after Keith and Sanoo. But people were always at war, blowing each other up, he needed change something deeper. From anyone else the talks would've been offensive, but Brad had his way of revealing true Vince to misguided Vince. He'd convinced Vincent uncontrollable rage to be actually a deeper passion. One to be guided in a new direction. Had that fractal angel been giving Brad a push? Rather than lashing out at the world, he could grow that energy of his true nature into activism. The passion would speak for itself, Brad said. He could satisfy those inner drives without punching walls.

Was he a lifetime oil patch employee? So many bells rang unhappy on that. Bonded to a carbon polluting salary and spending habits—values never his—he found no exit door. That high road to an ever bigger house would crash one way or another he now knew. His father's archaic ladder of traditional success might fulfill his wife's dreams, but to acquiring another warehouse stocked with the latest consumer items to ship in, catalogue and rotate out to the landfill would never work for him. Me must accept that truth. So why not pick his own path? Why not decide himself what he would do? Instead of conforming to the business plan of some oil corporation executive.

One persistent line of thinking told him politicians could sure use a new story. The ones who made decisions seriously needed strategic advice. Yet in the strange way of people, that advice had to come in such a way as a court jester informing his king. The ones voting for those decision-makers needed to be educated too, to keep the wily political manoeuvres on the straight and narrow. He could become an information source.

Somehow.

He pulled a chair over to the window and sat elbows on knees with chin resting on hands. Now he saw only the riveted steel of the bridge, and slow traffic flow crossing.

All that mind chew rattling about the back of his mind. That cloud base tour, that ride up Brad's magic air elevator. All those words, others out of Jeri, and from Tamanna's soft voice. Such insight freely give by Brad in everyday chatter. A career change. No shit! The solar powered streets of Vauban flashed through his brain like an infogram guide pointing out a fact. But facts for people needed extra guidance, suggestive stories *about* their true insinuations. He could be the one telling those stories! If he could get the right words flowing and add meaningful touching drama to flow past or around barriers to true understanding. Numbers were his fractal gift, that had always been a given, but not so for most. Everyday people tuned out any list of figures. Numbers dried up like light rain on a hot metal roof. He needed to actually translate, yes, numbers and facts into story-time rhythm. Tales that caught the inner child's ear could help influence decisions. Not just for the benefit of deciding now adults but for everyone's future. For someone like his daughter and all other children now and to come.

His hands fell from this chin, and he felt the fingers of one hand begin drumming on the window sill. He leaned forward to stare straight down the hotel wall, as he had from the paraglider or as he would have as a child.

Take any old number...take the amazing low cost figure for this project. He had never ever before worked on such a low cost to impact ratio. The climate cooling effect was cheap! All due to the sulphur leveraging factor—a geoengineering basic. That Harvard professor had published that leveraging power of sulphur at a near million-to-one advantage. In simpler story words, you knocked off a million tons worth of carbon warming with only one ton of sulphur cooling. He'd confirmed the chemistry through infograms more than once. If he could build chemistry into story background he knew that million number resonated with people. Win a million and all that.

His fingers stopped drumming, and he leaned back kicking his teenager-like feet up against the wall.

Tami's measure was cool, the climatologists' heating figure in watts for every global square meter. The eye catching image of a Christmas tree drew a picture familiar to crowds. That Space Agency climate scientist told you a 240 watt bulb shining on every planetary square meter gave you an energy balanced Earth. Next frame, you add in not many extra watts and the impact got scary. Or should get scary, that being a problem. The scariest thing was no one did get scared. You double the atmospheric carbon load, a happening fact, and you get only 4 watts extra. That's less than 2 percent. The tree bulbs got slightly brighter but no one really noticed. The story had to be rewritten, those numbers recast.

Just how would you talk up any dry numbers into spin? First of all, 'spin' carried a lot of political innuendo so never mention that word. Scientific, though truthful, carried that unreadable factor. A better story, keeping the truth word from science, had to come from somewhere in between.

But how?

He pushed the chair back, standing to stretch. He slowly leaned side to side, straining to pace the cramped space in front of the window.

Take the science of the Fifth Assessment report Tami handed out. Right there in the title the number 8.5 meant watts per square meter. So you snuggle in an extra little eight and a half watt bulb beside each two hundred forty. That added decoration on Merry Christmas tree Earth should catch glances. But still the average Joe could shrug and say 'whatever'. And that whatever attitude now scared Vince the deepest. He had to somehow convert those extra little bulbs into flashers.

He needed more air—he had to get out of this room. He had to lighten up. Absently grabbing his jPad, he walked out the door musing his way down the hall. He thought of Annalise. What's a pirate's favourite letters? "R, daddy. R." The Arr5 report, the Arr6 and Arr7.

Christmas went with children and that Christmas tree had potential. But you needed a real connection to the global warming temperature. Another challenge. You needed to translate light bulbs into thermometer degrees. Easy math there, as you take three quarters—the latest climate sensitivity estimate—of the 8.5 watts and you get six degrees Celsius. How to get those numbers into everyone's head? That much warmer by the year 2100 should raise howling concern. Was the end of century too far off for people to care? He needed to translate each degree C into a six shooter shell, for a round of the traditional game Russian's play with a revolver. Or was fear not the best motivator?

That global game of roulette needed more work. Trepidation might at least be woven into intrigue. He stepped into the elevator and selected main floor.

How about that jester's humour to lighten the message? People love funny stories. That animation he'd watched with his daughter followed a trio of now extinct critters through Ice Age adventures. That type of show held out all fun and games for characters and viewers alike, yet the noticeable background presented in depth detail of an abruptly changing climate. Would people notice that? A Disney moment or a deep rising scream.

That moment needed control; he needed keep his escalating scream contained. One minute a happy ending after lunch at the border, the next a fire hole. And a partner babbling about how that changed everything. He could not ignore the memory in any way.

He stepped off the elevator on the main floor.

The line warning danger had been pegged at Copenhagen as anything over two degrees. Others, like the Space Agency scientist, said anything over one degree screamed too much of a change. All while people lived their inadvertent lives seeking out the latest housing, an automobile identity and jet set vacation thrills anywhere in the world, not to mention the latest Martian romance. Any story had to somehow get in there as a competitive attention-grabber.

Eagerness building, he stopped for a minute. As a practical engineer he knew he needed to systematically review his basic options. Boring for others. But just what were the real options on his list? He had to be rational, objective and analytical. He could do that part, no sweat.

Pushing his way through the glass door, he wandered over to the pool. He stared into the late evening light glittered across undulating wavelets.

He certainly had option one, to struggle on with this engineering life. He could keep up all pretence in just the way things had always been, calculating this chemical compound product and that expansion coefficient. Or option two, he could turn a sharp corner. A tangible corner. This sulphur in the sky dump could be his turning point like a catalyst stimulating a new reaction. His wife would be pissed, but what was new about that? He'd make changes according to what he knew to be right and let the cards fall where they may. Top of the priority list would be Annalise and her desirable future. Unlikely she'd be off to Mars. With home planet Earth as her real place of residence, he needed help that place be happy ending livable. Healthy and getting healthier, not despoiled and chaotic.

What had Tami said when chatting about Venus? How each star had its surrounding habitable zone, and how Venus formed like Earth from the same interstellar gas and dust. How the initial composition of Venus held enough water to form oceans, and earlier in time with a dimmer sun had been within the sun's habitable zone. Venus lost all water gradually into space as ultraviolet radiation split off hydrogen atoms. Today anywhere on the Venusian surface you measured the heat of a blast furnace. Whatever planetary history played out on Venus, no known biological life form could exist there. Yet the fact that Venus had at one time been like Earth would speak to peoples' imagination.

He turned from the pool, and glancing out to the palm shadows, strolled along an imagined, redefined arc.

That Tami loved to compare the reality of now with her paleoclimatic data. What history revealed. That thermal maximum happened long before people were around, like 55 million years back. But even if no people lived then, the climate could be compared solidly to a what-if-people-burned-all-the-hydrocarbons scenario. That Paleocene-Eocene Thermal Maximum came about at natural speed, people were wrapping a carbon dioxide blanket around their planet at human technology speed. Confirming evidence to a wiped out world at that temperature came from the climate models concurring with the historical record. Carbon dioxide at five times preindustrial brought you an environment that could at best be described as desolate.

Back to fear. Do people change their behaviour if you scare them? Epidemics of contagious disease or fear of overseas or homeland terrorists bent on destruction did get people going. Respectful trepidation could be arranged.

He could convert the bars of Venusian surface pressure brought on by high carbon atmosphere into a story of horror. Or say the survival struggle of terrestrial life during that Paleocene-Eocene Thermal Maximum…god, that Paleocene-Eocene could sure use a nickname. And some drama, but the dinosaurs were gone by then and the ensuing creatures unfamiliar to people. Venus, say an ancient Venusian civilization on an Earth-like planet dealing with climate change—that had potential. A runaway Venus effect on home planet should catch the human imagination. The Venus effect could be easily imagined, just like snowball Earth but in temperature reverse. In that younger solar system the Venusian civilization may have even visited an uninhabited glittering snowball Earth. Snowball Earth—he loved the feel of that phase, along with the shimmer of terror brought on knowing geoengineering could cause the same by mistake or design. Too much terror, he needed tone back. How about translating the boring chemistry of weathering terrestrial rock that normally stores carbon in carbonates on the ocean floor into a tale of how that little snowball planet had warmed up again. That would be a based-on-truth story according to science theory. Would a children's type story be noticed? Maybe partially. What would the politicians pick up on?

Past apex, and reaching his arc's end point at the edge of the lighted grounds, he strolled back under a parasol to one table and placed his jPad before him.

What was the true story back home? So much global outlook had come out through his project research. With crisis evidence scattered around the globe, simple deduction told you not only the Sahel would be having situational issues. He had come upon enough to deep down suspect he needed first to rewrite the Alberta story. With investigative eyes, you didn't need to look far to uncover a different truth.

Local news always covered the weather, yet media back-story was editor chosen. Checking southern Alberta weather records, he found a recent trend towards stronger winds. Gusts began to blow the roofs off buildings. Howling downtown Calgary winds brought out emergency fire ladders to rescue window cleaners. Newsworthy events, these had been reported yet with no inference to climate change. Selecting a guide nudged to source the alternate, he found an infogram recasting news stories to count climate associated deaths. Fatal incidents always caught the public attention, and the guide took him back to the first likely. During a 'freak' Calgary storm, reports said then, naturally caused and not to bring any extra concern, an older fellow drowned under his car. Along 4th street north west; Vince vaguely recalled that local torrential rain event. That poor fellow would be the first climate fatality in Calgary, with all the missed potential of an iconic hero cast as a warning.

Three years after that storm, came that extensively covered southern Alberta flood. A significant rush of river and rain had flushed right into downtown Calgary. The guide revealed how the media cast the event as a hundred year flood. No reference was made at the time to the probability increase due to climate change. Displaced residents were never referred to as Calgary climate refugees. Of course not Vince thought. That term would only be used for faraway places. Adaptation became the only Alberta buzz word he ever heard. The province built a diversion channel around that regional town to the south and that super reservoir drain right under the city to the Bow River downstream. The next flood tested those new flood mitigation efforts to their limits—the year Annalise was born. Local flood mitigation, local media reported, with little mention of the cause behind the floods. Or what really needed to be done—the climate change words were never spoken. All part of that politically touted adaptation strategy.

He glanced away from the jPad.

He'd noticed a couple things back home now that he thought about it all. Migratory crows hadn't returned to Calgary in January because they were lost. They came to nest early. Could be they instinctively recalled shortening winters at the end of the last Ice Age. Those early September snowstorms that broke so many urban tree branches still green with leaves had happened more than once now. A climate change aware person would think that could very well be due to a destabilized polar vortex. You could call it a freak storm if you wanted to stay unaware. Most people preferred to keep pretending, or stay in denial altogether, that's what Jeri said.

Good old Alberta, and the Alberta tradition. With an oilfield mentality wrapped around tar sands and frac jobs the province was determined to squeeze the last drops of oil from the ground. Even when prolific and globally restated assertions came out that four fifths of proven reserves had to stay in the reservoir to keep below that two degree line. That being true, why would any fossil fuel company have an exploration department? But they did, based on their traditional business model—a reserves to production ratio to keep them solvent in the eyes of investors. The business model required continuous atmospheric carbon dumping. How would a story converting displaced residents into climate refugees ever fly in a backdrop of politically touted adaptation strategy and Alberta culture? Tough hard working frontier cowboys worked everything out with a gunfight at the southern Alberta corral.

What corral? The frontier was long gone, replace by a new challenge. An alternate outlook infogram compared historical tradition of Genghis Khan and his horse-riding invaders. After the atrocities of their conquest, even those riders had to eventually join the settled. There wasn't enough hay growing room to feed all those horses and that rider mentality. Not in that historical setting nor would there be in a climate changed world.

Feeling his eyes droop, he pushed to read on.

The guide took him to an infogram revealing an early century peak oil prediction equating to peak economic growth. Naturally running out of oil would solve the climate problem it had been assumed then. But horizontal drilling and fracking had thrown a wrench into that version of peak oil. All that happened when the need for emissions to peak no later than 2020 became a globally known fact. Much better that they peak in 2015. The budget approach gained some carbon accounting attention. People had room for a trillion tons of carbon in their atmosphere to stay below the 2 degree danger line. The two critical parameters were the peak date and the rate of emissions decline after the peak. The super steep decline rate now required suggested that information had been ignored. With required crisis not arising then to stimulate action, the schedule needed to keep within that budget now called for a scrambled approach. Where had people been? Playing the fiddle as the Titanic went down.

A nonsensical laugh escaped his exhausted lips as he pictured those making music on a sinking ship. He could appeal to peoples' daring childish side a giddy thought told him.

He had his analogy of Russian roulette. So first the children played a game with one blank shell, then more daunting came a game with a rubber bullet—now that would hurt, and now, now after a few more taunts across the sandbox, at least one chamber out of the six was loaded. With a real live climate change shell. Click, click, another click, then bang—statistically the most likely sequence. But keep statistics out, this needed story appeal. Anyone could figure you get a bang with the first trigger pull. Just the ensuing brains-on-the-wall scene was not for children, and neither did adults like that image. He wanted to cry.

He put his hand to his mouth, unable to hold back his yawn.

The global picture was a no brainer when you thought for a minute, one climate, one planet. But that one planet came with these people, and their behavior. People, who waited for a crisis, and then even if they caused it, wanted only to adapt. Or try to. All of Tami's talk on how that global mitigation agreement failed year after year. She now put higher odds on a five degree planetary shift to be the new stabilized climate. That British Gaia scientist may have predicted correctly. Five degrees would be five shells in the six shooter.

He fumbled with his jPad and headed back to the hotel.

Fractal math, calculated in the hollow inner clutching of his heart. He could tell a climate change story, anything from a Christmas tree, to a death count, to a six shooter bullet. But who would want to hear? Where would he get an audience? Back in Alberta? Wherever, he had to find and accept his own path. Like Tami, to make some hard decisions, take some losses, but reap the rewards as well.

He walked back into his room, smiling groggily. He saw them again, though he knew them so briefly. Keith and Sanoo, doing exactly what he was, one minute there, and the next exploded away. Brad's infectious upbeat grin cut hard to harsh pain yet now ingrained into him. He rubbed at emerging grin lines, facial pain subsided, yet screaming the bridge fractals message. Do something!

All he could do at the moment was sleep, mind filtering switched on. He'll talk to that Tamanna again, and gather more data beyond, far beyond his father's engineering. Ambling over to the bed, last thought promising to take action, he drifted off exhausted.

Chapter 27

"We never took this on, Jake" Tami bit her lip hard. "I met them once and now they're both dead. They had families, children, like you and Anna. Like my cousins."

"I know," Jake nodded, his head hovering in the Holo-Skype cube on the table in her room. "Legal reminds we have an exit clause Tami. We can drop this contract."

"No!" Tami said, then more quietly. "No Jake."

"Still your choice."

"Yes, thank you."

Tamanna sat on the bed's edge, her hands folded on knees.

"Remember Copenhagen?" Jake asked. "You hooked on to that ice-bubble story Anna told. You had her tell that one over and again, like a little tot. Then you followed that bubble trail back and forth on a time adventure through what I term as annual ice deposition."

Tamanna nodded, staring into the cube.

"Anna tells great children's stories," Jake went on. "Remember how she connected the bubbles to the pirates of the Little Ice Age. All you got from me was science literature."

Tamanna sighed. On the street curbs of Copenhagen, locked out of meetings, Jake had talked, and never stopped talking about the climate change research coming from the NASA Goddard space centre. Mostly authored by that New York scientist. She'd always been motivated by this American—a voice calling for change in human created forcings.

"I too get the science better," she said. "But those stories Anna told, they somehow grab me."

She had time, sitting there on the concrete, to read the literature he forwarded, especially the one on the Antarctic Vostok ice core. That one got her hooked on history, climate history.

"I hope Anna tells stories to your children," Tami said. "Sometimes I picture Captain Vos and his pirate mates when I talk on climate sensitivity or the record of the Holocene."

The bubbles in that ice core became the research topic for her PHD dissertation. Those little ice-trapped bubbles of gas told a story, a record of times past merging into the reality of now. Paleo spoke of the ancient, the Holocene when humans developed record keeping and the prehistoric before. That narrative from the distant past revealed so much of what was happening today. That paper had been a turning point in her career as a paleoclimatologist. Each tiny bubble revealed part of the all-important climate sensitivity, based on the account from long ago. That data confirmed and enhanced what the climate models could and could not show. The atmospheric samples grabbed by that frozen water, each year over thousands of years, revealed a backlog of the planet's carbon measure—each bubble holding a micro chapter on the climate for that year.

"Copenhagen went it's way," she said. "Along with the Holocene."

"Maybe for the COP story," Jake said. "Not for ours."

Slightly charmed and somewhat hopeful, mind set on a PHD, Tamanna met Jake and Anna at COP 16 in Cancun. While Anna told enchanting stories she felt her charm washed away and most hope dashed as scientists with facts were drowned out by industry lobbyists. And totally ignored by timid politicians. She realized gradually how a sudden awakening by governments could well come too late. At Durban COP 17, when Canada and Japan dropped out of the Kyoto protocol, a sinking reality set in on political agreements. They left that conference disillusioned with the political process, intent on finding another way. Any further COP attendance turned to a matter of gaining relevant experience only, and finishing research for her dissertation.

"When you sent that missile insurance advert I laughed," Tami said. "Drone missiles were a joke, nothing more."

"I sent that to legal for an opinion," Jake said. "No response yet."

"Climate change is not a joke," Tami said.

"That, we know."

The COP agreements and emissions targets up to Copenhagen, even if fully met which was a big if, placed the planet on a mean global warming trajectory of well over three degrees Celsius. Better than the A1F1 scenario that saw intense fossil fuel use with high economic growth on a business-as-usual pathway. That scenario put the planet at well over four degrees just after mid-century. Better, but not enough—simply put, still a world war scale crisis with no foreseeable victory.

"COP meetings were the joke."

"Still?"

"I dunno, Jake."

COP would be in Florence a few short weeks hence. Though likely another laugh, the meetings could prove valuable as a staging grounds for their contract outcome. She speculated there but Nishat had alluded to as much.

"Why don't people get it? We have given up our gift," Tami said. "The Holocene, why not our *precious* Holocene? Like in a child's eyes."

The climate of the Holocene, that geological age allowing civilization to develop, had officially ended. Knowing that drove Tamanna. Civilization, that which allowed her life as it was. The climate gift of the Holocene, that which kept her Bangladeshi cousins above the rising seas. Most had no idea what the Holocene was—how could she, a scientist, educate them? Now, this chance.

"Anna tells the children a story," Jake said. "She gets them into the Age of Blessings, like the Holocene, and she does call it a given wonder. From some Ultra Being she imagines up."

All children now were born and lived lives after the now forsaken Holocene. In the new Anthropocene, geoengineering had premium potential. To send a message on behalf of children, a noticeable voiceless signal to adults.

"Nishat needs press release material," she sighed. "But the lost Holocene? That wouldn't cut it any better than my spiel on the Volstok ice core. People just don't follow the graph line of a bore hole down through a glacier."

"Don't ask me, Tami," Jake said.

"A bore hole rates as boring in popular culture," Tami said. "People don't hear that. Life is not linear. And Jake, I am not a story teller."

"I'll try running that by Anna."

Neither spoke for a moment.

"People roll the dice and look for action," Tamanna said. "Seeking excitement." Jake had seen the dice rolling infogram in the cube in her office. But NASA statistics didn't translate well into people story either, no matter how hard that scientist tried. Natural forcings and infogram volcanic eruptions caught her and Jake's attention. Wide eyed, they had discussed how certain volcanoes cooled the planet, but the raw data didn't go over well for public consumption.

"People are people," Jake said.

That rolling dice infogram concisely illustrated the science of a changing climate. That message—the thirty years before 1980 established a global average temperature base equal to the Holocene. Then, the shift in statistical probability of extreme weather events decade by decade so clearly showed the climate's transformation. Climate forcings, human caused, came out in each roll. NASA's consistent conclusion: that temperature would rise further due to human caused climate forcings.

They knew that, but how would others?

"Nishat speculates I search out a storyteller," Tami said. "Maybe, Jake, I talk to one engineer Vince tomorrow."

Chapter 28

They sat across the table from each other, the afternoon sun filtering in a soft dance through poolside palm fronds. "Sulphur dioxide is an opaque gas in the upper Venusian atmosphere." Tamanna spoke to Vince over her coffee cup. "But the sulphur scattering effect is totally overridden by the CO_2 impact of layers below. Though sulphur gas reflects and diffuses incoming sunlight, the carbon dioxide strata keep the surface temperature hotter than any planet in our solar system. That same sulphur gas forms the thick Venusian clouds blocking our view of the landscape."

"Huh." Vince was picking up more on the chemistry and climates of other solar bodies. The chemistry between him and the soft face before him need be his only to know. No romance imaginings allowed, he needed drama contrasting the Earth of today, or before the steam engine with any Earth of the future.

"Venus may have had a climate similar to ours at one time," Tamanna said. "But now, not at all. Venus is essentially isothermal, whereas planet Earth has wide variations in temperature." The diurnal cycle of day and night and the high latitude seasonal fluctuations. With all these coolings and warmings science needed speak in terms of a mean. That explained the 2 degree danger line as a global average.

"Right. So what about that 2 degree line." Vince needed more on home planet. "What's the danger?"

So that two degrees global average, Tami told him, was based on thousands of weather stations measuring temperatures for decades, a significant number back to the 1880s. "At an Oxford conference I heard the satire: 'who needs coral reefs anyway?' A pretty divisive remark." She frowned. "A crude joke, perhaps, but totally true. That's a loss we get with 2 degrees." Water temperature and ocean acidification were not friendly towards coral; the temperature killed off the polyps and the acid ate up the little houses each one built. "So even if we don't exceed our 2 degree danger line, we still kill off our reefs. The Australian Great Barrier goes; bleaching they call it. And even if tiny resilient reef patches survive, global reefs face significant biodiversity loss. Even if we don't pass 2 degrees, we mess up our planet."

"Yeah, shit," Vince said. "And if we do go past two?".

"Well, that Oxford conference went under that title. *'Why we should completely avoid a 4 degree world.'* In a world like that, the temperature increase on land would be one or two degrees hotter than 4, as land heats up more than the ocean. And the northern latitudes double that heat load, as higher latitudes capture more heat than the mid-latitudes. We'd be approaching the Miocene-like world of 25 million years ago"

He stared.

"That was an ice free world." She held her coffee cup in both hands, looking at Vince. "That would only be an overview without getting into much detail."

"People. What about people?"

"A 4 degree world this century would kill a lot of people. More poor than wealthy, but everyone would feel the impact."

"Brad found a 4 degree global map," he said. "The Sahel dries right up. North Africa becomes a no go zone."

"Yes."

"Not good."

"No. And temperature change would not be uniform. The Arctic gets over 10 degrees warmer, and in the continental United States more than 6 degrees higher. The Palmer drought index measures cumulative balance of precipitation and evaporation relative to local conditions. In other words, what's locally normal. Or, what would have been normal preindustrial—now we work with a floating normal. A huge part of our planet is prone to drought. Like the Sahel."

"So doing nothing carries a lot of risk." Vince voiced his thoughts carefully. "But this project we're working on must have risks too."

Tamanna nodded, sighing. "Take a hypothetical global geoengineering scenario."

"Hypothetical," he said. "Right."

Tamanna listed off the risks of geoengineering. Natural volcanoes could occur unpredictably at the same time as artificial geoengineering. Say another Pinatubo in Malaysia started billowing extra sulphur dioxide. You get double the effect for an uncertain period of time, so how do you compensate? The whole process, even if global in design, might slow down a monsoon somewhere.

"Countries of different political persuasions take on this or that unsynchronized geoengineering plan concurrently," she said. "Another risk."

"That would be crazy," Vince said wide eyed.

"The HICCC offers the best option to avoid that," she pointed out.

He listened, and she went on.

Picture sulphur emissions emitted towards target, all organized and on track to offset continuing carbon pollution. Then some political disagreement comes up causing unexpected project termination. An abrupt cessation of sulphur would create an abrupt increase in temperature. Political players like Russia might sit on the sidelines cheering on any warming scenario. Canada acted as if wanting a warmer world too, she looked wryly at Vince. Russia appeared wishy-washy on climate change, as one might say to their perceived advantage. Time was on the ex-soviet nation's side if nothing was done and carbon kept building. Canada's too if a warmer planet proved out to their benefit. Most science doubted that, but this was politics.

Vince stared into his cup, then at his cup, slowly focusing on that globe icon. He caught a fractal instance of Annalise there with her kindergarten smile.

Even with a global geoengineering plan, there would be regional negatives. If they cool only the polar region, they cause regional droughts and flooding precipitation. Or any country, any cooperating states opt out of the global plan. At any time. Or add in their own regional version of a desired global thermostat setting. Say the Sahel countries formed a cooperative group, and they had their own plan. To dump extra sulphur to get 1 degree *below* preindustrial levels and attempt to really green the Sahara. Lousy science, but the idea might sound good politically.

"A little Ice Age." Vince said.

She nodded, telling him more. Carbon had already slowed down ocean circulation, thermohaline circulation like the Gulf Current and this combined with a Sahel plan like that might work in conjunction to bring about a massive cooling—an unintended Ice Age. Messing with the climate was tricky business, but people had already taken on the job when they industrialized.

"Snowball Earth," he tried the sound of it, looking for her reaction.

"With even a slight error," she simply agreed.

"My guide took me to one infogram last night," Vince lamented. "The Haber-Bosch process allows us to create inorganic fertilizer. That's the real reason we have the population we have today. We could have chosen a lower population, but we didn't. That would have made a big difference now."

"Population," Tami nodded. "The untouchable subject." She told Vince that a couple in North America deciding not to have a child equaled fifty couples in Bangladesh making the same decision. "A child anywhere in the world does not equal another child anywhere in the world."

"Yeah, I was talking with Brad about that," Vince said. "The real equation comes out as Population times Affluence. The result makes for total impact."

"Bangladesh may have a high population," Tami nodded. "But according to that equation, a very small total impact."

They sat quietly for a minute, each looking out the window, then back at each other at the same moment.

"You took on a personal change," Vince looked down, then directly at her again. "Was that a political move?"

Her eyes brightened when he said political and she said COP right off. As a mainstream but idealistic student, she'd attended those Conferences of the Parties, those gatherings of nations struggling to globally cooperate on addressing the climate changing Earth problem. Filled with excitement to begin with, she hadn't understood the sense of disillusion with COP15 in Copenhagen. But the youthful idealism filling out her sails gradually subsided. By Warsaw 19 the reality of the official plan became clear, going formally close to nowhere. As a distant observer she had by then become more passenger than crew.

"So you changed then?"

"Not quite," she said. "I realized you could try to influence political will directly. Or you could give the politicians social license—the voice of the people."

She watched the functionaries gather up steam on their road to Paris. Too-late Paris, many said, but-at-least-something others remarked. After that number twenty one in France, the next year turned out benign for Tamanna. By then she was committed to influence through social license.

"Like this project?" Vince asked.

"Just a few countries dumped the vast majority of carbon disproportionately causing the problem. They most need political will, yet social license could come from those most affected."

Paris pronounced an inadequate-to-say-the-least agreement at COP21 and to top it off a five year delay before coming into effect. A colossal mark of human inadequacy. In her view, an attempt at crisis management or mismanagement as the laws of physics patiently exacerbated the crisis. Later, post-Paris infograms confirmed her solemn vow never to return.

Now that carried story to Vince's ears. Tami had lived out a frame of reference for him, Vince thought, as she had made a decision on a different path. He could follow.

He wanted to talk on his latest infogram tour and he didn't. He looked at Tamanna. Geoengineering science had been likened to the Manhattan Project. He wasn't totally sure what to believe yet, but Harvard said any nation could now play politics like North Korea. Right beside nuclear arms, geoengineering was there for any country to take. You didn't need high cost bombers or fighter jets either, no intercontinental missiles, just a few balloons and a guy like him to estimate the sulphur tonnage. Then you dictate your back off terms to the world. The thought stabbed Vince with a deep knife blade anxiety. The calculations were simple; the cost quite low. The scariest thing was how people would react. Countries weren't exactly friendly when it came to global cooperation.

"Our politics are not overly helpful in many ways," Tamanna said.

Vince shook his head. "Nope," he said softly. But, his heart shivered, his daughter needed a friendly future. She truly did. He needed to act. "So you traded what you were with what you are now?"

"More like I swapped what I was for what I really am."

He stared at her, eyebrow raised.

"My play role satisfying others went on the block, in exchange for what felt true for me. What feels right, that was the indicator."

"So what bottom line made you switch? I mean, really, why?"

"My people, those I know I can do something for. My mother was the youngest child and I have uncles and aunts, and some cousins living in Chittagong. On the Bay of Bengal in Bangladesh, they are fortunate to have hills. So many Bangladeshi have lost delta farmland and live in Dhaka slums. These refugees bear living witness as a global canary in the coalmine." She looked at him directly. "And I know I can help them sing louder. I wasn't given this highly functional brain to play games, I was given an opportunity. To act responsibly."

Vince stared, thinking again of Annalise. His daughter would be a canary too. A canary of the near future.

"But there's something else too. It's hard to describe, but when I look at the green woods growing, or at any living ecosystem, I breathe differently. I hear a quiet voice speaking to me deep inside."

"Yeah, me too," Vince nodded. "Like an angel or something. My voice talks math—I see fractal images at times, and they tell me Pi defines a pure universal balance. I think I get it."

Vince looked out the window, at the water and palms. "A lot of things in my life are less than perfect, you know. Sometimes I wonder about that God of creation idea, but one gift keeping me going is my daughter. Whenever anyone tells a story of importance it makes me think of her. You do, kinda." He wiped at his eyes as he spoke, looking at Tami unabashed.

She waited.

"Anyway," Vince said. "When you talk to someone not well-versed in your profession, you almost have to speak to them like a six year old child."

"Yes," Tami said. "That could be."

"I want to be a part of that voice. That HICCC voice," Vince said. "That louder voice of the coalmine canary."

"Oh," Tami beamed. "Brilliant."

Chapter 29

Vince sat with Brad around the morning table in the meeting room downstairs waiting on Jeri. Vince was going on about how Southern Alberta had flooded, yet how most oil company employees ignored any reference to climate change. They just kept living their oil company lives, talking about reservoirs and production and barrels of oil. He heard that talk in the streets of Calgary.

"Like Jeri said, people are crisis managers," Vince said. "On that I totally agree."

"Say managers are the crisis," Brad said. "Leaders don't lead."

"Political leaders?"

"Who gains, who loses?" Brad's face held no smile. "Who took out Keith? And why?"

"Jeri picks China," Vince said softly. "She says they want to send a mixed message. So they took out Keith's SUV after you got out. They didn't want to kill two Americans, sorry bud, so they waited for one to step out."

"Yeah, think logistics," Brad's face went dark. "With a high altitude missile you don't have that kind of timing control. You ascertain target, you confirm and you obtain release authorization. That takes about a minute and anything can happen. Luck of the draw for me that day."

"Russia's Jeri's second pick," Vince said. "Say they take on a new national cause—they want to warm the planet—and they want China to look bad too. Say in Africa. They get a double hit. They keep carbon emissions going and they make China look like they're playing war games in Africa."

"Jeri's spinning her wheels," Brad glared. "Like I said, when it comes to Keith, who knows? So much for brotherly fucking love."

"People in the street are not proactive. They talk about their day to day stuff in a wait and let-it-happen mode. Then when it happens, they freak out and scramble into action. I think she's really got that one pegged. Explains a lot about what we're doing right here right now."

Vince scrunched his eyes at Brad.

"Right," Brad nodded. "Look Vince, on managing our own little crisis I found us a safety feature."

"We, the engineer target crisis?"

"Yeah. I found us a missile warning device," Brad said. "Aahil's seen it yesterday and we installed the hardware in the Nissan. Here, check out this image." He swung his visiscreen towards Vince.

Vince read the label on the dash mounted device. Drone Detector. The warning below stood out in hard lettering—You have ONE minute to RELOCATE.

"One minute."

"You don't get much time," Brad's face fell. "Better than what Keith had."

Vince looked to Brad's pain, keeping quiet.

"So this device detects surface drone communication signals and warns when you're locked as a target." Brad said. "Look, if it sounds, you move directly away from where you are as fast as you can. And get behind anything solid."

"Right," Vince said softly.

Brad told Vince more. Once launched from their Marauder drone platform, a Hellblazer missile took only seconds to reach a target. Solid rocket fuel made them only a little slower than a bullet. So that one minute warning was a pilot decision time estimate, and depended a lot on the delay to identify and confirm a lock target. The device took advantage of the process time between surface drones and drone cameras high above.

"How does it warn?" Vince looked at his friend.

"Aahil picked a siren blast setting." Brad looked directly back. "You'll get an earful you can not miss."

"Alright Brad," Vince said. "Good idea, I think."

"We picked a side, bud, no going back," Brad said. "We gotta take on whoever got us in their sights and get this contract done."

Vince nodded.

"Back to people philosophy," Brad said.

"This geoengineering project comes in as an eleventh hour response," Vince said. "Climate change was all over the media for decades but people never noticed. Not enough to vote for anything but their economy. Then there's who they vote in. Politicians postpone any real problem and selectively suppress media so they can strategically pass big issues on to the next ones elected. They only make any real move if it makes them look good. Not like I'm saying we're playing any hero role here but once they have a good solid crisis, they bring someone like us in to design a poorly thought out solution. They need someone coming in on a rescue mission at the last minute like in some *goddam* movie."

"Oh yeah, man, that's us." Brad's smiled past half. "We come riding in on our big horses, guns a blazin'."

"Yeah, well in this movie we ride in for the HICCC underdog. Kind of atypical for a Western."

The two engineers sipped at their coffees.

"That Jeri got us people nailed down pretty good," Brad said, putting his cup down.

"Oh yeah," Vince picked up on the topic. "She's got good insight. We've got economies based on free carbon dumping grounds. Man, I hear that free word all the time from my wife. Rings a consumer bell...people come running when they hear free. Then there's freedom. That one works on citizens, so politicians get good mileage out of that. Reminds people of the time they threw rocks of revolution at the king's castle, or when they toppled their dictator."

Brad found a piece of paper, and began folding together an aeronautical design.

"Then there's her intelligent fear." Vince watched him fold. "She says people aren't afraid of climate change same way they have no intelligent fear of driving seventy miles an hour. You remember? They hear about traffic fatalities all the time, so why aren't they petrified? Truth be told lotta people ride roller coasters to get a speed thrill—they enjoy fear. People need a respectful caution on climate change. I mean look at the impact so far, and then look at that 4 degree map. Our dangerous future. So Brad, how do you teach climate caution?"

"Natural disasters," Brad shrugged. "Gets more attention than traffic stats. When a natural volcano erupts, people notice. Mount St. Helens blew a decade before I was born, but even when I was a kid there was still a lot of talk. They'd chatter on about the layer of ash spread over the streets of Spokane. Everyone noticed 'cause it was right there in their face. On their lawn, actually. And who knew how long the eruption was gonna go? People are gonna notice our sulphur dump like any volcano."

"Yeah," Vince said. "We need that better in-your-face visibility."

"The president knows that. That's why we've got balloons going up all around Niamey."

"So we need media up at Agadez. Or we move operations from Agadez back to Niamey. The HICCC decides on visibility...that's their call. And...depends how far they go with this make-a-volcano project."

Jeri came in through the door.

"Hey Jeri," Brad said. "We were just talking about you."

"Yeah," Jeri glared. "Like what about?"

"Like all those things you say about people," Brad said. "We figure you got us figured right out."

She wandered over to the coffee machine. "What's the latest drone report?" she asked. "We got Ms. Tamanna talking?"

"She doesn't get told either," Vince said.

"She refuses to talk on any other projects," Brad said. "I'd say Chad, Mali and Burkina Faso each have a Phase I design right now. Ready to roll."

"You were right there? In Burkina Faso?" Jeri asked. "With Keith."

"Luck of the draw," Brad scowled. "We stepped out of the vehicle minutes before the missile hit."

"Keith was an American citizen," Jeri was adamant. "That's an act of war."

"And Sanoo? Just because he wasn't? That's old thinking," Brad said calmly. "They knew the risks of overseas work. Like us."

Pin drop silence reigned for a moment.

"Did you get that last set of numbers for your CMIP5?" Vince said. "That would be Phase I, now complete. About a thousand tons released mostly here around Niamey."

"Yes I did," Jeri poured her cup of coffee. "My chimp's responding pretty much as expected. That'll be excellent data for her calibration to the rest of the national launch."

"The president's office sounded pretty happy," Vince said. "Last kwikgram from Tamanna says people flooded out in the streets last night. Lots of people watched, waving presidential posters. Good politics."

"One fresh green Sahara, on the way." Brad whooshed his hand outward. "Aahil's wound up."

"Yeah," Jeri walked back to the table, coffee in hand. "Real world check, what's our project status?"

"Engineering progress report," Vince said, looking at Jeri. "I fly to Agadez to supervise the next phase. We've got seven thousand tons to launch for Phase II requirements, and that should be complete in four weeks."

With the other two looking at him, Vince wondered at his own words. The project had deviated from standard engineering practice, and expanded in scope more than once already.

"We get the rest of that sulphur up high, and we're set," Vince said. "So we send Phase II up in the stratosphere over those beautiful Ayăr Mountains, and the Ténéré beyond and that'll be it. Our client has Niger national done as requested, so we all go home."

They sat for a minute.

"You guys even think they hired us for alternate reasons?" Jeri wiggled up straight in her seat. "Like what else they knew about us…besides direct project related qualifications?"

The interviewers, it turned out, asked both Brad and Jeri hypothetical questions on how they'd respond to media in certain situations. Vince nodded along. He told them of not just the questions he got on media response but queries into his political views. All in a roundabout way, by mentioning specific political figures. He hadn't paid much attention at the time. As the other two chatted on, Vince wondered if this political consortium carried out research on him that he hadn't. Had they looked into his high school literature class work or those math classes? Some fractal influence past engineering skills leading him to a new career.

"I'm thinking they wanted me for messaging as much as for model analyst." Jeri looked to Vince. "There must've been news cameras out there last night, right? I mean, the world's gonna notice this release, you can't keep something this big out of the news."

"I dunno," Vince said. "Could be."

"Well, they called a press conference this morning," Jeri said calmly. "That's where I go next."

"No kidding," Vince said. "What you gonna tell them?"

"The truth, the God honest truth." She stared at him. "That's what comes out of my mouth. Anyone listening to me for a minute can tell that. So you could presume that's what they want going to media."

Vince and Brad looked at her, waiting.

"Listen up! You, building your political career, you capitalist, you consumer. You will wake up and smell the coffee. Now." She thumped her fist forcefully on the table. "Yeah okay, they won't want my rant, but when they ask their questions I'll be rattling off the truths coming out of our climate model. Any detail they want, any implication on any HICCC national security issue."

"A lotta people have their own versions of truth," Brad said. "They'll say it's just a model."

"I've heard that a million times over," Jeri said. "The question is, you got something better? Like a spare planet for experimental control?"

"Talk on volcanoes." Vince felt an inner shiver. "Just tell them we are engineering an artificial volcano."

"Yeah, possibly," she said. "That would certainly be true."

"They'll pick up on that better than a model analysis," Brad said. "Your pet chimp, or not."

"And, give our volcano a name," Vince said, enthusiastic. "You talk about tons if you keep the numbers simple. Like global numbers, in millions. We'd put up 16 million tons for this global scenario, right, and good old Pinatubo, remind everyone of that volcano from 1991, blew up 8 million. Easy math, that's double!

So we name our artificial volcano Pinatubo the second, or Pinatubo II. You need to get personal with a name to make good story. Especially for kids; we had that chat on human maturity, remember?"

Vince felt his internal rush as he talked. Right in there with waking-up-to-smell-the-coffee he knew the time had come for adults to grow up. Period. Semi-barbaric children needed to mature into forward thinking adults. And yet at the same time, keep some purity of little children, like his daughter. To set out and make friends with the others in the global sandbox. As children do, yet, all around the planet. And not tomorrow, but now! Tough call, that, but what other choice did they have?

"This'll be my lifetime moment in the spotlight," Jeri said. "And I've been rehearsing for so long."

"You'll do great," Brad grinned.

"You need to tell everyone," Vince said. "The world needs to hear what you've been telling us."

"We got us some serious competition out there," Jeri said. "Last night news has it Jackie's gonna be having a baby. They're talking names already. Jessi, if she's a girl."

Vince and Brad looked at each other. Brad looked to his jPad.

"No shit."

"Crowdsource chat talks about sending a nursery," Jeri said.

"That's a nine month trip," Brad said. "And they're what? Six months out? So this Jessi girl will be the first Martian born kid."

"Another crowdsource chat wants to bring Jackie back to Earth."

"Just her?" Vince said. "What about Haydon?"

"They didn't develop return technology for anyone," Brad said. "The Mars Mission was a one way trip from the get go – they all signed contracts."

"Yeah, we'll see what crowdsource funders wanna pay when there's a baby," Jeri said. "That Jackie's our social experiment with an outer space darling."

"Okay, so at least Jackie's gonna keep people glued to the news," Brad said. "They'll catch you too, Jeri."

"Right, who's gonna notice my rants?" Jeri said. "They'll be following the first human ever conceived off planet. The Jackie and Hayden love story."

"But that's only one world story, see," Brad said, spinning his jPad screen around for them to see. "You got room right in there next to Jackie."

Vince understood, but wasn't sure about Brad's enthusiasm. The Nigerien national design was in place he knew and the Agadez release would be starting next. It'd take a few days or even weeks for the international media to notice, but up at edge of the Sahara desert didn't cut it as a high profile part of the world. He wondered if Jeri would be speaking to local news only. And the outside world won't be noticing at all.

GREEN SAHARA

Chapter 30

Tamanna sat before her visiscreen in her London office, door closed. Nishat had caught her off guard making contact so soon. Not only the call, but her appearance surprised Tamanna. The Minister of HICCC Negotiations looked horrid with her wire frame glasses tumbled to one side, as if she'd been dabbing at her eyes. Tamanna knew she needed check in before the third Sahel circuit tour, but she wasn't leaving for three days. Tami sensed a new tone behind Minister Jabbar's weary voice, a new urgency.

Nishat began on a notation of lament, so unusual. The confidence she exuded any other day seemed shaken. She waved a cherished World Bank report she'd kept over the years she'd been leafing though. A special graph she originally noticed in *Turn the Heat Down,* had an explicit subtitle warning *Why Avoid 4 Degrees,* one that had held hope for her. More hope than others, much more, when the report first came out; a withering wish as the years had passed.   The intrigue of a vision wrapped around easy-to-understand numbers. If the people of the globe had abruptly ceased all emissions as of 2016, that would have marked the historical point when they may well have contained the temperature rise below one point five degrees. But that year, along with that warming and that wish, were well past. Now, looking back, and as predicted by the pragmatists of the time, that very symbolic turn of events had not come anywhere close to fruition.

Tami looked wistfully into her elder's eyes, no she knew, that wish had no real chance of fulfillment. Carbon gas could be sequestered directly from atmosphere, but cost and will of the people had disallowed all. Nishat straightened her hair, adjusting her spectacles. Heart more at peace, she regained her disciplined composure and got back to politics.

The High Impact meeting with Economically Cooperating nations, in their HI/EC negotiations, had finished their fourth day, and with but one day to go, agreements came nowhere close to High Impact Countries' minimums. A dreamed of sign off, even an eleventh hour grand finale, could not realistically be expected her advisors agreed. They needed a new tactic—a consequential bargaining chip.

"We must initiate another option," Nishat stated. "But first, I wish to speak with you on some background my child."

So first, acceptance. That the global North would share with the global South out of higher human goodness, well, as nice as that might sound, they needed pragmatically forget that possibility. In this era of humanity, you still needed patriarchal power to hold up as a threat, a warning to bring about a certain nervousness in others around the table.

Take China. With so much coal, and so many coal burning power plants, they had a global voice. They were also fully aware of their serious climate change situation; that truth came out repeatedly in national agricultural reports at least back to first decade this century. Their vulnerability index ranked close to the top, somewhat offset by their significant economic power to adapt. Agricultural reports translated directly into food issues and Chinese citizens needed secure nutritional sources. The potential of a Green Sahara appealed to the Chinese, but that option needed to appear realistic. Political wild cards floated about too. North Korea might drop technically challenging nuclear arms development, switch to a chlorofluorocarbon factory and shift their threat to augmenting the carbon warming effect. Who could predict? Even if North Korea's climate vulnerability index ranked right up there with China's. Enhancing climate change appeared as insanely self-destructive as their nuclear arms program. Then there was Russia. Say the Russians build one of those CFC plants. To save spending on fur coats, the Minister's face turned into a wry half smiled.

Tamanna adjusted her visiscreen view, her multiple tasks to-do racing through her mind. The Minister must be getting at something.

Developing countries had clout, Nishat said, when it came to climate change voice at COP. Especially populous countries like India or China. Tamanna winced at the COP mention, but listened. Either nation could burn coal for as long as they so decided, giving them significant negotiating power. So now, Nishat stated with pride, the HICC had a geoengineering project to hold high in their bartering hand. They must strategize how best to use this newly designed bargaining instrument.

Tamanna shuffled her chair forward, excited.

"We reveal our African project."

"Possibly, my child." Nishat touched at the side of her spectacles. "The question at hand being the manner to best do so."

According to Nishat, the OECD at best had vague awareness of some Green the Sahara initiative—not a new idea. But a climate engineering aspect remained publically contained—unfathomable to many ears. Surface drones if snooping about detected nothing officially. Details had not been released, nor any information publicized towards the true nature of what the HICCC was doing. Officially, the Sahel enterprise was recognized as an extensive yet benign scientific research effort, hinged on an attempt to make rain with cloud seeding aerosols, any atmospheric release a dated technology effort to stimulate precipitation. This was just how the HICCC wanted to keep things. At least until now.

"The industrial countries may have a large military, with many planes, tanks and soldiers. But we challenge all of that with our African project." Nishat appeared calm. "Please, then update the status of our climate cooling project."

Tamanna brought up the report she had just composed, reviewing the highlights. Each of her five countries in the Sahel was on, or close to being on schedule. The Niger regional test was technically completed just days ago. Politically emblazoned balloons floating above the city of Niamey, had gained the slightest of global attention, international media paying minimal attention to the inner workings of an obscure country like Niger. The more hidden away balloons around the Ayăr Mountains had recently gone skyward, achieving release requirements calculated by the engineers, and confirmed by the climate model analyst. She glanced at the Minister. The Niger team now referred to their project as Pinatubo the Second.

The other four nations, two on each side of Niger east and west, had completed test releases, synchronized enough to say the Sahel regional Phase III option was good to go. Aircraft design quotes from India and Brazil for the mid-Atlantic release had received notification, and would be confirmed in days. Those redesigned planes would be required, if the HICCC wanted optimal effect for the Phase III regional project. And, engineering teams would have to know about each other. "To gain that extra ocean impact on stimulating the monsoon," she paused to emphasize. As things stood, Niger had extra release capacity, and as the centrally located country had potential to be the only release point. Niger's solitary discharge was technically a backup, knowing sulphur would spread east and west across the Sahara on its way towards the Mediterranean.

"Excellent." Nishat nodded. "We have become a precipitous and serious hazard to the industrial nations—or as they might term it, a clear and present danger."

Tamanna pulled her chair up tight to her desk, leaning forward to listen.

"We do plan to re-engage the OECD," Nishat's said. "But our High Impact consortium will first invite these wealthy countries to act in a less than traditional fashion. We will reveal our climate cooling initiatives to all governments and simultaneously to their citizens through last minute press releases to global media."

With the Sahel project as a pivotal playing card, the HICCC would, during the critical final hours, let it be known they had a proposal for the OECD at the next Conference of the Parties. That began in but two days making an opportune staging ground for further news releases.

Nishat had been discussing the idea of a messenger with her advisors and what had been suggested as almost radical initially, had been gaining momentum in her mind and the minds of her advisors.

"We must choose one of the OECD members as a messenger."

"A messenger?"

"Yes, my child. We select a country best suited to bring our communiqué before other high carbon delegates at COP," Nishat said. "My advisors have spoken at length and narrowed it down to two. I would like your feedback."

"Which two?"

"Russia, or Canada."

Tamanna scrambled to find that data from Vince. She pulled the global digital map from cloud to screen, carbon figures floating over each respective country. The two Nishat mentioned leaped out from the model as the most extensive in national borders. She made her screen available to the Minister.

"These two northern countries might benefit from a warming climate." Nishat spoke to Tamanna's pointing cursor. Perhaps in controversial ways, and not identical, but benefits none the less. Especially relative to other parts of the world. Two Arctic nations extensive in land mass, two of a kind in a non Nordic way. Their coastlines ran long on the Arctic Ocean, and each had a huge agricultural bread basket with a short growing season. They had claims laid on extended economic zones for resources under the now disappeared Arctic ice. A longer growing season, and for some Nishat heard conversation, a longer golfing season.

Nishat highlighted points on the Canadian record, their elevated level of consumer-oriented energy use, over consumption really, especially when compared to the cold and northern Nordic countries. In a country like Sweden or Norway, one third of the energy consumed by any Canadian was transformed through lifestyle into carbon emissions by each Nordic citizen.

"Do we talk carbon per person or for all the people of a country?" Tamanna asked.

"Both are relevant," Nishat said.

As she listened, Tamanna glanced over the data Vince had mapped for each country. She placed Russia next to Canada to view the geography beside carbon emissions. Russia had five times the Canadian population, and yet interestingly only triple the current annual emission rate. By default, then, Canada had higher emissions per person. Even with Russia's history showing cumulative emissions over time, the ex-Soviet nation had four times that of Canada. With five times the citizen count, carbon dumping was still lower than Canada's when you looked to each citizen.

"I need to hear the science from a climatologist," Nishat was saying. "How would you compare the climate outlook for these two nations?"

Tami went over what she knew about projections for mid to high latitudes, as that encompassed both Russia and Canada. Globally there was a slight projection of crop increase for local mean temperature increases of up to three degrees, depending on the crop of course. After the benefits of that warming, however, the gains decreased with further temperature rises. For the ex-Soviet's situation specifically, the Eastern European heat waves since early century had become a measurable phenomenon, with significant loss of grain exports and the noticeable Russian deaths attributed. EuroWatch reported distinct differences between the Eastern European political voice and the negative climate associated impacts. One must consider adaptation time to shifting climatic zones, shifting crops and agricultural production. On the ground trends showed Russia had not been keeping up with Mother Nature, no matter what the economics theory or political platform. If mother Russia thought higher agricultural production risk worthwhile, they might want to reconsider. Checking Vince's data Tamanna found Russia to have a higher climate vulnerability risk than Canada. Based solely on risk index, Canada had the most to gain from non-action on climate change.

"Listen to this." Tamanna came upon one of Vince's notes. "The World Bank predicts an increase in the scale of population displacement. So many triggered population moves and a higher likelihood of conflict over diminishing resources such as food, water and energy." Tamanna read the script out loud. "That conflict could unfold in a way that would roll back development across many countries. In any region where poverty and precarious conditions are the norm. They qualify that conflict a threat multiplier."

"Yes." Nishat nodded knowingly.

"The largest loss of crops are expected in Sub-Saharan Africa, then the next food production loss happens in China and the United States."

One political stickler, Nishat pointed out, was that Russia had for decades been a nuclear armed nation with a permanent position on the UN Security council. Russia needed to score ongoing political points, to show its prominence as a global power house much more so than America's neighbour to the north.

"Canada, then."

What more did they know about Canada? The only country to ratify and then subsequently drop out of the Kyoto protocol. That put the North American nation in a politically unique situation, with a globally recognized reputation. Except for the Montreal protocol under earlier political circumstance, Canada had become a plague on the global environment. If it ever came about that destructive actions towards the global life support system came to an internationally recognized court, crimes against climate stability would easily be the charged against the Dominion of Canadian.

"I believe the 'Dominion of' to be a historical name for their country," Tamanna said.

"Set a time context, my child," Nishat spoke carefully. "The country bases policy on knowledge from decades in the past."

"Oh, I see. So speak to their now obsolete name." Tami felt excitement grow with her political prowess. "To highlight what should be obsolete policy."

Going forward, and having given the OECD a clear opportunity to act on the better-for-all option, Nishat explained, required the High Impact consortium to hold in place a challenge. With that, Bangladesh and others less powerful would gain real voice.

"One of the engineers in Niger comes from Canada, Minister," Tamanna said. "In fact, some of the data I am looking at right now comes from his research. You know Nishat, to be honest, he seems to be gaining interest in the project far beyond his contracted tasks."

"The one you mention in the latest personnel report," Nishat said. "Does he speak French?"

"Yes, he is bilingual." Tamanna smiled, nodding. "He is married but not happily."

"What is his name?"

"Vince."

Nishat looked at her carefully. "Be careful, my child."

"Oh Nishat." Tamanna blushed. "Look, he talks of the adaptation focus in his Canadian province."

"And does he realize the delusional danger of that response?" Nishat said. "Adaptation alone is a maladaptive idea. Delusional in the global long term, even towards the government structures now in place. Political research tells us adaptation alone will push past social tipping points, where democracy would be too cumbersome to deal with."

"He speaks as if open to knowing, Minister." Tamanna said.

"Many people today need move or die," Nishat went on. "Not only in our Bangladesh, but other places. There may be shifts in Vince's province."

"He knows houses demolished on his city's flood plain," Tamanna said. "He understands how climate increases flooding."

Nishat described the overall human outlook; many with less adventurous spirit would die before moving. On surviving a hurricane, or a major flood, people tend to believe more highly in their survival ability and become firmer in decisions to stay. Recent rhetoric sounded much better than reality. For these stubborn ones, mitigation was the only hope.

Tamanna smiled cautiously. Reality, with inherent fears would be gaining audience. The long running global justice deficit would certainly have a new voice.

"Would you agree with our selection of Canada then?"

"Yes," Tamanna nodded. "I would. The Dominion of Canada."

The little man with the puffy chest, Vince joked once about his own national government. This North American nation to be instructed as their messenger. And their designated Sahel project message delivered directly from one to other wealthy industrial nations.

"COP takes place in Italy this year?"

"In a city called Florence," Nishat said.

Recalling Copenhagen and Paris, Tami hesitated, but knowing this voice to be new, and strong, she shrugged off her dismissal of COP.

"Tamanna, adjust your next circuit to arrive in Niger last," Nishat directed. " And set up a meeting with that Canadian engineer. This supersedes any other priority. Be in Niamey a week Friday."

Chapter 31

Vince wiped at his face, at a grin spreading through his being—Brad contagion but more. His gaze drifted beyond the pool as he sipped at his morning cup of Ténéré dark. He caught himself at times waving at any unseen drone spy, knowing full well of the Hellblazers above. This time in Niger stood in such stark contrast to his chemical engineering past.

Back and forth to Agadez each week over the last three, twice with Brad, once alone, they were getting that latest sulphur release lifted above the weather zone. Routine engineering procedures or not, the underlying purpose now had him wrapped in its grasp. A shivering thrill swirled in with fear ran up his spine day in and day out, reminding him of his daughter's storybook hero discovering what she was born to do.

Most sulphur would drift at a slow pace north, cooling the Niger Sahara as a thin solar management parasol began shading the sands below. As the sky blue faded around space station astronauts, the desert would transition to the green color of life and they should notice. Soon. And along with the planetary tint transition, that something else inside him had found its true color.

Lately, he couldn't keep hypothetical scenarios out of his mind. For what real purpose, or optional purposes, would the HICCC calculate a Sahel regional or a global plan? To be able to bluff politically made sense, kinda. That Niamey release was clearly for show, to appease the growing angst of Nigeriens and get them politically onside with their president. But now, Agadez. The real tonnage required to bump the volume up to required engineering specs was mostly hidden from the public eye. Whatever the strategy, much Nigerien national sulphur was now working on the laws of physics up in the stratosphere.

Process in place, they had but to wait. Was the known chemical time delay calculated into political strategy? As Tami said, it took weeks just for nature to convert sulphur dioxide and water into the form of the light scattering aerosol. Release elevations selected by Tami's consultancy, the bottom of the stratosphere, would mix with enough weather zone to wash out before reaching the Mediterranean, and then Europe. Mostly. Still, there was nothing now but a pass-the-time game before measurable effects would appear, and those measurements would take months, and then years. The political effects were a different question; he'd heard Tami's repetition of how, having dissimilar agendas, physics don't negotiate with politics.

The question now was why he and Brad and Jeri didn't have plane tickets yet...they should be on their way back home. Another possibility then and he could only guess, but his and Brad's numbers could be providing the HICCC another alternative. The consortium needed the engineering to expand to a larger scenario, so the Nigerien project could have an impact on a larger part of the Sahara. That mid-Atlantic release? No way. With the Nigerien sulphur spreading east and west along the Sahel were they worried about neighbouring Chad and Mali? Mid-desert national borders of Algeria and Libya to the north would be breached, but mid-Sahara, who would notice? Where the sulphur spread was based on high elevation winds and risk analysis. Then, he speculated, from all other things going on they'd most likely been calculating that global scenario for solid practical reasons, like an engineer would. Not just to publish for someone like the IPCCC. But politically? A global release? Absolutely not. It had to be that Atlantic release, to get the monsoon coming farther in over the desert sands. As it was, the regional plan would cool the desert in the winter only, a more limited effect the model runs showed.

On that map hanging on the meeting room wall, he'd lately seen arrows sketched in over the ocean. Were those wind and current directions? Or weather pattern movements in some Jeri Tami discussion? He knew the sulphur target zone to be out in the middle of the Atlantic. Tami said to increase the West African monsoon, to truly bring back the Green Sahara, a real boost would be to engineer a significant cooling effect over the mid-Atlantic.

Engineering planetary tilt to increase insolation—to have the sun positioned more directly overhead—well, the thought alone rang obtuse. But that natural tilt *had* heated and greened the desert for the Dabous giraffes, Tami said. So strategically, they could leave the Nigerien Sahara summer sands hot and cool the Atlantic. If they kept the winter Sahel release going as they had it now—that fit as an extension of their current plan.

The heat didn't have influence so much as the temperature contrast between the Sahara and equatorial Atlantic. That he now knew, the temperature differential would bring in more monsoon. Cooling one was the same as heating the other. Most effective to cool the ocean when the Sahara was naturally at its hottest, during summer. Were they here to cool the mid-Atlantic?

He rose, wandering over to the shade of a swaying palm. So weird, counterintuitive, but more summer heat in the desert sucked in more rain off the ocean. Bigger temperature and humidity contrast made for a bigger vacuum effect on the rain clouds. Aircraft, not balloons, worked better for the mid-Atlantic release—he'd have to chat with Brad more.

He couldn't keep a dreamy thought from slipping in. Would not a Green Sahara be good for everyone, for the whole world? To engineer a bread basket out of what were now essentially uninhabited sand dunes? Aahil, his cousin, and their tribal desert tradition might be lost...or would they rejoice? Presidential support was there, no question.

Asia showed an ever growing interest in a Green Sahara. Aahil had been talking to his cousins, Brad said. Asians were actively speculating land deals on the sand dunes around Agadez. The Chinese may have subsidized biochar for agriculture, that looking acceptable in the public eye, but a bigger monsoon in the background would certainly help that biochar effect. Really in the end, Tami said, the Chinese monsoon was reducing in size due to carbon-warming, giving China a rice growing problem. They might want data on a monsoon modification trial. The Chinese would be keeping an eye too on enhanced food production in a place like the sulphur-cooled Sahara. How many Chinese could be planning to immigrate to the newly greened Sahara to set up shop?

Or political negotiators signing long term trade agreements on a potentially huge food export market.

He pulled his Jeenyus, checking messages.

The last kwikgram from Annalise wondered about the color of the sky. What color to make it in her drawing, and if she should get a new pencil crayon. Looking up at the sky and wiping at his eyes he took a resolute breath. She'd been going with mommy on house shopping expeditions, and they spent a lot of time at granpa's house. *At Rocky Vew. Mommy really likes to look at lots of houses. Hr favrit size is big. She wantz a house like granpa. I miss you daddy. Wen will you com home?* Another house the size of his father's was just what his daughter's future did not need. *Goddam it.* That's not gonna happen, not if he can influence.

Walking back under the parasol, he sat back in his chair. He tossed his Jeenyus onto the table before him with a clatter, and let his head drop into both hands.

To drop out of the insanity of the baby boomer mentality, his father's outlook and the lifestyle ideals that came along. He had to. To redefine what it meant to be prosperous—his wife would never get that. But he didn't need to be his father's son, to play a cast role. Could be nothing but a good personal move, even if he was to join the many divorced. Something else he'd have to explain to his daughter later, so many trade-offs in life. So much more he could do at this professional level, even if he ended up talking to his daughter through a Holo-Skype cube and kwikgram a whole lot more. Even back in Calgary. Yeah, even if his father decided to add a department of atmospheric sulphur to GeoChem, that still wouldn't cut it. He had to find a new way.

He held his eyes closed for a moment. Based on their ground actions so far, the HICCC was not bluffing. And this whole game was deadly serious, not only for their client. Who knew politically? Like Tami, he would follow this new feels-right lead. He would do what was right. A career change had been looming for ages, well, that would begin now. Back home oil patch work was out. Forever, as Annalise would say. And something else would fall into place— the next short time would tell.

#

Vince pushed his way back through the glass doors from the Gaweye pool and out the front. Brad had called, and wanted him to go up in that passenger balloon again to test a redesigned release. Aahil would drive them to the storage yard. The Nissan pulled up just as he came down the brown cobbled steps. Brad wanted to launch from outside the storage area this time.

"Hey, just thinking," Vince said as he got into the back seat. "If they keep speculating on that mid-Atlantic. I dunno if I should plan extra sulphur storage close to the Niamey airport. Or bump up the trucking availability."

"Yeah maybe," Brad said. "Your call."

Vince looked at Brad, eyebrows furrowed. "So tell me, how could an Atlantic component run independent of a global plan? Out there in international high seas airspace above unclaimed ocean?"

"Tough to get airspace agreement, that's sure," Brad said, scrunching his cheek. "But if they do...I'd say they'll classify that as a Phase III regional plan expansion."

"Been learning more on the stratosphere," Vince said.

"Oh yeah." Brad lifted his chin. "Talking to that Tami?"

Vince ignored him. "You know most atmospheric movement over the mid-Atlantic ocean goes south. Towards the Antarctic pole, and down the middle of the Atlantic. You could argue our sulphur design harms no one. Just like over the Sahara, a Green Nigerien Sahara makes a lot of people happy and no one gets disturbed cause no one lives there."

"Yeah okay." Brad nodded. "But what happens if...say we do expand our regional and go poking a sulphur release out over mid ocean. Then say our client tries talking as if no global interests. I dunno, lots of airspace interests gonna scream global. And what if military interests wanna poke back?"

As they crossed the bridge lined with presidential posters, Brad talked on ocean lift and release engineering. Out there in global airspace they'd best use a small fleet of high flying modified business jets with dispersal technology. They could easily get those designed by Embraer in Brazil or Hindustan Aeronautics. Turnover time would be short—months."

"Should've put in a strategic order."

"Maybe they did," Brad said. "Could be on order right now, how would we know? Our client doesn't tell us everything, that's sure."

"Yeah," Vince said. "Maybe."

"Hey Aahil," Brad said. "That the president's men behind us?"

"Yes," Aahil said. "It is so."

"They wanna have a chat," Brad said.

"No," Aahil said. "We do not speak to them and they do not speak to us."

"Huhh."

Brad went on about business jets. Not much higher tech than desert balloons, just extra susceptible to drone or even fighter jet interference—those planes could simply be shot down. On an expanded Phase III regional, Brad thought, they'd fly jets out to ocean centre south of the equator and release sulphur at one focal point. Assuming non-politicized engineering interests could somehow be had free of interference.

Assuming good engineering only, Vince pointed out, released sulphur drifting south towards Antarctica would spread, but never east and west enough to influence the rest of Africa or South America. All effects would remain over the ocean. Minimal impact on anything else, so still pretty regional.

Of course political reality rolled out other dice they agreed.

The dark vehicle with the president's men pulled over outside their yard. They both looked at Aahil, but he held up both hands, shaking his head.

"Looks like we ignore them and let them watch."

"Yeah."

They loaded a balloon into the back of the Nissan and heaved a helium tank in too, leaving it to stick out over the tailgate. They wouldn't be going far, but still hopped back in the Nissan so Aahil could drive them out of the yard.

But as they pulled out through the gate, Aahil's eyes grew wider staring at the dashboard, and then at Brad. Hitting the gas hard like never before, he braked the Nissan to an abrupt halt in the lot beside the storage yard wall.

"You crazy today?" Vince asked.

Aahil turned off the engine, pointing to his dash screen.

"We must listen." Aahil said, punching at volume control.

The flash of a full screen blinking red glared out the installed target lock device, and as Aahil pushed his finger hard to turn up the sound, a mounting siren blare blasted its warning in synch with the screen flash.

Before Vince could think, stunned, he felt Brad's arm dragging him out the passenger door. Aahil scrambled out the driver's side, and around the Nissan to dash after them. The American engineer pushed Vince hard towards the wall corner. "Gotta move it," Brad was shouting. Vince stumbled, but regaining a precarious balance tore along with the other two around the corner. He plopped down breathless on the ground beside them.

"Like what?" Vince asked, heart hammering.

What would the president's men think of this chaotic rush, his mind raced, looking at the black SUV parked just down the road.

Vince looked at Brad, stunned by an expression not on his face since the Burkina border crossing. Aahil cocked an ear to the now distant siren, counting seconds on one hand. Prying his back from the wall, Brad wormed his way to the wall's end. Just as he was about to peak around the edge, the Nissan siren stopped, and he flopped back against the wall waving their heads down. Then, in the still of the moment an ear piercing explosion roared out from the parking lot. And another blast a millisecond later. As seconds of stunned silence passed, sprinkles of sand settled down around them from two directions.

"Fuck!" Brad groaned, lifting his head.

The three edged along the wall, glancing around the corner together. The Nissan was no more, replaced by a smoking dark crater in a ring of scattered dirt chunks.

"Jesus," Vince said softly.

"Good lead Aahil, I came behind you half guessing," Brad said. "Where's the other hit?"

Vince glanced down along the road, where the second blast had seemed to come. He pointed at another fire hole spewing fumes. Where the president's men had been parked. The three fell back to sit again, shaking. Vince struggled to speak sense but, "No balloon ride today," was what he heard himself say.

"No chat with the president's men," Brad said.

"Some do not like our president," Aahil said matter of fact. "Or what we do."

"A Marauder drone could hover up above us for half a day, and might be anywhere five miles away." Vince listened as Brad spoke to the world as if lost in some military manual he once read. "And could be from a base six hundred miles from here. A drone missile used to come out of a helicopter, so the old Helicopter Launched acronym made sense, along with Fire and Forget. Now we got the Hellblazer, still clocks in at Mach one point three, meaning seconds to arrive. That app detected the surface drone lock signal, so that's how we got that minute to move. Off by a few seconds, but, pretty accurate."

Vince grabbed Brad, giving him a light shake.

"That, my friends, was likely an AGM114 Hellblazer missile." Brad's grin half returned. "I sure did like that balloon in the back. We gotta order us another."

Vince watched the others' faces closely.

"Sorry about the Nissan," Brad said.

Aahil nodded, keeping a deep desert silence.

"Why didn't those guys get out?" Vince pointed at the second fire hole. "Why didn't they have a siren warning app?"

They all sat for a moment.

Through the resonating ringing in his ears Vince spoke first. "Another question is," he said in a calm voice. "Who would want to knock us off?" He should be terrified, he knew that, but that thrill rush rippled up his spine. And an almost passively curiosity came on, like he'd arrived to play a fitting role in some gangster story.

"Anyone with drone capacity," Brad said. "And that's a long list. The real answer to that question is: Who knows? The only thing I would say for sure would be, not our client. Likely military, but not the HICCC."

Even so, if the HICCC played a serious tussle of turf wars, and was not bluffing, Vince figured there'd be others with an opposing persuasion. A clique just as serious. He'd have to find his way in this strategic game attentive to how it developed.

Chapter 32

Tami scurried about her flat, awaiting a last minute Holo-Skype with Nishat. Light frocks for the dry Africa heat lay piled into her suitcase. Needing be out the door in one hour, she glanced over her trip list of must-haves. The HI/EC negotiations finished today, and she was sure the update from Minister Jabbar will include a reaction of sorts.

They spoke briefly yesterday, and that discussion held a serious tone. No preferred happy ending came up at all; quite the opposite, as Nishat reviewed harsh real world threats. What one could almost term climate conflict, with multilateral politics proclaimed to be working vying in direct opposition with other political pacts. While on the sidelines potential unilateral actions of populated and powerful countries adjusting the global situation to accommodate national interests waited.

Quite sad. But as the Minister said, she needed consider all global possibilities in any decision going forward. Even scenarios that one could only imagine come to that. Many situational circumstances remained unknown, undiagnosed, unfathomable.

Tamanna had compared select messenger Canada with the countries on her circuit. Lower latitude regions, seasonally dry and tropical like the Sahel, stood to lose crop productivity at temperature rises of even one degree. Sub-Saharan Africa as a whole was projected to reach new temperature normals well above any current heat wave extreme. Projected heat extremes, and especially their influence on the hydrological cycle, would have huge impact on ecosystems and agriculture. Sahel country economies being highly dependent on agriculture dictated a people economically with very low ability to adapt.

As Tami counted the minutes, she imagined a charismatic HICCC speaker. And what that one might say. Well, you

Europeans and you of European descent you have come, you have occupied and taken possession of our lands, your corporations have invaded and economically colonized our communities, you have taken our resources, and to top that off now you destroy our climate. All while you act only to insulate the effects of climate change from your own citizens. You, the Economically Cooperating world have dumped carbon into our common atmosphere, floating across our borders into our airspace. Well then, in return, our sulphur has been sent forth to mingle above your lands, to mix into your atmosphere.

Charismatic... or maybe not. One must somehow turn voice to an inspiring *we,* not an accusing *you. Our* geoengineering project will bring about *our* wellbeing and restore *our* national security, and we certainly regret any negative outcome affecting you. You will cooperate if you wish or you will not, but we will at this time do as we see fit. You no longer hold the advantage of whatever barbaric attitude of indifference to our welfare you have chosen in the past. Her voice would best not be the one speaking. The message must be much more practical, much more political. In a truly succinct and pragmatic sense, they needed the world to know their global cooling release would be reduced in direct correlation with measured reduction in OECD climate warming emissions.

Time digits flipped—when would the Minister call??

She'd double checked her adjusted final Sahel circuit bookings. Coastal Nouakchott in Mauritania still first, and then inland to Bamako in Mali, but she then leap frogged over Niamey to N'Djamena in Chad and one desert hop further to Khartoum. Her final flight returned from the Sudan to Niger in the middle.

The short long two tone audio signal began, and Tami stepped up to her kitchen table to accept. Nishat's face flickered into focus in the cube and Tami stared at the Minister's stress-ridden face.

"The meeting has not come off as we wished," Nishat said, resolutely.

Tamanna listened, snapping her suitcase closed.

"The Russian economic scientist calculated all political and economic benefits to Russia of further climate change." Nishat spoke urgently. "He went so far as the 5 degrees quick shift scenario. Some Russian grain fields wither to dust, but he showed cost benefit analyses offsetting any negative with abundant political benefit estimates. While he spoke of a balmy St. Petersburg, our HICCC delegates rose in concert and filed out of the meeting room."

"You walked away from the negotiations?" Tamanna said. "There will be no more talks?"

Nishat waited for Tamanna to return to the table before looking at her directly. She told Tami keeping the HICCC plan under wraps no longer held benefit. Everyone must know, the whole world must know, but first the contract personnel.

"You will tell them, all of our African project personnel," Nishat said. "You will tell them of each other, and you will tell them we will fully implement Phase III, the Sahel regional release."

"The mid-Atlantic business jets?"

"We have quotes, an option, yes."

The HICCC represented the voices of one third of the global population she reiterated. They had sufficient internal cooperation. Now they must become as equally indifferent to the OECD desires as those countries had been to their wellbeing. The colonial past carried significant political weight, popular support among citizens. Tamanna gave one last nod and signed off with Minister Jabbar. Her overwhelmed mind raced as she grabbed her bags, stepped out and locked the door behind.

At each circuit stop she must tell engineers to ramp up Phase I from whatever level to full Phase II national, combined to become the Sahel regional sulphur release. Her mind scrambled to recall, but yes, she was sure Jake's latest operational reports analysis confirmed the time target achievable. Right, she'll need each national team to know, now, of all other Sahel engineers and how her business partner in London had compared their field test results. Projected numbers looked mutually supportive. She'd explain how the purpose had been to confirm outcomes with identical specs through independent tests—good science—but now the combined effect would be implemented to create the desired Green Sahara. They'll need adjust their calculations accordingly.

She had minutes to join the Heathrow train.

Chapter 33

Harry strolled around his desk, edging up to the window. As he stared down at early Sunday morning taillights journeying along Kent Street, he mentally reviewed the day ahead. 'Call home' he voiced his jPad. This COP trip would be his fifth—the first back when Jase and Sten slapped a foam puck around the kitchen with plastic sticks. His travel bags rested beside his chair.

"Hey Angie. Thanks for pressing my shirt last minute."

"Oohh Harry," his wife said. "Why don't we give you a ride in the Lexus."

"Just like last time, honey. We grab a cab from the office here straight to the Ottawa international airport." He watched the foot traffic move as the lights switched to walk." We meet Minister Kendall and his team at Hanger 11 for our pep talk, and like I said, they never let personal vehicles though there. Security, sorry." He turned back from the window.

"We'll miss you Harry."

"Listen Angie, if you can get the boys to their hockey practices that would be so cool." He stooped to grab the handles of his two bags and made a quick visual check around his office. "All their gear is sitting in the Lexus and all you have to do is drive." He sauntered out his office door. "Think about St Lucia after Christmas. I'll give you a call when we're in the air babe."

"I love you."

Harry voiced 'Sign off' as he walked the aisle and into André's office. "Ready to go my man." The taxi would be out front in ten minutes. They followed each other out the entrance door and down the hall into the elevator. The conversation today, intermingled with a final review of their policy positions had been dancing around André's latest research. The bottle had been broken and construction was underway in Edmonton, Alberta. The oilfield industry had jointly agreed to finance the installation of a new carbon capture research facility. All effort driven by market forces with no added taxes, a moving forward initiative.

They tossed their luggage into the taxi trunk at the corner on Kent and escaped the cold into the back seat. A left onto Laurier merged them into traffic. The rat-a-tat of snow pellets on the glass ebbed with the wind gusts. The red-yellow-green traffic lights sequenced as they left downtown, and at Queensway underpass they sped as congestion spread out. The Airport Parkway appeared just over the river bridge.

Harry gazed out the window as André read a paper printout. This part of the job he could kinda do without. So much time away from his wife and boys. He'd be missing the live Sens game tonight, but oh well, thank God for NHL net. The game action would be coming in via hologram. Harry turned his look back inside and let André know about his sons' hockey games. How they were playing this year so far. André' had no children yet, Harry knew, but he talked of his NHL team Montreal. Talking kept up team spirit.

The driver turned onto Tracker, the private road leading to the Canada Reception Centre in Hanger 11. Harry waved his coded Government of Canada card over the scan bar and the security access gate opened for their taxi. Once parked, they pulled their bags from the trunk and hustled through the snow into the VIP Reception Building.

In the strategic pep talk room Harry and André shook hands with Paul and Sophie, two ministerial assistants they knew. Sophie pointed out their home contact team member when he entered with the Minister.

Climate Minister Kendall called all attention to outline what he wanted on policy strategy. Brazil and Mexico were to be engaged with on the side towards a Latin American free trade agreement. Indonesia's rising voice would be recognized similarly. Articulate the same position with China, with India. The global economy would certainly solve any problem. He ended briefly mentioning the HICCC walk out from the HI/EC meeting two days ago. That was to be kept as a minor issue. One old negotiating rule Harry knew—economically developing countries, like those in that high impact consortium, held little sway at the bargaining table. Downplay any rumour anything significant was up, the Minister told them. The Prime Minister had few concerns—there would be no media release. Sore losers, Harry quipped, and he got laughs and a smile from Minister Kendall. That self-proclaimed consortium initiated the talks, had they not? The OECD had nothing to lose.

With the Minister having voiced his spiel, chatter shifted to previous COP meetings. Historical Copenhagen and that supposed pivotal meeting in Paris all those years back. Harry could feel his engagement energy rise. He learned a guy he met from the Italian negotiating team would be at the bargaining table. Italians were not hockey players, but the guy did talk up *la vita*.

When Minister Kendall raised his phone hand they all fell silent; the pilot was ready to go. Harry recognized the Minister's let's-do-it look for his negotiating team. They filed out after each other through the boarding gate ramp onto the plane, picking up on the chatter again.

#

As their last in-flight prep meeting finished, Harry stood to stretch in the onboard conference room. André slipped eye covers on and leaned back. The last discussion turned to Canada's need for extra energy due to a cold climate and the long travel distances due to the great expanse of the country. How to respond to comparisons made to Nordic countries. Copenhagen with all those bicycle riders. Canada had a transnational cycling trail that would take an Olympic rider an entire summer to traverse. Proving the point of long distance. Bicycle trails in Ottawa functioned fine for the young and the athletic, Minister Kendall said, before retiring to his private room.

Harry glanced at the time. Half their ten hour flight had passed so their plane must be somewhere over the mid-Atlantic. And so very close to game time.

"You ever been on the Prime Minister's plane, Harry?" Paul walked up.

"Never have," Harry said, turning.

"Sophie has. She says they've got an oval office conference area. Chairs are connected to that hologram All-Round-U system," Paul said. "A full Float'n'Hover sound system."

"Yeah?" Harry said. "That'd be so cool for watching a game."

"Oh yeah," Paul said. "Like you're right there in Scotia Place."

Harry felt a glow of camaraderie watching Paul's expression. "You want a drink?" He grabbed two and another for André before sitting again. Flicking the remote for this plane's older hologram projections, they tuned in to adgram beers, babes and buster trucks rolling through the back country. A dancing icon counted fifteen minutes of pregame left, and then game time! Excellent.

"Gonna be a lot warmer in Italy than Ottawa." Paul took his drink from Harry.

"Yeah...still not as warm as the Caribbean," Harry said.

"You go south for the winter?"

"Oh yeah, we love it there. We've got tickets booked for St Lucia early January." He told Paul they might squeeze another trip in too. That place they heard of other side of the Dominican. "We've got a family excursion map posted in our downstairs rec room. So every place we explore gets a green pin and a yellow for all the wanna go places we haven't been yet. My boys miss a couple of their junior league games, but they love putting up those pins." The map was just above the pool table. One reason they needed to buy a bigger house, so they'd have space for that twelve foot table.

"We got it tough," Paul said. "Living up in the cold north."

"Warmer than Mars," Harry laughed. "Wonder what they've got for vacation spots on that planet?"

"My wife sent a hundred bucks to the bring-Jackie-back fund," Paul nodded. "Leave Haydon there, she says."

"Ah, my wife figures Jackie would get lost in the crowd back here." Harry shook his head. "Keep her famous, she says. So she sent a couple hundred to the send-a-nursery fund."

They checked the screen. Still a few minutes before the game.

"Yeah, man, Canada's the best by far but life can get tough." Harry went on. "My family's happy enough when we grab our scuba gear and hop a plane for a bit of reef swimming. Those resorts are the perfect place to clear your mind. You know, you laze around on a sandy beach for the day. Great way to relax and get away from the snow. You?"

"Ah, been south a couple times," Paul said. "We've got skidoos and we downhill ski a lot."

Noise in the crowd signalled pregame over, and the game beginning.

"You must be a Sens fan," Harry said.

"Bruins," Paul stated. "They'll be taking this game and any other."

"André's got the Habs." Harry shook his head. "I feel sorry for the guy."

André pulled his eye covers, lifting one fist. "Montréal." He rolled the name out in his first language French.

"Spezza's gonna take the Sens into the playoffs easy this year." Harry told Paul. "Then, the real and only team takes it from there."

"That's Ottawa's captain?"

"Absolutely."

"Hey, game's starting."

The game came and went fast as Harry fell into the comfort of his cheering zone. He rose from his seat at a couple hard hits, and when the game ended in overtime his loud cheer and Paul's belated groan echoed around the boardroom. With a couple hours yet until arrival, they held the game's excitement talking over the best plays until Harry felt his energy sag. He could see the same in the others. Flight hours and the European time change kept a team, international hockey or negotiating, adjusting for jet lag. But the best trick was setting the game time delay, Harry told them, just as if you were watching that evening. You trick your circadian rhythm with the greatest game on Earth.

Late Sunday evening Florence air traffic was light as their plane circled. Harry rubbed at his tired eyes. Angie and the boys would be eating breakfast.

As they followed each other off the plane, their Climate Minister gestured over at a Challenger coming to dock at the next terminal. Harry felt the cool Italian night air refreshing his spent face. That would be the Prime Minister's plane he vaguely heard Paul say.

Chapter 34

They sat around the downstairs meeting room, chairs at scattered angles, each nursing their coffee cup. Tamanna had called together a Holo-Skype conference and Nishat was scheduled to be in attendance. Tension hung heavy in the air as they waited.

"You guys sign that contract extension?" Brad asked.

Vince nodded, but Jeri was silent.

"Not for the bonus, I just gotta stay." Vince grimaced. "Like you said, we're probably on multiple drone lists now."

"You guys are so lucky to be alive." Jeri spoke in an unnaturally subdued voice. "We don't need to be here you know."

"We'll be out of here soon," Brad said. "With or without the real story."

"No matter what," Vince said. "I kinda like it here, drone listed or not."

"Like Jackie," Jeri said flatly. "You guys know there's gonna be a Martian kid? And the voting audience wants a say on bringing her home. What do you do with a baby on Mars, or a bonus when you're dead?"

"You'll be getting more model numbers like you always wanted," Brad said, looking sideways at Jeri. "That's what I think is gonna happen here."

"Give it a break." Jeri shook her head. "Nothing past Phase II on this project, no way."

"You guys ever meet Tami's boss?" Vince asked.

"Nope," Brad said. "Couple times I saw her profile, but she keeps a blank icon photo."

"Here's Tami remote," Vince said, waving at the cube. "I wonder where she is?" His voice trailed off.

Tamanna came through from a simple desk in a one colored room. No clue on her location, Vince noticed. She briefed them on their time with Nishat. Two minutes, no more. Listen only, she told them, no interactive questioning. "If you have any questions, direct them my way afterwards."

"What's that all about?" Jeri asked.

"Yeah," Brad said.

"On our project while we wait." Tamanna ignored the comments. "Speaking strictly to the global scenario, for reference only as we all know, we take that as a slow start build up scenario. Remember the natural event we model—Pinatubo emitted eight million sulphur tons over several months, and netted a global temperature reduction peaking at zero point four degrees. That was over an eighteen month timeframe. For our Niger scenario, we want to reduce the temperature by double Pinatubo within the first year. We adjust that temperature drop on an ongoing controlled basis using incoming satellite infrared emissions measurements over the next months."

Vince looked at Brad, and they both shrugged. They'd be relying on those satellite measures, but no change there. Jeri had become more attentive.

"But now, based on discussions over the global, we want another scenario calculated. Still based on Pinatubo. We now realize we can design artificial volcanoes to reduce temperature, or, we design to adjust precipitation to pre-industrial. We realize those to be two distinct targets, similar, but not identical. So we want a global scenario to target an offset of half the carbon temperature effect. Why? Two reasons. First is we would want to avoid precipitation loss by cooling the planet too much. Model runs show that happening. Then second, however empty this effort may seem at times, we still want to take a chance on people acting responsible. We still want to leave global incentive for carbon mitigation efforts which, as we all know, is the real solution."

"Mitigation *was* the real solution," Vince said. He knew mitigation, even in the optimal scenario with a rapid carbon dioxide reduction program, would only moderately offset climate change. Carbon already emitted would continue as the primary effect on climate change over the next many years.

"Mitigation will still be one atmospheric lever available, still having significant potential to bring back the planet we once had,"

Tamanna said. "Making our geoengineering project all the more important. The benefits we bring, even mitigation can't supply."

"If we had taken on mitigation decades back, you could have called that a solution," Vince said. "Now, carbon's in the atmosphere." Carbon already in the air had committed the planet to a distinctly modified climate.

"Barring any carbon capture from thin air technology developing," Tamanna said.

"Biochar," Vince said. Biochar was one good way to create a carbon sink and reduce desertification. Absorbing and retained moisture and nutrients, biochar helped create soil. But someone had to initiate and coordinate the project globally, or regionally—not happening. What was happening, right here in Africa, was the offset of one pollutant with the intentional introduction of another pollutant.

"So, what's this new scenario about?" Brad said.

"Sulphate cooling doesn't precisely offset carbon warming," Vince said. "So there's change no matter what. Carbon insulates all the time, but sulphur only reflects when the sun shines. So you get effects like cooler days and warmer nights."

"Aahil might like that," Brad said. "What about back home?"

"Just like sulphate cooling actually happens only in the day time, it also happens more in the summer time, you know, whenever there's more sunshine. So up north, we'd have cooler summers and warmer winters."

The image of Minister Jabbar appeared, coming almost into hazy focus. "Good day High Impact Country Climate Change contractors," Nishat said. "We congratulate you on your work so far and we apologize for any inconvenience. Thank you. We all understand our wish for sulphur-driven cooling to counteract carbon-driven warming." Nishat spoke as if she were reading from script. "Ms. Meacham has informed me each one of you has agreed to stay until our project is complete."

For a further set term, yes, Vince thought. The contract wording had been selectively ambiguous.

"What we now wish is that you calculate and deploy a revised sulphur release plan what we have referred to as the major regional Phase III. Specifically, this revision will now include your national release combined with any country bordering your assigned nation." Nishat's face formed a pixilated smile. "Cooperating with sister countries, we wish to see Phase III in three days' time. Our global scenario must also be revised to reflect the changes made in this Phase III plan. The Phase IV global remains for reference only. Thank you again." Her image blanked out.

Vince and Brad looked at each other.

"She's not talking just to us," Vince said. "That was a blanket statement."

"Yup," Brad said. "No brainer there."

"At least we had a visual of the boss woman," Jeri said.

"Okay, this will be something of a transition," Tamanna said. "But we've been preparing along these lines, so it should all go smoothly. Any questions?"

"Three days." Vince shook his head. "I mean, what about that mid-Atlantic release?"

"Not included. As you deduced, we'd never have the aircraft design time," Tamanna said. "Our HICCC Minister Nishat Jabbar wishes to keep that as part of a full global scenario tagged in with balloon launch. Political risk there she sees fitting with global. As things stand, other Sahel countries are near identical to Niger with strong regional interest in a Green Sahara. So we calculate mid-Atlantic as per previous, and for Phase IV reference only."

"We have a refined Phase III scenario," Jeri said. "If we include these other nationals into the model, I can tell you that modifies the run somewhat. Question: do we still include a percentage of ocean surface for each country, and the land surface of the non-HICCC world. Proportional to each country's area and GDP?"

"Correct," Tamanna said. "Nothing changes there."

The three looked at each other, each with doubts. They would have to rely on other engineering teams they'd never met and assume correct calculations and sulphur releases, and to synchronize their balloons in the air accordingly. Jeri's model would now be linked in to the actual release tonnages for each neighbouring country, in fact, all major countries across the Sahel.

"Burkina Faso?" Vince said, glancing at Brad.

"Mali covers that," Tamanna said.

Brad nodded.

"So speaking now for Nishat, I can tell you we have been running independent tests in other Sahel countries identical to those here in Niger." Tamanna said. "We will link you in to a common database and you can source any test results there. Your data will be posted also."

"They must have infrastructure in place," Vince said.

"Yes, with design variations, the same basic model as Niger." Tamanna said. "In fact, if you look to your visiscreens, you'll see you've secured access to another cloud."

"So to summarize." Tamanna appeared about to sign off. "We assume a Sahel regional release. To be initiated three days from now. We also want to assume an attitude of trust—that all members of our consortium have the same desired outcome, and that we are all acting in a coordinated fashion. Each Sahel country has a vested interest in a Green Sahara. And finally, we want to adjust our reference Phase IV global according to this new regional scenario."

"Explains that balloon Aahil's cousin found," Vince said quietly.

"Yup," Brad said. "Sure does."

"To start, this will have an impact on our Niger volcano," Jeri said, pointing at the paper wall map. "With a shoulder release each side of Niger, Mali to our west and Chad to the east, this will have significant influence on our model output. Our sulphur effect will funnel a lot better going pole ward, and we won't be leaking out the edges."

"So, Jeri you'll have to run our Niger model, and then run that again assuming these other countries participate." Vince glanced at the wall map. "Niger is the middle country and we need release numbers from Mauritania and Sudan on the outside edges too. I'll need that model output to recalculate our output and coordinate maintenance tonnages." He smiled. "Now I see the Sahel sisters on the map, all wanting a Green Sahara."

"Yeah, I'll get you that." Jeri held her lips firm. "This Phase III Sahel release is gonna give our model a lot better numbers to extrapolate that global. Improved start data there, and a major region has much better climate zone reality than any defined by a national border. That makes our global, Phase IV, a significantly more accurate estimation."

"I told you you'd be happy, girl," Brad said.

"Not totally." She frowned now. "It's still possible we get a polar regions only cooling effect. The model's not perfect, by any stretch. A regional change can have negative impact. Best to have a reliable cooling of those mid-Atlantic waters in play. Or your biochar, Vince, en masse."

They looked at each other.

"Nothing simple, man."

"Like the climate."

"Like people."

"Another thing I wanna mention," Jeri said. "With this major regional model solidly defined, Phase IV becomes nearly a one button push. Alright, alright, hypothetically 'cause that totally assumes all HICCC countries actually cooperate. We'd need accurate synchronization."

"Assume some major Asian country's been organizing all along," Vince said. "Could be. Niger project's pretty organized."

"When'd you take on this optimism," Brad said.

"Right," Vince said, nodding. "Reality check. We've been less than informed on project scope the last few weeks. If we are now not the only, but a sister Sahel country, our Phase III may well not be the only major regional."

"Yeah, that's my man." Brad smiled.

"Think for a minute on our regional logistics," Jeri said. "Take moving sulphur tanks and launch balloons, and past that, can we realistically coordinate that much sulphur into the stratosphere? You engineers you."

"No worries there," Vince said. "We've got contingency sulphur coming out our ears—we could bring back the Ice Age, or make a snowball earth the truth be told. The real issue is gonna be peoples' reaction. Once the world knows what's going on—that's when shit flies."

"Or here's another one," Jeri said. "Say someone makes a gross error in calculations, or our whole project has a theoretical error. Like the NASA satellite measure that detected the Antarctic spring ozone hole, but the data was coded into the software as instrumentation error by default, and tossed. The error then was belief, blinded by theory 'cause the measurement they were getting wasn't believed possible. Yeah, people do make errors."

"Anything else Jeri?"

"Look guys, you been great at playin' the card game," Jeri said. "But I can work the model from back home just as well. I'm relocating. Next time we talk, you'll be lookin' into your Holo-Skype cube."

"Yeah," Brad sighed. "Drones?"

She didn't answer, nodding silently.

CONFERENCE Of the PARTIES FLORENCE

Chapter 35

As they walked the stone courtyard to the last afternoon meeting place, the Tuscany sky radiated a paradisiacal portrait, a splash of celestial blue on a fantastic day. Moments like these reminded Harry full well why he had chosen this career. Meetings were smooth wins, all anticipated flack on Canadian energy policy successfully deflected. They played the game of soft touch politics, always underlain by fierce competition—the part he most loved. Canada, negotiating around Alberta's influence on much needed global energy supply, held sway in close to all offensive plays on Ottawa priorities.

He loved any kind of win; when you had home ice advantage, you took it to the fullest. The Senators would be on screen playing the Bruins back in his room that evening, well, the game finished hours ago but he'd catch the action delayed-live on NHL.net. A relaxing finish to a sensational day.

He'd been practicing his persuasive tone, inviting André to come watch just one Senators game.

"Didn't you play junior hockey for Ottawa?"

"*Oui,* also for Quebec City."

"One game, then." Harry added smooth appeal to his enthusiastic undertone. "C'mon, you don't wanna miss out on great hockey."

The innuendo on André's face made it clear he'd be sticking with his Montréal hockey and their Philadelphia game. Harry squinted and winked. A new angle, a negotiator always kept a back pocket strategy when it came to convincing others. When their teams faced common foes, yes, then. In the next Leafs series both the Sens and the Habs had it in for Toronto.

As he grabbed the hardwood handle to the meeting room door, Harry felt his pocket buzz. He stepped aside, and pulled his Jeenyus. His eyebrows rose at call display. Minister Kendall? Wasn't he meeting Asian reps? He waved André in, and stepped over under a portico arch.

"Yes Minister?" He touched up volume.

"Harry. Are you familiar with a deputy minister's role?"

"Yes sir."

"We have a situation and I need your negotiating skills. The HICCC has invited my office to a meeting in Africa."

"Africa, Minister?" True surprise mixed into Harry's questioning tone. "The HICCC?" In the drone zone! Jesus!

"Take the Challenger to the city of Niamey. Bring your assistant," Minister Kendall directed. "We have PMO clearance on the jet."

"Of course, Minister. But can I ask—these countries invited your office?" As senior contract negotiator, Harry knew he had a tiny wiggle room, even with the Honorable Minister. "Does the Prime Minister's Office even recognize this HICCC consortium?"

"My office will be counting on your consulting firm. I personally chose Harold Heine services for my office negotiations."

"Yes Minister. We are fully aware of your priorities." He paused. "If I could voice one minor concern, Minister." This was the last play of the game. Time to strategize. "How specifically will we speak to your absence, sir? You, having been personally invited, and not attending?"

"The situation doesn't warrant my direct attention. Look, Harry, I'll send my executive assistant Paul Dion along. That will cover all bases for my office. Have Paul contact me directly on any significant issue."

"Yes Minister." He squeezed his lips. His questioning tone insinuating team needs had come off just right, given the situation. Paul was an extra player advantage. "Thank you sir." His mind switched gears as the Italian dial tone started beeping, and he slowly returned the Jeenyus to his pocket. So much for that relaxing evening watching the Sens play on NHL net. Or was there a way, to see the game at least? He fought to keep the day's fading glow, imagining the crowds on their feet for home team, cheering the winning goal.

Niamey. He rolled the name off his tongue. In English, then French. Lewis, that's where Lewis had been, on that goofball HICCC tour, yes, that same city. In Niger, yes, French. *God.* Maybe he could swing an overnight stay. To enhance clear minds anticipating next COP days he could say. He'll have to check with Sophie. Right, grab an overnight bag and get to the Peretola airport. And actually, all games should be there to watch on the Prime Minister's plane with its snazzy All-Round-U holograms.

He opened the meeting door, waving André back out.

Chapter 36

Vince gripped his jPad in the back of the jostling scout truck bumping along up the wadi. Brad kept his eyes glued on the developing GPS pattern of morning balloons first returned to ground. "Looking pretty good," Brad said, grinning. "I'd estimate we get an easy ninety percent recovery. See that one." He pointed at the visiscreen map. "Aahil says the guys coming in on motorbikes can get in further than the trucks. They stuff the balloon in a carry bag, hook the bag on the front of the bike, and drag the helium tank back out with a towrope."

As they approached the first balloons, Vince followed Brad's glance out the window for a visual ground check. A splash of green lettering marked one empty balloon, and another deflated piece of feather-web fabric lay draped across a rocky outcrop. One more stretched over the sand to hang partially from a scrubby bush.

"Wind picks up later in the day, right?" Vince asked.

"Today we keep launching, no matter what," Brad said. They'd been given the go ahead on keeping balloons going up all day. Each emblazoned with Green Sahara, for the president's campaign and his vision for Niger. "Today's Friday, the peoples' day off and their president wants them to celebrate the second coming of their Green Sahara. We seek Redemption, my man."

"You are peculiar Brad. You got this upbeat stance on everything, all while you prepare for the Apocalypse."

"Look around your world, dude. What clearer sign would anyone need of a global climate crisis? And you of all people know about people! Think of the potential shit to come, Vince." Brad had been trying to convince Vince to purchase a piece of land on the British Columbia side of his mountain valley. Think of it as insurance, for your daughter if nothing else he'd been saying.

Vince had resigned to the topic and the conversation, even interested. "So you look at the basics of food and shelter first? Security in a local community."

"Yeah man."

Picture our children in a generation, Brad would say, when they're our age. Easy proposition. His bright grin seemed conducive to what he wanted for his boys, a better, more people friendly scene. A more nature friendly community, and by extension a whole world with the same outlook. The climate of the future, meteorologically and culturally, was not on its way—the change had arrived. With no end in sight to extreme weather events, unless these sulphur injections into the stratosphere worked, people would react. People *will* do something. And Brad stressed thinking on how what people did might not be too pretty—they did have a track record. When it came to climate change, the chance at a global wise move had come and gone, too late, and how much too late was the real question to ask. So at a personal level, best to focus on how to survive the climate change transition. Brad got into the details of the Mad Maks movie world, one he really hoped against. But possible. A real world scenario came from the transition by prehistoric people from the last Ice Age to the Holocene. He watched the transition dramatized by animated extinct characters with his sons. You could laugh at the antics of critters like a sloth and a mammoth, but if you looked carefully, you saw reality issues abounding in the setting and the background. A climate transition involved a significant lifestyle adjustment.

"Food's number one," Vince said. "Sounds like that valley of yours has an excellent growing climate. And a low risk climate change projection."

"Correct. Soft fruit trees grow there," Brad said. "An indicator of high productivity in the colder north."

"Couldn't you store food from a current agricultural source," Vince asked. "In my grandfather's time, a guy carried a fifty pound sack of flour to the homestead and fed a family for months."

"Yeah, starting to think about that," Brad said. "A couple hundred pounds of stored rice. Aahil does that in their house."

Food storage would be essential. Brad, with no green thumb, imagined specializing in refrigeration or water systems design. Irrigation required water flows to the right places at the right time. Being a non-gardener, he thought about long term self-sustaining food sources, like a yard full of nut trees. To get a family food storage facility in place would be top priority. History taught the basics of root cellar function, but solar power allowed a heat transfer system. He dug one pit on their valley property, lined with Styrofoam insulation. A summer long test revealed the pit's ability to keep vegetables cool and ice frozen throughout the summer valley heat. Your grandfather did something like that, he told Vince. Big question, though, would a guy be standing guard over his vegetable patch with a shotgun? Something to keep in mind, and ideally not.

"Soon as I get home, I'm gonna dig another pit. You gotta come out there Vince, and see the place. Check out the land for sale. Not too far from Calgary," Brad said. "I've been sketch designing another rain capture system, so I'm gonna do an install on that next summer too."

Brad even had international dreams for the valley, as valley geography overlapped the Pacific Northwest and British Columbia. Spectacular views made the valley appear as paradise but on a pragmatic tone kept the place isolated. On either side, high mountains kept unwanted factors out.

"Civilization contained within," Vince said, looking at Brad. "The unconverted world stays out."

"The valley's inland off the main California to Alaska route," Brad said. "Movers best travel along the coast, if they veered inland to Spokane they hit a lot tougher route. So a guy keeps out of their way."

"You see that happening Brad?" Vince asked. "Climate refugees coming north in our own countries."

"A lot of scenarios run through my mind." Brad squinted. "Distinctly plausible."

You needed a Wild West covered wagon plan, Brad summarized. Always the basics: daily nutrition essential, and a shelter to stave off winter cold. Good strategy suggested two shelters, like an urban house and an emergency survival cell. If he moved stock and barrel to the valley, he'd still set up another survival cell up a mountainside or on that valley lake. Quality modern clothing lasted a long time, so a good stock kept you warm and dry.

Next was community. In fact, that would and should be the ultimate focus.

"So a valley community," Vince said. "Like a town, and all the rural people up and down the valley."

"Community making can be a blast." Brad's smile flashed wide. "Dancing jigs around that covered wagon camp. Or really, how about building a better community model of the future? Out of the way of any coming climate change crazies."

All sorts of neighbour problems came up for Brad's cousins in the northern Idaho towns. But still, they kept a pretty solid community spirit. Neighbour helping neighbour, that's what you needed. Internet had to be there as a solid connection for not just neighbours, but with the external world. Wireless telecommunication, all devices were essential technology—no going back to the covered wagon on that.

"What's your biggest concern?" Vince asked. "As a potential threat?"

Wild fire danger, Brad was clear. Increased regular forest fires came with hotter drier summer weather. Learning from those cousins he'd designed his land and building accordingly. They said build a fireguard; you chop down all trees close to any structure. But Brad wanted to keep the place hidden, and forest worked for that, so he removed select trees.

But, second threat ran with a massive climate refugee influx. "What do you say to a million people moving up from California? Escaping their parched valley, they come knocking on your humid valley door?" Brad asked. Some bloggers speculated on no place to run to except Planet B. Those more down to earth wrote on regional population shuffles. Like what Tamanna said on Bangladesh—refugees struggling to enter India and the closest big city of Calcutta. That scenario ran him a spinal shiver, Brad said. Far from the Pacific Northwest, Asia, but what people did there told you what people do anywhere. Sadly, what could a guy do for

Bangladesh from the mountain valley but stay in touch through the web?

"All an adventure to you, right Brad?" Vince knew of the glimmers in his friend's eyes.

That adventure would be impacted by whose side had the edge in the struggle to control the climate, Vince thought. Brad would leave the climate struggle to national governments, thinking what could you really do there anyway? Build his community of the future out in the valley. If something like this geoengineering helped give offset time and the world got its shit together, excellent. If they effectively transitioned to a low carbon economy, and re-stabilized the climate, bonus. But that would still take decades, Vince knew, so you couldn't blame the guy for taking it as opportunity, and building a little valley community model for future reference. He thought of his daughter's future more often now.

#

Balloon recovery went well that release-day morning, with only a light wind blowing. Having checked field operations, Vince rode with Brad in the back of a scout truck to the warehouse. Having deciding on lunch back at the Gaweye, Vince asked the driver to take them into the city.

"A ton of sulphur for each balloon, now up in the stratosphere," Brad said, laying back. "Makes for easy accounting, no?"

"Yeah, good lift design," Vince bantered along.

"How're we tracking the sulphur, post release?" Brad asked.

"Satellite imagery partially," Vince said. "Partly Jeri's model. Still weather happening at the bottom of the stratosphere, Tami says. If we did mid-Atlantic we'd go higher, and the process would go smoother."

"We'll be doing that Atlantic." Brad squinted. "Just wait."

Vince had put together a tentative plan to store liquid sulphur for the mid-Atlantic, with a rough calculation to compensate for any loss to drones. But shooting down a plane in international airspace, Brad said, that would scream political. The Atlantic release floated as an add-on option, officially still for reference calculation. Their desert released tons officially cooled the

Nigerien climate only. Ridiculous to think a border contained atmosphere.

Vince thought of that first balloon ride with Brad. The smaller test balloon had rocketed skyward spewing sulphur and helium, finally emptying two kilometers higher like a volcanic eruption. But with both gases colorless, the eruption had been invisible just like carbon gas.

On a contract that could have ended then, Vince mused, here they were launching hundreds of daytime balloons aloft around Niamey, all for local politics. Over the next weeks, they'd reach their target of five thousand tons. Then every autumn for a decade, depending on larger than local politics.

Past the engineering and climate science, the impacts of a successful launch brought in people, and the real political game. The laws of physics not caring about national borders as Sahel sulphur thinned, it would approach Europe drifting north towards the pole. Some impact would arise everywhere, all around the globe—like Krakatoa impinged on England— the Sahel sisters would affect his daughter's Calgary life.

As they drove further into the city, they noticed the noise of people building in the streets. Looking, they saw groups on corners everywhere cheering, some waving at their truck as they drove past. "Hey man, they're cheering the balloons." Brad waved back out the window. "That's what it is. The president's gonna be happy today." The farther into the city they got, the more they noticed crowds. Horns blared on the bridge, and they crossed the river, amidst a tumult of bicycles flying green flags high, and pedestrian masses wearing green armbands.

"Amazing."

"Stunning."

"Aahil reached Agadez?"

"Yeah, he left a kwikgram earlier," Brad said. "He's gonna pick us up at the airport there tomorrow. I told him to launch the Agadez urban balloons this afternoon."

"He's got the procedure down?"

"He picks up on things quick, Vince." Brad said. "But as we know, anyone could be doing this in their back yard."

It really came down to that, Vince knew. Wouldn't take much for any small country to build an artificial volcano. You could talk about a volcano, but invisible brought extra challenge when telling a story. Harvard said for every ton of trash going to landfill, forty tons of carbon got dumped into the atmosphere. If carbon was a stinking mass of human refuse, people would have cleaned it up right away. But you didn't see carbon. Unlucky or unfair, but a lot wasn't fair. The sky color change might be a visible sign, or would people notice?

"Let's hope people find a hazy sky as repugnant as garbage," Vince said.

"Yeah," Brad shrugged. "Got doubts."

"They get blazing sunsets first. The hazy blue comes more gradual," Vince said, looking at Brad. "Yeah...they'll paint a sunset picture, and talk about the weather. Like another day in Russian—or Canada—just a nice warm day."

Making atmospheric carbon trash visible by proxy might bring attention to the invisible, but too beautiful perhaps, not disgusting enough. Vince felt a buzz and he glanced to visiscreen. Why would Tamanna be calling? He answered, listening.

"She says they invited a Canadian Minister to a meeting tonight," Vince said, pushing end call.

"Here?"

"Yeah, here in Niamey. And she wants me at the meeting."

"Hey, Vince good on you man!" Brad slapped his back. "I told you, you got more going for you than engineering. All that time and interest you got in people, people engineering man, you gotta use that."

"Yeah." Vince felt the grin on his own face forming

Chapter 37

Harry sprawled out in the back of the hybrid limo, tight lipped. Riding with his diplomatic entourage in a presidential car, elation might have been the mood. But not with *la vida* left behind and after an exhausting flight to this obscure African city. Niamey.

To top it off, the Senators lost the game on the plane by one goal; he was pissed. And the hockey highlights had been obscured by their scramble to review recent interchange with these High Impact Climate Change Countries. This HICCC. A bunch of snivelling countries who couldn't keep up. And who would destroy what everyone wanted—a first world lifestyle.

Representing Minister Kendall's office would be enough of a crapshoot. And thoughts of drones snuck out of the penalty box, no matter how he slammed his mind's door. *Shit!*

André and Paul stepped with him out into the heat, Hotel Gaweye commissionaires opening the limo doors. Presidential guards escorted them up the stone steps, and then up elevators to the door of the executive meeting room.

Harry prepared his look for entry, as there would be introductions. Paul had reviewed the Minister's reminder list on priorities—Canadian energy exports first. Of course. He also mentioned a name, a Ms. Tamanna Meacham. First name Bangladeshi, André's research told them, but a Welch surname. Peculiar. Drop assumptions, interpret carefully, read her position. As always, scan for anything personal. They stepped through the door, and he assessed the room at a glance. A brown woman, and a Caucasian man, both dressed casually, sat at the conference table. He led his team in single file to the chairs directly opposite. Harry, now flanked by his team, turned on his winning Scout smile along with his career-building likable squint. They placed their slim cases down beside them and took seats.

#

"Good evening gentlemen." Tamanna spoke. "As you have been informed, we represent Her Excellency Nishat Jabbar, the High Impact Climate Change Countries Minister of Negotiations. My name is Tamanna Meacham, this is Vincent Patel. Any issues with an audio record?" She glanced around, finger poised.

With no disapproval, she left it recording.

"Lovely, let's begin. Both Vince and I are consultants; as a paleoclimatologist I consult on climate change issues and Mr. Patel is a chemical engineer. Thus, you will find us speaking in pragmatic terms."

She returned smile to their man in the middle. "I should think you are the Canadian Climate Minister then?"

Harry assessed her light accent. British, with a colonial hint.

He leaned forward slightly, his polished look expressing empathy and regret. "Unfortunately, the Honorable Minister was not able to attend due to other pressing charges. However, my name is Harry MacLean, and this is my assistant André Garneau; we are political negotiators, consultants like yourselves. And this is Paul Dion, the Minister's executive assistant. We are fully commissioned to represent the interests of the Minister's Office and of the Minister."

Tamanna's face twitched.

"I see."

She glanced at the assistants, then directly at Harry. "Her Excellency deferred on meeting your Prime Minister, but insisted we speak directly to your Climate Minister. She was specific."

"With all due respect to the High Impact Countries." Harry picked his words. "Minister Kendall conveys his deepest apology. The Honorable Minister regrettably has some high profile engagements with other national ministers and his presence is not possible at this time."

"Our message was quite clear."

"Our apologies."

A shrewd look came over Tamanna as she slowly released her breath. With eyes of ice, she spoke in a calm voice.

"Your Minister Kendall may have just made the political clanger of his career."

The air conditioning fan hummed through the silence. Harry sat back, his practiced face wavering only slightly as his nape hairs bristled. He said nothing.

She spoke again. "We require a recess—to consult with Her Excellency on how she wishes to proceed." She touched audio pause and rose to her feet.

"Absolutely, no problem." Harry's eyes bored into her yet he held the swallow in his throat.

Vince followed Tamanna out.

#

"Pretty dramatic." Vince glanced up at Tamanna as they sat in the next room.

"We negotiate. Nishat insisted on a mature conversation, with someone able to comprehend when and where cooperation becomes an absolute necessity. With at least a national minister. She does not want more bickering amongst playground school boys over who wins." She slapped her fingers on the table edge. "She wants us to speak directly to the truth, about where responsibility lies, and about the real impact of climate crisis. Based on non-politicized science."

She leaned forward, eyebrows furrowed.

"Despite our best intentions, Vince, that was rubbish. But we take it as opportunity. I twig now why Nishat didn't attend. She always has more than one strategy. She now depends on her messengers, and she needs our message to be crystal clear." Her look hardened more. "If she decides to proceed, your presentation will be critical."

Vince nodded.

Tamanna raised her device and selected a number, holding her forefinger up as it buzzed.

Vince stood, drifting back to the window, to the starlit evening…his device buzzed and he pulled his eyes from reverie to Jeenyus, reading. *Daddy I saw my furst star I see tonite.* His face softened. *I made a wish but I'm not telling it.* He thumbed in his reply, *Okay baby, your secret. But tell me, what color was the sky?*

He pushed *send.*

Much talk here on how they had but one planet, with one atmosphere and one climate. Impact of some type will show up everywhere. Some effect will transform life back home.

The buzz. *The sky was bluey darc. But Daddy, my star wuz whit.* The times he picked her up from school, he could hear her happy laughter; almost feel her tiny hand in his. He struggled to keep it together, blinking hard. How would he tell her, one day, what her Daddy's time in Africa meant? Physics explained the change of sky color, but it's the sky of her future too. The why-of-it-all raged at him, with his little daughter's life hanging out in the storm. He felt torn, what he did now either way, no question, would have consequence. He'd take on the risk of an eco-terrorist label, not claiming ignorance, an engineer following contract specs. To take the right side and take on a role cast as the bad guy, never again on the do-nothing side. One day he'd explain to her, somehow.

Was he responsible? The *furst star,* the one his daughter always waited on as the sky darkened before bedtime. If he could have found that same twinkling brightness...he had a wish for Annalise. Amidst the back and forth, among the swirl of terror and tension, the political drama did nothing but enhance that inner pervading elation. A game changer, and he'd play the game for what's real, for his daughter. The idea of acting as negotiator, sure storyteller, had brought that on. He'd become an ex-oil company engineer—or eco-terrorist depending who was talking.

Chapter 38

Back in the conference room Tamanna restarted audio record. Nishat had suggested tactics on ensuring the Canadian Minister was best informed, and ways to go forward with this negotiator. National pride, especially for men, could allow a subtle affront.

"Her Excellency has decided you may represent the Minister at this time," she intoned. "For the Dominion of Canada."

Harry lifted his head, catching the inflection. He ticked off a score; they would not be returning empty handed, and he sat back. Yet his lip twitched into the slightest of smirks, one he concealed with his winning smile.

Tamanna, however, knew she had him.

She stared his way, then prodded. "Was it something I said?"

The smile held. "Oh, nothing really. Look, just to be clear, we refer to our country as Canada. *The Dominion of* was dropped some time in the past." Many decades back. These sorry third world countries, to call them developing was too polite. So backwards, so uneducated. Still, stay submissive.

Tamanna nodded slowly. "Perhaps Her Excellency refers to an earlier name to set a time context. One more appropriate. Back when your country's lack of knowledge might explain its dated climate change policy."

Harry's eyes narrowed. "Oh, I see." But he forced his practiced smile wider. He looked at Tamanna and then Vince, emphasizing compliance. "We remain willing to represent the Honorable Minister."

The sound of shuffling in chairs pervaded the room.

"Before we begin, then, Her Excellency's office requires it be made a matter of record that the Canadian Minister was officially invited by Her Excellency and has chosen to be otherwise represented."

"Yes." Harry gave a reassuring nod. "Duly noted."

Tamanna began again. "The first point of business, then. Your Minister Kendall must realize that negotiations between our consortium and yours, the Organization for Economic Co-operation and Development—the OEC—can no longer continue as previously. The situation has changed. Significantly."

Harry settled back, falling into his practised listening mode.

"Minister Kendall must know that the HICCC decision to act came about due to OECD non-response to repeated requests. Our appeals to basic human interests and a globally focused solution have not received adequate response. Further to this non-response, a decision has been taken on a project we expect *will* be noticed."

Harry became vaguely aware of some sort of challenge. What could they possibly have? "You realize that while Canada does hold OECD membership, our country does not represent the OECD as a whole," he said softly.

"That may be the officially recognized state of affairs, however, we are about to reveal a unique opportunity for your country. With your membership, Canada will play the role of our messenger to the OECD as a whole." Tamanna looked at Harry calmly.

Harry said nothing.

"So we can speak in metaphor or stick with scientific terminology, what would be your preference?"

"We can be flexible," Harry said.

"Brilliant." She looked to her jPad visiscreen. "We will touch on both then."

She stood, straightening her skirt.

"First, let us point out that we all share one planet and that to a certain degree, we have common interest in our mutual wellbeing. Her Excellency wants to truly emphasize those two words, *mutual* and *wellbeing*." Tamanna paused, looking directly at Harry. "With wellbeing in mind, we must all understand the true value of nature, our biosphere, that being our mutual life support system. We inhabit only one planet."

She paused, touching her visiscreen. "Any comment?"

Harry shook his head absently.

"Now, there was a time when nature was big, and society was small, yet today those circumstances have reversed. A basic fact. While nature may still seem ample in northern latitudes, when we measure our planet globally, we find significant carbon footprint overshoot. Led by industrialized countries such as members of the OECD. These measurements, with repeated scientific confirmation, speak negatively to our *wellbeing*."

She paused again, waiting. The Canadian team remained silent.

"Not to beleaguer the point, but simply put, this sets our context. Like all countries, members of the HICCC have specific interests in the *wellbeing* of their citizens. What we emphasize here, are the effects our *mutual* now altered atmosphere has on climate change—also *mutual*. Our project, we believe, will help move negotiations along."

Harry kept his look cordial.

"Now, our engineer."

She nodded towards Vince as she sat, and he rose.

"Okay, so...once upon a time there was a volcano." Vince gauged initial reaction. "The first volcano in our story was named Pinatubo. One day, on a peaceful island covered with dense forest, a lava leak sprung and blew up into the sky to form a naturally active volcano." He detected interest, the human ear innately tuning in to story. "Now, you may have heard of Pinatubo 'cause that eruption was recent. You may not be aware of are the atmospheric effects, some of which jump out on any global temperature graph. What do we know? Volcanic eruption can, in fact, have a cooling effect on our planet, albeit short-term. And from Pinatubo, we get our project name, Pinatubo II."

Vince's felt that spinal tingle permeate his being.

"So our Pinatubo II venture, really, can be called a make-your-own-volcano project, and our HICCC client has defined five different volcanoes of interest. Each comes with increasing size, and by default, each has a greater effect."

He held a hand up, five fingers extended.

"So, we classify our volcanoes geographically. We've got local, regional, national ..." he held his hands close together, moving them wider as he went down the list, "major regional and even a hypothetical global." He stretched his hands far apart.

"Major regional would be a group of countries." He moved his hands back in from the widest. "More than one country stretches into the Sahara desert, as you may know, so an area like North Africa."

The Canadians watched, with increasing attention.

"At this time, our client's Minister Jabbar has directed we carry out sulphur release tests for both the local." He returned his hands quite close. "And the regional." He shifted them a step wider. "So we've already created both of those volcanoes."

He opened his hands to hold them at middle size.

"And, we now have the green light on a Niger national release. The first country to create its very own volcano." He paused. "I'll let my colleague speak to this, but I believe the Niger volcano has solid political support." Tami nodded confirmation. "Just to give you some project engineering insight, the Niger national sulphur release has an expected initial effects timeframe weeks from now."

"Okay, wait, wait, sulphur release?" Harry began tapping his pen on the table. "Create a volcano? Can you please clarify."

André leaned towards Harry's ear, pointing to his visiscreen, speaking quietly. "Geoengineering. What I have been telling you, Harry. High or low, this has been a building risk as time has passed." Harry stared at his assistant, then back at Vince. He turned his pen sideways, tapping now in staccato bursts.

"Vince, can you explain the impact of sulphur dioxide release in the stratosphere as you summarize the Nigerien national," Tamanna said.

"Sure, no problem. So back in school, we all learned how a volcano works. Later, any earth science class would teach a little on plate tectonics. Now, our natural Pinatubo eruption took place *geographically* in the Philippines, recently yes in 1991, when a dormant volcano erupted unexpectedly. Pinatubo importantly sits *geologically* on the edge of a subducting oceanic plate. And to help our story explain let's bring in a second volcano, Krakatoa, which erupted back in 1883 in Indonesia. But importantly for us, also on one of those subducting oceanic plates."

He paused, eyes on Harry's bouncing pen.

"While Pinatubo adds significance because she blew recently giving us enhanced records, Krakatoa gave us noteworthy data due to her size. Now to that sulphur question. One emissive substance, when volcanic eruption occurs on a subducting oceanic plate is sulphur dioxide. And this sulphur gas can be blown clear up into the stratosphere, that portion of our atmosphere way above the weather zone. Skipping all the boring chemistry, once up there, sulphur gas turns into a haze, or an aerosol. And that haze blocks a certain portion of the sun's rays, like a super thin sunshade parasol. Global cooling, again, all natural."

The Canadian delegates appeared to be following, no glazed over eyes.

"So our Pinatubo II project basically replicates that process." He spoke slowly now. "We reproduce that haze in the stratosphere and block a calculated portion of the sun's heat. We engineer a cooling effect." He took on the demeanour of a cartoon salesman. "We can design-a-volcano for any client, for anyone actually, anyone with an interest." More serious, he held up a finger. "When I say replicates, well, there are actually some differences. Unlike natural volcanoes exploding, artificials keep silent. In the secret night time only if you wish, when everyone's faaast asleep. And invisible. So unnoticed, kinda like no one wants to notice the global-average temperature."

Vince looked at Harry, dead serious.

"So that's the sulphur release we're talking about."

Harry stared at his now motionless pen. "What you're talking about will screw up our entire climate." His voice rose. "Completely."

"You're screwing it up right now." Vince matched tone. He had practiced this.

Harry glared, but caught himself. "We need to discuss this more...we can speak to specifics."

"Sounds like you already have been speaking. A lot. Minus any real action."

Harry began the pen tapping.

"One more fact," Vince went on. "In spite of our story volcanoes both being local, that is, at a one mountain location, they each had significant global effects. People in Europe felt the Krakatoa cooling, but what they noticed most was a different colored sky. So, our project design, at this point our Niger volcano, will impact the global climate due to aerosols blocking out sunshine, mostly but not entirely above Niger."

Vince almost did a spin-around like his daughter after ballet class, but he held it in and sauntered professionally over to the window.

"If you can bear with me, just a couple baseline numbers."

He turned to face them, hands behind his back.

"For Krakatoa, gentlemen, global thermometers recorded a drop of over one degree, precisely 1.2 degrees. Celsius." He paused, scanning their faces for comprehension. "Good, we all speak Celsius here. For Pinatubo, the cooling effect was less than half a degree, 0.4 degrees. So we now need to offset the global warming effect of current greenhouse gases emissions." He grinned. "And...we can do that with Pinatubo II." He raised a paper report to show a title. "Or Pinatubo 2.0 if you like."

"Okay, hold on." Harry cut in. "Remind me, how much warmer are we now?"

"Now? Yeah, well, triple Pinatubo, or 1.2 degrees so far, same as Krakatoa."

"Yet two of your 0.4 volcanoes makes only 0.8 degrees," André spoke. "The math is not good."

"Yes, excellent observation," Vince said. "Technical risk reasons explain that. But also Pinatubo II instead of III gives you guys wiggle room to act—gets political there."

"But really." Harry went on with his suggestive look. "How much difference would one or two degrees ever make?"

Vince looked at this man of the political world, wondering what he might or should know. He came up on his toes against the wall, and spoke slowly. "Most trend estimates agree the carbon *already* released into the atmosphere will *double* that temperature increase. So we are committed to 2.4 degrees. When that happens, we'll need even more multiplications of Pinatubo."

"But I mean, give me a break. That kind of temperature change happens all the time." Harry spread his palms wide. "I'm no engineer, but I'd guess that kind of heat change happens here in this room at the touch of a button." He waved towards the air controls. "Or even more, outside in this African heat. We all know that. Right?"

Vince looked Harry over. He could hear his wife's nonchalant voice telling him of the new Bow River valley after the Calgary floods, freshly formed channels, gravel bars shifted to new places…quite pretty actually, she had said. He toned his language down more, to a child's level, still with precision, yet keeping it simple. "Look, no one feels the global-average climate. You must base what you know on a measure, like a ruler or a thermometer. You gotta be smart enough to know the change is there based on that measurement. Are you familiar with two degrees? What impact a global two degree increase will actually have?"

Harry looked to André, who slowly shook his head to keep silent. He turned his pen to bounce on end.

Vince took a deep breath, and began his spiel on the Intergovernmental Panel on Climate Change defined two degree danger line. He emphasized danger, making direct reference to the high-risk game being played by humanity, and the many global feedback loops waiting to be touched off just past two degrees. Or triggered even below two, that being a Russian roulette game of chance. With a warmer world, the hydrological cycle intensified. Extreme weather events increased out of proportion to regular temperature changes. Thermostat settings like the one on the wall didn't count; he searched their faces for understanding. Simply put, evaporation forms clouds, which comes down as precipitation and lots of rain makes for a flood. Lots of heat makes deserts, and extra heat spreads deserts with droughts. Still, quite unpredictable, and erratic. In semi-arid southern Alberta where you'd expect drought, the new normal brings on floods. Floods also come with rising sea levels, for any ocean-front property.

Harry kept glancing at André, holding silent.

Vince ended with the socio-political turmoil likely to come about, not just globally but in each country. And locally, he winced thinking of Annalise in Calgary. He could only imagine climate refugees moving en masse into western Canada, people in the streets turning to crime, god, that there could be such events in a place like Canada. Were these guys hearing, even the basics?

André leaned into Harry's ear. "Sulphur gases are cheap commodities." He tightened his lips. "Any rogue nation could do this, just what he is saying."

Harry held his pen up, speaking back to André. "We budget for an improved media campaign." He tossed his pen on the table. André shook his head slightly. "I would caution our domestic believability may be quite stretched." Harry shook his head. "Well there's no flooding in Ottawa. Let Alberta deal with their own problems." André leaned back, silent.

Vince sighed, watched them with interest, somewhat exasperated.

"So, our Nigerien artificial volcano replicates Pinatubo aerosol creation, only less conspicuously," he said in summary. "Two last items. First, we design the long term impact based on a continual sulphur release over a proposed ten year timeframe. We make adjustments every six months depending on satellite temperature measures and seasonal evidence-based impact such as the greening of the desert. Second, we have strategic release locations spread all across this country. So up north here, that would be the Sahara."

He walked back to the table. "And, just to reiterate." He pulled his chair out. "As you would have deduced from Pinatubo, or Krakatoa, any local sulphur release has a global impact. As will the Nigerien national. Assuming cooling would impact the Nigerien landmass only is a grossly incorrect supposition. But that's where engineering becomes politics." He waved a hand towards Tamanna. "So at this point I step out, and Ms. Meacham steps in."

The room fell into silence, and as Vince sat he could hear the air conditioning fan squealing in its cage.

"Lovely. What Mr. Patel stated is correct," Tamanna said. "Niger has an initial ten year plan. While the president wants one release close to Niamey for citizens to see, other release points will not be disclosed." Tamanna rose, looking at Harry. "This plan, however, is available for adjustment into the foreseeable future as climatic and political conditions warrant. With your minister now informed, Her Excellency proposes further talks on a global climate change agreement."

"Okay, Okay, just a minute here," Harry said. "To start, I find it difficult to accept you actually represent the country of Niger. You are nothing but technical support. But just assuming you do, is Niger familiar with international agreements? Does Niger realize how irresponsible this action will be seen by the international community?"

Tamanna looked at him.

"We can review the responsibility of other national actions, say those of your country," she said quietly. "We could discuss the carbon pollution your country has chosen to release into our atmosphere, our *mutual* atmosphere, the carbon now causing direct climate change impacts. Missing monsoon rains dry up Nigerien rice fields, enhanced ocean storms cause the Ganges delta exodus in Bangladesh, and it sounds like floods have come to your own Alberta south. In fact, we would really like to compare notes as we negotiate. Carbon emissions per capita for Canada versus say, Niger. So please, yes, bring that topic to the table."

Harry retrieved his pen, squeezing it tightly now.

She went on.

"Might I also mention that at this time there is talk in Niger, as well as in other high impact countries, of a global temperature reduction. Below that of pre global warming. As citizens here learn cooling to be possible, they rally around the idea of their own volcano and what that might do for them."

"Below? Why would anyone want a colder planet?"

"National interests." Vince put in. "Hungry people."

"Politicians want happy citizens," Tamanna said. "Political points, you know. The Canadian or Russian citizen may be happier on a nice warm day, however, the Nigerien people cheer on a cooler day. And let Minister Kendall know, this outlook is not unique to Niger."

"Not unique," Harry parodied, chin dropping slightly. "But only Niger now, correct?"

Tamanna smiled, and went on. "Did you know that during the last ice age, when Canada was covered by a kilometer of ice, the Sahel was not? Not long after that time of ice sheets, the Sahel became wetter, much greener. So now, the president of Niger gains a lot of political traction when he reminds citizens of the Green Sahara. Especially when he talks of how he will bring it back."

"Are you threatening us? What, are you threatening to throw Canada back into another Ice Age?" He glared at her. "Destroy our country just so you can have a little more rain here?"

"As you must have perceived from our presentation, modifying our mutual climate can bring about unpredictable results," she replied evenly. "Yet rain is good for crops, don't you agree?"

"Canada is not just an OECD member, we're a NATO member." Harry scowled. "We'll easily put a stop to your pitiful African president."

"As one Canadian to another," Vince broke in. "I'm telling you we've got to have a *real* look at what we're doing. To our children's future, to our own future."

"Canada has an extensive carbon capture research program, with many Alberta energy companies on board. We have ongoing breakthroughs from our research teams—there's a new lab under construction in Edmonton." Harry spread his hands. "We'll have a market solution any day."

"How many tons?" Tamanna's voice was loud and clear. "How many have you captured so far?"

Harry glared at her.

"Look," Vince matched Tami's voice. "I've spent most of my career as an oilfield engineer. So don't try telling me about Alberta. Moving that liquid carbon dioxide would need a pipeline system as extensive as the entire Alberta oilfield production and transmission lines we have now. So who's going to finance that? Carbon capture had potential, especially with Alberta's coal burning electric system, but too late. A province with natural gas coming out its ying-yang produces over half its electric power burning coal! Typical symbolic action."

"Nearly all the energy driving our civilization remains hydrocarbon based." Tamanna kept her tone. "We have a dodgy situation in that our economy needs energy and we demand that energy be cheap."

"I've learned a few things from this non-oilfield project, another perspective on the politics of climate change," Vince said. "The first world lifestyle, Canadian like mine, like yours Harry, is highly subsidized by a free dumping ground for hydrocarbon emissions. In this situation, what we're *gonna* do doesn't count anymore." Vince could almost hear his daughter's not fair voice. "These countries may not be doing the best thing for our mutual planet, but they never caused climate change in the first place. And now, they *are* doing something."

"Everyone wants that lifestyle," Harry said smoothly, shrugging back and forth between them. Then, subdued in his confidence, he repeated, "Everyone."

"At what cost?" Vince demanded. "There are people dying here in Niger and in Bangladesh and a lot of other places specifically because of that lifestyle, not that we ever cared much before. But now it's global. Think, man, the carbon in the air here in Niger is the same in Canada. Now four hundred twenty parts per million. So I, for one, am thinking about here and back home too. I have my daughter's future to think about."

"I have two boys," Harry said.

"Good. So take it from me, you're raising them on a lifestyle they can't have."

How could an engineer be such a moron, Harry thought, of course they can. "My boys play hockey, didn't you? Now that's Canadian, that's our lifestyle and we'll never let that be taken away." He glared. Hockey equipment might cost a lot, but a kid has to play. "Not from my country, not from me, not from my boys."

A pin drop might have sounded as loud as a pounding fist.

Harry spoke again, strategically. "How big is this Pinatubo II project?" He looked from Tamanna to Vince with his determined show-nothing face.

"At this time, we are authorized to speak of Nigerien national, but," Tamanna dropped her voice, "a little political insight. There are other high impact national interests. Take what we have told you to your minister."

The air conditioning fan wound down into off cycle.

Harry took a breath. "I would like to request a recess to contact Minister Kendall."

"By all means." Tamanna lifted her hand in a small flourish.

Harry rose and followed as his team filed out.

Chapter 39

With the room cleared, Tamanna spoke one word. "Nishat." Finger in the air as her device buzzed, she thought back on one of Her Excellency's strategies. Find a project engineer, a Canadian, and one with our voice. She watched Vince move to the window, as Nishat answered.

As he looked out, the light middle of the night bridge traffic flowed across. Tami had first told him of her vision of a game changer global discussion. The Bangladeshi canary would screech from its coal mine, she had said, no longer signaling via sacrificial death. And no more farce negotiations, dominated by the historical essence of colonialism.

The truth was really starting to sink into him. The numbers were always plain enough, but he actually got it now. Not just in his head, but in his gut, even in his heart. Acceptance, Tami had said. The Canadian lifestyle, his lifestyle, that was the real carbon dumping issue. A deep dragging guilt swirled into his tumultuous feelings heap. His own time in the candy store had left the shelves bare for Annalise. So what about her and the other kids? How does he pay back?

Along with these Africans and their kids, his daughter loses. Will the Martian kid get the spotlight? Annalise gets to pay for that party, for his party…unless he gets this right.

He had told Tami of southern Alberta tradition, the pioneer focus on rebuilding after the first flood, little change after the second flood eight years later, in spite of triple Calgary over-the-dam flow rates. Prioritize repairs, build bigger berms, dig a diversion channel around the town of High River. And then the third flood, yet even after a downtown underwater for a month, many argued normal forces of nature. Her stories of Bay of Bengal cousins resonated with similarity, just other waters forcing other peoples from their homes. All effects of this *mutual* problem.

He'd listened intrigued to the story line of Her Excellency's shopping trip for a fall guy. Final selection came down to Canada and Russia, Tami said, Nishat's primary candidates. A proposition arose—why not bring a new guy on stage, how about an easier pickings bad guy? Calgary came up, his city noted famous for the largest carbon footprint per citizen among Canadian cities. That kind of free advertising helped, along with global media attention focused on Alberta tar sands. Nishat had called for a scapegoat, and now that goat was here, entangled. Negotiating, that could be his new career—his oilfield enthusiasm long drifted away anyway. But under the eco-terrorist label, no doubt.

#

The Canadian team walked into the next room to group around the table. "Shit! Minister Kendall should have been here." Harry looked from André to Paul. "Any suggestions?"

"We must speak openly of what I tell you, Harry. Better that we told Minister Kendall these things years ago." André spoke emphatically. "Geoengineering by any nation or alliance has been an increasing risk. And now it happens. Now we have it here before us."

Harry said nothing.

"We contact the Minister immediately," Paul said. "We give him the update André suggests. I would further recommend we judge his true reaction. From that, we interpret how he wants us to act."

"Call him up on Holo-Skype. We need to read him face-to-face."

"Also," Paul said. "We must anticipate Minister Kendall's contact with the Prime Minister's office."

"Absolutely, let's keep developing that thought too," Harry agreed. "For now, among us, we step back. We play the go between role, nothing more." He looked at the other two. "Okay, here's the Minister."

#

Tamanna pushed *end* on her device, letting her breath out slowly.

"So?" Vince came over. "We expand our story?"

"No, well possibly." Her eyebrows creased. "Remember I told you I would never walk through the doors of any totally shit COP meeting again? Ever? Well, we may be flying out with these gentlemen tonight. So if that happens, and then only outside Nigerien airspace." She looked at him. "If all that comes about, then we'll have another look."

"Look at what?"

She took a breath. "Piss it!" She looked directly into his eyes. "Right, look Vince, we never told any HICCC contractor, so you're the first to know. The Sahel countries are not the only artificial volcanoes on the go. Sulphur balloons are releasing across all High Impact countries. Tonight."

Vince's jaw dropped, a deep cave hollow swirling into place. Back and forth in his head, car crashes resonated to the rhythm of a cuckoo clock—this couldn't be real—they were so fucked. He had known, he should have known. *Oh Christ.* They were going global, and that would include the mid-ocean release. Tami had been clear; that was the only way to get a Green Sahara. *Fuck!* He somehow knew this might happen, no, would happen.

He dug deep into the internal churn, Okay, decision made! He took a deep breath...*fuck it*! Oilfield dead, he had a career beyond negotiating, he would bring real voice to Alberta, he would tell the world—he would do anything he could for this HICCC. And for his daughter Annalise.

#

The other Canadian's returned, and Vince stared at the opposition as they sat at the table.

Harry began, "Our Climate Minister Kendall wishes to speak directly to Her Excellency Nishat Jabbar."

"Too late. Did I not say clanger of his career?" Tamanna shook her head. "Her Excellency will not be available." She paused, "However, she has suggested we accompany you back to COP in Italy. Due to time constraints, and as we have more to disclose, we propose reconvening this meeting on your plane."

"More to disclose." Harry stared.

"Yes."

"The two of you."

"Vince for logistics, myself for contact with Her Excellency."

Harry looked at his team, his eyes falling. He glared sideways at Tamanna, but spoke evenly. "Yes, follow us to the airport. Here are my contacts, in case we need speak between cars."

"Brilliant. Her Excellency assumes your Minister Kendall will be communicating with your Prime Minister. Her Excellence has strongly suggested we speak to that."

#

Harry stepped into the back of the presidential hybrid limo. What chaos! He held his device on the ready for any call, scrambling to judge the situation. "André, what time is it? In Ottawa?"

The next play had to be good.

"Okay, André get me through to Harold Heine."

"And Paul, call the Prime Minister's pilot. Tell him we will be flying out, now."

"Sure thing," Paul nodded.

Of one thing Harry was sure. He would never, could never allow this craziness to happen, not to his boys. Not on his watch.

He slumped back in his seat, wanting so bad to be somewhere else. But he had to get a conversation going.

#

Vince rode beside the climatologist in the other presidential car listening to Tamanna expand on the politics. The fact that five Sahel nations could synchronize national volcanoes together would send a clear signal, a powerful signal. And that those volcanoes all released then, in the early morning hours of influence, must be revealed strategically.

"On the plane, Vince, when you talk." Tami's voice was soft. "If you can, create a picture in their minds, so when we land, what they remember seeing out the window of the plane, was a string of volcanic explosions down there, all across the Sahara. And then a ring of fire around the world too. We want the color of conflict, of challenge, imprinted in their minds."

Vince looked at her, nodding, then away. He couldn't tell thrill from terror—so what was a terrorist anyway? He stared from the limo at that horizon, knowing the string of invisible-fire volcanoes blasting off must grab world attention. To start, the line of fire was not just here on the Niamey outskirts, not just in Niger, but on the urban edges of Bamako in next door Mali. Had the Malian president been out in the streets, with cheers and green flags? And others would be soaring high across the western deserts of Mauritania, then the sands of Chad to the east, and throughout the mountains of the Sudan.

His mind raced, forming all into a storybook picture. Tell it as you would a seven year old, but twist it into political pitch. Not one right here, but five, smoking holes in the planet, like gunshot wounds with the smell of gunpowder drifting. A short burst of gunfire. Five blossoming North Korean fire-bursting volcanoes. Then the other High Impact countries, an automatic gun burst of invisible smoke holes circling around the globe. But not North Koreas—not dictatorships with an isolationist obsession, but presidents democratically popular with their people, cooperating hand in hand…this must be his daughter's best chance for a friendly future.

They sat in silence. Tami with her secret directives from Nishat. Vince, with his developing career. Personal policy came clear—he would take the global assumption to heart, face all fear, and do whatever it took.

Chapter 40

Aahil accelerated out the gate of the Agadez storage compound, caught in the swirl of a many day rush. He drove his newly delivered Toyota, a gift said to be from the president's office. But contacts told how the Asians financed his exploded Nissan replacement, along with the newly installed target lock detector. He left the yard behind, uncomfortably scattered with half and fully emptied crates, metal cylinders and boxed balloons.

Turning west, he viewed the desert city fully and the highways running into the emptiness beyond. His foot lost push for the pedal and the Toyota slowed until coasting to a stop in the road's middle. Reaching to turn off the key, he pushed the window buttons allowing a dry breeze to wisp at his turban. The sun touched ground where the road wove through the whispering sands among scattered bushes. Before him the endless desert, the shifting Sahara, and he could almost see the twinkling eyes of Tuareg faces.

Agadez stretched to the south, past the Stade where the urban launch began that day. There, the N11 began a winding path across the desert to Ingall. At the Cure Salée, the Tuareg met the Wodaabe as the rains ended each year. Late September brought that Festival of the Nomads, reviving their common wandering spirit. In times past, a greening desert brought many years promise of the good life for any nomad. If all goes well, the Sahel will have its Green Sahara.

He stared as the last sliver of sun disappeared below the rocky road. Two of his cousins drive scout trucks this night, seeking spent balloons returning to the ground. Familiar with terrain and wadis among and around the Ayăr Mountains, they gain retrieval bonuses with ease. Business will be good in their camps; they will eat well for some time. As long as this struggle of world forces continues. For him as well, the driver contracts look prosperous. He checked the surface drone target lock—life here had always had its dangers.

Shadow highlights of the road winding down from the Ayărs— the N25—trailed north along the mountains to the Dabous Giraffes. As tourist dollars arrived, the allure of the Dabous Giraffes could replace the Cure Salée. In whatever way it was to be, Tuareg people believed the Green Sahara would be returned to them, the one of so many millennia past. What was he to tell his cousins of the Ténéré? As his engineering friend said, a sway in the ways of many people had come, perhaps shifting as dunes back to the ways of old. A nomadic gathering now blown by new winds, and the changing season of the rains. The Dabous celebration may invite more than nomads. Those cheering their hero president would arrive, the one whose political friends brought true the green Sahara promise.

In a green savannah first the antelope and skittering Darcus gazelles will spread from the mountains. Followed by the cheetah and the Barbary sheep. The date palms, the Acacia trees. Desert elephants, and one day giraffes restoring to life the ancient rock wall paintings. Where once there was but sand.

In Niamey, people of the city will gather to cheer for the promise of cheaper rice, of sorghum, millet and peanuts in the markets. They will look to the urban night for the president's Green Sahara balloons floating skyward, or to their visiscreens to watch this huge desert launch. They will understand how the rains came and they will vote for the one who brings them the good life, the green of the future.

His cousin Aksil, to the northeast in the middle of the Ayărs will closely watch this fleet of balloons rising up to expand his green pasture, banding up with him to plunder grass from the rock and sand. The rains in the Ayărs will bring nothing but good fortune to the pasturelands of his cousin.

The darkening desert sky stretched out to the edge of a bright orange horizon. Watching, he sensed the desert sands about to rise and replace the darkening evening with billowing sandy balloon plumes. Volcanoes, they said, but these appeared as a mysterious morning sun, rising on the wrong horizon to overtake the desert and the desert sky. First tens, then hundreds had, and now thousands ascended with their sky-changing loads.

His eyes glimmered at the twists in events. He never had to try influencing the engineers, with money or trickery. The president would get what he wanted, or perhaps more. A new story was being written, to be told in times ahead. How as the Sahara greened, the Nigerien people found balloon work, and food came to grow in abundance all around them. If the story played out well new lakeside land markets would arise. For the people of Asia, or any who would come to live in a Sahara among free roaming Dabous giraffes.

His eyes caught slight movement, and he shifted his gaze upward. As the sands of the Tinarimen rose before him, so his life had been carried aloft with the lives of the desert Tuareg, along with the life of his American friend, and the lives of the world beyond. Yet, could the descendants of European conquerors who have taken the world befriend the new power from Asia? He glimpsed the motion expanding. Lead balloons now touched sunlight as they rose faster than the setting sun, the main fleet close behind and the stragglers trailing to last find the light.

He stared in awe.

How will all things be for his engineering friend in his western end of the world? This fellow global citizen who piloted this fleet up. Can a Tuareg relocated to his African city, the Canadian from the oil city and the American from the most powerful nation join with the good ideas of his and their ancestors? What will be their common future, or will they have one at all?

Aahil turned the engine key. The balloons would soon be descending, in the dark, and he must be there to refill for their next trip to the sky. He sped off down the road, back into the rush of the times.

Chapter 41

Tamanna watched the streetscapes swish past on her last auto ride to the Nigerien airport. Men mostly walked the Niamey late night, leaving daytime to women and children. So many children, she sighed, like other cities across the Sahel. From Bamako to Khartoum, these born here were the least responsible for a sweeping global climate crisis. Yet these people paid the price, each meal eaten at a dearer cost as their rice fields dried with the shrinking monsoon rains. Like her cousins on the Ganges delta—how soon will they be leaving for crowded Dhaka? At least now they will together have a voice and an address to their misfortune. No longer will their officials attend global conferences as stage props. Every word they utter will be closely noted at the negotiating table.

The two presidential cars passed through the car park, pulling onto the runway beside the Canadian jet. Harry got out first, stepping up beside the boldly labeled Challenger 604. White with a blue stripe the aircraft pointed folded vertical wingtips up beneath the airport lights. She and Vince stepped from their car, and she watched Harry's practiced wave to the pilot as he usher them up the steps into the jet. André motioned them to the plane's midsection and the oval office conference chairs. Like those of the Gaweye boardroom. The trappings of luxury, Tamanna noticed, but now on a Canadian VIP business jet. They selected seats on the far side of the circle.

The plane taxied out along the runway, and Tami leaned over to Vince listening as he spoke in hushed tone. He wanted her evaluation of his simple numbers metaphor at the Hotel, and his volcano story's attempt to drop engineering lingo. Tami winked and nodded, showing she'd been impressed. She felt the wheels lift off from the runway. Their ears popped as the plane gained altitude and then gradually leveled off allowing the seat belts sign to dim.

She glanced at Vince, then over at the Canadian representatives speaking among themselves on the other side of the circle of chairs. She leaned back, and forced her eyes closed for an imagined moment of Gunnersbury woodland tranquility. She must rest for what lay ahead.

#

"Should we wait any longer?" Vince spoke softly.

Tamanna came alert, and he pointed at the flight visiscreen map. They were passing outside Nigerien airspace.

"Right." She beamed. "Let's do it."

He followed Tami across to the Canadian political team who fell silent as they took their seats. He waited as she turned on her recording device and began the tone setting questions required by Nishat. Do you now represent the office of the Canadian Climate Minister? *Yes.* Is your Minister in attendance at COP 33? *Yes.* Is your Prime Minister in attendance at COP 33? *No.* Will your Minister be speaking to your Prime Minister? *We can ensure that.*

"Okay, then," Tamanna said. "We speak for Her Excellency Nishat Jabbar, Minister of Climate Change International Negotiations for the HICCC. We've been instructed to supplement your information on the HICCC position—our engineering consultant will now fill you in further."

Vince looked towards Harry and his official team, feeling that spinal shiver. Harry had what might have been a practiced firm smile on his face. "So geoengineering," Harry said. Vince took a breath. "*Oui.* We will stick with English if that suits you. For the sake of the *mademoiselle ici.*"

Harry's face twitched, but he nodded. "Yes, we can do that."

"As Ms. Meacham has stated, the HICCC Minister wishes to fill you in completely on the Pinatubo II project. We have described the Green Sahara scenario—we also have a planet wide scenario."

Vince noticed drop dead attention.

"If you will imagine the geography of the HICCC nations, they are scattered around the globe, and each has a citizen count and a land and sea area. By now we agree, they and all countries share one common planetary atmosphere. With only HICCC nations participating in a global scenario, we have calculated a sulphur dioxide release to cool the entire planet. Simply put, we divide the sulphur release among members proportional to their area and population as well as the extra planet they will have to cover for non participants."

"Planet wide! Global!" Harry's voice rose. "You're talking of the whole planet now."

Tamanna and Vincent nodded in unison, and spoke together as one voice.

"Yes, global."

"Okay, listen up on this brief," Vince said. "A country like Niger releases just over three percent of the global target. All sulphur will be released within Nigerien air space and Niger expects completion within weeks. Expand that to cover all HICCC countries, and the total release comes out at double that of Pinatubo. We expect the global average temperature will be measurably lowered over the next six months at which time we will re-evaluate our maintenance releases for adjustment."

"Jesus!" Harry stared at the wall, shaking his head.

"So, Pinatubo II," Vince said. "Easy name to remember."

"Please, please, then to confirm," André said, looking back and forth between Harry and Vince. "The global sulphur release has started tonight? Did you say so?"

Tami and Vince looked at each other, then back at the Canadians.

"Yes," said Tami. "Tonight."

"Correct," Vince said, nodding in agreement.

This event will catch the attention of those who did nothing or impeded progress at COP all those years, Vince thought. Something real to talk about now. He turned to Tami who appeared to have more to add.

"As I alluded to earlier," Tamanna said. "The HICCC has a fully global ten year climate cooling plan."

Vince watched the Canadian team. They appeared disjointed, looking anywhere but at each other.

"To expand on Vince's geography and add in the politics," Tamanna went on. "One fifth of the planetary land area where a third of the planetary population resides are participating. Sulphur release may or may not be flexible, depending specifically on the direct action taken by the OECD. To consider any change, we need measurable and confirmed reductions in rich country carbon emissions."

"Do you understand?" Vince asked. He hoped one fifth and one third were not too numerical.

Silence.

"Also," Tamanna said. "Our Minister Jabbar has stated the HICCC invites the OECD to the negotiation table. We have a new set of terms to offer."

"Please, to one more time confirm what you say." André spoke again, looking briefly at Harry. "You have initiated a global cooling effort. Yet the HICCC wishes to resume climate change negotiations with the OECD under these new terms."

"Precisely." Tamanna put in. "And due to the late time and the need to directly inform your Minister, we suggest adjourning this meeting until we land."

"We're still available for consultation on your messaging," Vince said looking to Tamanna. On this political stuff he couldn't help but poke in more. "The message we strongly suggest Canada release openly at the COP conference."

"What are you saying now?" Harry said under his breath as he rose and walked away muttering in his own space. "How can you be doing a *global* project?"

"You could spin Pinatubo II through a global ramifications perspective, like you might even if Sahel countries alone were acting." Vince turned to Paul and André. "One way to look at this situation could be the current carbon release by OECD countries. But in reverse. A country like Canada now dumps global climate warming carbon that directly messes with the climate of Niger. Now Niger dumps global cooling sulphur that directly messes with the climate of Canada."

#

Harry feigned attention to his jPad at a corner table, using every ounce of effort to keep control. Hearing André voice the negotiating words he should be speaking felt so disjointing. He loosened his tie yet could still feel his wet shirt inside his suit jacket, in spite of the cool air in the Prime Minister's plane. His mind repeated over and over the cardinal rules of negotiating. When on defense, show concern, listen attentively yet defer judgement and postpone commitment into the political future if at all possible. Great theory. *God, shit, fuck!*

What they'll tell Minister Kendall's office was hard to fathom. *Fuck, fuck ,fuck.* The brain storming session in the limo with Paul and André had not gone off well. When he asked for ideas on what could be said to best inform the Minister, all he got was André's most recent research on geoengineering. The implications were horrendous. Extreme weather events past adaptation he kept repeating. The southern Alberta floods. Why did he keep harping on those? Predicted long ago to be brought on by climate change, André said, and they could supposedly be reduced by global cooling. So the HICCC could even be perceived to be helping Canada. That was such bullshit! "Why didn't you keep me up to date?" he had demanded. "You would never respond," André said. "You showed no interest in my reports." Harry had scowled. *There were no floods in Ottawa!* But he couldn't help thinking now of their Ottawa house and their planned move to a new neighbourhood. Should they move to higher ground? Was Vanier North above the flood plain?

Focus.

He looked across the oval conference room. His assistants appeared to nodded their heads as they listened to the engineer. At least they would gather information. *God, fuck, shit.* Not just to disclose to the Minister's office, but Minister Kendall was going to require solid suggestions on how to speak to the Prime Minister's office. Minister Kendall's office will be grilling him on that soon. He could only imagine what the Prime Minister or whoever he assigns to speak would say at COP for Christ's sakes.

#

Vince sat beside Tamanna across from André and Paul at a side table in the oval conference room. André keyed into his device, while Paul scrawled with a pen on a paper pad.

"We know something about global drone capacity," Vince said. "We calculate the NATO drone fleet will be overloaded by the thousands of balloons we have ascending in any night time release. Like the barrage balloons cluttered the skies with cables and nets to damage dive bombers in the World Wars."

André and Paul listened attentively.

"I am administering the Sahel region," Tami said. "We will release enough to take care of most of North Africa, and the appropriate part of the ocean. Other HICCC global regions will be organized from other regional centres." She paused. "Your Minister Kendall might wish to approach the HICCC directly after Canada delivers this message."

André hammered at his keyboard, nodding.

"The negotiations have potential," Tami said, shrugging and nodding. "They will, I believe, be centered on the maintenance of the HICCC ten year release schedule. On a positive note, if sulphur emissions are terminated, the atmosphere will gradually revert back to a natural state within a couple years, just as it did after the Pinatubo eruption. All of this would depend on measurable actions taken by the OECD."

Paul scribbled furiously.

Absorbing the scene, Vince glanced away, his eye catching the flicker of a wing light on a window edge. He felt a soaring need to get up and dance. How inappropriate. But that tingle within would not stop swooping about, high among the sky-angel clouds within. Elation, to a power of who knows what fractal factor. A jet airliner was more enclosed than a balloon and certainly had less exposure than a paraglider, but this flight tonight felt so detached like a trip to the stars.

Stars, right he sighed, like his daughter's wishing star. Yet in spite of all the fallout and chaos likely coming, this was what for sure he had needed to do. If not for his math angel, at least he had acted for his daughter. At least he had that.

His new found terror label closed in on the swirling euphoria as he leaned back in his seat, eyes closed. Annalise might need a lighter hazy blue crayon for the color of her near future sky. At least his face didn't hurt anymore when the smile came, and that inner trembling whatever its source had gained growing room. He could almost feel his daughter sitting there next to him, her tiny hand in his.

Made in the USA
Charleston, SC
21 March 2016